"This novel skillfully tackles the dark topics of depression and suicide as well as the often misguided way Christians treat mental illness. It asks the hard questions such as how one should support a loved one who deals with this disease and what to do when our best intentions are ineffective in providing help and solace. Beautiful and haunting, *Shades of Light* is a heart-wrenching and necessary read that ultimately offers hope."

Elizabeth Musser, author of *The Long Highway Home*

"Sharon Garlough Brown uses the vulnerable, sensitive, compassionate, and creative character of Wren to sympathetically immerse the reader into her valiant struggles of coping with depression and anxiety. With Wren's deep insights into the life of Vincent van Gogh, we are invited to participate in the illuminating potential of visio divina to experience the comforting aspects of Vincent's art. Sharon succeeds in revealing what hides beneath the surface of the two wounded and kindred spirits—Wren and Vincent—namely, their compassion and their spiritual and intellectual depth. This is a book that compels us to be more compassionate and less judgmental."

Carol A. Berry, lecturer, author of *Learning from Henri Nouwen and Vincent van Gogh*

"Sharon Garlough Brown's *Shades of Light* is a rare and beautiful study in contrasts. Faith and doubt, control and surrender, acceptance and resistance—all are woven into the darks and lights of a story so real and provoking that you will find yourself aching, wondering, hoping, and even praying alongside her luminescent characters. The struggles of depression and anxiety, of parenting and being parented, of loving and losing aren't tied up in easy answers or simple narratives, but are lifted up for what they are: the beloved brokenness where God's light and love get in."

Tara Owens, author of *Embracing the Body*

"*Shades of Light* is a beautiful, moving story filled with Sharon Garlough Brown's deep, spiritual insights. As a fan of artist Vincent van Gogh, I loved how the main characters, Wren and her mother, Jamie, drew from the faith this 'companion in sorrow' as they faced the challenges of Wren's depression. Brown offers no pat answers to the questions raised by mental illness, but shows how joy and suffering are held in delicate balance through faith in the 'Man of Sorrows,' who is 'sorrowful but always rejoicing.' This is a powerful book, triumphant with hope."

Lynn Austin, author of *Legacy of Mercy*

SHADES

OF

a novel

Light

SHARON GARLOUGH BROWN

An imprint of InterVarsity Press
Downers Grove, Illinois

InterVarsity Press
P.O. Box 1400, Downers Grove, IL 60515-1426
ivpress.com
email@ivpress.com

InterVarsity Press® is the book-publishing division of InterVarsity Christian Fellowship/USA®, a movement of students and faculty active on campus at hundreds of universities, colleges, and schools of nursing in the United States of America, and a member movement of the International Fellowship of Evangelical Students. For information about local and regional activities, visit intervarsity.org.

Mark 9:14-20, Psalm 139:1-6, and Psalm 102:1-7 are quoted from the New Revised Standard Version. All other Scripture quotations are taken from The Holy Bible, New International Version®, NIV®. Copyright © 1973, 1978, 1984, 2011 by Biblica, Inc.™ Used by permission of Zondervan. All rights reserved worldwide. www.zondervan.com. The "NIV" and "New International Version" are trademarks registered in the United States Patent and Trademark Office by Biblica, Inc.™

This is a work of fiction. People, places, events, and situations are either the product of the author's imagination or are used fictitiously. Any resemblance to events, locales, or actual persons, living or dead, is entirely coincidental.

Cover design: David Fassett
Interior design: Daniel van Loon
Images: brush stroke background: pexels.com
    blurred lights background: © Peter Zelei Images / Moment / Getty Images
    blue watercolor background: © kentarcajuan / E+ / Getty Images
    fairywren: © Andrew Haysom / iStock / Getty Images Plus
    wren: © Andrew Bensch / iStock / Getty Images Plus

ISBN 978-0-8308-4658-0 (print)
ISBN 978-0-8308-6526-0 (digital)

Printed in the United States of America ∞

InterVarsity Press is committed to ecological stewardship and to the conservation of natural resources in all our operations. This book was printed using sustainably sourced paper.

Library of Congress Cataloging-in-Publication Data

Names: Brown, Sharon Garlough, author.
Title: Shades of light : a novel / Sharon Garlough Brown.
Description: Downers Grove : InterVarsity Press, 2019. | Series: Shades of light set | Includes index.
Identifiers: LCCN 2019019916 (print) | LCCN 2019022038 (ebook) | ISBN 9780830865260 (eBook) | ISBN 9780830846580 (pbk. : alk. paper)
Subjects: | GSAFD: Christian fiction.
Classification: LCC PS3602.R722867 (ebook) | LCC PS3602.R722867 (print) | DDC 813/.6—dc23

LC record available at https://lccn.loc.gov/2019019916

P   20   19   18   17   16   15   14   13   12   11   10   9   8   7   6   5   4   3   2   1
Y   36   35   34   33   32   31   30   29   28   27   26   25   24   23   22   21   20   19

For David, my beloved son

You inspire me with your courage,

compassion, and wisdom.

Words can't express how much I love you

and how proud I am of you.

The light shines in the darkness,
and the darkness has not overcome it.

JOHN 1:5

If I say, "Surely the darkness will hide me
and the light become night around me,"
even the darkness will not be dark to you;
the night will shine like the day,
for darkness is as light to you.

PSALM 139:11-12

CONTENTS

Part One

EVEN

THERE

Where can I go from your Spirit?
Where can I flee from your presence?
If I go up to the heavens, you are there;
if I make my bed in the depths, you are there.
If I rise on the wings of the dawn,
if I settle on the far side of the sea,
even there your hand will guide me,
your right hand will hold me fast.

PSALM 139:7-10

It's so beautiful here, if only one has a good and
a single eye without many beams in it. But if one
has that, then it's beautiful everywhere.

VINCENT VAN GOGH,
LETTER TO THEO FROM LONDON,
JULY 31, 1874

PROLOGUE
February

It was the sighing, the news article read, the awful sighing that caught the woman's attention in the half-light of morning and led her down to the beach. She said the young whales were the worst, their splashing frantic, their moans tortured.

Wren Crawford closed her laptop and pushed her sandwich aside on her desk.

She knew better than to spend her lunch break reading stories about whales beaching themselves by the hundreds half a world away. She could barely manage her own daily intake of sorrow working with traumatized women and children at Bethel House. She didn't need to read about another potentially futile rescue mission. Her current therapist, Dr. Emerson, would agree: limit exposure to faraway tragedy and anguish as much as possible. Her job provided more than enough for anyone to absorb.

She fixed her attention on the many children's drawings and paintings taped to file cabinets and tried to shake the whale image, but it was no use. All she saw were the volunteers with their buckets, laboring to keep the survivors cool and damp by dousing them with water, desperately cooperating with a high tide to turn the creatures upright and coax them out into safety. Then they would form a human chain and try to keep the rescued ones from stranding themselves again.

Already the carcasses were strewn for hundreds of yards along the New Zealand coast. It would be several days before they could assess whether any of their efforts had succeeded.

She picked up her phone to text Casey, her best friend since middle school. He might tease her for being sensitive, but he wouldn't condemn her.

Need a mental reset, she wrote.

What for?

Beached whales in New Zealand.

How about kittens somebody dumped in the alley?

Wren punched his number. "How many?"

"Three."

"Where?"

"Inside the dumpster. Heard them crying when I took out the trash."

She would never understand cruelty. Not to animals, not to children, not to any who were vulnerable. "Where are they now?"

"Playing with my shoelaces. And ow! Biting me. Hey, hey, Theo. Here—play with this."

"You already named them?"

"Just one."

"Does Brooke know?"

He laughed. "Not yet. Not sure how she feels about cats."

Wren hoped his long-distance fiancée would approve. "Well, you're a good man, Casey."

"Or a sucker for cuteness."

"Either way . . ." A coworker appeared in her doorway with the familiar *Sorry to bother you but there's an emergency* look on her face. Wren held up a single finger to indicate she'd be there soon. "I've got to go. But maybe you can investigate whether there's a no-kill shelter or a cat rescue agency? And they'll probably need to go to a vet. What's your schedule like? I've got to work late."

"It's okay. I got it. We're not shooting anything today." Casey, a freelance videographer, had been working for months on a project highlighting human trafficking in West Michigan. "But come by after work, okay, Wrinkle? I need to talk to you about something."

"Okay." She took one final bite of her sandwich. "But if there isn't a safe place for them . . ."

"I know, don't worry. Then I'll keep them here until we can figure something out. And hope they don't destroy my couch in the meantime."

"Thanks, Casey. You're a star."

"Each of us lighting our own little corner of the world, right?"

Yes, she thought as she hurried down the hallway. In the midst of all that was crooked, dark, and despairing, *Shine*.

There was a sketch by her favorite artist, Vincent van Gogh—a pencil, chalk, and ink drawing of a gnarled tree with exposed roots, half torn up by a storm, yet clinging to the earth. Vincent had seen within the tree roots an image of the struggle for life, for hope. He understood it.

That was the picture that came to mind as she listened to her coworker recount the story of the latest referral: a mother beaten up by a boyfriend who had been pimping out her four-year-old to his friends. She'd come home from work early and discovered it.

Wren wasn't sure if she was going to faint or vomit. She only knew she had to find a way to cling to something solid. Like Vincent's tree roots. She gripped the edge of the table where she and Allie were sitting.

"You need a minute?" Allie asked.

Wren nodded.

Allie set aside the police report. "I keep thinking if we were in Chicago or Detroit, I might not be surprised by all of this, but Kingsbury . . ."

Exactly. In college Wren had been stunned by statistics on abuse and human trafficking in West Michigan. That's when she had decided to put her compassion to good use and be part of the rescue mission in Kingsbury and beyond. But the darkness was relentless.

She bit her lip. She was not going to cry. Because if she started to cry, she might not be able to stop. *Is that happening a lot?* Dr. Emerson had asked her a few weeks ago. *Crying that won't stop?*

Not a lot. But some.

At work?

No. She managed to hold it together at work. But it was exhausting, always being on high alert, always bracing for the next crisis, always living on the verge of losing control and crumbling.

She stared at her hands and pictured Vincent's precarious tree.

Would you be open to getting some more help? Dr. Emerson had asked. *Maybe taking a break from work?*

She couldn't. They were already understaffed, and still, the kids kept arriving at Bethel with their moms. She glanced out the window at the February gloom. "The baby whales are the worst."

"What?"

She didn't realize she'd said it aloud. "Nothing."

Allie paused, then said, "Are you okay? I mean, not just about this, but in general. You've seemed a little off lately."

Wren tried to receive the observation as concern rather than criticism. "Just feeling a bit overwhelmed by everything."

Allie nodded. "Well, don't let the enemy drag you down. This is frontline stuff, right? You've got to take up your shield of faith and fight back against the darkness. That's what we've all got to do."

Wren sighed. "Some days I don't have much fight left in me."

"I know. Me too. That's why we've got to keep renewing our minds. We've got to take every thought captive because otherwise"—Allie motioned toward the hallway—"all this will pull us under."

And on the days when she didn't have the energy to take thoughts captive and renew her mind? On the days when the undertow of grief and fear was too strong to resist? Then what?

Allie seemed to be reading her thoughts. "It doesn't matter how we feel. We've got to stay grounded in the Word. It's the only way to survive. The only way through is to pray. Constantly."

That was exactly what Wren found hardest to do whenever the

darkness pressed in. She didn't have the energy to read the Word or pray. But she wasn't going to say that to Allie. She didn't need guilt and judgment layered onto her sorrow. She pushed back her chair. "I should get in there, meet Evelyn and her mom."

Allie eyed her with compassion. Or was it pity? "Tell you what— how about if we swap places today and I do the intake for this one?"

Wren was going to argue. She was going to assert her competence, demonstrate her resilience, and prove to Allie she was emotionally and spiritually fit to push back the darkness and fight the good fight. But she didn't have the strength for bravado. And besides, with all the legal and medical complications involved in this type of case, she couldn't risk missing something. Or falling apart in front of everyone. So she said, "Thanks, Allie."

"You'd do it for me." Allie picked up the folder. "You've still got time on your lunch hour. Why don't you head to the art room? Take a deep breath, center yourself."

Good idea. Wren retrieved her phone from her desk drawer, then went to the art room and closed the door behind her. She would paint and listen to music. That would help center her. She chose a few tubes of acrylic paint from the storage closet, set up an easel and a small canvas she had already primed, and selected one of her favorite songs, "Vincent," for inspiration.

Starry, starry night, Don McLean sang as she squeezed cerulean blue onto her palette. Like Vincent, she could paint in blue and gray.

Look out on a summer's day with eyes that know the darkness in my soul.

Vincent knew. He understood. He was a companion in darkness.

She mixed the blue with a bit of violet until it was almost black. Then she spread the gloom onto the canvas with thick impasto strokes, sculpting the dark into shadowy mountains and caverns. Strokes of contrasting yellow would brighten the sky, but she didn't want it brightened. The purple darkness soothed her.

She stepped back and scrutinized the scene. She would blur the violet with gray and smudge the clouds into a brooding haze. Nothing luminous about it. Not like Vincent's dark, which shimmered with light.

"Let it be what it is," Dr. Emerson might say. "At least you're painting."

She needed to create space for doing it more often, especially when she felt stressed. Art had always helped her to be well—not only her own art but also Vincent's art. As a child she had fallen in love with his paintings and for years had studied and savored the honest poetry of his letters. She'd even written her college honors thesis on the potent spirituality of his art and the chiaroscuro of his sorrowing, rejoicing life, the shadows of despair streaked by what he called "a ray from on high." In his letters, in his sketches, in his paintings—even in the darker ones—beamed the hint of radiant hope.

With eyes that watch the world and can't forget . . .

She wished she could see and forget. She set down her palette knife and brushed a strand of her short, dark hair away from her eyes. She envied those who could see and forget. But that had never been, and likely never would be, her gift. Social workers, artists, care-givers, people of faith and compassion—theirs was the call to see and not flinch.

She rinsed off her brushes in the sink and pinched the bristles to dislodge remnants of dark sky. Maybe she would have the kids paint rather than draw today. She could analyze their use of color, study their subject matter for indicators of trauma, and note her observa-tions in their case files.

She rubbed her tinted hands with lukewarm water and glanced over her shoulder at her work. What would someone conclude about her if they saw it? What might Dr. Emerson note in his file? She turned off the faucet, went back to her palette, and dipped her broadest brush in gray. Then she smeared paint over the entire canvas, erasing every bit of evidence.

She didn't have margin for melancholy. The children needed her to be strong. The women needed her to be hopeful. She could pull herself together and be resilient. She had done it many times before, and she could do it again. In the midst of all the chaos and churn, she could cling like Vincent's roots. And press on.

1

October

"Time for your medicine, Wren." Kelly, one of the kinder nurses, entered the room with a little plastic cup of pills and a glass of water.

Wren set her pencil down on the bed. She had been so immersed in drawing she hadn't heard the summons to the nurses' station for morning medications. Kelly, thankfully, wasn't one to scold.

"That's really good," Kelly said, studying the sketch of a woman carrying a bucket. "I didn't know you're an artist."

"Just an amateur."

"Well, I can't even do stick figures." Kelly handed her the cup. "I'm glad you're drawing."

There wasn't much else to do. Sleep, sketch, attend groups. Now that the immobilizing lethargy had lifted and the racing, terrifying thoughts had begun to quiet, her creative impulses stirred again. She swallowed her pills dutifully.

"The others just went down to breakfast," Kelly said. "I'd bring you a tray, but Dominic wouldn't like it."

No, he wouldn't. Her new case manager had given strict instructions about the importance of engaging with community as much as possible. "I'll be right there."

"I'll walk you down. Come find me at the nurses' station when you're ready."

She waited for Kelly to exit the room then returned to her sketch. If she couldn't expunge the image of the whales and the rescue mission, even all these months after first reading the news story, then she needed to work with it.

That's what Dr. Emerson had recommended during their last appointment together, just before he retired in June: be open to what the image might want to reveal. And get on the schedule with one of his colleagues. But she had never bothered to make an appointment with another therapist. She was tired of change, and it required way too much energy to start over again with someone new. If she could even find a good match. That was always a challenge. And then if you found someone good, they might move away. Or take a maternity leave and not return. Or not take your new insurance. Or retire.

She shaded the woman's hair with the edge of her pencil. Maybe it wasn't a rescue mission. Maybe the woman was carrying a bucket to make a sandcastle with a child, like the red plastic ones she and her mother carried years ago whenever they walked the Australian coastline near her childhood home, looking for shells. The purple ones were their favorite.

But her grandfather always warned her that blue-ringed octopuses lurked in the tide pools, concealing themselves in shells or beneath rocks. She had to be vigilant because with one bite they could paralyze a girl and knock her unconscious and make her unable to breathe. Pop knew a girl who—

She needed to breathe.

—was looking for starfish with her grandfather when—

Breathe.

She placed one hand on her chest, the other below her rib cage, and inhaled slowly through her nose to allow her diaphragm to fill, just as a therapist had taught her years ago. She tightened her stomach muscles as she exhaled through pursed lips. Keep the chest still, very still. Once. Twice. A third time. There. Settled.

See? You're fine. Just keep breathing, nice and slow.

After her morning group she would draw a relaxing day along the shores of nearby Lake Michigan, where no whales could beach themselves, where no venomous octopuses lurked in shadows, and where children could skip and play and build castles to their hearts' content, happy and carefree children, not terrified or traumatized or abused like the ones who came to Bethel House, but laughing and splashing, innocent and protected and safe.

She tucked her notebook inside her pillowcase so her current roommate wouldn't find it as the last one had. Then she fastened her shoes with a plastic grip that had replaced her confiscated shoelaces and shuffled toward the nurses' station.

As Kelly escorted her to the dining hall, it was impossible not to overhear an anguished groan and cry of protest from behind a closed door, the same groan and cry of protest that had run on a continual loop in her own head the past few days: *I shouldn't be here. I don't belong here. Please help me.*

For the last several months she had convinced herself that with more than ten years of therapy and six different therapists behind her—not to mention her training as a social worker—she had collected all the tools she needed for fighting the good fight whenever her nemesis reappeared. But she was mistaken. She'd also been naively hopeful, thinking she could wean herself off her medications without talking to her doctor. Some would say it was her fault, not being proactive about pursuing care when she needed it. But she thought she could manage on her own.

And she had, at least for a while. She'd made it almost four months without Dr. Emerson and eight without Casey. Some might say she deserved a bit of credit for lasting that long without breaking, especially with the ongoing strain at work. All the whales. Too many mama and baby whales.

Scattered along the hallways at Glenwood Psychiatric Hospital and on countless remote beaches lay God-only-knew how many helpless ones sighing and moaning, dazed and disoriented, hoping for a mission of mercy, a cup of cold water, a rescue from destruction, a resurrection from death.

For the past three years she had been one of the rescuers. Now at twenty-seven she was one of the stranded ones, weary of fighting against the rip currents of fear, despair, and the sensitivity that could morph from gift to crippling liability without any warning. If others knew the mental battle required just to keep from disintegrating under the daily burden of sorrow and stress, maybe they wouldn't be surprised she had landed at Glenwood. They might even be compassionate. But she hadn't told them. Her friends and fellow social workers thought she was on a much-needed vacation.

She would have told Casey the truth, and he would have understood. He had needed rescuing himself. Many times. She had often been the one to help lead him to safety. But no more. That was his wife's job now. She hoped Brooke would be vigilant.

She spooned firm scrambled eggs onto her plate, poured a small cup of orange juice, and sat in the corner with her back turned toward the other patients gathered at rectangular tables near the center of the room. Chewing slowly, she stared at the framed art, no doubt designed to compensate for the cheerlessness of artificial light and window views of a brick wall. She wondered if those who chose the prints understood the significance of selecting Van Gogh's sunflowers and irises and wheat fields and gardens to decorate a mental hospital. Maybe they didn't know he had painted some of them during his own stay in an asylum. Maybe they selected the paintings without giving thought to the context of his work, how he accessed his pain and channeled his suffering into the creation of something shimmering and transcendent, capturing the sacred in the swirling light of stars or in the weathered face and weary posture of a peasant laborer.

However the art came to be on the walls, Wren was grateful for the presence of beauty in the midst of desolation. Here, in a place where she hadn't touched a blade of grass or a tree in five days, Vincent could be her eyes to the radiance of the natural world, reminding her there were places where her soul could breathe, like in the walled courtyard where she was permitted to sit twice daily and where a patch of blue or gray sky above the concrete walls was a little square of infinity that beckoned her and gave her hope that someday she might be free of the oppressive darkness pinning her down like a boulder on a dragonfly.

Vincent, at least, had been permitted to take supervised walks around the picturesque grounds of the asylum and paint outdoors when he was well enough. She wondered who had determined that patients in a mental hospital like Glenwood would benefit more from austerity and scarcity than from beauty and abundance. If only there were a garden to sit in with green and growing things to tend to. If only there were flowers or birds or a pond. Something alive and enlivening.

She set down her plastic spork, its tines blunt and harmless, and stared at Vincent's golden wheat fields under a whirling sky, the vast blue calling to mind the Australian sky she had loved as a child. That was a scene where she could travel in her memory and imagination—to her grandparents' house, where she and her mother lived until she was ten, a house that kept evolving, growing new chambers like a nautilus as Pop added on a veranda here, a bedroom there. He'd built it on land he'd cleared in the bush, the eucalyptus trees dense around the paddock where the horses grazed. She pictured herself there, a little girl reading under the willow trees that rimmed the pond. She watched Pop carve bristly banksia pods into wooden balls and bells to adorn Christmas trees. She lay beneath the Southern Cross, scanning for shooting stars to wish upon. There she was, happy and at peace.

But inevitably the shadows would descend, tainting the picture of joy and contentment. The relentless, ominous dark would press in as it had for Vincent, the storm clouds gathering, the crows hovering, the destroyer lurking at noonday and breathing menacing threats, always prowling, always encroaching, always obscuring the halo light of the sun. She hadn't had words for the darkness then. Later, she would learn them. *Depression. Anxiety.*

"Groups are starting," a voice called from the doorway. Though the multiple daily groups were not mandatory, attendance was necessary to demonstrate progress to the case workers. She hadn't missed one yet.

With a final glance at Vincent's skies, she scraped the rest of her eggs into the trash, poured out her juice, and followed the other patients down the hall.

"Wren? What kind of a name is Wren?"

Every single day, the same exact question from the woman who rocked constantly in her seat, wringing her hands.

"Leave her alone, Sylvia," the man beside her muttered. "It's a good name."

"It's a bird name. The name of a bird. Like a little birdie. She's a little tweety bird. Tweet tweet."

Wren stared at the floor, trying to summon pity and patience while she waited for Krystal, the social worker, to take control. At Bethel House she had led many groups like this one, with adult outpatient clients and temporary residents who arrived troubled and traumatized, some of them battling demons of addictions as well as the anguish of domestic violence, some a danger to themselves and, on the rare occasion, to others.

She didn't belong here. They had promised her at the intake exam that it would require only a few days to get her mood stabilized with medication, and she could gain some new coping strategies for stress. Then she would be free to go. She was exhausted, she told them, mentally and physically and emotionally and spiritually exhausted, and all she wanted was a brief respite from her life, a place where she didn't have a cell phone, where people didn't constantly bombard her with their needs and their heartaches, where she wasn't continually assaulted by chaos and tragedy on every street corner around the globe.

"Tweet tweet, little bird."

Wren rubbed the side of her nose.

"Little bird, tweet tweet." Sylvia laughed, long and hard. "Did you see a puddy tat? Get it? Get it, Tweety Bird?"

Stop, Wren silently commanded. *Stop it.*

Sylvia leaned forward so her face nearly touched Wren's, her breath thick and sour. "Tweeeeeeet! Tweeeeeeet!"

Wren jumped to her feet, hands clenched, nostrils flared. Someone grabbed her from behind, pinning her arms behind her back. She struggled to free herself but couldn't twist out of the vise grip. *Tweet! Tweeet!* The taunting shriek pierced and sliced through her like a serrated blade, and she dropped to her knees, pleading, shouting for all of it, all of it, to stop.

An hour later, Dominic appeared in her doorway with his clipboard. "Okay to talk a minute?" he asked, then entered without waiting for an answer. He hooked the desk chair with his sneaker and dragged it closer to the bed.

Wren pulled her knees to her chest and lowered her gray sweatshirt hood like a monk's cowl over her head, her fingers in search of the drawstring, a lifeline to tug, an umbilical cord to ground her. But the string had been confiscated along with the shoelaces. "I wasn't going to hit her." Her thin voice sounded as if it had arisen from a much younger version of herself.

He scribbled something without looking at her. "Dr. Browerly is going to want to see you when he gets in after lunch."

She knew what that visit would be about: Was she noticing an increased fluctuation in mood swings? Aggressive thoughts? Did she have a history of assaultive behavior? She knew the checklists.

"I'm not sleeping," she said, realizing too late that this would be noted in her file, with yet another medication prescribed. How could she sleep with the flashlight safety checks every fifteen minutes, a roommate who snored, and the nocturnal wanderings of a patient from down the hall who sometimes slipped past the nurses' station without being seen and stood in her doorway, silent and staring? What hope did she have of making progress with her anxiety when everything fed her sense of helplessness and vulnerability?

She wanted a rest. She wanted to sleep and sleep and not wake up. "Please don't send me back to South Hall." South Hall was where the severely mentally ill were kept. Wren had spent three hellish days there, not because her presenting symptoms warranted such a placement but because that was the only bed available. "Please, Dominic." Her South Hall roommate had brandished dark stitches on fresh wounds up and down her arms and would sometimes scream with night terrors. Daily, Wren had begged to be moved to North Hall and daily was told, "Probably tomorrow."

She stared at her wristband. That was her name and birthdate printed on it. But this was not her life. This couldn't be her life.

"Krystal indicated to me that you were provoked by someone else in the group, that your reaction seemed to be a post-trau—"

"No." She knew all about post-traumatic stress disorder. She didn't have it. Though she might develop a good case of it if they sent her back to South Hall. "I'm tired. That's all." Not crazy, she added silently.

He looked up at her. "Were you hurt when the other patient restrained you?"

"No, not bad. I mean, no." She had insisted to herself and others that she wouldn't have struck Sylvia, that she would have maintained control, that she had only leapt from her chair because she wanted to escape the taunting and flee the group. But maybe the other patient had saved her from doing what she didn't think she was capable of doing. She didn't know what she was capable of anymore, she was so tired. "Please don't send me back to South Hall. I just want to sleep."

Dominic scribbled a few more notes, then rose from the chair. "Everyone else is in groups right now. Maybe you can get some rest before lunch."

She waited until he left the room, then rolled onto her side, determined not to cry. Because if she started to cry, she wasn't sure she could stop.

"Dominic said I could bring you lunch."

Wren pushed back her hood and scooched herself up in bed.

Kelly handed her a tray with chicken salad, a cup of melon, and a whole grain roll, then sat on the edge of the mattress. "How are you feeling? Looks like you slept for a while."

She rubbed her eyes. "I guess I did." She glanced across at her roommate's empty bed, the sheets rumpled. The two of them hadn't had much conversation. The more normal someone appeared, the less likely they seemed willing to disclose the reasons for being there. "If I could get a few good nights of sleep, I think I'd feel a lot better."

"It's hard for that here, I know."

If she had known how difficult it would be, she might not have come. But her reliable coping strategies had stopped working. And she was scared. She didn't know what she was capable of, she was so tired. *Your fault,* the voice inside her head reminded her. *If you hadn't stopped going to counseling and taking your medications . . .*

She hated the thought of needing drugs in order to manage her life.

Only Casey and her parents knew about the cocktail of antidepressants and anxiety medications she had started taking in high school. Casey had been on his own cocktail for bipolar disorder. Whatever stigma was attached to mental illness, they'd shared it together. It had eased the burden. And complicated it.

"Dr. Browerly wants to meet with you before your next group," Kelly said. "And I thought maybe you'd like to have a bit of time in the courtyard after you finish eating. It's nice outside. Cool, but sunny."

"Okay. Thanks." Clouds, rain, hail, it wouldn't matter. A bit of fresh autumn air and a place to breathe without music videos or news blaring from the television in the common room across the hall would be a gift. If she had ever needed to be recalibrated with a sense of gratitude for small things, then confinement at Glenwood had already accomplished that.

Periwinkle. Cornflower. Aquamarine. Turquoise. Azure. Cerulean. Blue, oh, the wonder and glory of blue! She leaned her head
back and looked up, the white clouds brushed in thick impasto
strokes like Vincent's churning skies. She shut her left eye and traced
two fingers along the brow of a cloud, imagining the feel of her
palette knife as she mixed and molded white with violet and a bit of
citron yellow, spreading the paint like icing on a layer cake. Sweep,
swish, swirl. There were no palette knives or oils or canvases in the
art room at Glenwood, only watercolors and soft brushes and sheets
of white computer paper. But at least there was paint. For the first
time in months, she felt a desire to return to an easel and create
something beautiful. That, her case manager would probably say,
was progress.

"Hear that?" a voice from behind her asked. She turned to face a
gray-haired man who was pointing toward the sky. "Wait for it," he
whispered. "Wait for it . . . there! There! Did you hear it?"

Wren heard only the sound of a light wind rustling through
unseen trees that had by now, she imagined, become flaming torches
of amber, vermilion, and copper. "No. Sorry. I don't think so."

"Listen. You got to listen. Close your eyes."

Unsure how safe that was when she was in a confined space with
other patients, she squinted.

"Listen for it now, okay? Like a cough. Churt-churt. Churt-churt-
churt."

And then, just as he'd described it, the call sounded. She opened
her eyes. "Yes! I heard it that time."

He nodded his approval. "Red-bellied woodpecker. They've got
a different call this time of year. Usually, it's kwirr kwirr." He closed
his eyes. "Cardinal. Blue jay. Chickadee. Woodpecker again." While
she'd been reveling in clouds, he'd been reveling in birdcalls. "Know
the most important tool for birding?"

Wren thought a moment. "Binoculars?"

He made the sound of a buzzer. "Your ears! That's how you know what's around. Even if you can't see them, you can hear them. You have to know how to listen."

She hoped he wouldn't ask her name. She didn't want to reveal that a woman named after a bird knew so little about them.

"Michigan," he said. "This is a good place to be, right on the migration path. You get them coming and going." He scanned the patch of sky. "They'll be going soon, some of them, anyway. Heading south once the weather turns. You seen the way the geese fly in those *V*s, how they take turns being the leaders?"

Wren nodded.

"Know why one side of the *V* is longer than the other?"

"No."

"'Cause there's more birds on that side." He laughed, then signaled to a staff member that he was ready to go back indoors.

Wren sat down on a bench, eyes still fixed on the patch of blue, ears now tuned for a variety of songs she couldn't identify. Her mother probably knew some of the calls. She loved birds. She loved telling the story of how a bird had saved her. Or rather, how God had saved her by sending one.

Maybe she'd call and ask her mother to tell her the story again, to remind her she wasn't alone, that God was with her. Despite how it seemed.

2

Oh, her sweet little bird.

Jamie Crawford gripped her phone to her chest and leaned against the bannister. It took every ounce of strength not to hop on the next plane from North Carolina to Michigan and wrap her oldest daughter in her arms. But Wren had again insisted this was a journey she needed to make on her own. She didn't want her family seeing her like this. *Not here, Mom. Not now. Maybe after they send me home.*

"Are you all right, Mommy?" Five-year-old Phoebe, her surprise baby at forty-two, had stopped coloring at the table and was staring at her, brow furrowed. Even speaking in code from the adjacent room hadn't been enough to conceal heartache and worry.

"Fine, love." Jamie set her phone down on the kitchen counter and pulled up a chair. "Tell me about your pretty picture."

"I'm making a card for Wren."

"Are you?" Nothing got past that child.

"Since she's sad."

"That's so thoughtful, Phoebe. I know she'll love getting a card from you."

Phoebe scrunched her nose in concentration as she peered into her box of colors. "She's so sad because her friend moved away."

Jamie reached for a blank piece of paper from the stack in front of Phoebe. She would need to be more careful what she communicated to Dylan when the kids were around. "Well, I'm sure your pretty rainbow will make her very happy."

"And I'm drawing a fairy. Like the one that landed on your tummy."

Jamie removed a royal blue crayon from the box. "Phoebe, when Mommy's on the phone, sometimes it's to talk about grown-up things you don't need to worry about, okay?"

"I know. Daddy tells me that all the time."

Much as Jamie would have liked to change the subject entirely and let the fairy misunderstanding drop, if she didn't correct her, Phoebe would likely wander around Fellowship Hall on Sunday morning telling people about the fairy that God sent her mommy when Wren was in her tummy.

Jamie sketched the outline of a bird before coloring its plump little body and upright tail. "It wasn't a fairy that landed on Mommy's lap. It was a bird called a fairywren, a tiny little bird that's bright, bright blue like this, see?"

Phoebe pressed her hands to the table and leaned forward. "That doesn't look like a bird."

"No, I'm not a good artist like you or Wren. But this is like the little bird that landed on my lap one day when I was praying. They have lots of these birds in Australia. I'll show you a picture of a real one later."

Phoebe lowered her head and sighed dramatically. "I'm just so sad."

Dylan entered the kitchen, holding his favorite sermon-writing mug. "Why's my girl so sad?"

"Because I'll never ever get to see a real fairy bird or koala."

He cast Jamie a *Where did that come from?* look.

Jamie mimed "big ears" and "Wren."

He patted Phoebe on the head. "Maybe when you're older we'll all take a trip to Australia, and you can see where your mommy was born and where I first saw her and fell in love with her. And you'll get to see lots of wallabies and kangaroos and koalas."

"And cassowaries that will rip your guts out," twelve-year-old Joel called from the family room.

"Ewwwwww!" Phoebe exclaimed.

"Not on my watch," Dylan said. "Nothing's going to hurt my girl."

Joel appeared in the doorway, holding his science book, head-phones draped around his neck. "You think they're cute, but koalas will rip your face off."

Dylan held up his hand. "Joel, that's enough."

"Just saying."

"Enough."

Without another word Joel slunk back to the couch.

"Phoebe, put your crayons away for now and go upstairs to play, okay? I need to talk to Mommy."

"But I want—"

"Now. Please."

"We'll finish our coloring later," Jamie said. "And here, I'll put your rainbow on the fridge, so we can all enjoy it before we send it to your sister."

"I need to draw the fairy."

"Okay, take it with you. But color on your desk, not your bed, okay?"

"You too, Joel," Dylan said. "Upstairs for a while. Let me talk to Mom in private."

They waited until they heard two bedroom doors close upstairs, one more angrily than the other. "She hates missing out on conversations," Jamie said.

"And I hate her eavesdropping. We're going to have to start having all our important conversations in my office or something. Either that, or tell the church we're done living in this old manse and find a house that's big enough." Dylan had been making that threat ever since Olivia, now sixteen, was in elementary school. The house hadn't been designed with a growing family in mind. But the view over the valley was priceless, especially when fireflies winked like a thousand sparkling lights, or when hot-air balloons rose from the valley floor to float over bronze and scarlet trees, or when morning mist hung like a gauzy veil on the evergreens. Wren loved the view as much as Jamie did. She often painted it during her visits.

Dylan emptied his mug into the sink. "So, fill me in. What's the latest?"

"She still doesn't want me to come."

"I know she says that, but . . ."

"She says it will be too upsetting for me." No matter how hard Jamie had tried to convince her otherwise, Wren was unpersuaded. "I told her it's not about me, that it's about her, about loving and supporting her. And she says this is how I can best do that, by staying away. I want to honor her wishes, but . . ."

"Has Kit been there?"

"She didn't say. I didn't ask."

"I'll call her and see if she'll go visit."

Jamie shook her head slowly. "No. Wait." Even though Kit, Dylan's favorite aunt, would be a prayerful, compassionate presence, Wren hadn't given permission to share any details about her hospitalization. "I feel like we'd be betraying her, especially if she hasn't told anyone where she is."

"But Kit's got experience with these kinds of things. Wouldn't you feel better knowing she was there?"

"Of course I would, but . . ."

He picked up his phone. "Blame it on me. We're calling her."

No, Kit said, she hadn't heard from her. She'd last seen her at Kingsbury's art festival, where Wren had exhibited one of her paintings in the corridor of a downtown restaurant. "Her seascape was gorgeous," she told Jamie, "but very dark. I'm no painter, but it felt turbulent. There were a lot of people around, though, and I didn't have a chance to talk with her about it. I wish now that I'd followed up with her. I'm so sorry."

Jamie had seen a photo of Wren's entry, the tumbling waves and stormy skies thick with Van Gogh-esque brushstrokes but lacking her usual vibrancy of color. Though Wren had insisted it was a good experience to exhibit in the public vote competition, she had also intimated how vulnerable she'd felt sitting next to her work while people feigned interest or passed judgment on it with an averted gaze or a perfunctory compliment. Jamie regretted not flying out for the event. But Olivia had been preparing for her driver's exam, and Phoebe had been sick with strep, and Dylan had been away at a ministry conference, and Joel—there had been something happening with Joel too, but now she couldn't remember what it was.

"I'd love to visit her," Kit was saying, "if she'll put me on her list."

A science fair. Joel had had a big project due for a science fair, and with Dylan out of town . . .

"Do you want to check with her and see?" Kit asked. "I know the visiting hours are usually pretty limited, but I'd be happy to rearrange my schedule and get there whenever it's open for her."

"I'll call her," Jamie said. "But honestly, she probably won't be happy we told you. Nothing against you, I mean . . ."

"No, I understand. These things are so hard. And the feeling of shame makes it worse. Poor girl." She paused. "I'm so glad you let me know. At least I can be praying. Is there anything else I can do?"

Jamie couldn't think of anything, so she thanked her, told her she'd keep her updated, and handed the phone back to Dylan.

How many hours had she spent over the years trying to make sense of Wren's depression, trying to identify some root cause, some inciting event, some maternal failure or oversight that would lead a beloved daughter to question whether she could live the life she'd been given? Would it have been easier to accept her daughter's illness if she'd been able to explain it? Even if she could have explained it or understood it, that didn't mean she could control or prevent it. Though, God knows, she'd tried.

And what about this latest round? For years Wren had insisted she didn't need to be hospitalized, that she could press through her struggles with depression and anxiety with the help of counseling and medication. It hadn't been easy, but she had managed. Even with the stress of being a social worker—a career choice Jamie had always worried would crush her—Wren had managed and had even, at times, thrived. Helping others gave her a sense of purpose.

She's sad because her friend moved away, Phoebe had observed.

No doubt about it, Casey's sudden move and marriage had hit Wren hard, not because there had ever been any romantic attachment between them, but because they had been like siblings. After sharing so much of life together, it was understandable that Wren should grieve his absence. But was that enough to explain her descent into severe melancholy and paralyzing anxiety?

Then again, Jamie reminded herself, who was she to stand in judgment over someone else's sorrow?

If Wren knew what had precipitated her latest decline, she hadn't shared that information with her family. She'd only said she was too tired to fight against the darkness and needed radical intervention. She was frightened, she said, frightened enough to seek admission to a psychiatric hospital.

Jamie stared out the window at streaks of clouds twining above the valley like tendrils.

Her daughter was in a psychiatric hospital. Her daughter was suffering from mental illness. There was nothing she could do to fix it, nothing she could do to alleviate the pain, nothing she could do.

You can pray, some would reply. *You can trust God.*

She did. But that didn't mean he would fix it, either.

3

No matter how old she got, Wren never tired of hearing the narrative of what her mother called her "holy visitation."

She propped a pillow behind her, opened her notebook, and sketched the outline of her winged namesake.

When she was small, Wren would sit cross-legged in the pasture and hope one of the little fairywrens flitting between the shrubs surrounding the paddock would decide she was a very good girl and come sit on her lap too. But her stillness never persuaded them, which made what happened to her mother seem all the more magical and mysterious.

She shaded the tail with her pencil edge.

One of her favorite childhood nighttime rituals had been curling up with her mother beneath the attic bedroom skylight, the two of them tucked beneath her grandmother's quilt, her mother's voice lilting and lovely, soothing fears and anxieties by assuring Wren that she was safe, that God watched over her, that God himself had knit her together—not with long needles like Gran's, but with love. Wren hadn't understood what it looked like for God to knit with love, but she had a sense that she was special and chosen, that she was known and seen, even before she was born.

"But what did the bird do after it hopped into your lap?" she would ask.

Her mother would reply, "It looked at me as if to say, 'I've been sent to deliver a message from God.'"

"What message?"

"'Don't be afraid.'"

So Wren would lean her head against her pillow and try very hard not to be afraid. Because if God had said, "Don't be afraid," then she shouldn't be afraid. Not of anything.

But she was still glad Pop carried his snake stick whenever they walked the bush together. Because an eastern brown snake had struck and killed one of the dogs before Wren was born—Pop had told her the story so she would be very careful and watch for them in the garden—and she worried that Tangara, her favorite sheepdog, would someday be bitten and killed too. They were fast and aggressive, the eastern browns, and Pop said they had a bad temper, that they could rear up like a stallion and strike with venom powerful enough to paralyze a small girl. And her mother would motion for him to stop telling her such things, but he would say, "She needs to know so she can be prepared."

So, whenever her mother's head disappeared beneath the trap door as she descended the ladder with a final, "I love you! Sleep tight!" Wren would barricade herself behind a wall of stuffed toys, burrow beneath the covers, and try to spot the Southern Cross through the skylight, because if she could see it, she knew God could see her.

She shoved her notebook under the blanket just as her roommate entered. Maybe after Monica fell asleep, she would sketch a pregnant woman with a bird on her lap. She wished she had brought her tin of graphite pencils, but those would probably have been confiscated along with the shoelaces and drawstring. She ought to be grateful she was allowed to keep a single pencil. Poor Vincent van Gogh, he'd had his pen confiscated at the asylum. His materials, too, after he swallowed oil paint and turpentine during one of his attacks. He suffered from temporal lobe epilepsy, his doctors said, with terrible seizures and hallucinations that terrified him and could last for weeks. Poor tormented Vincent, wounded and stranded and frightened, longing for a cup of comfort, for rescue, for peace.

Wren cleared her throat and said hello when she noticed Monica staring at her.

Monica mumbled hello. Then she shuffled toward her bed, removed her pajamas from beneath her pillow, and disappeared behind the bathroom curtain to change her clothes.

Wren hoped she would be able to sleep without being awakened every half hour by Monica's snoring, even with the in-ear headphones Kelly had supplied. She ought to feel compassion for a fellow sufferer—whatever her suffering was—but instead she felt only desperate exhaustion.

That's how she had framed her struggle to her mother when she called a second time: yes, she'd been having frequent panic attacks and was feeling depressed, but she knew if she could get some sleep, and if they could get the medications regulated again, she would be okay. And no, it wasn't necessary for Kit to come during visitor hours. She just wanted to focus on attending her groups and trying to get well enough to go home. In the morning she would submit her written request for discharge, and then she would be kept a maximum of three more days, which, she'd assured her mother, was more than enough time. Especially when the cure sometimes felt as hard as the affliction.

Mental illness.

She suffered from "mental illness." She had tried to come to grips with that label when she was first diagnosed with anxiety and depression in high school. "There's no shame in this," the doctor had said, handing her the first of many prescriptions. "If you were diabetic, you would need insulin."

But that logic seemed lost on some Christians she'd met who, though it never would have occurred to them to judge a diabetic for taking medication, insisted that the depressed and anxious should be able to "pray their way out of it" or "memorize more Scripture" and be cured. That's what one small group leader had told her when she confided during her junior year of college that she was struggling to cope. "Anxiety and depression are all about a lack of faith," the leader said. If she would just repent and trust Jesus, she would be fine.

"And you wonder why I don't go to church?" Casey had said when she told him. Then he ranted about Job's comforters being alive and well, spouting their pious platitudes to those who sat in dust and ashes. Wren regretted telling him. He didn't need more fuel for his resentment about church.

Shortly after that she stopped attending the small group and changed churches. She also decided she wouldn't speak again about her affliction to anyone except Casey, her parents, and her counselor. She couldn't risk further reproach. If she could have "believed Jesus" for a way out of the darkness, she would have. For years she'd tried. But being told her anxiety and depression were rooted in sin or lack of faith or spiritual warfare only made her more anxious and depressed.

The curtain swished along the metal rod, and Monica emerged in striped flannel pajamas, clutching her jeans and sweatshirt like a life preserver to her chest.

"Your socks," Wren said, pointing. "You dropped your—"

"Oh. Thanks." When she stooped to pick them up, she nearly lost her balance.

"Are you okay?"

Monica looked up, mouth twisted in a wry frown. "Are any of us?"

Unsure if this was an opening for conversation—unsure if she wanted an opening for conversation—Wren tried to squeeze the tip of her pinkie finger through the hole where the sweatshirt drawstring belonged.

"All of this"—Monica swirled her hand in front of her face—"all the masks, all the 'I'm fine, everything's fine, it's all good,' it all comes off whether we want it to or not. It comes off in a place like this. And they say I'm brave. Brave for what? For leaving my kids with my mother so I can take a break from being one? That makes me brave? It makes me sick." This last word she spit with disgust. "And as for the psychiatrist, Breyer, Bauer—"

"Browerly?"

"Yeah, Browerly. What a waste of space he is, sitting there at his computer, not even looking at you while he types away. It's all so . . . so . . ."

Wren waited for her to find the word.

"*Dehumanizing.* A number, I'm a number. His 'two-fifteen' or 'ten-thirty' or 'one-forty-five.' I'm an appointment, that's all." She kicked off her slippers. "Just part of another billable hour so he can have his cottage at the lake or take his cruise or whatever."

Wren cleared her throat again. "Kelly's nice."

"Yeah, Kelly's fine. But Kelly isn't the one making the decisions about me being here, Browerly is. And when you actually want to see him, that's when he avoids you. Have you noticed that? How if you want to see him about getting out or if you have a complaint about something, he's"—she signed air quotes—"'unavailable'? Have you noticed that?"

She had. But Dr. McKendrick, the other psychiatrist everyone seemed to prefer, was full. She had asked.

"All a big racket, the whole thing," Monica said. "I never should have agreed to come here. And what do they say, that ninety percent of us will end up back here? No, not me." Her eyes lit with fierce determination as she flung back the blanket and crawled into bed. "Not me."

No, Wren thought. *Not me, either. Please, no.*

She drew her knees tightly to her chest and waited until she heard Monica's breathing settle into an uneasy rhythm of sleep before she removed her own pajamas from beneath her pillow and tiptoed toward the bathroom curtain, making sure to pull it quietly behind her. *Not me. Not a statistic.* She would prove the statistics wrong. She wriggled her right arm out of her sleeve and pulled the sweatshirt upward. *Now, breathe.* She lingered, face covered in the dark shroud, and focused on filling her diaphragm.

Dr. Browerly hadn't looked her in the eye the entire fifteen minutes she'd sat in front of his vast, untidy desk that afternoon. A small, anxious child summoned to the principal's office for interrogation, she hadn't bothered to correct him when he called her by the wrong name. *No, sir,* she didn't think she had a problem with anger. *No, sir,* she hadn't experienced a sense of rage like that before. He changed the dosage of one of the medications and sent her away.

Breathe.

She couldn't remember how to breathe.

She tried to yank the sweatshirt off, but her left arm felt like dead weight, and she was pinned, flailing, her throat constricting.

Breathe!

She couldn't swallow. She was choking.

Help!

No words, no breath. Her heart was pounding. Her chest was going to explode. She could feel her throbbing pulse in her ears. She was going to die. She ripped off the sweatshirt, then her T-shirt, leaving her torso bare, shivering, sweating. This time she was going to die. She was floating, swirling. She lowered herself onto the cold tile floor and surrendered to the consuming dark.

No. No sedative. She didn't want any more medications. These panic attacks, they came in relentless waves, and sometimes she didn't know what triggered them. Those were the particularly terrifying ones, the attacks that ambushed without apparent cause or correlation. "Let me take a shower," she said to Bree, the night shift worker who'd found her huddled and hyperventilating behind the curtain on one of the fifteen-minute checks. "That will help relax me."

Monica, who had been awakened by the commotion, turned over in her bed, sighed loudly, and pulled the covers over her face.

"I'm sorry," Wren said. And then silently added, *But you've kept me up plenty of times.* She wrapped her sweatshirt more tightly around herself and lowered her voice. "Please, Bree."

"Are you sure you don't want to see a nurse?"

She wasn't sure about much of anything right now, except that she didn't want to lose any more control. "Just a shower. Please."

Bree hesitated, then said, "Okay. You'll need to press the button—"

"I know." She wasn't a newbie, and she hadn't forgotten the drill: press the button on the wall every thirty seconds to keep the water flowing so the staff knew you were still alive.

A few minutes later she stood beneath a spray of water, hand poised beside the button and tears streaming down her cheeks. *My God, my God,* she murmured. *Why?*

4

You've got to fly out there," Dylan told Jamie as he straightened his tie. "If she won't let Kit come visit her, then you need to go."

Jamie ran the lint roller over the back of his suit coat, meeting his gaze in their mirrored closet door.

"The kids and I will be fine," he said. "Olivia can help around here, and we can recruit some people to help out in the office." Ever since the longtime church secretary retired, Jamie had been volunteering several days a week.

"That's not the issue," she said. "Wren still insists she needs to face this on her own."

Dylan shrugged slightly. "Yeah, but she needs some support, even if she says she doesn't."

"But what would we tell the congregation? She won't want any of this public."

"No, I know. Sad, isn't it? If she'd been hospitalized with gallstones or appendicitis or something, we would've put it on the prayer chain."

"Put what on a chain?" Phoebe chirped from the doorway.

"Nothing, Phoebe. Let me talk to Daddy, okay?"

"C'mon, Feebs," Olivia said, grabbing her hand with a knowing glance at her mother. She had obviously been eavesdropping too. "You need to get dressed for church."

"Mommy needs to pick out my clothes."

"I'll help you today."

"Thanks, Liv," Jamie said. Olivia nodded and closed the bedroom door.

"See?" Dylan said, tugging on his collar. "We'll be fine. And if anyone asks, I'll say Wren has been under some stress lately and wants time with her mom. End of story. People know she has a stressful job. They won't ask questions."

He was probably right. "Stress" was a far more socially acceptable label than "nervous breakdown." People were generally sympathetic and understanding about stress.

She tore off the lint-covered sticky tape and crumpled it. If only she had caught on to some of the warning signs earlier. If only she had asked more questions, been more attentive, more proactive. If only, if only, if only. "Okay," she said. "I'll call the hospital."

It was late afternoon before Wren returned her call, her voice thin and tired. "You know I'd love to see you, Mom, but now's not a good time."

Jamie closed the bedroom door and sat down on the edge of her bed. "But I hate the thought of you going through all this alone."

"Even if you came, visiting hours are only twice a week. And I'm really hoping I'll only be here a few more days."

"Did you submit your request to be released?"

"No. Not after the episode last night. I'll give it another day, see how the medication adjustment works."

"Sweetheart, I wish . . ."

"I know. I wish you could make it all better too. But you can't. No one can."

Jamie smoothed the blue patchwork bedspread, her fingers lingering on her mother's hand-quilted stitches. "What about after you get home? I don't like the thought of you being alone in your apartment. What if I come then?"

"Maybe. But honestly, I can't even think past today. I don't feel like I can make any plans right now. I'm sorry."

"No, I know. I don't want to put any pressure on you. I just want to do whatever I can to love and support you through this."

"I know, Mom."

"Are you sure you don't want Kit to know? She would come see you, I know she would."

"No, it's okay. I called the church. My pastor's coming tonight."

"Oh, that's good, honey." *Thank God.*

Someone was shouting in the background, a man with a voice raised in cursing anger. "I should go," Wren said. "Hallway phone and everything."

"Right. But you'll let me know about when—if it's okay for me to come? You know I'd be there in a heartbeat, but I don't want to intrude. I don't want to push."

"I know. Thanks."

Sometimes eight hundred miles felt like ten thousand. "I love you, Wren."

"I love you too."

Then she was gone.

Jamie set her phone on her nightstand and stared at the panoply of family photo collages adorning the wall: six-year-old Wren, her dark bob pinned back with two pink plastic barrettes, lying on her stomach beneath a willow tree, reading *The Velveteen Rabbit* to a favorite sheepdog; eight-year-old Wren, her new black suede riding helmet firmly fastened beneath her chin, her large brown eyes wide with wonder and a bit of fear as she sat atop the gentle mare, Bramble, Pop holding the reins to lead her around the paddock for an inaugural ride; ten-year-old Wren dressed in white satin and lace, wicker flower basket in hand, shyly smiling up at Jamie and Dylan on their wedding day at the stone church outside of Sydney; twelve-year-old Wren pushing baby Olivia in a stroller at a park in Kingsbury; sixteen-year-old Wren, thin and diminutive in her sapphire blue prom gown, standing on tiptoes to pin Casey's corsage. Jamie leaned in for a closer look, seeking again to discern when the shadow of sadness had first entered her daughter's eyes. But hard as she tried, she couldn't find its origin. The wariness had always been there, the apprehension shading even the deepest moments of joy.

"An old soul," Pop used to say. "Wren was born knowing the measure of things."

For months after Wren was first diagnosed with depression and anxiety in high school, Jamie had tried to find a straightforward explanation for it. Was it the result of being raised by a single mom for her first ten years? But other children endured that trial and didn't inevitably suffer with mental illness. And Wren had been surrounded by love and care as a child, adored by her mother and grandparents.

Was it the adjustment of welcoming a stepfather into the family? But Dylan had from the very beginning regarded her as a beloved daughter, adopting her as his own. And there hadn't been other siblings to compete with, not in those first days of being a new family.

There was, of course, the upheaval of the international move when Dylan, an American, felt called to return to his roots in the States and start seminary, so they left Australia for him to commence his ministry training in Kingsbury, Michigan. That had been hard on Wren, leaving behind the only world she'd ever known, saying goodbye to grandparents and pets and friends. It was hard on her, leaving behind the spaciousness of the farm for a studio apartment in Kit's basement, where they stayed a few weeks before moving into a marginally larger apartment near campus.

It had all been hard. But Wren's accent was a novelty at her new school, and she quickly made new friends. And by the time Dylan finally finished his training and took his first post as a solo pastor in North Carolina, Wren was already well established at Kingsbury University. Saying goodbye to her family might have been stressful then, but many college students lived on campus, far away from home.

"You always do this, you know," Dylan said as he and Jamie straightened up Fellowship Hall later that night.

"Do what?"

"Try to explain it, try to assign blame."

She brushed cookie crumbs off the buffet table. She would vacuum in the morning. "I'm not blaming her."

"I'm not talking about blaming her. I'm talking about blaming yourself."

"I'm not blaming—"

"Jamie . . ."

A lump rose in her throat. A counselor had told her the same thing years ago. And still it was her default position whenever Wren became unwell.

Dylan set a folding chair onto the metal rack and reached for another. "Tell me this," he said. "Which part of the story would you change?"

Immediately, her mind raced to what her parents had referred to as her "indiscretion," a single romantic evening spent beneath a pearled night sky on a soft sandy beach in Fiji. She and a few university friends had flown there from Sydney for a short holiday. She met him at a bar, where they drank way too much. She only ever knew his first name. She didn't know where he was from. There was no finding him, even if she had wanted to. And she hadn't wanted to. Overcome with shame and regret, she withdrew from the University of Sydney, where she was training to be a teacher, and kept the baby. She kept her Wren. Thank God she had kept her Wren.

Dylan leaned his head sideways to look her in the eyes. "Yank one thread—remove one single dark thread—and what else unravels?"

5

In Glenwood's main lounge, patients gathered with their designated visitors around tables with puzzles and board games or in chairs clustered together in an attempt at private conversations. A few sat in front of a television set, staring blankly forward rather than at one another, words spoken from the sides of their mouths. Wren waited in an upholstered chair in the far corner of the room, hands folded in her lap, watching for her pastor to arrive.

Ever since Casey's departure she had been a regular attender at Wayfarer, eager to use her spare time to volunteer at the food pantry or help coordinate clothing and toy drives. But though she was on friendly terms with the pastoral staff, she had never sought their care. She hadn't intended to call the church now. But she was desperate.

"Okay if I play?" a voice called from the blond spinet piano. With murmurs of assent around the room, the courtyard birder rolled up his sleeves, and began playing "Tomorrow" from *Annie*.

"Oh, gawd!" Sylvia yelled from a table where she was assembling a puzzle by herself. "Anything but that!"

"You know any Sinatra?" someone called.

Another voice said, "No Sinatra. Play a hymn."

"No! No hymns. Jazz."

The birder stopped up his ears and yelled, "No requests!" before playing a classical piece Wren didn't recognize. The piano badly needed tuning. Or maybe it was beyond tuning.

"Wren?"

She turned to face her pastor, Hannah Allen, who was holding a bouquet of sunflowers. Rising to her feet, Wren blinked back tears. "How did you know?"

"Know what?"

Know how desperately she had longed for something natural, something beautiful, something cheerful, something that declared, *I know where you are and what you need.* "Sunflowers," Wren said. "They're my favorite."

Hannah smiled. "Oh, good. I'm glad."

Wren clutched them to her chest. Vincent had loved sunflowers too, in all of their life stages, from nascent to hearty to withering bloom. He painted them to cheer bedroom walls, welcome a friend, and shine like sacred flaming candelabras in the dark.

Hannah gestured toward the bouquet. "I'm sorry about the paper towel. I had them in a glass vase, but I didn't think about . . ."

"It's okay. They probably have plastic ones around here somewhere. I'll find something."

Hannah settled into her chair, feet crossed at the ankles. "I'm so glad to see you, Wren."

How did she know?

How did Hannah know how deeply she longed for her name to be tenderly spoken by someone other than her mother? How did she know?

"I wasn't going to call the church. I mean, no offense or anything. I just . . . being here . . . I wanted to keep it private."

"I understand. Pastor Neil is the only other person who knows I'm here. Well, Neil and my husband. But I won't share any details."

"It's okay. I don't mind them knowing."

The birder, having finished his classical piece, was playing "Tomorrow" again. Sylvia jumped up and started cursing. "Ah, leave him alone!" another woman said. "Let Bud play what he wants."

"I'm sorry," Wren said as multiple voices rose in anger. "There's no quiet place to talk." While those for and against the music argued, Bud soldiered on.

Hannah tucked a wisp of her short gray hair behind her ear and leaned slightly forward, deep compassion filling her eyes and etching her brow. It was one of the first things Wren had noticed about her when she started attending Wayfarer—how Hannah, the minister of congregational life, always seemed to be fully present to the person in front of her.

"Have you been here long?" Hannah asked.

Wren mentally calculated the days. "A week tomorrow. But it seems a lot longer than that. And I thought I'd be feeling better by now, but I'm really not." In the presence of compassion, the words poured out faster than she'd expected. "I hate staying here, but I don't trust myself to go home. I don't trust myself to make any decisions right now, not when I'm so churned up and exhausted. I thought this would be a rest for me, a break from my life. But it hasn't been the break I was hoping for." She shifted in her seat. "I was desperate, that's why I came here. I couldn't turn off the dark thoughts, no matter how hard I tried or how much I prayed. And then I spent a whole weekend in bed, and the crying wouldn't stop, and I got really scared. I've had bouts with depression before—it's kind of a cloud I've learned to live with—but this time was different. I felt like I was going under, like I'd never feel hopeful again, and then that just made my anxiety worse and it all spiraled from there."

"It sounds terrifying, Wren. Exhausting."

"Yes. It is." She rubbed her hand against the damp paper towel, then pressed the bottom of the stems against her palm, creating tiny temporary circles on her skin.

"I'm so sorry you've had to suffer like this. It's such a hard road, depression. Anxiety too. It's all hard. And it can feel so lonely."

Exactly. And the sense of isolation made it worse.

Casey had understood it firsthand, the intense and wearying and consuming battle fought inwardly, day after day, month after month, year after year, the inner screams for mercy no one heard. And some days you wondered if God heard. People who hadn't suffered through it couldn't comprehend the strength, the resiliency, the courage, the energy it required to put one foot in front of the other and perform even the simplest of daily tasks. If they could see, they might be in awe. Or filled with compassion. They would never say,

Snap out of it. That's what people had often said to Casey. Even his parents. They didn't know how to deal with him, how to help him. She hoped his wife did.

"Is there anyone alongside to support you in this?" Hannah asked.

She wasn't going to cry. She wasn't going to think or talk about Casey and his absence. She couldn't. "My family," she said. "They've always been really supportive. But they live in North Carolina. My mom wanted to come out and help, but there isn't anything she can do for me right now, and I don't want her to see me here. Maybe after I go home. I'm kind of freaked out about going home, about being by myself again."

"You live alone?"

"Just me and my cat. The neighbor thinks I'm away on vacation. She's feeding him for me."

"Is there anywhere else you could go, anyone you could stay with for a while?"

"No, not really. My friends all have roommates, or they're married, and it would be awkward." She thought a moment. "There's my dad's aunt, Kit. We lived with her for a few weeks when I was younger, but she's allergic to cats, and I'm not giving Theo up. Some days he's the one thing that gets me out of bed. Well, Theo, and not wanting to let anyone down at work. My job has kept me going. But also worn me out."

"I can understand that."

A middle-aged man had joined Bud at the piano and was singing along with gusto to the show tunes he played. The arguing had stopped, and many in the room had paused their conversations to listen to his sweet tenor voice. *Sunrise, sunset, sunrise, sunset, swiftly flow the days.* Bud swayed as he fingered his swelling arpeggios. Even Sylvia had closed her eyes and was moving in her chair to the rhythm of the lyrics, momentarily soothed.

"I'm not sure I can keep going." Wren looked down at the flowers in her lap so she wouldn't see shock or disappointment in her pastor's eyes.

But Hannah's voice was gentle. "Going with . . . ?"

"With anything. Work, life. I know it sounds awful, but sometimes I wonder if I can keep going with my faith, whether I can keep holding onto God."

"Oh, Wren."

Two syllables spoken with compassion rather than condemnation broke her open. Her chest began to heave in muffled sobs.

Hannah's hand rested lightly on her shoulder. "It's not your grip on God. It's his grip on you. Especially when you're too tired to cling."

A cliff face. That's what Wren saw when her pastor prayed for her—a treacherous cliff face she was trying to climb. But she was tired, so desperately tired, and her grip wasn't going to hold. And then, as she watched in her imagination, the cliff became an enormous upright hand, and still, she tried to climb, to fasten herself to something solid so she wouldn't plunge to her death. Beneath her loomed a dark abyss. She tried not to look at it. She tried to keep her gaze fixed on the creases in the hand where she might grab hold. But she was slipping and gasping in terror.

And then—

The hand shifted from vertical to horizontal, becoming a bowl, a cradle, a nest. And she was caught. Held.

A gift, Hannah said after Wren described what she had seen. She'd been given an image that was a gift from the Spirit, something to help when she felt like she was plummeting. Hannah scanned the room. "I had to leave my phone and my bag at the check-in desk," she said. "I wonder if they've got a Bible here somewhere."

Wren pointed toward low bookshelves on the far wall. "Over there, probably." She hadn't bothered to bring her Bible to the hospital. Reading the Word the past few months had felt like chewing cardboard. She wondered if her pastor would understand that. Or maybe, like Allie and her former small group leader, Hannah would remind her of the importance of reading the Word, especially when she didn't feel like it. Maybe she'd remind her that when you're sinking, you need a firm, solid place to stand. Because, she might say, if your life isn't built on the foundation of the Word, you'll be swallowed whole. You've been given the mind of Christ. You've got to work hard to renew it.

But that was like commanding a quadriplegic to run a marathon. When your mind was broken and ill, you couldn't work at much of anything.

Hannah had retrieved a Bible from the shelf and now sat in front of her again, flipping through pages. "The image you saw reminded me of something from one of the Psalms. Thirty-four, maybe." She skimmed the page. "No. Not that one, though that's a good one too." She turned a couple of pages slowly, still scanning. "Here it is. Psalm 37, verse 24. 'Though he may stumble, he will not fall, for the Lord upholds him with his hand.'" She looked up. "That's like what you saw. God's hand upholding you."

Uphold.

Wren liked that word. If she had her phone, she would look up the meaning and origin of it. But her phone had been confiscated too.

"Years ago," Hannah said, "back when I lived in Chicago, I was holding a baby before the congregation, getting ready to baptize her. And the little one had her hand wrapped around one of my fingers. From her perspective, she was the one holding me. What she didn't see, what she couldn't yet know, was that I was the one holding her."

Wren let the picture form in her mind: the tiny fist clinging, the hands and arms undergirding. "I don't think I know how to trust that right now. I don't even know how to ask for it, how to pray."

Hannah nodded. "It's okay. You don't need words right now. You can groan or cry or be silent. For now, let the Spirit pray for you. In you. That's a deep kind of trusting, a deep kind of consenting prayer, saying yes to being held."

Wren had never heard prayer described that way before. Prayer was work. And when she was overwhelmed or anxious, she needed to pray harder. Pray harder and read more Scripture: that was the standard prescription for Christian health and maturity. *Because feelings aren't facts*, a college mentor had reminded her many times, so she ought to disregard them. Master them.

That strategy hadn't worked. And maybe—maybe her feelings clamored more loudly because they hadn't been regarded or heard.

Bud was playing "Tomorrow" again. Other visitors were rising to leave as the top of the hour approached. Patients, some of them tearful, were saying their goodbyes. Hannah closed the Bible. "I'd love to come visit again if you're up for it," she said.

"I wish you could. But we don't have visiting hours again until Thursday."

Hannah smiled. "Special dispensation for pastors."

"Really?"

"Really. You let me know what time, and we can work it out for tomorrow. In fact, if you'd like, I can bring communion to you."

Wren was going to decline. That was the kind of ministry reserved for the sick or homebound or dying. Then she remembered where she was, confined and ill. How humbling. "Okay," she said. "I think that would be good."

"Great. What time works best for you?"

"After dinner? Maybe seven?"

"I'll be here," Hannah said.

Wren mustered half a smile. "So will I."

6

While the rest of the morning group discussed mindfulness strategies—or rather, while the social worker attempted to engage them in conversation about what helped them focus on the present moment—Wren held her notebook at an angle on her lap to conceal her sketching. Hands had always been difficult for her to draw in detail, the intricacy of the fingers confounding her. She erased her third attempt and brushed the residue off her paper.

"Do you have some thoughts, Wren?" Krystal asked.

She felt as if she had just been caught passing notes in junior high. "No." She shifted her foot to cover the tiny pink eraser flecks now visible on the brown vinyl floor and resumed her sketching. If Sylvia could snore and drool through the group, then she could draw. She slid her chair a few inches to the left so Sylvia's head wouldn't droop onto her shoulder.

Across from her in the circle a slouching twentysomething guy glanced toward the door, nodded, and held up one finger to signal he'd be there shortly. This he did every day, in every group. As he rose, she looked him in the eye. He winked, then sauntered to the hallway.

She wondered what he was in for.

Did any of them wonder what she was in for?

She tried again to sketch a thumb. But what she needed was a model sitting in front of her with a hand cupped like a nest. Casey had often modeled for her. In her apartment were sketchbooks filled with drawings of Casey with his camera or his storyboards, his gray

knit "inspiration cap" pulled down over his red hair. He gave that
beanie to her when he moved away. And little Theo. "Brooke can't
stand cats," he'd said. "You'll take care of him, won't you?" Of
course she would.

The woman next to the vacated chair sat with her hands opened
flat on her lap, eyes closed. She was probably trying to practice one
of the breathing mantras or body scans Krystal had recommended.
Cup your hand, Wren silently commanded her. C'mon. Close it just
a little bit.

The woman stretched her shoulders and leaned her head from
side to side but kept her hands still. Wren peered around the circle
to see if anyone was cooperating. No. No one. Drawing the hand
would have to wait.

She could draw the empty chair instead. Vincent, inspired by a
painting of Dickens' empty chair after he died, had painted a couple
of chairs, his own and artist friend Gauguin's. They were a symbol
of an artist's mortality, he wrote, a symbol of absence and the work
they left behind.

And perhaps, Wren thought, of the work left undone.

She adjusted the angle of her notebook. She would do a blind
contour drawing like Mrs. Hoffman had taught in tenth-grade art
class: fix your eyes on the object and quickly sketch its outline without
looking at your paper. Mrs. Hoffman said they needed to learn how
to see things in their true form, which required paying close attention to the object rather than drawing what they expected to see
when they heard the word *desk* or *tree*. Though the students had
laughed when they shared their distorted renderings of desks, trees,
chairs, and windows, the results were strangely beautiful in their
abstraction.

She fixed her gaze on the ordinary upholstered stacking chair,
placed her pencil point to the left of her page, and followed the line
of the top of the chair upward to the right at a slight diagonal, down
and slightly curved where the back met the seat, jutting out again
and then down to catch the narrow metal leg, then up straight and

back to the left along the bottom of the seat, down to catch the other front leg—

"Whatcha drawing?" Sylvia was awake again, and her loud, hoarse whisper caught the entire group's attention. "That chair over there?"

Wren ignored her. Her mild OCD tendencies meant she couldn't leave the chair unfinished, even if everyone was watching. She had to close the line.

"That's a good chair," Sylvia said. "Now draw mine. Draw me in my chair."

Krystal said, "Let's leave the drawing for now and bring our attention back to the group."

Evidently, the social worker was not an artist and did not appreciate the mindfulness drawing entailed. Wren did not say this aloud.

"Draw me," Sylvia whispered again. "Draw me in my chair."

Wren closed her notebook.

Sylvia tugged on her sleeve. "Draw me, draw me, draw me."

Wren inhaled through her nose, then exhaled slowly.

Sylvia nudged her with an elbow. "Hey. Draw me."

"Sylvia," Krystal said, "nobody's going to draw right now."

"Later. She's going to draw me later. Right?"

"Okay," Wren said. "Later." That might keep her quiet.

"She's going to draw me," Sylvia announced to the man sitting on her other side. He crossed his arms. She leaned in front of Wren, her crooked smile wide and open. "You're going to draw me."

Wren pictured Phoebe, her eyes lit with anticipation and delight, and said, "Yes. I'm going to draw you."

Since she didn't want to be scrutinized by others gathered in the lounge area waiting for lunch, Wren motioned to a corner near the nurses' station. "How about standing there?"

"Right here?"

"Yes, that's good. Right against the wall. And you'll need to stand still, okay?"

"Okay." Sylvia wiggled her shoulders, arms, and legs as if she was dancing the hokey pokey, then suddenly went rigid as a statue. "Like this?"

"Just like that." Wren opened her notebook to a blank sheet of lined paper. Then she took a good look at Sylvia: round face with puffy cheeks, mouth lines carved like deep crevices from her nose, short unkempt gray hair cut in jagged bangs, double chin, and dark gaps between yellowed, misshapen teeth.

Sylvia smiled broadly, her eyebrows rising like pointed peaks. Wren quickly drew an outline of her head, keeping her eyes on her subject as she moved her pencil. The woman hardly blinked, her smile frozen. "Like this?" Sylvia asked between clenched teeth.

"Yes." Lines for the eyebrows, the nose, the mouth, shading for the hair and eyes, lighter lines for the hint of shoulders, and there! Finished. She tore the page from her notebook. "Here you go."

Sylvia stared at it in silence, brow furrowed in concentration before exclaiming, "I'm beautiful! Look at me!" She shoved the paper in front of Wren's nose, then scuttled toward the lounge, flourishing the portrait above her head and calling out to any who would listen, "Hey, look at me! I'm beautiful!"

"My companions in misfortune," Vincent had called his fellow asylum patients. The phrase had caught Wren's attention years ago when she first read his letters to his brother Theo. Once she returned home, she would read them again, if she could manage the concentration. Her three-volume unabridged set had been a Christmas gift from her parents when she was in high school, the pages dog-eared and favorite passages underlined. Even at fourteen she had recognized within the anguished painter a kindred spirit. He kept her company now as she sat in the dining hall beneath his sunflowers, swirling her tomato soup with her spoon.

If only she had thought to bring her Van Gogh art books with her to the hospital, she could sit in her room with the plastic vase of sunflowers and feed her soul with his drawings and paintings. But she hadn't been thinking. That was the problem. She hadn't been thinking clearly about anything when she came to the hospital. Maybe it was a special gift that Vincent was already there, a reminder she wasn't alone.

Sylvia was circling every table, still holding the hastily drawn portrait next to her face. "My friend drew me. Look! Do you see me?"

Some murmured polite praise, others ignored her completely. A few tracked her pointing finger toward Wren, who pulled her sweatshirt hood over her head and slouched lower. But it was no use hiding. Soon Sylvia was tapping her firmly on the back and saying, "Draw my friend."

Wren swiped her last bit of bread against the bottom of the empty bowl, then chewed it slowly, head down.

Poke, poke, poke. "Hey! Draw my friend. She's beautiful too."

Wren looked up. Beside Sylvia stood Monica, who, with a half-shrug and self-conscious smile, communicated a silent message: *Sorry, will you humor her for me?*

"Oh, okay. Sure." Wren pushed back her chair and picked up her notebook and pencil.

"Where should I stand?" Monica asked.

"There," Sylvia said, pointing. "You can stand against the wall right there."

It was as good a place as any. Monica stood beside Vincent's sunflowers, fidgeting with her hands.

"You have to hold very still," Sylvia said. "And smile. Like this." She demonstrated a wide plastered grin.

Monica opted for a subtler approach with lips curled slightly upward but closed. Wren made a quick observational scan of her face, trying to find the main lines so that with a few well-chosen strokes she could capture something of her essence: square face, angular jaw, high brow. Dark shoulder-length curls, two dark moles on her left temple, dark circles cushioning heavy, sad eyes. Beneath the physical features were deeper realities of despair, weariness, and longing. *My companion in misfortune.*

After several minutes Monica visibly wilted under Wren's silent concentration, her face flushing with color. "It's okay," Sylvia said, reaching for her hand. "You're beautiful. You'll see."

"My girls will love this," Monica said after Wren finished shading her curls and handed her the sketch. "Thank you."

Sylvia bounced on the balls of her feet and clapped her hands. "I told you. See?"

It was no Van Gogh, that was for sure. But Vincent might have said she captured a bit of Monica's strength and dignity. He had been a master at finding beauty in the ordinary, beauty in the suffering, beauty in the broken and the poor, in the wounded and the neglected, in the forgotten and the discarded. Vincent knew how to see. Like Sylvia.

Teach me, Wren said silently. *I want to see beauty again.*

7

Dominic was gone—there were never any explanations given for changes in case managers—and the new one, Thomas, found her in the art studio, where the afternoon therapy group had been instructed to assemble "life collages" from clipped magazine photos.

"Sorry to take you away from your group," he said after summoning her into the hallway, "but I'd like to go over your file with you. Is that okay?"

She nodded, then mentally sketched him: bald head, round face, short dark beard starting to gray, dark eyes that smiled with his mouth. Congruity. Kindness.

"There's no one in the lounge right now. Would you like to sit there or come to the office?"

"The lounge, please." With most of the other patients in group sessions, the hallways were quiet too.

"Pick a comfortable spot," he said when they entered. Wren chose the corner where she and Hannah had sat the night before. Thomas pulled a chair forward a few inches before sitting down. "I've been going over your notes, and it looks like you're making good progress, Wren. How are you feeling?"

She shrugged. "My pastor was here last night, and that helped. I think I slept okay. That always helps."

"No more panic attacks?"

"No."

"No other incidents with the other residents?"

"No." She wondered what Dominic and Dr. Browerly had recorded about that.

He looked down at his notes again. "So, you came here a week ago, feeling overwhelmed, depressed, anxious, exhausted, feeling like you couldn't manage your life . . ." He looked up for confirmation. Wren nodded. "You spoke about racing thoughts you couldn't control, suicidal ideation . . ." He paused. "Sorry. I know it sounds like I'm reading a checklist, but I want to make sure I cover everything."

"It's okay." Thomas, at least, called her by the right name and appeared to care about her responses.

"Where would you say you are with the suicidal thoughts?"

"Okay, I guess."

"Tell me more."

She cleared her throat. "I don't think I would have gone through with anything, but there were dark thoughts I couldn't turn off. And that scared me."

"So, no planning—"

"No. Not like that. More like, I wouldn't mind if I closed my eyes and went to sleep and didn't wake up."

He nodded and scribbled a note. "And now? Do you still feel that way?"

"Not as much. But sometimes."

"How frequently would you say?"

She shrugged. "I don't know. A passing thought a few times a day?"

"But no specific plans to harm yourself?"

"No."

"Or anyone else?"

"No."

"And no history of chemical dependence?"

"No."

"How do you feel about the medications you're on? Does it seem like they're helping?"

"Yes, I think so. I mean, a couple of them I've been on before, and they seem to help."

"You understand the importance of taking them?"

"Yes." The despair she'd felt over the last few weeks had been enough to frighten her into committing to a disciplined regimen of therapy, medication, and pastoral support.

"Tell me about your job, Wren. It says here you're a social worker, that you work with domestic abuse victims."

"Yes, at Bethel House."

"That's tough work. Stressful."

She nodded. It was like constantly trying to save poor disoriented whales who, no matter how hard you tried to get them out into safety, might end up stranding themselves again on the exact same beach.

"How do you feel about going back?"

"I'm not sure. I mean, I want to, but I've been scared the past few weeks."

"Scared of what?"

"The responsibility, the pressure. I'm scared I might miss something important, that someone could be harmed if I make a mistake."

Thomas scribbled more notes. "Recovery is hard work. Maintaining good mental health takes a lot of energy. It might be worth thinking about some extended time off. Or even something more radical, like a job shift. Even temporarily."

She couldn't do that. She needed to pay her bills. She needed healthcare benefits, prescription coverage, counseling. It would be hard enough to afford all these things as a full-time employee. And who knew what the hospitalization would cost after insurance paid its portion? When she parsed her options that way, the decision was clear: she needed to find a way to stay at Bethel.

"Did Dominic talk to you about our daytime outpatient program?"

"Yes."

"What do you think about that? Are you willing to do it? It's an excellent program, a great way to transition from inpatient care to home."

Wren shook her head. "I think I've already gotten what I need and that I need to get back to my life, back to work."

"You're sure?"

"Yes."

He paused as if considering how hard to press. "Okay." He scrawled another note. "We'll send you home with information in case you change your mind. And there are other support networks locally that we recommend. We'll send you home with that information too."

"I'm going home?" Her heart began to race.

"Not today, no. But it could be as early as tomorrow, depending on what Dr. Browerly says. We typically say seven to ten days here for treatment. And you seem to be doing pretty well, so, once you fill out the safety crisis plan form and have that approved . . ."

Her ears buzzed.

"Wren?"

Her hands began to tingle. *Not here. Not right now. Breathe.*

"Are you okay?"

She nodded and filled her lungs from the diaphragm. *Breathe.*

In.

Out.

In.

Out.

"Wren?"

"I'm okay," she said, trying not to gasp for air. "I'm okay."

She wanted to go home. She did. So why had she panicked when Thomas gave her the good news she would soon be released?

She poked through the leftover jumble of magazine photos and word cut-outs on the art table while the others sat in a circle, some of them willing to show their collages and explain why the images spoke to them.

Thankfully, she had managed to avert a full-blown panic attack in front of her case manager. In fact, Thomas had commended her for using "good coping strategies." She had plenty of strategies. Sometimes they worked.

A photo of a lush English cottage garden, a riot of colors and blooms, caught her attention. She liked it because it was jumbled and haphazard and attracted birds and butterflies and bees. She could try to formulate a profound connection about how her life or her longings mirrored the garden, but she was too tired for the deep thought that required. Enough to say it was beautiful, and she was attracted to beauty. Beauty fed her soul. She laid the photo on the cardstock and kept rummaging. A bird in a nest. That was for her. A paintbrush—also hers. She set them on the cardstock. A little girl on a bicycle. She picked it up, surprised by the strong emotional response the image evoked. A little girl, maybe seven or eight, with long dark hair beneath a pink helmet, was riding with an expression of keen concentration mixed with terror, her father running alongside, beaming.

It was for her. She wasn't sure why it was for her, but it belonged.

"Monica?" a voice called from the hallway.

Wren glanced up as her roommate exited with her collage tucked under her arm. When she returned to their room before dinner, Monica's belongings were gone, and a white-haired stranger was sitting on her bed, clutching a battered teddy bear like a talisman to her chest.

"Hi," Wren said.

The woman, her gaze riveted upon the open pages of her book, mumbled hello. Wren slid her collage under her pillow, picked up her notebook, and walked to the dining room to sit beneath Vincent's skies.

It was a game she'd played as a little girl. Whenever she felt sad or anxious, she pretended she could jump into paintings, like the children in *Mary Poppins*. But she always made sure to jump into oil or acrylic paintings, not chalk drawings that faded or smeared or washed away with the morning dew or a passing thunderstorm. Not watercolors, either. Watercolor paintings were too insipid. Wren preferred bright

colors, the kind of colors you could smell, touch, taste. The kind
of colors that thrummed with life. Gran painted with those kinds of
colors, with blues and yellows that could make you weep.

In Gran's studio were stacks of postcards of famous paintings to
inspire her creativity: Monet's *Water Lilies* and *Japanese Bridge*, Renoir's
Young Girls by the Water, and dozens by Van Gogh. Wren loved playing
Poohsticks on Monet's bridge or reclining in a straw hat in Renoir's
meadow, whispering secrets to a best friend. But her favorite painting
to inhabit was Vincent's *Starry Night*, where she would listen to the
pulsing rhythm of the stars that swirled and danced above her. She
would lie all night on the hillside beneath those stars and not close her
eyes for an instant because she wouldn't want to miss a drop of beauty.

She looked up at those skies now and sketched the outline of
Vincent's dark cypress tree in her notebook. Vincent had learned by
copying too. He would copy favorite paintings by Millet, Rembrandt,
Delacroix. Then he would add his own twist. Some said his *Starry
Night over the Rhône* might have been inspired by Millet's painting of a
night sky. But this *Starry Night*, the more famous painting that later
captivated the world, was all his own—a radiant mystical vision con-
ceived behind a barred window at the asylum. She filled in her tree
with curving vertical lines.

Gran was the one who first introduced her to Vincent. Gran also
taught her how to paint. Watching Gran paint was like watching a
sculptor at work. She'd squeeze out the colors onto the canvas and
with her palette knife, she'd swirl and scrape and shape them into
rivers or suns or trees or cliffs or clouds. As she painted she'd blend
and blur and create new colors unlike any in Wren's crayon box.
"Whatever you can think of," Gran would say, "you can do. You just
have to begin." Watching Gran create something from nothing was
like watching a miracle.

"Be brave!" Gran would say. "Bold! If you don't like it, you can
paint over it. That's what the old masters did."

"But how do you know when you're done?" Wren would ask.

Gran would smile and say, "When I'm done, I sign my name."

"Dinner!" Sylvia called from the buffet. "We're having lasagna!"

Wren finished filling in the cypress tree, then joined the others in line.

As promised, Hannah arrived promptly at seven o'clock with juice, bread, and a chalice. "Your communion cup is beautiful," Wren said after they settled themselves in the only unoccupied corner of the lounge.

Hannah passed it to her for a closer look: mottled olivewood with hand-carved flowers, a cross, and a star. "My husband and I took our son to the Holy Land when he graduated from high school, and we bought this in Bethlehem."

Wren wished she had the courage to go on a trip like that. Some of her friends had gone with a tour group during college. Seeing their photos afterward fueled her regret.

She gave the chalice back to Hannah. "Thank you for coming again."

"I'm glad to." She opened the plastic Welch's grape juice bottle. "Sorry it's not very elegant, but I think I'll go ahead and pour it now, and then we can begin. Does that sound okay?"

"Yes. Thank you."

Hannah poured the juice, then pushed the bottle beneath her chair, out of sight. She placed a small round loaf of bread on a linen napkin and set it on her lap.

"Whatcha doing?"

Wren stiffened in her chair. She had been so focused on watching Hannah, she hadn't seen Sylvia approach.

Hannah smiled. "I'm serving communion to my friend."

"She's my friend too." Sylvia pulled up a chair. "I like communion."

"Do you?"

"Uh-huh. Jesus is in my heart."

"That's wonderful," Hannah said.

Sylvia cupped her hands, ready to receive. Hannah looked as if she wasn't sure what to do. "I'm Hannah. What's your name?"

"Sylvia."

"Tell you what, Sylvia. Let me have a quick word with my friend Wren, okay?"

Sylvia laughed and said, "Tweeet! Like a little bird. A cute little bird." She patted Wren on the shoulder. "Wren's my friend. She's a good friend."

"Yes, she is."

Signaling for Wren to follow, Hannah rose with the chalice and bread and stepped out of Sylvia's earshot. "It's okay with me," Wren whispered.

"Are you sure?"

Sharing communion with another patient wasn't what she had pictured, but she wasn't going to deny someone the opportunity to receive it, especially someone as childlike and eager as Sylvia. "I'm sure. But I don't know what the rules are here, whether you need to check with somebody first or . . ."

Hannah nodded. "Okay. If you'll sit with her a minute, I'll go find out." She set the chalice and bread on an end table, then said, "Sylvia, I'll be right back, okay?"

"Yep."

Wren sat back down and stared at the cup. Then at the wall. Then at her sketchbook, which she had placed on the floor. Sylvia rocked in her chair, eyes closed, humming quietly. At first Wren thought it was a hymn. But it wasn't. It was "Feed the Birds" from *Mary Poppins.* *How did she know?*

How could Sylvia have possibly known that she had only just been thinking of that movie an hour ago when she imagined herself entering Vincent's vision of the skies?

Sylvia opened her eyes and grinned. "Do you get it?" She pointed to Wren, then to the bread and the cup. "Feed the birds!" She laughed long and hard before warbling the words. "Feed the birds, tuppence a bag. Tuppence, tuppence, tuppence a bag." She was still singing the same refrain when Hannah returned with a staff member.

"Sylvia," he said, interrupting her music, "this is Pastor Hannah."

"I know."

"She's here to serve communion to Wren."

"I know. And me too."

"You want to have communion?"

"Yep."

He nodded to Hannah. "I'll be out in the hall if you need anything."

"Thank you."

And so they began again, Hannah speaking the words Wren had heard many times, that on the night Jesus was betrayed, he took bread, and having given thanks, he broke it and gave it to his disciples, saying, "Take, eat. This is my body broken for you." As Hannah held up the loaf and broke it in half, small crumbs fell to the carpet. Sylvia bent over to collect and eat them.

"In the same way after supper," Hannah continued, "Jesus took the cup and said, 'This is the cup of the new covenant, sealed in my blood for the forgiveness of sins. Take, drink, and remember me.'"

"Amen," Sylvia said.

"These are the gifts of God for the people of God," Hannah said. "Let's pray together."

But before Hannah could speak a word, Sylvia grabbed each of their hands and began to pray. She thanked God for taking care of her. She thanked God for her friends. She thanked God for her food. She thanked God for little birds and trees and flowers and music. She asked God to forgive them for their sins and help them to forgive others. And when she finished her prayer, Hannah said, "Amen."

"Amen," Wren echoed.

Hannah held out the bread and the cup to Wren. "Wren, this is the body of Christ broken for you." Wren broke off a small piece. "This is the blood of Christ, poured out in love for you."

"Amen." She dipped the bread into the cup and chewed slowly, trying to picture the life of Jesus coursing through her, wishing something mysterious and wonderful would happen to her while she chewed. But the bread tasted like ordinary bread, and the grape juice made it a little soggy, and she felt nothing special when she swallowed.

"Sylvia," Hannah said, "this is the body of Christ broken for you." Sylvia closed her eyes and opened her mouth. After a moment's hesitation, Hannah broke off a piece of bread and placed it on Sylvia's tongue. Sylvia chewed slowly. "This is the blood of Christ, poured out in love for you." Sylvia took the cup in her own hands, tipped it to her lips, and drank.

With her arms bent, the loose sleeves of Sylvia's sweater shifted, revealing a trellis of scars like many crosses carved into tender flesh. "Amen," Sylvia said, handing the chalice back to Hannah and straightening her sleeves. "Jesus—he's so beautiful, isn't he?"

Wren nodded.

"Don't you think he's beautiful?" Sylvia said again, her face close to Wren's, her smile crooked and open.

"Yes."

Sylvia sat back in her chair with a sigh of satisfaction.

Wren observed her in silence.

She would sketch her again, and this time she would sketch her with loving compassion and attention, the way Vincent would sketch her. The way Jesus would. This time she would look more deeply to capture not merely a physical likeness, but the light and life within her. "Hannah, is it all right if Sylvia holds your chalice while I draw?"

"Of course!"

There was no wide smile plastered on Sylvia's face while she sat with the chalice on her lap. Like the Madonna with the Christ child, she gazed at the cup with an air of deep peace and devotion. She wasn't posing for a portrait. She was praying.

Wren sketched the soft lines of her face, her relaxed brow and reverent expression. Then she drew her left hand wrapped around the chalice stem and her right hand cupped beneath it. Visible on her wrist, just below the hem of her sleeve, was a single cross etched into her skin. Wren drew it there. And signed her name at the bottom of the page.

8

Jamie stared at her laptop screen in the church office Tuesday morning, trying to distract herself by editing the monthly newsletter. In the past thirty-six hours she had left a couple of messages for Wren, with no response. "You're on her emergency contact list," Dylan had reminded her several times. "If something happened, a staff member would call."

Every time he said, "If something happened," she felt the pit in her stomach widen. "If something happened" was code for any number of horrifying scenarios, the worst of which she couldn't allow herself to imagine. The hospital was as safe a place as any, right? They were monitoring her. Every fifteen minutes, Wren had said, a visual check on her location and physical safety. And they would notice if she was agitated or detached.

She stared at her phone again, willing it to ring.

Suicidal ideation. That was the phrase that terrified her. And though Wren had insisted they were only fleeting thoughts that were now mostly under control—*mostly,* she'd said, which wasn't an entirely reassuring word—she could lose control at any moment. Anything might push her over the edge.

But the staff closely controlled the administering of medications, and they had confiscated any potentially dangerous items. She would be safe while she was at Glenwood. They would keep her safe. That was their job.

But what about after she was sent home? How would they know for sure that it was safe to discharge her? What if the decisions

were driven more by insurance coverage or the need for beds?
What if Wren convinced them she was ready when she wasn't?
Then what?

If she could remember the name of the church Wren had been
attending, she would call and ask to speak to the pastor. She opened
her browser. But she couldn't remember the name of the pastor,
either. She typed "female pastors Kingsbury" but didn't find any
information.

Good thing, probably. She knew better than to ask a pastor to
breach confidentiality.

It was surprising, though, that Wren hadn't contacted her after
her pastor visited. What if it hadn't gone well? What if the pastor
had only quoted Scripture verses at her and told her to have more
faith? That would have left Wren feeling even worse about herself.

A voice from the doorway startled her. "Is Pastor here?"

Jamie shut her search window and spun around in her chair.
"Good morning, Trudy."

"I called his cell phone, but he didn't answer."

"He's in a meeting right now."

"In his office?" Trudy peered over Jamie's shoulder at his closed
door.

"Yes."

Trudy set her purse on the floor before sitting down. "I'll wait."

Jamie stifled a sigh. Someone ought to put "bouncer" in the job
description for pastor's wife. "He's going to be a while. Is there something I can help you with?"

"I was out of town over the weekend, just got back last night, and
found out there wasn't a rose on the lectern Sunday morning."

"Sorry?"

"A white rose. For the birth of my granddaughter, Alexandra
Jolene Harper. I talked to Pastor about it last week, and he said he'd
put one out. He didn't mention it to you?"

Maybe he had. With everything else on her mind, it was impossible to say.

"It's a tradition here," Trudy went on. "Every time a baby is born we celebrate with a white rose. On the communion table, it used to be. Before Pastor changed it."

There were many such traditions at the church, and it had taken years to decipher and remember them. The few changes Dylan had managed to make had come about only after significant battles. He had the scars to prove it.

"Every single one of my babies and now my grandbabies has had a white rose in worship—until Alexandra. Now, I told my daughter that Pastor probably didn't do it deliberately—"

Jamie stiffened. "Of course not."

"—and that I would talk to him about it as soon as possible. Because you know how these things can fester."

Yes. She did. She arranged her face into a suitably sympathetic expression and gave herself a beat before responding. "I know Dylan feels strongly about the importance of celebrating all the births in our church family. So please know it wasn't anything deliberate. I'm sure he would be happy to talk with you and your daughter to apologize." Oh, how she wished she could say that there were far more important things in this world to be concerned about and that she was dealing with a few of those far more important things right now.

"I want to speak with him today," Trudy said.

"I'll be sure to give him the message."

Trudy pushed back her sleeve to look at her watch. "What time will he be done?"

"I don't know." Dylan was counseling a couple on the verge of divorce, and it wouldn't be appropriate for Trudy to be sitting there when they exited their appointment, especially if their emotions and body language were easily read. That would provide fresh grist for the rumor mill. "He's likely to be at least another hour."

Trudy exhaled in frustration.

"And, actually"—Jamie turned toward her computer again and scrolled through her planner—"he's booked solid in meetings today, so he may not be able to get back to you until tomorrow." She took a certain measure of satisfaction in saying this. "But I'll let him know you're upset and ask him to call you."

"As soon as possible," Trudy said.

Oh, they couldn't hire a new secretary soon enough. "As soon as he gets a chance," Jamie said, "I'm sure he'll call. And congratulations to you and your family. We'll be sure to put a rose on the lectern Sunday."

Trudy thanked her and exited the building.

Jamie leaned back in her chair.

Babies. That's when motherhood was straightforward. Exhausting, but straightforward. She glanced at her phone. *Ring. Please.*

Maybe Wren had had more panic attacks. Whatever new cocktail of medications they'd put her on obviously wasn't addressing that issue. Maybe she would never be free of them.

Over the years Jamie had tried to pray and coach Wren through many attacks, both in person and over the phone. Some of the episodes Wren concealed or navigated more successfully than others. But even with all the good counseling strategies she had learned for working through them, they couldn't be prevented and could strike at any time.

"It's like all the guardrails on your life are gone," Wren had once explained to her. "You think you're going crazy because you can't trust what your body is saying. You feel like you're going to die, like you've completely lost control, and you don't know if you're safe or not. And it doesn't help when someone keeps saying, 'You're okay,' because you're not okay."

Jamie wished she had understood that when Wren, who would have been about eight, started complaining of having trouble breathing. Thinking she was suffering from asthma or allergies, Jamie took her to the doctor, but there was nothing physically wrong with her, and no one identified it as panic disorder. Given how fearful and sensitive Wren was, Jamie blamed herself for missing the signs. She should have been able to name it and get her help sooner. Instead, she had often tried to talk Wren out of the attacks. On her good days

Jamie was measured and patient with her. But there were days when she'd told Wren she needed to pull herself together, that it wasn't real, that it was all in her head. That had only made things worse.

She stared at Dylan's closed office door, remembering one particularly bad episode when Wren, a sophomore in high school, pushed her chair back from the dinner table, hand to her neck, complaining she couldn't swallow. Her throat was closing off. Before Jamie could attempt to calm her down, she was heaving in hyperventilating gasps and pacing the apartment, stopping periodically to brace herself against a wall. Dylan was in class at the seminary, and Jamie, pregnant with Joel and trailed by a frightened three-year-old Olivia, followed Wren from room to room with arms outstretched, trying to help, but her efforts were as futile as coaxing a trapped and frantic bird to land. When Wren finally stopped pacing and curled herself into a fetal position in the corner of her room, Jamie tried to cool her perspiring face with a damp cloth. But Wren swatted her hand away. Even Olivia had tried to help, offering a favorite teddy bear. But Wren shoved the bear back to her and yelled, "Stop!" That's when Olivia started wailing, "I'm dying too!" Given the commotion, it was a wonder the neighbors hadn't called the police. Or child protective services.

"I'm not crazy," Wren had said over and over as she rocked herself in the corner. No matter how hard Jamie tried to soothe her with reassuring words of help and presence, nothing penetrated. It was as if Wren were in a locked room surrounded by a force field that deflected every kind of consolation. Jamie had never felt so impotent, especially in her prayers.

"That sounds demonic," another seminary student's wife had commented when Jamie shared the terrifying experience as a prayer request at their monthly small group meeting. "'God hasn't given us a spirit of fear,'" the woman quoted, "'but of power, love, and a sound mind.' So you need to rebuke the spirit of fear. Cast it out. Jesus has given you that kind of authority. You need to walk in it. As her mother." But the woman's insistence that Wren, who loved and trusted Jesus, was oppressed by an evil spirit only made Jamie feel more helpless and confused. And ashamed her faith wasn't strong enough to help her daughter.

It was the last time she shared any struggles about Wren with that group. Wren was fine, she said whenever they asked, so much better. And they said, Praise God.

She watched the screensaver photos scroll by on her computer: Phoebe blowing out birthday candles on a cake, Olivia holding up car keys after getting her license, Joel and Dylan playing catch. She needed to get some more recent ones of Wren, maybe a few of her painting. She always looked happiest when she was painting. Or when she was with Casey.

Phoebe's words returned to her: *She's so sad because her friend moved away.*

Just because Jamie hadn't viewed Casey's departure as a traumatic event didn't mean it hadn't been to her daughter. In fact—and she never would have confessed this to anyone but Dylan—she had actually been relieved when Wren told her he was moving.

Jamie hadn't seen Casey since he and Wren graduated from high school, but she knew from what limited details Wren had shared over the years that he had his own mental health issues that could easily overwhelm others. Not that Wren had ever complained about offering him support. But Jamie had hoped that after he left for Nevada to be with his fiancée, Wren might invest herself in some healthy friendships that didn't require so much emotional and mental energy. Instead, she'd thrown herself even more fervently into her work and had seemed, even with all the upheaval, to be relatively stable. That's what was so hard to understand. If she had checked herself into the hospital right after Casey left, it might have made sense. But now? Why now?

Her phone rang, startling her. *Glenwood!* "Hello?"

"Mom?"

Jamie exhaled a breath she didn't realize she'd been holding and pitched her voice to calm and casual. "Hey, love, how're you doing?"

Wren was well enough, it seemed, to go home. Possibly no later than tomorrow. The visit with her pastor—two visits, she said—had been a gift of encouragement to her. Jamie was relieved. At least Wren would have strong pastoral support once she got home. And she was drawing again—always a good sign. Now, if she could find a counselor . . .

"I'll call Dr. Emerson's office today and set up an appointment with one of his colleagues," Wren said. "I need to do that before they'll release me."

"Even if it's not a good fit with whoever that is," Jamie said, "it's important to keep trying."

"I know. I will, Mom."

"And you're sure you're ready—I mean, you feel like you've gotten what you need. The medications, groups . . ."

"Yeah."

"You'd tell me if—"

"Yeah."

"And if you want me to come out—"

"I know. Thanks. But I'll be okay. I just want to get home and get back into my routine."

Jamie felt herself deflate. She had hoped to spend a few days with her. But she ought to be relieved Wren didn't need her. She pitched her voice to cheerful. "Well, that sounds like a positive thing."

"I have to get to my group," Wren said. "But I'll call you once I know for sure what's happening."

"Thanks, love. I'll keep praying."

Just as she finished the phone call, the office door opened, and Dylan emerged with the estranged husband and wife, the wife clutching her purse to her chest, the husband with arms crossed. Jamie pretended to type so they wouldn't feel self-conscious, then smiled and said, "Take care," after Dylan told them he'd see them next week. As soon as they disappeared down the hallway, Jamie said,

"Sorry to throw this at you right now, but Trudy was here, upset because there wasn't a white rose celebrating her new granddaughter on Sunday."

Dylan cursed under his breath. "You know what? Hang the tradition. I'm gonna buy fake ones to keep in the storage closet. If the deacons can't take care of something simple like that, I'm not doing it anymore. It shouldn't have to be me. It shouldn't always have to be me."

"I told her it wasn't deliberate and that you'd call her."

"Yeah. Okay. Great."

"And that you were booked solid today and probably wouldn't get back to her until later."

"Thanks. How about never?"

"Yeah. That'd be nice."

"I swear, the things people get upset about. Some days . . ."

"I know. I'm sorry."

Dylan raked his hands through his dark hair and sighed, eyes fixed on the ceiling.

Jamie ran her finger along the edge of the desk. "Wren called. She's doing well. It all sounds very positive."

He took a moment to reply. "At least something's going right today." With a shake of his head, he returned to his office and closed the door firmly behind him.

9

While Wren waited in the classroom for the social worker to arrive for their group, she tried to fill out the crisis safety plan worksheet Thomas had given her. She wanted to go home, didn't she? She'd been saying to herself all week that she shouldn't have come, that she wanted to leave. But now that her release was imminent, she wasn't sure what she wanted.

She wanted to see her cat. She wanted to sleep. She wanted to paint.

She needed to work. She needed to find a good counselor. She needed to reconnect with friends.

Identify your triggers, the instructions read.

Change, she wrote. That was a significant trigger for her anxiety and depression.

"Paint your feelings," Gran had told her in the studio the day her mother gave her the news they would be moving to America. She was eleven. She loved her mother. She loved her new stepfather. She loved Gran and Pop and the house and the paddock and the horses and dogs and willow trees and ponds and—"Pour it all out on the canvas," Gran said. "What color is sadness? What color is fear?"

Wren squeezed blue and violet and gray and black tubes directly onto the canvas and with her palette knife spread them into one swirling, jumbled mass of chaos.

"I'll paint my feelings too," Gran said. "This is my 'I'm sad you're leaving.' And my 'I'm happy you have a new dad who loves you.' And my 'I love you, and I'll miss you very much.'" Gran painted with browns and reds and golds and citron yellow rays of light. She and Pop would visit America, she said. And they did, many times. Until she had a stroke, and Pop couldn't leave her. They died within a few weeks of each other, just before Wren graduated from college. She'd painted her feelings then too. Blue and gray, violet and black, with streaks of citron yellow rays of light, because that's what hope looked like, and Gran would have reminded her to paint hope along with the sorrow.

She should have painted her feelings the night Casey gave her the news he was moving to Reno to be with Brooke. It was the same February day he found the kittens, the day she read the story about the whales. "It's not like I'm moving to some remote jungle in South America," he'd said. With all the easy ways of staying in touch, he said, it would be as if he'd never left. "You'll come visit us, Wrinkle. And don't worry, I'll be back to work on film projects and stuff." She should have painted the jumbled mass of feelings—her "I'm so happy because you're happy," her "I'm so sad because you're leaving," her "I hope this doesn't change our friendship."

But everything had changed. Change, loss, grief, a sense of losing control—all familiar triggers.

She stared at her worksheet again. *Identify the warning signs you need to pay attention to,* the instructions read.

Numbing out, she wrote. Crying uncontrollably. Losing hope. Withdrawing from community. Finding no pleasure in things she usually enjoyed, like painting. Not responding to beauty. Feeling dead inside. Not being able to sleep. Racing, obsessive thoughts.

"If you all can take your seats, please," the social worker said as she entered, "we'll get started." Wren tucked her half-completed form back into her folder. But when the social worker took her place in the circle, Wren felt sick to her stomach.

They knew each other. They had trained together. They had both worked at Bethel House after getting licensed, but Samantha had left after a year to take a job at a hospital.

Their eyes met, and Samantha, trying to cover for the shocked expression on her face, looked away.

Wren didn't bother pretending she was being summoned. She snatched up her folder and dashed out the door, nearly bumping into Thomas in the hallway.

"You okay?" he asked.

She wasn't sure what to say. She didn't want any notes made in her file that could delay her release. After a moment's hesitation she said, "I left something in my room." Thomas nodded and returned to his conversation.

But it wasn't as if she could hide somewhere, not with the safety checks every fifteen minutes. She could either go to her room and have it noted she had not attended the session, or she could try to press through her sense of shame, trust the HIPAA privacy laws, and tick the remaining boxes so she could go home. Possibly even later today.

She walked halfway down the hall, feigned finding what she needed in her folder—just in case Thomas was watching—and returned to the classroom as Samantha was passing around blank sheets of paper with envelopes. "Welcome," Samantha said. "And you are?"

Bless her. "Wren."

Samantha made a note on her attendance sheet. "Wren, I was just explaining to the group that you're going to write a letter of encouragement to your future self—something that will be mailed to you on the date you choose. Maybe a few weeks from now, or a few months, but pick a time when it will be good for you to be reminded of some strategies you've learned while you've been here, anything to help you practice good mental, emotional, and behavioral health."

Across the circle from her, a middle-aged woman who had never spoken up in any of the groups began to sob. What use was it? the woman cried. What did she have to offer her future self if she had no future? All she saw as she looked ahead was emptiness and darkness. Sure, she could parrot all the coping strategies, but none of them had worked before. And why would it be any different now?

Others in the group tried to speak hope and encouragement to her, but she would have none of it. Still weeping, she packed up her folder and left the room.

"I've got to go to a court appointment today," a teenage girl said, breaking the uncomfortable silence. "If I don't get away from my dad, there is no 'future me.'"

One by one they took turns and spoke of their despair and their fears. One by one they told some of the same stories they had recounted multiple times over the last week, stories of abuse, trauma, grief. Now that her own stupor had lifted, Wren heard the details of their catastrophic losses with fresh ears.

Her companions in misfortune.

She had begun to think of herself as belonging to a larger community of misfortune, but what misfortune had she experienced? What trauma could she point to, what heartache could she identify that could compare to what the others had suffered? She almost envied them—not because they had suffered. No, never that. Not for a moment would she covet their trauma or abuse. No, she envied them because they could identify reasons for their hopelessness and fears. Their depression and anxiety had causes. They could explain it, justify it. And people might listen sympathetically. They might nod and say, "Of course you suffer from depression. Of course you have panic attacks. Look what you've been through!"

But hers?

The best any counselor had ever offered was the observation that some people were "genetically predisposed" to mental disorders, and that though there was typically a trigger that could incite the onset of illness, the greater a person's biological vulnerability, the less stress required for triggering it.

What explanation could she give for the latest onset?

That she had a stressful job? Many people had stressful jobs.

That the suffering in the world overwhelmed her? Many people felt overwhelmed.

That she felt left behind by friends who were getting married or having kids? Many people were single.

That her best friend had moved away and gotten married? Many people had endured far more difficult transitions.

She was not going to cry.

Not for herself.

If she needed to cry, then it should be for the ones who had truly been afflicted. She had nothing to contribute to the conversation. She didn't belong here. She wasn't worthy of the community of sufferers.

She glanced around the circle. She knew what she had to do. She would muster every bit of mental and emotional strength and convince Thomas and Dr. Browerly she was ready to go home. She had to go home.

As the others continued to share, Wren wrote herself a letter, addressed and dated the envelope, and left the room before anyone could ask her any questions.

No, she told Thomas at their meeting later that morning, Samantha hadn't created any issue. It was her own discomfort at attending a group led by a former peer.

Thomas said he understood. "Your crisis plan looks good, like you have some good support in place, good self-awareness, good emotional and spiritual resources to draw from. And you've got an appointment with a counselor?"

"Yes." She had taken the first available appointment with one of Dr. Emerson's colleagues.

"Okay." Thomas scanned other notes. "And I know we talked about the outpatient program before. We really recommend that you participate—"

"I can't."

He raised his eyebrows. "Most insurance companies will—"

"It's work. I need to go back."

"You mentioned the stress of that when we talked before."

"I know. But the groups here were really helpful, and I've already gained so much. I feel ready to go back." She commanded herself to smile. "You've got a really excellent program here."

He paused, then returned her smile. "Well, that's good to hear, especially coming from a social worker."

She felt herself relax. She was acing her exit interview. *Crushing it,* Casey would say.

"Dr. Browerly has already signed off on your release form. And we'll set up an appointment for you to meet with him again next week so he can continue to supervise your medications."

Wren nodded. She would tick that box so they would send her home. But then she would find someone else who could learn and possibly remember her name.

Thomas slid some forms across his desk. "I'll have you sign these papers here, we'll retrieve your belongings for you, and you'll be all set."

Wren signed her name, dated the forms, and shook his hand.

"If you change your mind about the outpatient program—"

"I know where to find you," she said with another smile.

"Right. I've circled the information"—he gestured toward the top sheet—"and like I said, it's a great way to reinforce and strengthen the work you've done here. You and Dr. Browerly can talk about it next week and see how you're doing."

Aloud, she said, "Sure. Okay." But to herself she said, *Nope. Not gonna happen.*

She went to her room to pack up her things, then called her mother from the hallway phone. She would have liked to have thanked Kelly for her kindness, but she hadn't been on duty the past couple of days. So she left her vase of sunflowers at the nurses' station. She would have liked to have said goodbye to Sylvia, but the groups were still in session. Maybe her roommate Monica had the right idea, just slipping away.

On her way toward the lobby with Thomas, she passed the truant group member in the hallway. He saluted them with a grin. "Leaving so soon?"

"Yeah."

"Good luck," he said.

And she said, "Thanks. You too."

She was free. Like a bird from a cage.

She exited the building with her duffel bag and squinted at the bright sunlight. Now what?

She stared at her shoes, still fastened with the telltale plastic grips. First, she would thread her laces. She sat down on a bench near the entrance. But that was too close. She walked to a tree. It was yellow, sulfur yellow against a bright blue sky. She touched the trunk. It was rough. It was gray. But also brown, with silver and lilac and lime streaks blending together. She touched a leaf. It was smooth. But also crinkled, with small holes like bronze eyelets. She sat down on the grass. She removed her laces from her bag. She removed the plastic grips. She stared at her shoes. She stared at her laces. She couldn't remember where to start. She took off her right shoe and stared at the eyelets. She stared at the lace. Over or under? Under, she decided, and began to thread. It was not even. She tugged at the crisscrosses. They were too tight. She tugged again. She pulled and pulled until the laces were even. Then she put on her shoe. If she didn't think about how to tie it, she could do it. She closed her eyes and trusted the automatic response of brain and fingers working cooperatively.

There. One shoe done.

Chicka-dee-dee-dee. She looked up. *Chicka-dee-dee.* Such a tiny bird. White, black, gray. Little bowler cap, bandit mask. It flitted from branch to branch. *Chicka-dee-dee-dee.* Bud would be proud of her for listening.

A well-dressed couple and a teenage boy got out of a parked silver car and walked toward the entrance. The woman put her arm around the boy, spoke in his ear, and kissed his cheek. He wiped off the kiss. The man held the front door open for them. They disappeared into the brown building. Such a drab, inconspicuous building. How long had she lived in Kingsbury without noticing it? The sign at the entrance said only *Glenwood Hospital.* People might pass by and never think about the anguished, despairing ones battling for life inside those walls. She had passed by many times without thinking of anyone inside.

She stared at her left shoe. This one would be quicker. As she laced it, she debated how to get home. She could take a bus or—she looked up at a fleet of clouds drifting in a sea of periwinkle blue—she could walk. After eight days of being confined, walking a few miles would be a gift, an opportunity to re-enter her life gradually. She would not turn on her cell phone. Not yet. There would be too many messages and texts and emails. She would need to take small bites and chew slowly before she could face the demands of real life again. When she got home, she would change into fresh pajamas, curl up with little Theo, and spend her evening reading Van Gogh's letters.

On second thought, words might be too much to process. She would look at prints of his paintings instead.

With a final glance over her shoulder, she turned left out of the parking lot and headed home.

She was on a journey, she reminded herself as she walked, not just physically but mentally and emotionally and spiritually. It was a good metaphor to embrace. People passing in cars might assume she was homeless or a hitchhiker, her bag slung over her shoulder. Or maybe she looked like one of those people who trekked across the country on foot, raising money for a good cause or trying to get in touch with something they had lost or forgotten. But no. Those pilgrims traveled with backpacks, not duffel bags. She would not be mistaken for one of them.

Casey had trekked the Camino de Santiago last year. He had hoped to reignite his faith, to rediscover the passion he'd once had for Jesus and to "find himself." During his six-week journey along the ancient way in Spain, he'd sent her regular updates and photos: views of fields, roadside stands selling figs, blisters on his feet. When he returned, he said he passed people on the sidewalks in Kingsbury and felt the impulse to say, "Buen camino!" Have a good journey.

He'd had a good journey—though none of it, as far as she could discern, had anything to do with encountering Jesus. Instead, his buen camino had everything to do with meeting Brooke. They met and fell in love while they walked and got married six months later in April, in Aruba. Wren was not asked to be in the wedding party. "You would have been my best man if Brooke had let me," Casey had said. It was okay, Wren had assured him. She didn't have the money to go.

She would not think about Casey or Brooke. She would fix her eyes on the road ahead. She would feel the rhythm of her steps and the pleasure of endorphins coursing through her body, quickening her senses as her feet pounded the concrete. She would inhale the fragrance of a pasture, savor the voices of children at play, and marvel at the glory of October.

The autumn colors were even more stunning than she had remembered or envisioned while at Glenwood. She lingered on a street corner where an orange maple tree rose in bold relief against the blue sky. Vincent would have painted it. He would have recognized the power of complementary colors that intensified one another and made each other shine. Like a husband and wife, he wrote to his sister, completing each other. He knew how to use blue and orange, red and green, yellow and purple, with great emotional effect.

She shifted her bag to her other shoulder, picturing Vincent traipsing through the countryside with his easel and canvas and paints, alone. A madman, they called him, painting the way he did and muttering to himself. He was teased and disregarded and scorned. But still he painted. He had to paint. And still he longed for community, longed to be loved, to be appreciated, useful, good for something.

She stooped to pick up a leaf.

There was a line in one of Vincent's letters to Theo that made her cry whenever she read it, that though there was a great fire in his soul, no one stopped to warm themselves by it. All people saw was a little wisp of smoke rising up from a chimney, and they passed by.

She was not going to cry. She might not be able to stop.

She held the leaf up to the sunlight, marveling at the intricacy of its veins, the subtle blends of color. It was not uniformly orange. It was citron yellow and tangerine and pumpkin and—

"Hey, stranger! Need a lift?"

Wren spun around. Sophie, who lived in the apartment directly beneath her, was smiling broadly through her open car window.

"Oh—I . . ." If she equivocated too long, it would seem suspicious, especially since she was lugging a travel bag. "Thanks, Soph. That'd be great." She tossed her bag into the backseat before sliding into the front.

"Did you break down somewhere?"

"No." Evidently, Sophie had forgotten she didn't have a car. She hated driving. Too stressful. Especially with all the distracted drivers. "I was going to take the bus home but decided it was too nice a day."

"Yeah, it's gorgeous out. I'll have to go for a run later." Sophie could often be seen jogging through the neighborhood in her turquoise tights, never breaking a sweat. She motioned toward Wren's bag in the back. "So, where've you been? Haven't seen you lately."

"No, I was away all week."

"Someplace fun?"

Think. Fast. "Not really. More like continuing education."

"Oh. Not fun."

"No. Not fun at all." Quick. Change the subject. "How about you? What's new in your world?"

Sophie smiled. "Oh, not too much, just—" Still holding the wheel, she wriggled the fingers on her left hand to show off a glittering diamond.

"Sophie! Congratulations!"

"Thanks! Tyler put together this amazing scavenger hunt all over Grand Rapids with all these clues along the way, and then at the end he was standing down by the river, waiting for me and . . ."

Blah, blah, blah. The pictures were posted on social media, they'd uploaded a video on YouTube, they were having a destination wedding in Hawaii. All the way to the apartment, Sophie's lips kept moving. Wren offered appropriately enthusiastic and supportive interjections—mostly monosyllabic ones like "wow," "great," and "oh!" Sophie didn't need more than that to keep gushing.

When they arrived at the apartment complex, Wren removed her bag from the car and pulled out her key. Sophie pointed to her wrist. "Were you on a cruise or something?"

"What?"

"Your bracelet."

If Wren could have commanded the ground to open and swallow her whole, she would have. "Oh, that!" she exclaimed, trying to sound casual. "Conference ID band. Guess I forgot to remove it." She tugged her sleeve downward. She could either be grateful or alarmed that the lies flowed so readily.

Sophie stopped at the mail kiosk. Wren decided not to open her box. She'd deal with the stack later. Right now, she wanted as quick an escape as possible. "Thanks again for the ride."

Her neighbor didn't look up from thumbing through envelopes. "Yeah, sure. Any time."

At the top of the stairs, Wren set down her bag and unlocked her door. "Hey, Theo," she called as she entered.

Normally, he came running as soon as a door opened. She scanned the room. Maybe he was punishing her for being gone.

"Hey, kitty-kitty-kitty, I'm home." She tossed her bag onto the sofa and slipped off her shoes, leaving the laces tied. Thank God she had replaced the plastic grips with her shoelaces before she left the hospital. Sophie definitely would have noticed those.

"Theo?" She checked his cat tree by the sliding glass door. Empty. She looked in her room on the bed. Not there. "Here, kitty-kitty. Treat, treat."

She went to the kitchenette. Odd. His dishes were gone. She checked the bathroom. His litter box too. Mrs. Kramer must have decided it was easier to watch him at her apartment. Wren tore off her wristband, put on her moccasins, and padded across the hall to knock on her neighbor's door, which immediately opened.

Mrs. Kramer threw her arms around her, then motioned for her to come in. "I'm so sorry. I left messages for you, but . . ."

"It's okay. How's he doing?"

Mrs. Kramer stared at her. "You didn't get my messages?"

"No, sorry, I didn't check." She stooped down to pet Misty, who was rubbing against her jeans. "Hey, sweet girl. How's your friend, huh?" When she looked up again, Mrs. Kramer was crying.

"I'm sorry, I'm so sorry! I opened your door a few days ago, and he raced out before I could catch him, and the UPS driver had propped the front door open, and Theo ran right out—so fast, straight out toward the road and . . ."

No, no, no. This couldn't be happening.

"Wren, I'm so sorry. I feel devastated. And then when I couldn't get ahold of you . . ."

No. No. No. Please, God. No. "So he—uh . . . he . . . ?" Her hands started shaking. Her throat was burning. She was having trouble breathing.

Mrs. Kramer took her hand. "He ran right in front of a car. The driver tried to swerve—she felt awful about it."

Her ears were ringing. Her stomach clenched.

"I didn't know what to do when I couldn't reach you, so I brought his things here. I didn't want you to get my message and then walk in and see his dish or his box. I thought maybe . . ."

Oh.

Oh.

She probably thanked her. She probably told her it wasn't her fault and that she shouldn't beat herself up about it. She must have carried his empty bowls and litter box back to her apartment. She must have changed into her pajamas and turned off the lights. She must have. Because early the next morning she awoke on her couch, Theo's bowl and favorite mouse toy pressed against her chest and Casey's cap on her head.

Part Two

WORN

OUT

I am worn out from my groaning.
All night long I flood my bed with weeping
and drench my couch with tears.
My eyes grow weak with sorrow;
they fail because of all my foes.

PSALM 6:6-7

Our nature is sorrowful, but for those who have learnt and are
learning to look at Jesus Christ there is always reason to rejoice.
It is a good word that of St. Paul: as being sorrowful yet always
rejoicing. For those who believe in Jesus Christ, there is no death
or sorrow that is not mixed with hope—no despair—there is
only a constantly being born again, a constantly going from
darkness into light.

VINCENT VAN GOGH, SERMON, 1876

10

The fragility in Wren's voice struck terror in Jamie's heart. Of course she would come. She would book the first available flight. "But who can you call right now, love? I don't think it's good for you to be alone."

Wren started to cry again, a wailing sob that pierced her.

"What about Kit? I'm sure she'd come. Can I call her for you?"

Gasping, wheezing.

"Wren, I want you to stay on the phone with me, okay? And Dad"—she motioned to Dylan, who was standing in the kitchen doorway, listening—"Dad can call her right now, okay?" Dylan grabbed his cell phone from the counter and punched the number. "Just stay with me, sweetheart. Stay on the phone with me. See if you can take a deep breath. A deep breath—that's it. Try to take a deep breath, Wren."

"Kit, hey, it's Dylan . . . sorry to call so early, but we've got an emergency we need some help with and . . ."

Jamie was going to tell Wren, You're okay. But that was the wrong thing to say. She wasn't okay. So she said, "I'm here, love. I'm staying right here with you."

"No," Dylan said, "she's home from the hospital, got released yesterday. But when she got home . . ."

Jamie leaned her head against a kitchen cupboard. He didn't need to go into all the details, just ask if she could get to the apartment. Fast. "How're you doing, love? Still with me?" No reply. "How about another deep breath? See if you can slow it all down. You remember the trick? Put your hand on your abdomen and—"

"Mommy?" A drowsy Phoebe was standing in the doorway.

"Hey, Phoebe-girl. Not now, okay? Mommy's on the phone."

Dylan said, "We're worried about her being alone today."

"Mommy, I peed in my bed."

"Okay, here, love." Jamie reached out her hand. "Take off your pajamas and your undies, and I'll wash them for you, okay? That-a-girl." She held Phoebe's arm as she wriggled out of her clothes. "Wren? You still with me?"

Her breath was rattling, the sobs quieted to a plaintive whimper.

"Oh, could you really?" Dylan said. "That would be great. Really great." He looked at Jamie. "She can head there now. Thank you, Kit. Thank you so much."

"Wren, Kit's on her way. She'll be there in about—"

"Fifteen," Dylan said.

"Fifteen minutes, okay? Can you buzz her in when she gets there? I'm going to stay on the phone with you until then, all right?"

"Mommy!" Phoebe was jumping up and down, half naked.

"Phoebe, stop! I'm on the phone. Go upstairs and put on clean clothes."

"C'mon, kiddo," Dylan said. "Let's go. I'll help you find some."

"I need to take a bath!"

"Okay, Daddy will help you. Go on." She shooed her upstairs. "I'm sorry, Wren. Phoebe had an accident."

"Sorry." It was only a faint whisper of a word, but it was a word.

"She's fine. Dad's got her. How are you?"

"I don't know."

"Kit will be there soon."

"Okay."

"While I've got you on the phone, I'm going to find a flight, okay? Something that gets me there today."

"I'm sorry."

"Don't be sorry, sweetheart. I'm glad to come. I'm just sorry you're going through all of this." On top of everything else Wren had endured, to lose her beloved Theo was too much. It was all too much.

The bathtub faucet began to run upstairs. She could hear Phoebe protesting it was too hot.

"Okay, I've got my browser open, and I'm going to do a search." Jamie described which windows she was clicking, which flights were available, the connections that would get her there most quickly, anything that might keep Wren mentally occupied until Kit could arrive. "I think this is the best one. I can connect through Baltimore and be there by six. How does that sound?"

"Okay."

Phone still pressed to her ear, Jamie retrieved her wallet. "Okay, I'm just entering all my details here, passenger name—come on, Jamie, spell it correctly—address—you okay?" A slight murmur. "Oops—North Carolina, not North Dakota. Here we go. And credit card info here. Oh, my eyes are getting worse"—she tilted her card toward the light—"time for a new prescription. Security code on the back. Okay. Expiration date, here. And . . . done. We're all set."

Upstairs Dylan crooned, "Rubber Duckie, you're the one," while Phoebe clamored for more bubbles.

Jamie checked her watch. Kit should be there in a few minutes. "Tell me what you see out your window." It was a strategy one of Wren's first therapists had recommended using whenever she was ruminating on a distressing thought or image: pan back for a wider view. Shift the mental focus. That sad thing exists, but so does this precious thing. So does this beautiful thing. "What are the trees like there?"

With a small voice, Wren said, "Orange. Yellow. Some red."

"The red are my favorite. What about the sky?"

"Gray."

"What kind of gray?" Wren had many words for colors.

A long pause and then, "Pewter."

That was a good word for her to find. "How about squirrels? Any squirrels?"

Silence, then a gasping sob.

Jamie silently cursed her stupidity. Theo had loved to watch squirrels and chipmunks and birds. "I'm sorry. I'm so sorry. Stay with me, love. Just a little longer." She was trying to find a different focal point for Wren to describe when a buzzer sounded. *Thank God.* "Is that your door?"

No reply.

"Can you let her in, Wren?"

Jamie heard the sound of shuffling, a lock being opened, and a soothing voice greeting Wren. *Thank God.* "Jamie?" Kit said, speaking into Wren's phone. "I'm here."

Phoebe, still wrapped in her robe, appeared in the bedroom doorway as Jamie was packing her suitcase. "Where are you going?"

"To see your big sister."

"Why?"

Jamie patted the bed. Phoebe hopped up. "You know how you were saying the other day that you wanted to draw Wren a picture because she was feeling sad?" Phoebe nodded. "Well, I thought I'd take your picture to her. What do you think?"

"And then come back?"

"After a few days."

"How many?"

"Not sure yet, love. But Daddy will be here. And Olivia and Joel. They'll take good care of you while I'm gone."

"I want to go with you."

"Not this time." Jamie embraced her and kissed the top of her head. She smelled like strawberries.

"Why can't I go with you?" Phoebe's bottom lip began to quiver.

She cried all the way through breakfast. Since a goodbye at the bus stop would be impossible, Jamie drove her to school, eventually persuading her to take her teacher's hand and join her friends in the classroom.

"We'll be fine," Dylan said when he loaded Jamie's suitcase into the trunk of the car later that morning. "She'll be fine. What about you?"

"I'll be fine. It's Wren I'm worried about."

He did not say, She'll be fine. Instead, he said, "I'll be praying for both of you." But the words did little to fill the hollow, fearful place in her soul.

All the way from Raleigh to Baltimore, Jamie reminded herself that her daughter was in good hands. According to the last phone call just before she boarded, Kit had canceled her appointments for the day and had persuaded Wren to pack a bag with toiletries and clothes. They would spend the day at Kit's house doing whatever Wren wanted to do—movies, food, art, sleep—whatever would help. "Come straight to my place," she'd said. "I'll have dinner waiting for you."

Kit would provide a soft place to land, for both of them. She was no stranger to grief. For decades Dylan's aunt had served in ministry, first as a chaplain and then as the director of the New Hope Retreat Center. Not only was she accustomed to companioning people in crisis, but she had also experienced her own significant heartaches. Jamie didn't know many specific details, only enough to appreciate that Kit had been shaped by sorrow and loss.

While Dylan was training for ministry in Kingsbury, Jamie had participated in as many spiritual formation retreats, seminars, and conferences at New Hope as she could, benefiting from Kit and others who offered wisdom and guidance about traveling deep into the heart of God. Years ago, at Kit's recommendation, Jamie had immersed herself in the biblical narratives about desperate parents seeking Jesus on behalf of their children. Jamie understood their agony and urgent pleas. If Jesus didn't come quickly, if he didn't speak a word of authority, if he didn't respond to their cries for mercy, where else could they turn? What hope did they have apart from him? "If you can do anything," a heartbroken father cried out to him, "have compassion on us and help us."

Us. Plural. Not "Have compassion on him," but "Have compassion on us. Help us." This was a father who knew firsthand the particular pain of being helpless to alleviate a child's affliction. This was a father who experienced the reality of co-suffering, who knew what it felt like to be tormented as he watched his beloved child tormented. This was a father who understood. She reached under the seat in front of her, removed her Bible from her carry-on, and turned to his story in the Gospel of Mark, chapter 9. The nameless dad could be her companion again.

> When they came to the disciples, they saw a great crowd around them, and some scribes arguing with them. When the whole crowd saw him, they were immediately overcome with awe, and they ran forward to greet him. He asked them, "What are you arguing about with them?" Someone from the crowd answered him, "Teacher, I brought you my son; he has a spirit that makes him unable to speak; and whenever it seizes him, it dashes him down; and he foams and grinds his teeth and becomes rigid; and I asked your disciples to cast it out, but they could not do so." He answered them, "You faithless generation, how much longer must I be among you? How much longer must I put up with you? Bring him to me." And they brought the boy to him. (Mark 9:14-20)

She stopped reading and pictured the scene. Here was a father looking for Jesus, and the nine disciples who hadn't been invited to go with him up the mountain and were perhaps smarting about it—the nine who didn't get to witness his transfiguration before Peter, James, and John—failed miserably in Jesus' absence to use the authority he had given them to cast out demons and heal the sick in his name. While the father's suffering was compounded by disappointment, the nine stood around and argued with the scribes. No wonder Jesus was exasperated.

What were they arguing about? The root cause of the boy's affliction? The disciples' authority to attempt such a miracle? Whatever the squabble, the boy and his father had lost their personhood, reduced to object lessons in a theological debate.

"Teacher, I brought you my son."

Oh, the poignancy of those words. Jamie felt them in the depth of her soul. She watched the father come forward to answer the question the disciples wouldn't answer. "Teacher, my boy's the one they're arguing about. You see, I brought him to you. My boy can't speak. He's got this spirit that has taken away his voice, and sometimes—we never know when it's going to hit next, but sometimes the evil spirit comes upon him and tries to destroy him. It thrashes him to the ground, and my boy can't even cry out in pain. He just foams at the mouth and grinds his teeth and goes rigid. And there's nothing we can do to help him, Jesus. Nothing. Your friends couldn't help, either."

And then, as if to demonstrate its power, the spirit did exactly what the father described. It convulsed the boy, and the boy fell on the ground in front of all of them and started foaming at the mouth. But—this is what had caught Jamie's attention and surprised her years ago—rather than immediately casting out the spirit, Jesus turned to the father and asked him, "How long has this been happening to him?"

Her eyes stung with tears.

"Tell me the story," Jesus said to the despondent dad. "Tell me how long your son has suffered. Tell me how long your own heart has been breaking. Tell me." Because Jesus knew there was also healing in telling the story and having someone listen with concern and compassion. Jesus didn't need to hear the details; the father needed to speak them.

Just as Jamie had, over and over again. She closed her eyes. "It's been years, Lord. She's suffered for years. Sometimes it goes away for a while, and we think she's well, that she's whole. But then the depression strikes again without warning, and it seems like it will destroy her. Please. Are you able to do anything, Jesus? Can you help? Can you deliver my daughter? Can you heal her? If you're able to do anything, please. For both of us. Have mercy on us."

"Jamie," she imagined Jesus replying, "what do you mean, 'If you are able'? All things can be done for the one who believes."

"Lord," she replied, "I believe. Help my unbelief!"

How often that had been her prayer over the years. Like the nameless father, she was a walking contradiction, an amalgam of hope and despair, faith and doubt. She believed. She believed Jesus had the power to deliver Wren from her affliction and make her completely well. She knew he was able. She wasn't sure he was willing.

She closed her Bible and tucked it back into her bag. Years ago, a struggling friend had said with a sigh, "I always want the power that delivers, not the grace that sustains."

That's what Jamie always wanted too. But which one did God desire to give? And if she had enough faith, would it make a difference what he gave?

11

As soon as she landed in Baltimore, Jamie called for an update. "She's sound asleep," Kit said. "I asked her to keep the door cracked open so I can check on her every once in a while. She didn't object."

"That's good." Jamie found an open seat in the gate area and set down her bag. "I can't thank you enough. Just knowing she's with you . . ."

"I'm glad she was willing to come, poor girl. She hardly seemed to know where she was when I got there."

"How does she look?"

"Tired. Thin. I mean, she's always been a slip of a thing. But maybe a little thinner. A bit skittish. I noticed she jumped at any little noise. I wonder how much she slept at the hospital."

Jamie sighed. "I don't know what to think about her being there. I don't know whether it helped or hurt."

"They do their best," Kit said. "Glenwood has a good reputation, but it's not an easy place to be. She's safe, though. They kept her safe. And that's no small thing."

"Right." They did what they were supposed to do. Jamie was grateful for that.

"Ooh, I think I hear stirring upstairs. Call me when you land."

"Thanks, Kit. I will."

"We'll see you soon."

Jamie checked the time and set her phone down. Dylan would be leading a Bible study at the nursing home. The kids would still be at school. She had promised Phoebe she would Skype with her before she went to bed. "Wren too," Phoebe had said, sniffling.

Jamie hadn't been able to promise that. "Wren might go to bed before you, sweetheart. She's very tired."

"And she's so sad."

"Yes, she's feeling very sad." They hadn't told Phoebe about Theo. That would have made her cry harder. Phoebe loved animals as much as Wren did.

Her phone chimed with a text from Dylan: *Call me asap*

She pressed his number.

"Hey," he said. "You're at the airport?"

"Yeah, just landed. Everything okay?" In the background she heard Phoebe's voice. "What's up?"

"Got a call from the school while I was at the nursing home. Phoebe's sick."

Oh, no. "Sick-sick? Or just . . ."

"Not sure. She wants to talk to you."

"Okay. Put her on."

"Here you go," she heard Dylan say as he handed over his phone. "Mommy?"

"Hey, sweetheart. How're you feeling?"

"I puked my guts out!"

"You did?"

"Yeah. All over the whoooooole carpet."

"Oh, honey. I'm sorry."

"It smelled really, really bad."

Her poor teacher. "How are you feeling now?"

"Really bad."

"So, Daddy's taking you home?"

"Yeah. When are you coming?"

"Not today, love, remember? I'm going on an airplane to see Wren."

"But I'm sick."

"I know. I'm so sorry. But Daddy will take really good care of you, I know he will."

Phoebe gave an exasperated sigh. "But I'm really, really sick. And I'm really, really sad."

"Phoebe, listen. I know you're sad. I know you don't feel well. But I can't come home right now. I promised your sister I would visit, and I haven't seen her in a while, remember? And when we make promises, we need to keep them. She's waiting for me."

"Well, I'm waiting for you too."

"I know, honey. I know it's hard. And I'll be back soon."

"When?"

"I'm not sure. About a week, probably."

She sighed again.

"I love you very much, Phoebe-girl. And we can Skype tonight before you go to bed, okay?"

"Promise?"

"Cross my heart."

"'Kay."

"Put Daddy back on the phone, all right? I love you."

Silence.

"Hey," Dylan said.

"She's mad at me."

"We'll survive."

"But what if she's really sick?"

"We'll figure it out. I've got tomorrow blocked off for sermon prep, so if we need to"—he quickly spelled "call a sick day"—"it'll be all right." Even now she could picture their daughter, nose scrunched, trying to figure out what he had just spelled. "Hey, Phoebe," he said, "how about a m-i-l-k-s-h-a-k-e?"

Phoebe cheered.

"See?" Dylan said. "We're good."

"Wait. No. She can't have a milkshake if she's got an upset stomach. It's not good for her."

"Oh. Sorry, Feebs. Mommy says no milkshake."

She could hear Phoebe's protest. "Don't make me out to be the bad guy, Dylan. Explain to her why and offer her something else. She can have popsicles."

"Mommy says you can have popsicles since milkshakes might

make you sick." Phoebe said something Jamie couldn't hear. "Ah, okay," Dylan said. "She says she's not that sick."

Ah. Well. "She's still got to wait."

"Popsicles and a movie, Feebs. That's the offer." There was a pause and then he said, "Okay, that's a thumbs up. We're good."

"I hope so."

"What? You don't trust me?"

"Of course I trust you! I just feel bad about . . ."

"About . . ."

She stared at the passengers coming and going. "Everything." Having such a wide age gap between her children often left her feeling pulled apart by their competing needs.

"We'll be fine, Jamie. You just focus on being with Wren."

"Okay. Thank you."

"Call us when you get there. Hey, say bye to Mommy, okay?"

"Bye, Mommy!" she called.

"Okay," Dylan said, "we've gotta go. It's movie time!" And Phoebe cheered again.

Jamie clicked her belt into place and settled herself between two businessmen who evidently knew each other but hadn't wanted to occupy a middle seat. She hoped they wouldn't be talking around her the entire flight.

She also hoped Phoebe wouldn't get into the habit of trying to be sent home from school. If she thought she would receive special treats any time her stomach hurt, she might. She certainly knew how to get what she wanted. They needed to watch that with her.

As a little girl Wren had suffered from a nervous stomach. Many times the school had called to alert Jamie that she was in the nurse's office. With Wren, though, it never seemed to be a ploy to come home. She enjoyed school. She excelled in her classes and was well loved by her teachers. But the pressure she put on herself to excel and to please others had fueled her anxiety. Jamie had watched for the same impulses in Olivia, but Olivia seemed to have a much more secure and confident self-image, much less concerned with what other people thought of her. Joel too. Jamie admired that. It wasn't easy growing up as a pastor's kid.

She and Dylan had worked hard to ensure that Olivia and Joel—and Phoebe, too, as she grew older—would have as much autonomy and freedom from crushing expectations and fishbowl scrutiny as possible. She might have said such scrutiny was the source of Wren's anxiety, but Wren had been in college when Dylan accepted the call to ministry in North Carolina, so it wasn't that.

There you go again, Dylan's voice said. *Trying to find the cause.*

Not unlike the disciples who asked Jesus, "Who sinned?" when they walked past a blind man. "This man or his parents, that he was born blind?" They didn't care, evidently, that the man wasn't deaf.

Aisle-seat businessman removed a stack of papers from his briefcase and handed them to window-seat businessman. "You sure you don't want to sit together?" Jamie asked again. "I'm happy to move."

"Nah, it's okay," Aisle-man said.

Window-man said, "I think it was a hint, Jimbo. She wants some peace and quiet."

Jamie smiled at him. If Dylan were between them, he would inquire about their work, their hobbies, their families. If they didn't ask directly about his line of work, he would casually mention he was a pastor, to test reciprocity or openness to dialogue. Identifying yourself as a pastor was either a conversation starter or ender. Jamie had watched the conversations start and end many times. Dylan received either outcome with genuine equanimity. That was one of Dylan's gifts: peace.

She could count on two hands the number of times she'd seen him truly riled up. But one of those occasions was a reaction against the "Who sinned to cause this?" mindset.

It was one of his early courses in seminary—Jamie remembered that detail because they had just moved into their apartment near campus and she was unpacking wedding china—and he came home from class raging after a guest lecturer's presentation. "Want to know what causes depression?"

At that point in her life she hadn't given it much thought. She shrugged.

"Sin," he said.

"As in, living in a fallen world?"

"No." He opened his notebook and read Jamie direct quotes from the lecturer, how depression was all about allowing your circumstances, thoughts, and feelings to become your god, that at its root was an idolatrous unbelief that declared, "God is not sufficient for me."

Jamie was angry too. Imagine telling that to someone who was contemplating suicide. Or someone suffering with mental illness because they'd been abused or sexually assaulted or traumatized in some other way. Basically, the lecturer had told a room full of future pastors and counselors that if a church member or client was suffering from depression, it was that person's fault. "And if we don't tell them to repent," Dylan had said, "then we're 'encouraging disobedience' and 'undermining the truth and power of God's Word.'"

"But I don't understand. Why would your prof invite him to speak?"

"He wanted us to hear what some of the theology is about mental health issues. He wants us thinking critically about it. But I'm guessing there were probably some people in class agreeing with the guy. And that scares me."

Not long after that Wren returned from a middle school youth retreat at a friend's church, where the speaker had told the students that if they were feeling anxious, they were breaking Jesus' command not to worry. She didn't want to upset Jesus, Wren tearfully confided to Jamie and Dylan. She didn't want to be disobedient. But she couldn't turn off all her worries. She couldn't make them go away, no matter how hard she tried. Was Jesus mad at her?

No matter how hard they tried to convince her otherwise, Wren was certain she had disappointed him with her lack of faith.

It wasn't the last time she would hear a message of judgment, shame, and guilt. There was no shielding her from it. *If you had more faith. If you prayed more. If you focused on giving thanks in all things. If you just trusted Jesus and repented, you would be healed.*

Jamie sighed and shifted in her seat, trying not to bump Aisleman's elbow on the armrest.

Not that repentance couldn't bring healing. She knew it did. The rhythm of self-examination, confession, and repentance was an essential spiritual discipline in her life and in her marriage. No doubt some cases of anxiety or depression had underlying spiritual roots that needed to be addressed pastorally and sensitively with compassion, discernment, and grace. Sometimes what needed to be named were disordered desires. Sometimes what needed to be confessed was a disbelief in God's goodness and a stubborn resistance to God's will and way. This she knew from personal experience. But to begin by assuming that the afflicted were suffering because they had sinned? No.

When it came to ministering healing and hope to the wounded and despairing, the church of Jesus Christ could do better than that. It had to.

She stared out the plane window. Here she was on her soapbox again, her adrenaline rising as she debated imaginary opponents. *My wife, the reformer,* Dylan would say. Maybe. Maybe about a few things. Amazing what you came to care about when it hit close to home.

12

J amie, welcome." Kit embraced her that evening at the doorstep
of her condo with the sort of fortifying grip that made her believe
all would be well. Somehow all would be well. "Come in, let me take
your bag." At seventy-five Kit showed no signs of slowing down.

"It's okay, I've got it." Jamie maneuvered her suitcase into the foyer.

Kit closed the door behind her. "I've put Wren in the guest room
upstairs. I figured you wouldn't mind the futon in the den."

"No, that's fine. Thank you so much."

"Here, let me take your jacket. And don't worry about your shoes.
You can leave them on if you want. Or I've got some knit slippers in
the basket there. Whatever's comfortable."

Jamie slipped off her shoes and chose a pair of turquoise slippers
with decorative floral print buttons. "How's she doing?"

"Still asleep." Kit hung Jamie's jacket in the coat closet. "Do you
want to go up and see her?"

She did. But she wouldn't. "It's okay. I'll wait."

"Then let me show you where you'll be and let you get settled in.
And how about something to drink before dinner? Coffee? Tea?"

"Tea would be lovely, thanks." Jamie picked up her suitcase and
followed her around the corner to a small room decorated in serene
blues and grays.

"Bathroom is right there"—she pointed across the hall—"and I'll
put the kettle on. Make yourself at home. I'm so glad you're here."

As Kit retreated to the kitchen, Jamie unzipped her suitcase. She
would brush her teeth, wash her face, change her clothes. Maybe by
then Wren would be awake. She checked her watch: six o'clock.

Wren had been asleep most of the day. Not a good sign.

"Milk with your tea?" Kit asked when Jamie entered the kitchen a few minutes later.

"Yes, please." She gazed out the window at woods and a small creek. "What a pretty view. Very peaceful."

Kit nodded. "I've been happy here. It was hard to give up the house after being there so many years, but it was the right decision."

"Have you got good neighbors?"

"Very good. We look out for each other."

"That's a gift."

"Yes, it is." Kit set two mugs on the table and sat down across from her. "I miss my garden," she said. "We get so many deer through here, I've decided not to fight them. I tried the first couple of years, but they plowed down even the things they aren't supposed to like."

"I guess if they're hungry . . ."

"Oh, they're always hungry. So I gave up the garden and decided to concentrate on birds." She motioned toward the feeders. "Lots of variety out there. I even saw a pileated woodpecker on that tree the other day, which is fine, as long as he stays on the tree and doesn't decide he likes the house instead."

Jamie smiled. "Do you ever see wrens?"

"Every once in a while. Mostly, you hear them. Amazing, how such loud songs can come from such little birds." She peered over Jamie's shoulder. "And speaking of wrens . . ."

"Hi, Mom."

Jamie jumped to her feet. "Hey, sweetheart!" When she enfolded Wren in an embrace, she could feel her shoulder blades through her sweatshirt. "I was wondering how long we should let you sleep." She brushed her daughter's dark hair away from her face and kissed her on the forehead.

"How about some tea?" Kit said.

"Okay."

While Kit rose to start the kettle again, Jamie pulled a third chair back from the table. "I was just asking Kit about her birds."

Wren looked so small and fragile. No light in her eyes, no color in her cheeks. No point asking her how she was feeling; everything about her declared the answer.

"Are you hungry?" Kit asked. "I've got beef stew in the Crock-Pot, should be ready any time."

When Wren didn't reply, Jamie said, "That sounds great. How about if I set the table?"

Kit opened cabinets and drawers. Jamie stared at the utensils. She didn't need to put out knives, did she? But there was no danger in putting them out, was there? She grabbed three spoons and three forks. "Do we need plates or just bowls?"

"How about bowls and small plates for bread?" Kit poured hot water into a mug. "Milk with your tea, Wren?"

Wren was staring outside.

"Wren?" Jamie said. "Milk with your tea?"

After a moment of silence, she said, "Okay."

Kit added milk, stirred, and removed the teabag. "Here you are, dear one." She set the mug in front of her.

Tears welled up in Wren's eyes, and she lowered her head into her hands. She was sorry, she said. She didn't think she could eat.

Eventually, Jamie coaxed her into taking a few very small bites of bread and a couple of spoonfuls of stew. "You've got to eat, love. Please try." But she couldn't. Or wouldn't. Jamie didn't know how to discern the difference.

"Does anything sound good to you?" Kit asked.

No. Nothing. She just wanted to sleep. So Jamie gently escorted her back upstairs and asked if there was anything she could do for her. Wren crawled into bed and pulled the blanket up around her shoulders. "Could you stay with me until I fall asleep?"

Jamie lay down beside her and stroked her hair in the dark.

At some point during the night, Kit must have entered the room to cover her with an afghan. Jamie yawned and squinted at the sunlight streaming through the window.

What time was it?

Careful not to disturb Wren, who still slept soundly beneath her blanket, she rolled over to check the clock radio beside the bed. *Eight.* She couldn't remember the last time she'd slept until eight o'clock.

Downstairs she found a note from Kit on the kitchen counter: *Early morning meeting at New Hope. Please help yourself to anything you need. I'll be home around noon. Holding you both in prayer.*

Jamie selected a single-serve coffee pod from the box on the counter and brewed her morning cup. Then she shuffled to the den to get toiletries and clothes from her suitcase. There on the futon was her phone, with several missed calls and texts from Dylan.

Skype with Phoebe? the last one read.

Oh, no.

She leaned her head back and exhaled slowly. She could see it now, Phoebe snuggling onto Dylan's lap in front of the computer to call Mommy, Dylan explaining that Mommy wasn't online yet, Dylan calling to remind her Phoebe was waiting, Phoebe asking where Mommy was and did she forget? Dylan saying, "Of course she didn't forget. I bet she's just busy right now talking with Wren." And they would wait a few minutes and try again. And again. And again. She pressed his number.

"Jamie, what happened? Is everything okay?"

"Yes. I mean, no. Wren's not doing well at all. But I'm so sorry! I fell asleep next to her last night." She ran her hand through her hair. "Was Phoebe upset?"

"Yeah."

"Did you keep her home today?"

"No. She ate fine last night, so I sent her. But I suspect I'll get a call from the school at some point."

"Dylan, I'm so sorry. I'm a bad mom."

"You're not a bad mom."

"I am. I can't believe I forgot to call. I promised her." *And when we make a promise . . .*

"You've got other things on your mind, hon."

It didn't matter. "Did she cry herself to sleep?"

He hesitated.

"Did she?"

"I stayed with her and read her some stories."

"Should I call the school and try to talk to her?"

"No. Let it go. But set your phone alarm to call later. If she ends up coming home early, I'll let you know."

This was the sort of thing a child would remember, the sort of thing that would erode trust. *Promise?* she heard Phoebe ask.

She was such a bad mom.

"So, fill me in," he said. "What's going on?"

Jamie sighed. "I don't know. She won't eat. She doesn't communicate beyond a few sentences and only wants to sleep. I don't know what to do to help."

"Do you think she needs to go back to the hospital?"

"I'm not sure. I don't even know how that would work, once you check out if you can go back right away or not. I don't know."

"Some of those places have outpatient programs," he said. "It might be worth investigating. Or ask her whether they offered something like that."

She wasn't going to ask her that. Not right away. "I don't know how hard to press her about anything right now. And I have no idea what's happening with her job. I think she's supposed to go back on Monday, but I don't see any way for that to happen, barring some miracle the next couple of days."

Lord, I believe. Help my unbelief.

Upstairs a bed creaked and footsteps padded along the floor. "She's up," Jamie said. "I'd better go."

"Okay, call me later. I'm home today working on my sermon. Or trying to, anyway. Remind me why I'm preaching through Ecclesiastes?"

"Because it's timely."

"It's depressing."

Jamie said, "That's the point, isn't it? That the kingdoms of this world come to nothing?"

"Yeah. 'Vanity, vanity, all is vanity.'"

She knew many people who had reached the same conclusion. Maybe Solomon was depressed when he wrote the book. "Let me know about Phoebe, okay? I feel terrible."

"She'll survive. Give yourself some grace."

Easier said than done.

"And give Wren a hug from me," he said. "Tell her I love her and I'm praying for her. And if she wants to talk later, I'm here."

She told him she would let her know. But it was hard to imagine her being able to carry on a conversation with anyone right now.

"Hey, sweetheart," she said when Wren entered the kitchen a few minutes later. "Did you sleep okay?" Wren shrugged. "Sorry I fell asleep on your bed. Guess I was tired too."

Wren did not reply.

Jamie cleared her throat. "What can I get you for breakfast? Toast? Eggs? French toast? I'm happy to make some."

Wren loved French toast. It had always been a favorite breakfast together when she was little. Jamie opened the fridge. "That sounds pretty good to me, French toast. What do you think, hon?"

Wren was staring out the window.

Jamie removed milk and a carton of eggs. "If I can find some vanilla, we'll be in business." She opened a narrow pantry door. "Vanilla . . . vanilla—here! Vanilla. And nutmeg . . . that's good. She's even got maple syrup, the real stuff." She held out the small jug. "Pure Michigan, look at that. What do you think?" She set it all down on the counter.

Wren did not turn around.

Jamie followed her gaze outside, where a squirrel was dangling upside down from a branch, stretching to snatch the feeder.

Maybe she was thinking about Theo. Jamie couldn't count the number of times Wren had texted her a cute photo or story about him. He'd been a bright spot in her life ever since Casey left, a source of joy and amusement. A companion.

Maybe she was thinking about Casey. One fresh loss could dredge up all the others.

Should she try to distract her, or engage her in conversation about her thoughts? Was it safe to acknowledge the grief, or would that heighten it? If she wasn't thinking about her losses, then asking how she was feeling about them would only fix her attention on them.

"That little guy is determined, isn't he?" Jamie commented. "They say squirrel-proof feeders, but . . ."

Still no reply.

"Kit was saying she gets quite a lot of birdlife here. We might see some good variety."

Watching her stare outside like that brought back memories of the days and weeks after her favorite sheepdog, Tangara, died from a snakebite. Wren didn't want to go outside, not even to her grandmother's art studio. Day after day she sat beside the kitchen window and wept. She slept with his collar. She would never love another animal like she'd loved Tangara, she said. Why would God let it happen? Why were there so many awful things in the world? Jamie hadn't had answers for her then. She didn't have answers now.

"What do you think, love? French toast?"

Wren turned around slowly. "Toast."

"Just toast?"

She gave a slight nod.

"Okay. Toast-toast it is." She put the other ingredients away. "Oh! Look how sweet this is, Wren—a little toast rack." She lifted it from beside the toaster. This might be a happy memory. "I haven't seen one of these in years. Gran and Pop had one on their table, remember? You used to love arranging your slices in it. And they had little jam pots on the table too. You loved the miniature spoons, remember?"

"I . . . don't know."

Jamie set the toast rack on the table. It had been too costly to ship all her mother's treasures from Australia after she died, so her cousins had kindly agreed to store the keepsakes until Jamie could collect them. Someday, she told herself. She was saving all of it for Wren, who might have her own house and family someday. Or not. Jamie had learned not to press those conversations for fear of increasing anxiety or depression. Especially now that most of her friends were married or getting married.

"I wish I had Gran's jam and chutney recipes," Jamie said. "But she kept it all in her head."

Maybe she shouldn't talk about her mother. Wren had been deeply attached to her. They had shared a common bond of art and painting and love for Van Gogh. Wren had felt her absence deeply. No doubt she still did. Grief upon grief.

Keep it to food, Jamie told herself. The other topics were potential landmines. She held up two loaves of bread. "White or wheat?"

From the blank expression on Wren's face, one might have thought she'd been asked to calculate a differential equation.

"What sounds good to you, hon? White?" Jamie held that loaf out. "Or wheat?" She extended the other.

Wren pointed to the wheat loaf.

"Wheat, it is." She put two slices into the toaster and adjusted the dial. "Hey, love . . . have you got some prescriptions to take?"

No reply, either verbally or visually.

"Did they send you home with medications from the hospital?"

A slow nod.

"Do you think you took any of those yesterday? I know you had a lot going on, but . . ."

Wren opened her mouth but didn't form any words.

"I didn't see any bottles by your bed, and I don't see anything here in the kitchen, so I'm wondering if they're still at your apartment?"

Wren appeared to be weighing this possibility.

"Tell you what—how about if you go upstairs and check your bag, okay? See if you put them in there? And if not, we can go get them, no problem. Or I can go get them for you." Jamie stared at the Scottish Highlands calendar hanging next to the sink. What day was it?

Thursday.

She counted backwards. So if Wren had been released on Tuesday with medicine she should have taken that night, but she was traumatized over Theo, and if she hadn't brought the meds with her to Kit's, then . . . "Can you do that for me? Can you go upstairs and check your bag?" Whatever cocktail they had put her on, missing doses for two days might account for what she was witnessing. "Or I can go with you. Do you want me to look for you?"

Wren shook her head and moved in slow motion toward the stairs.

Jamie cut the slices of toast into diagonal halves and placed them in the rack. She found the butter dish and a jar of strawberry jam. She put her forgotten, lukewarm coffee in the microwave and heated it up. "Any luck?" she called.

No answer.

Oh, God! She should have gone with her. Why hadn't she thought of that?

She was just about to bound up the stairs when Wren appeared with her duffel bag. Jamie tried to slow her heartbeat, which, in the split second of imagining Wren had harmed herself during her three-minute absence, was pounding in her chest. *Jesus, help.* "Did you find it?"

"Yes."

"Do you think you've taken any since you left the hospital?"

Wren's eyes filled with tears. "I don't know. I can't remember."

Jamie kissed her forehead. "It's okay, sweetheart. It's all right. How about eating something first? Or do you want to show me the medicine so I can see if there are special instructions about taking it with or without food?"

Wren removed from the bag four prescription bottles.

Dear God.

Jamie scanned the labels: with or without food, once a day at night, with or without food, at night as needed. She didn't recognize three of the drug names. Maybe she would go online later and investigate their uses and side effects. She wasn't sure if that would reassure her or terrify her. It was all a guessing game, wasn't it, trying to adjust the levels of dopamine and serotonin? *She'll be safer on the meds than off them,* a doctor had told her and Dylan years ago. But oh, how many changes and adjustments had to be made, not to mention the troubling side effects Wren had endured until they found a combination that seemed to help. It was no wonder some people gave up and stopped taking them.

She set aside the "at night as needed" medication and handed the other bottles back to her. "Looks like the easiest way to do it is to take these two with breakfast, and then this one is for nighttime. And then the other one is maybe to help you sleep if you need it?"

Wren nodded.

"If I were you, I'd get it all organized in one of those daily pill dispensers. Then you don't have to worry about having to remember if you took it or not. Have you got one of those?"

No reply.

"I can pick one up for you, no problem. But here—before your toast gets cold. Come and eat."

Wren sat and took a piece of toast from the rack.

"Butter or jam?" Jamie asked.

She shook her head and began to chew slowly. Jamie sat across from her, then jumped up again. "I forgot plates." She swept crumbs from Wren's placemat into her hand, brushed them into the sink, and returned to the table with two square white plates and a bread and butter knife.

The toast was cold. Jamie spread jam onto a single slice. "What else can I get you? Tea? Coffee?"

A slow shake of her head, back and forth. Back and forth.

"How about some juice? I saw orange and cranberry in the fridge. How about cranberry juice? It's cran-raspberry, I think." Jamie rose from her seat again to check. "Yes. Orange or cran-raspberry. Would you like some?" She removed two glasses from the cupboard. "Wren?"

A long pause, then, "No."

Jamie poured a glass for herself. "I talked to Dad this morning. He said to say hi and to tell you he loves you and he's praying for you.

Phoebe went back to school. Did I tell you she threw up yesterday? Maybe I didn't tell you that."

You're doing it again, Dylan might say.

But she did it anyway. She told story after story after story to fill the void, to keep Wren physically present even if she wasn't mentally or emotionally so. She talked because the silence felt terrifying. She told her own stories because she was afraid to ask what she really wanted to know: What was it like for you, being in a place like that? What is it like for you now? And how worried should I be?

13

She needed a mental reset. All Wren could think of as she watched her mother's lips move was the image of Theo, her precious little Theo, limp and lifeless. She hoped he died instantly, that he didn't suffer.

Casey had hit a squirrel once when she was in the car. It was a terrible little thump. She made him pull the car over. She watched its bushy tail twitch and twitch, and then with one last convulsion, it went still. Casey had a towel in his trunk, and he moved the poor thing out of the middle of the road so it wouldn't be hit again. She wept all the way home.

Such an awful little thump. Theo wouldn't have been much more than that. A little thump and maybe a twitching tail.

She set down a half-eaten slice of toast. She felt like she was going to be sick. She pushed the plate away.

The woman felt awful, the neighbor said.

The neighbor's name was—

The neighbor's name—

" . . . got to eat something." Her mother sounded like she was speaking from inside a tunnel.

The neighbor had a cat. Her cat had not run away. The cat's name was Misty.

Her mother's lips were still moving. She looked worried. She looked sad. Don't be sad. Wren shook her head back and forth. Don't be sad don't be sad don't be sad. Please. Don't.

Her body twitched. Her chest tightened. She couldn't breathe. Her mother was reaching for her, pulling her up and out and into her arms. She felt limp, lifeless. "I've got you," a voice said. "I'm here."

No. No. She didn't want to go to the hospital. No. She didn't need to go. Yes, she would try to eat. She *would* eat. A few bites of banana. Okay, a little bit of yogurt. But no hospital. No doctor. Yes, she would take each pill. She would. And the medicine would work like it did in the hospital. It would. She would just lie down for a little while again. She was so tired.

Her mother thought it might help to sit outside instead. See the patio? The nice view of the woods? She bet that little creek gurgled over rocks. And look, how blue the sky! Wasn't it beautiful, that blue?

Periwinkle, Wren murmured.

"What?"

"Periwinkle."

Her mother looked like she was going to cry. "Yes. You're right. It's periwinkle. Yes, it is."

Periwinkle. Jamie wondered if the word had ever sounded so beautiful to anyone's ears. It had never sounded so beautiful to hers. "How about if we go outside for a while?" she said. "I'll make tea for us, and we can go outside to sit. Just sit."

So they sat in Adirondack chairs on the brick patio, Wren wrapped in an afghan and taking slow sips from a sunflower mug, Jamie trying not to interpret body language or monitor every slight alteration in facial expression. Mostly Wren stared blankly ahead. Sometimes she glanced at the sky or a bird swooping in to snatch seed.

Beauty would feed her. It had to. Jamie pictured intravenous tubes pumping sunlight, birdsong, and color into her daughter's desperately dehydrated soul. Words were evidently too much for her to receive. Words were like rain pounding parched land that was so dry, it repelled the very water it needed. Jamie had seen that before, how sometimes after a forest fire the scorched soil couldn't absorb the water, so it pooled on the surface or eroded the ground. But beauty, with its unassuming gentleness, could seep into the cracks. Beauty demanded nothing. Not even appreciation.

She looked at her daughter. *Can you feel it?* she wanted to ask. But instead, she kept silent and closed her eyes, listening to the rustle of leaves and ripple of water.

An acorn—was it an acorn Julian of Norwich had seen in her vision? Jamie stooped to pick up a small nut near her feet, the tufted little beret still attached. Phoebe loved to ink faces upon them, sad or happy or surprised or angry. Her current collection resided on her nightstand. Jamie turned the acorn over in the palm of her hand, feeling the contrast of the smooth and the rough, marveling that the towering oaks like the one where Dylan had hung a tire swing for the kids had emerged from such a modest, inconspicuous container for a seed. She put it in her pocket as a reminder of her need for patience and faith.

It wasn't an acorn Julian had seen, though. Jamie remembered now. It was a hazelnut. Julian had seen a vision of something small in the palm of her hand, a tiny sphere no bigger than a hazelnut. It was so small, so vulnerable, and yet she perceived that somehow it represented all that God had made. And though she feared it could not last, that it was too fragile to persevere, Julian understood that everything had its origin in the love of God, and it would last because God had made it. God loved it. God would preserve it.

Kit was the one who had introduced her to Julian during a class on prayer at the New Hope Center. Maybe she should read Julian again. *All will be well. And all will be well. And every kind of thing will be well.* That was what Julian came to know and trust.

Lord, I believe. Help my unbelief.

The screen door creaked open. "You've found my favorite spot for contemplation," Kit said.

Was it noon already? Jamie checked her watch. Yes, it was. "It's beautiful here, Kit."

"Well, it's nothing compared to your view out over the valley, but it's my own little corner of tranquility."

Wren readjusted her afghan around her shoulders.

"I stopped at the orchard near New Hope and bought apples," Kit said. "Honeycrisp, my favorite. Are either of you ready for lunch?"

Jamie rose to her feet. "I can eat any time. How about you, Wren? What sounds good?"

A slight shrug.

Kit laid her hand on Wren's shoulder. "How about something simple? Fruit and cheese with soup and bread? We can eat out here."

To Jamie's surprise, Wren said, "Okay."

"I'll help get it ready," Jamie said, and followed Kit inside.

"If you can slice the apples and cheese, Jamie, I'll get the rest."

Jamie opened the bag on the counter and started rinsing apples, keeping an eye on Wren from the window above the sink.

"How's she doing?" Kit asked.

"I don't know. She was so out of it this morning, I thought I might need to take her to the hospital."

Kit shook her head in sympathy. "It's so hard to know what to do, how to help."

"I don't know what's what," Jamie said. "I don't know if her being so detached—catatonic, even—is connected with the medications or not, whether these are side effects we need to worry about, or whether it's because she forgot to take meds yesterday, or whether this is all about her grief over Theo or friends leaving or depression in general. I don't know. And it's all too much to ask her."

"Exactly. She can't process much of anything right now. I know I couldn't after I had my breakdown years ago. All I could do was try to keep going with even the most basic life skills. And some days even that was too much."

Jamie turned off the faucet and dried her hands. It wasn't something Kit had shared many details about, and Jamie had never pressed her for them. Dylan didn't know many details, either. He was away at college when it happened, and it wasn't something his parents had talked about—at least, not to him. But this seemed to be an opening for conversation. "How old were you," Jamie asked, "when you—when all of that happened?"

Kit removed a loaf of bread from the carved "Give Us This Day" wooden box on the counter. "Well, let me think." She held the bag to her chest. "Micah died in March of '82. How old was I then?" She paused. "Almost forty. Sarah was away at school, thankfully. It would have been awful for her, seeing her mother fall apart like that."

"You had plenty of reasons to fall apart," Jamie said quietly. "I can't imagine losing a child." She couldn't imagine it. She couldn't let her mind drift there.

"There were days I didn't think I would make it," Kit said. "But here I am. Here we are. By God's grace, here we are." She tilted her head and pointed out the window. "Hear it? That bubbly song?"

Jamie stood still, listening.

"That's a wren," Kit said. "Beautiful, isn't it?"

Jamie nodded. It almost sounded like hope.

She couldn't remember what the fairywrens sounded like. "But they're this exquisite shade of blue," Jamie said as the three of them sat outside with their lunch. "All different kinds of blue, actually." She turned toward her daughter. "You would be able to name all the shades of blue."

Wren dipped the edge of her spoon into her soup bowl.

"Let's pull up a picture later," Kit said. "I've never seen one."

"They're really tiny. And I couldn't believe it when it came that close. I think I probably stopped breathing at that point, afraid I'd scare it away. And then when it hopped right up into my lap . . ."

"That's incredible, Jamie. Birds don't do that. A chickadee, maybe, if you've got seed in your hand."

"No, I didn't have any seed," Jamie said, then smiled. "Well, come to think of it, I guess I did. I had only just found out I was pregnant, and I was scared. I was feeling alone and overwhelmed. Far away from God."

Wren looked up from stirring her soup.

Jamie said, "That little bird looked at me as if to say, 'I've been sent to deliver a message.' And it was like I heard God for the very first time, not in an audible voice. But an inner knowing. I knew God was telling me not to be afraid, that all would be well. So I went home and told my parents. And your Gran and Pop"—Wren was still looking at her—"they were wonderful. They embraced me and said they loved me, and they loved my baby. They loved you. We all did." Jamie set her empty soup bowl on the small side table, then turned again toward Kit. "I knew from the beginning that her name was Wren. Even if she'd been a boy, it would have been Wren."

"How did I not know this story?" Kit exclaimed. "Did you tell me, and I forgot?" She touched Wren's shoulder. "Old lady brain. Forgive me for not treasuring such an important story for the two of you."

"I may not have told you," Jamie said. "It's not a story I tell very often. Most people wouldn't believe it. I wouldn't believe it myself if it hadn't happened to me."

"It's a wonderful story," Kit said. "These are the kinds of things we can't make up." She reached for the platter. "Come on, now. Don't let me be the only one eating all of this. Wren? How about you? A little bit of bread?" And she held it out for Wren to take and eat.

14

Wren went back to bed after lunch. "Let her sleep for now," Kit said after Jamie privately expressed her concern. "Remember Elijah in the wilderness? The angel woke him up to make sure he had something to eat and drink, then let him rest again."

Jamie had forgotten that part of Elijah's story: the gutsy, victorious prophet on the run, exhausted and dejected, feeling abandoned and overwhelmed, wanting to die. He was finished. It was all too much for him. And God met him in his despair with tender compassion, not condemnation or disappointment.

She poured the leftover soup into a plastic container and put it in the fridge.

"I've got meetings this afternoon," Kit said, "and then I'll be back around five. How about if I bring pizza home?"

"That sounds good to me." Wren usually liked pizza. Maybe they could coax her to eat again.

"And you, dear one, you look tired. Why don't you lie down too? You both have a long journey ahead. I think it would be wise for you to eat, rest, and repeat."

Jamie thanked her, then retreated to the den to lie down. But before settling herself on the futon, she perused a collection of family photos on the walls and bookshelves: Kit on the steps of a steepled church, sporting a beehive and cradling an infant in her arms; Kit in a straw hat and swimsuit, standing beside a lopsided sandcastle with two small children, each holding plastic shovels and pails; Micah in baggy overalls beside his father, both holding German

Shepherd puppies; Sarah in a Girl Scout uniform, receiving a badge. The family history was narrated as much by the missing photos as by the ones that adorned the room: no photos of Kit and Robert's wedding, no photos of a couple growing old together, no photos of Micah sporting graduation gowns or a tux for a sister's wedding. The oldest he ever appeared in photos was as a teenage boy with pimples and braces. Jamie had no difficulty recognizing the cloud of sadness that shadowed each of his pictures, even the ones of him as a little boy. The melancholy spoke.

A bit of a loner, Dylan had said. The cousins hadn't spent much time together as children—only at the occasional family reunion or holiday get-together—and the athletic, popular Dylan hadn't shared much in common with the shy and bookish Micah. That's what Dylan had told her once with a hint of regret, that maybe if he had tried harder to connect with him, Micah might not have gotten involved with the wrong kind of crowd in high school.

There was never any point in playing the "if only" game, not about anything.

The front door squeaked open, then closed again. Kit would be on her way to New Hope. Once she felt a little more centered, a little less preoccupied, Jamie might ask her how she had survived it all.

Not without scars, Kit would probably say. Not without many scars.

Just after three o'clock Jamie was awakened with her buzzing alarm, reminding her to call Phoebe. "Hey, sweetheart," she said when Dylan put her on. "How are you?"

"You forgot."

"I know. I'm so sorry. You know how sometimes you're so tired you fall asleep wearing your clothes? That's what happened to Mommy last night. I fell asleep wearing all my clothes."

"Oh."

"But tell me about your day today. Are you feeling better?"

"Yeah. But my stomach hurts a little, so Daddy gave me more popsicles."

Oh. She would need to coach Dylan about using a different strategy. If he offered to take her to the doctor, for instance, she might suddenly be cured.

"Did you give Wren my picture?"

No. She had completely forgotten. "I'm saving it for a little later. Wren hasn't been feeling too well."

"Did she puke her guts out?"

"No. But she's very tired, so I'm letting her rest."

"Oh." Phoebe paused. "Can I talk to her?"

"I don't know, love. I think she's still sleeping."

"Can you check?"

Sure. She could check. Maybe Phoebe could get her talking. "Okay, hold on. I'll go upstairs and see." The door was cracked open. Jamie knocked softly. No answer. She pushed open the door. "Wren?" The bed was empty, the bathroom door open. "Hold on, Phoebe. I'm looking for her. She might have gone outside."

But she wasn't on the patio, either. "Tell you what, love. Let me call you right back, okay? Can you put Daddy on the phone again?"

"Hey," he said.

"I'm not sure where Wren is."

"What do you mean?"

"I mean, she went upstairs to lie down after lunch, but now she's not here. She must have left while I was asleep."

"She couldn't have gone far, right? A walk through the neighborhood?"

"Maybe."

"Try her phone, then call me back."

But there was no reply to her text, and her call went straight to voicemail. Jamie called Dylan again. "What should I do?"

"I'm not sure."

"I don't know what state of mind she's in. No idea. I shouldn't have gone to sleep. I should have known better, I should have kept watch." That's what she and Dylan had done, not long before Wren was diagnosed. Multiple nights they alternated keeping watch. They hid knives, locked away pills, and slept in shifts on the floor of her room. She had never tried to harm herself, thank God. She insisted she wouldn't but—

"Jamie . . ."

"I should have kept watch. Who knows how long she's been gone? I was asleep at least an hour. No. More than that." She'd heard the front door open. She had assumed it was Kit. But maybe it was Wren. That was at least two hours ago. She could be anywhere by now. "What do I do?"

"Deep breath, Jamie."

"What should I do? Get in the car?"

"And go where?"

"I don't know. Drive around the neighborhood? I don't know." She paced the kitchen floor.

Dylan said, "How about if I pray right now?"

She glanced out the window. She'd been encouraged by Wren sitting outside, eating with them, and appearing to listen to their conversation. She'd been lulled into a false sense of security.

"Jamie?"

"Okay. Fine. Pray." But as soon as he was finished, she would get in the car to search for her.

While Dylan prayed, she grabbed her fleece, her shoes, and her rental car key. What she didn't have was a house key. She should have asked Kit for a house key. And as safe as Kingsbury probably was, she shouldn't leave the house unlocked. Then again, even if she did have a house key, what if Wren returned to a locked house? Then where would she go?

"Amen," he said.

"I can't leave. I don't have a house key."

"Where's Kit?"

"In meetings. She won't be back until dinner."

"So, call her and see if she hides a spare somewhere."

"That won't work. I can't risk Wren coming back and being locked out." She stepped onto the front porch and scanned up and down the road. "I've got to go. I've got to figure this out."

"Jamie—"

"I'll call you when I know something."

"Jamie, listen. We've talked about this before, how you don't have control over any of this. You don't, hon. None of us does."

Easy for him to say. Wren wasn't his flesh and blood. "I'll call you later," she said, and punched "End."

Years ago, Joel had left a gate open during his morning chores and only discovered in the afternoon that one of the dogs had run away. He was beside himself. So Dylan and Jamie prayed with him, asking God to bring Murphy home. After they finished praying, she felt a nudge to get into her car and drive toward the school. Leaving Joel and Dylan to scour the neighborhood on foot, she inched her way there, panning the sides of the road while telling herself it was probably her imagination, that it was a ridiculously futile pursuit and they shouldn't have gotten Joel's hopes up by suggesting that God could bring their pet safely home. When she pulled into the empty school parking lot, there was no sign of the dog. Not that she was surprised. But then, just as she was getting ready to head home, Murphy trotted out of the woods. It was a miracle, they all said, a miracle that God had kept Murphy safe and led her straight to him.

She circled Kit's neighborhood, first on foot, then in the car, asking the Spirit to guide her. But she felt no nudges directing her anywhere. After a fruitless hour she returned to the house, half-expecting to open the door and find her daughter waiting for her. But she was not there.

What had Wren been thinking, leaving the house without saying anything? Didn't she have any idea the panic she would cause? It wasn't like her to be thoughtless or selfish.

But Wren wasn't herself right now.

No. That wasn't exactly true. She was herself. She was the self that terrified Jamie, the unpredictable self and fragile self, the self Jamie had naively believed had been healed years ago when she managed to go off to college, graduate at the top of her class, and train to be a social worker, all because she had a deep sense of mission, a sense of call to serve the wounded. She longed to make a difference in the kingdom. She *had* made a difference in the kingdom.

But mental illness was a dormant volcano. And if she had been paying closer attention to Wren's state of mind a few months ago, she might have noticed the small earthquakes or steam eruptions that indicated the volcano was active again. But she wasn't paying attention. Not nearly close enough attention.

Not knowing what else to do, she sat at the kitchen table and wept.

"What about her apartment?" Kit asked when she arrived home with pizza shortly after five o'clock. "She wouldn't have gone back to her apartment, would she?"

"I don't know. I guess anything's possible. Is it walkable from here?"

"Five miles, maybe? But there's a bus stop a couple of miles from here."

"Then I guess she could have." But why? If she wanted to get something from her apartment, she could have asked for a ride. It didn't make sense. But anything that didn't make sense was a possibility. A probability, Jamie supposed.

Kit turned on the oven to low heat and placed the pizza on the top rack. "How about if you wait here for her, and I'll take a quick drive over there?"

"No, I'll go, thanks. I should have thought of that earlier. I wish I'd thought of that earlier. And if she shows up here . . ."

"I'll call you."

Jamie retrieved Wren's address from her contacts and typed it into her phone. Six and a half miles each way. She drove slowly, scanning the sidewalks and side streets. Even if she had walked, there was no telling which route she would have taken. At least she didn't have a car. She wouldn't be safe driving. But was she any safer walking? Would she ever be "safe"?

As she wound through Kingsbury, Jamie tried to redirect her anxious thoughts by praying through the story of the unnamed father and his son. *Jesus, help. Please. I brought my child to you . . .*

If only Jesus would speak to Wren's affliction the same words he spoke to the deaf and mute spirit: depart and never return.

She knew the statistics, how once someone had experienced a major depressive episode as Wren had in high school, the more likely she was to experience another. And now that she had experienced another debilitating one, she was even more likely to be afflicted again. *Depart and never return.* She knew Jesus was able to speak those words to the illness that engulfed her daughter. She didn't know if he was willing. And how could you ever know for sure? If the symptoms seemed to subside, you might live in hope. But was it a true hope or a false hope? And if the affliction never went away, then what?

She would keep asking. That's all she knew how to do. Keep knocking, keep seeking, keep asking. *Please.*

When she reached the apartment complex, she buzzed Wren's unit. No reply. A young woman about her age was stretching in a turquoise tracksuit nearby. "Excuse me," Jamie called, "do you happen to know Wren Crawford?"

"Yeah, she's my neighbor."

"I'm her mom."

"Oh, hey."

"Have you seen her today?"

The woman shook her head. "Not in a couple of days, probably. I gave her a ride home from her conference the other day."

Her conference? "What day was that?"

"I dunno. Monday? Maybe Tuesday? But I haven't seen her since then."

"Oh. Okay. Thanks."

"You want me to let you in? You could go up and knock."

Maybe Wren couldn't hear the buzzer. Maybe the buzzer was broken. Other more frightening possibilities also swirled in her imagination. "Sure. That would be great." Jamie followed her inside, then vaulted up the stairs to knock. No answer. She leaned her head against the door and called her name. No reply. And no way to break down the door to see if she was inside. *You have no control,* Dylan reminded her in her head. *No control over what Wren chooses to do.*

"Not there?" the woman asked as Jamie exited the building.

"No." She needed to keep herself together. "But if you happen to see her, could you let her know I'm trying to reach her?"

"Yeah. Sure." She eyed Jamie quizzically. "Is everything okay with her?"

"Oh, yeah. I just flew into town, thought I would surprise her."

"Cool. If I see her, I'll let her know."

Jamie thanked her and got back into the car. Now what? Where else could she try? Bethel House was a secure location for the protection of the residents. Jamie didn't know where it was. And it was unlikely Wren had gone there. Also unlikely she would have returned to the hospital. *God, please.* She would make one more pass around Kit's neighborhood in the car and then walk the woods along the creek as far as she could go.

Why hadn't she thought of that earlier?

Maybe Wren had gone to the woods. She backed out of the parking space and turned right at the stop sign. She would file a report with the police as soon as she got back to Kit's. She should have done that right away. Even if they told her she had to wait twenty-four hours, she should have called. Especially if she thought Wren could be a suicide risk.

Oh, God. Why hadn't she called the police right away? She was a terrible mother. A terrible, horrible mother. She blinked back tears. If something had happened to Wren . . .

Oh, God. She'd never forgive herself.

Dylan said he was sorry. He thought it was a twenty-four-hour waiting period too. But he had looked it up online while Jamie was driving back to Kit's, and the "mentally ill" should be reported missing immediately.

As difficult as it was to accept the label, her daughter was "mentally ill." How many photos had she seen on newscasts or in papers of the mentally ill who had gone missing? If she reported Wren as mentally ill and missing, what would be broadcast on the media? A photo of a young woman who appeared to be well, stable, high functioning. Not homeless. Not unkempt. No vacant stare. Mental illness could be visible or invisible.

But once Jamie reported it, then what? Wren would never be invisible again. And was that what she would want in a community as small as Kingsbury?

"They'll want a full description of her when you call," Dylan said. "And whatever she was wearing when you last saw her."

She couldn't remember what she was wearing when they sat outside eating lunch. Think. Think. Gray. She was in gray. Gray sweatpants, gray T-shirt. The T-shirt probably said something on it. But she hadn't paid attention because Wren had wrapped herself in an afghan. She wouldn't have left the house wrapped in an afghan, would she? As soon as she reached Kit's, she would check to see if the afghan was in the house.

Her phone buzzed with an incoming call, and she held it out to look. "I've gotta go. Kit's calling." Her hand trembled as she answered. "Kit?"

"She's here, Jamie. Wren's here."

Jamie pulled the car over to the side of the road, pressed her forehead against the steering wheel, and sobbed.

15

When Jamie returned to the house, an unfamiliar blue sedan was parked in the driveway. Kit met her on the front porch. "She's okay."

"Where in the world was she?"

"She went for a walk without her phone, got disoriented, and ended up at her church. Her pastor brought her here." Kit grasped Jamie's hand. "Hard as it is right now, the fewer questions the better. She's safe. That's the most important thing."

"But—"

"Being frustrated with her won't help. Trust me. When you're in the darkness of depression, you do loads of things that don't make sense. You can cause lots of hurt and a lot of anxiety. Some of it you remember, a lot of it you don't."

Jamie stared at the streetlamp and took a deep breath.

"Come on in," Kit said. "I've just made all of us some tea. Her pastor's an old friend of mine. But neither of us knew we had Wren in common. Such a small world, Kingsbury."

Wren was seated at the kitchen table across from a gray-haired woman who rose when Jamie entered. "I'm Hannah Allen," she said, extending her hand. "I'm so glad to meet you, Jamie."

Wren did not make eye contact. Jamie kissed the top of her head before sitting. "Thanks so much for bringing her here." With her gaze still fixed on her daughter's expressionless profile, she vented silently. *Do you have any idea how worried I was? Any idea what you put me through?*

"Wren kept mentioning her great-aunt Kit," Hannah said, "but I had no idea 'Kit' was Katherine."

"And I had no idea Hannah was Wren's pastor," Kit said. "Imagine my surprise when I saw her get out of the car."

How could you do this to me? What in the world were you thinking?

"Katherine and I met—oh, how many years ago now?"

"Ten, maybe?"

"Yes, that's about right. Because Nate and I will celebrate our ninth anniversary next spring. Hard to believe it's been that long."

"Hannah was up here on sabbatical," Kit said as she poured Jamie a cup of tea, "and she came to one of the sacred journey retreats I was leading at New Hope."

"It was life-changing for me. Katherine ended up being my spiritual director. Then she did our wedding and trained us as spiritual directors . . ."

Can't you even look at me right now?

" . . . and she's still walking alongside. I'm so grateful."

"It's been a joy," Kit said. She glanced toward the oven. "I've got pizza for us. Or I can warm up some soup or beef stew."

"I can't stay long," Hannah said. "I've got a meeting at the church tonight. But I wouldn't say no to a bowl of soup before I go."

"Okay, good. How about you, Jamie? What can I get you?"

How could the two of them be so composed, so casual about everything? "Pizza's fine. Thanks, Kit." They weren't her mother, that's how.

"Okay, one soup, one pizza. How about you, Wren? What can I get you?"

"How about some soup?" Hannah suggested when Wren did not reply.

"Okay."

"Soup, it is," Kit said, and went to the fridge.

As Jamie watched Hannah interact with her daughter in the simplest, mildest way, she perceived with a mixture of gratitude and envy that this woman likely knew far more about Wren's current state of mind than she did. She could tell: Wren had confided things to her that a mother might never know, and a pastor would never reveal.

Don't be mad. Please don't be mad at me. That's what Wren wished she could say aloud.

If she had her sketchbook, she would sketch her mother: her lips pursed, her eyes sad and perplexed, her shoulders slumped, bowed down with the weight of despair and disappointment, like some of the grieving and poor Vincent sketched and painted.

Their eyes met for a moment when her mother looked up from the table. Wren looked away again. She couldn't bear her mother's pain—the pain she had caused.

She had only wanted to go for a walk. She had looked for her mother before she left and found her in the den, sleeping soundly. She did not disturb her. She would not be gone long.

But the more she walked, the farther she wanted to walk. She had to walk. She had to put one foot in front of the other and prove to herself she could keep going. She had to see whether the blue of the sky could still beckon her onward, whether the touch of the breeze on her cheek could feel like a holy whisper, whether the beautiful mystery of decay and decline illustrated by the falling leaves could still speak hope. She had to see, to see again.

And then she had to see again where Casey had first found Theo. She had to touch the dumpster in the alley where he had heard the mewing. She had to trace his steps back to the apartment where he had decided the smallest and weakest of them would be his. For a few weeks, anyway. And then Theo would be hers. Maybe Casey knew when he named him Theo that he would be hers. She wouldn't say no to keeping him. Casey knew that.

And then she'd lingered in the empty parking space where he used to keep his truck. The balcony had different furniture: a matching patio set, a pink tricycle. The window above the kitchen sink had curtains. That's where she was standing when she first heard the news. She was removing multiple leaning towers of dirty dishes to wash them. For years she had chided him, and it had never done any good. Casey did what he wanted, when he wanted. Maybe Brooke could train him on how to keep a kitchen and bathroom clean. That's what she'd been thinking when Casey said, Just leave them. I'm gonna pitch them anyway. And she said, Don't be ridiculous. Why would you pitch them? And he said, 'Cause I'm moving.

Casey was always moving. He was like one of those trucks with a warning sign on the back: "Caution! This vehicle makes wide turns." A studio apartment for a few months here, a futon in a friend's house for a few months there. The gig economy suited his restless spirit.

"Where to now?" she'd asked. He said, Reno. And her stomach, which had been in spasms all that day, ever since she read the story about the whales and Allie told her about Evelyn and her mother, clenched again. Casey had only ever moved around West Michigan. And once to Chicago, but only for a few months. Brooke was supposed to move to Kingsbury. He had told Wren that was their plan. But the plan had changed. Brooke had a stable job she loved in Reno, and he could do his freelancing work from anywhere. She should have known the plan would change. That was one of the few predictable things about Casey: he was unpredictable.

When she finally left the apartment complex, she couldn't find her way back to Kit's. She had walked too far. She had made too many turns. With no phone and no wallet, she walked to the one place she knew how to find. She walked to the church and into Hannah's office. Once there she should have called her mother. She wasn't thinking. Not about that. She was sorry. She was so sorry.

Tears began to stream down her cheeks. Her mother saw. And embraced her.

"You've had quite a day, Jamie," Kit said after Wren went to bed. "What can I do for you?"

Jamie shrugged. "Keep praying, I guess. It's a miracle I didn't lose it with her earlier."

"I know it's hard," Kit said. "But you did so well." She turned off the light above the kitchen table. "I'm going to settle in for my evening prayers. Care to join me?"

Yes. She did. So she followed Kit into the front room, sat down on the couch, and watched her light a Christ candle, something she had first seen her do when they were living in her basement. Each night of their three-week stay, Kit invited them to join her in a prayerful review of the day, to watch for the ways they had been attentive to the presence of God and the ways they had avoided God, to pay attention to the ways they had been brought to life and the ways they had felt overwhelmed or discouraged, to name their "consolations" and "desolations."

Wren had sometimes joined them in praying the examen. She named her consolations: feeling happy that Dad was in their family, feeling excited about coming to America, feeling grateful that God watched over all of them and kept them safe. Sometimes she named her desolations too: feeling sad because someone teased her at school when she mentioned her "mum," missing Gran and Pop and Australia, wishing she had friends. But then one day a red-haired, freckled boy named Casey said he liked the way she talked and gave her a nickname. She'd never had a nickname before, and she was happy to have a friend like him.

Lord, meet her in all of her desolation. Please.

Jamie stared at the flickering candle as Kit read verses one through six from Psalm 139: *O LORD, you have searched me and known me. You know when I sit down and when I rise up; you discern my thoughts from far away. You search out my path and my lying down, and are acquainted with all my ways. Even before a word is on my tongue, O LORD, you know it completely. You hem me in, behind and before, and lay your hand upon me. Such knowledge is too wonderful for me; it is so high that I cannot attain it.*

"Search us, O God," Kit prayed, "and know our hearts. Test us and know our thoughts. See if there is any wicked way in us, and lead us in the path everlasting."

Jamie took a slow, centering breath before silently naming to God her gratitude. Wren was alive. She was safe. *For now,* the voice of fear hissed.

Yes. For now. For today. *Thank you, Lord, for your gifts today, for sunlight and birdsong, for food lovingly prepared, for the gifts of family and friends. For all the ways you give and sustain life.* She reached into her pocket and clutched the acorn. She had forgotten. In the stress of the day she had forgotten Julian's reminder that God loved, God protected, God sustained.

She gripped the acorn as she prayerfully read her day backwards, asking for the Spirit to bring to mind the moments when she had been aware of God's presence and love. The first one was obvious: the moment Kit called to say Wren was safe. She had wept with gratitude and relief.

And there was the sharing of the wren story at lunchtime. That was a rehearsing of a significant consolation in her life. She needed to keep rehearsing those narratives, to keep recalling the ways God had revealed himself to her in the past so she could be strengthened in hope for the present. For the future. *Don't be afraid.*

There was the wren singing. That was another consolation, an increase in hope.

Periwinkle. The moment Wren spoke that word was a moment of presence, a tap on the shoulder when God said, "See? I'm here."

Lord, I believe. Help my unbelief.

The desolations of the day came to mind as well, the moments when she had been overcome by fear, the moments when God seemed hidden, the moments of anger, resentment, and envy. She named to God her sorrow and asked to receive his comfort. She named to God her fear and asked to receive his peace. She named to God her sin and asked to receive his forgiveness. And when she had completed her prayerful examination of the movement of her soul toward God and away from God, she pondered how, in light of what she had seen and experienced today, she might live tomorrow differently, with more attentiveness, more faith, more compassion, more patience, more rest, and more confidence in his love and care. She could keep the acorn in her pocket as a reminder. She could be quick to confess her frustration to God, quick to acknowledge her fear and ask for help. And she could watch for the moments to celebrate and give thanks.

"So, what did you see as you prayed?" Kit asked when they finished their time of silence.

Jamie removed the acorn from her pocket and held out her hand.

16

B ethel House was expecting her to come back to work on Monday. Wren had taken ten days of vacation. Her coworkers thought she was thoroughly unplugged at a resort somewhere. And she had no more days to use until after the New Year. Jamie managed to coax this information out of her over breakfast Friday morning.

No more sick days. No more personal time. She had used it all. Jamie didn't want to cause her any more anxiety, but she didn't see any possible way for Wren to continue, not in a job with that much stress, not without margin to be unwell. After Wren went upstairs to shower and get dressed—a good sign, Jamie reminded herself—she conducted her own online research about what type of accommodations Wren might qualify for, given her illness and diagnosis. After visiting a number of websites and making several phone calls, she thought she had the gist of it. And there was no time to waste.

"Bethel House doesn't have more than fifty employees, does it?" she asked Wren while they sat outside later that morning.

"No."

Okay. She wouldn't benefit from the Family and Medical Leave Act. "Do you know how many there are?"

Wren stared at her a moment, then said, "No."

"Do you think you could run it through your head? Count up the number of full-time employees? Just an estimate?"

Wren did not reply.

"Would you say you have more or less than fifteen?"

"I'm not sure."

Well, they would need to find out that information. If Bethel House had fifteen or more employees, she could be protected by the Americans with Disabilities Act.

She decided to share what she'd learned while it was still fresh in her mind. "I've been doing research this morning, trying to see what accommodations you might be entitled to at work and whether you could take a leave of absence, and it's possible. Taking time off could be viewed as a necessary accommodation for someone with a disability, which, by the way, is a legal term, not a medical one—"

"Mom—"

"Hang on. You would need to have a conversation with your boss and possibly grant limited access to your medical records to prove that you qualify. The guy on the phone was really helpful, and he sent me lots of links to look at. Now, the way I read it, there's no guarantee Bethel House could accommodate a request for a leave, not if that leave would cause them"—she signed air quotes—"'significant hardship.' But it's worth looking into. What do you think about that? Do you think you could call your boss and ask?"

Wren rubbed her temples. "I don't know. I can't think about it right now."

"But we'll need to move quickly to get the process started, and with the weekend coming, we're running out of time because—"

"Mom. Please. I can't."

Wren stared off into the woods and spoke slowly, softly. The fog of the past couple of days was only just beginning to clear, she said, and she needed a day just to be. To sit. And maybe to draw. She had left her sketchbook at her apartment. "Would you please go pick it up for me?"

Jamie hesitated. Was it safe to leave her? "How about if we go together?"

She couldn't, she said. She wasn't ready to see her place again. She couldn't bear to be—

Right. Of course. To be where Theo had been. To see the place where he'd been struck. Which meant she wouldn't even be willing to go and wait in the car.

Wren appeared to read her thoughts. "I'll be okay by myself. I promise."

Jamie couldn't monitor her constantly. She knew that. She had no control over the choices Wren made. She knew that too. She gripped the acorn in her pocket. "Okay. I'll go get it."

Wren thanked her. There were also some Van Gogh books on a shelf in her bedroom, she said, some volumes of his letters and a couple of books with his art. Could she bring those? Jamie was happy to. If Wren had art and Vincent on her mind, then that was also a sign of hope.

"And there's a gray beanie. It might be on the couch or in my room. Could you get that too?"

"Sure." Jamie touched her daughter's cheek. "But no wandering off while I'm gone, okay? Please?"

She would stay right there, Wren promised, and wait.

After what she'd put her mother through yesterday, Wren thought, it shouldn't come as a surprise, her trying to take control this morning. But she didn't have the capacity to make sense of the intricacies of medical or legal provisions. Not today. She hadn't even managed to check almost two weeks of texts and emails. That task alone seemed daunting enough.

She buried her hands in her sweatshirt pockets and stared up at the sky. She wasn't going to grant anyone at work access to her medical records, that was for sure. Her supervisor didn't need to know that one of her social workers had mental health issues and might be pushed over the tipping point at any time. It was a miracle that in the three years she'd served there, she hadn't publicly crumbled. Somehow she had always managed to conceal the panic attacks. And the depression had been under control—or at least, she had thought it was.

That only fed the anxiety—never knowing when the darkness might return and swallow her again. It took so much energy to keep it at bay. She was tired, so tired, still so tired.

"Let the prayers of others carry you right now," Hannah had said in her office. Like the paralyzed man whose friends carried him on his mat to Jesus. She needed to let others carry the mat for a while.

But how could she let others carry her on the mat when she needed to be carrying lots of mats come Monday? She didn't have the strength to carry anyone. So how could she possibly go back to work? But if she didn't go back to work, they wouldn't have enough people carrying mats for the ones who were traumatized. For the women. The moms. And the kids who had seen violence like she had never seen. Those kids needed to be carried and cared for. But a rescue mission needed rescuers with strong backs and shoulders. Strong stomachs too. Not someone who couldn't even bear to check her messages.

An orange maple leaf fluttered lazily to the ground near her feet. She stooped to pick it up, then traced the delicate veins with her index finger.

She couldn't risk returning to work and having a breakdown in front of all of them. Kingsbury was too small a town. But beyond the fear of personal shame and failure was the more important issue of the well-being of her clients. A rescue mission needed rescuers who could carry buckets, keep the stranded from suffocating, and coax them out into freedom. They didn't need someone who herself was still too weak to swim to safety. That would be a liability.

"This is frontline stuff," Allie had said. "You've got to be able to fight back against the darkness. You've got to be able to pray. Constantly. To fix your mind on Christ. You've got to be rooted and grounded in the Word. It's the only way to survive work like this. The only way."

It was true. And Bethel House had every right to expect she would be capable, dependable, and fit to serve. She was not fit. She was not mentally, emotionally, or spiritually fit. They needed better. They deserved better. Her case manager had been right. She needed a job change.

She went inside and got her phone. She would turn it on just long enough to call her supervisor and tell her she was resigning. If she pressed for reasons, Wren would say she had health issues she needed to attend to. That was the truth. She was sorry, but that was the truth.

What were you thinking? Jamie wanted to exclaim. She had been gone only forty-five minutes—forty-five minutes!—and to return to find out that Wren had quit her job? They hadn't even explored the disability provisions yet. There were accommodations that could be made, she knew there were. Wren couldn't have been fired for mental illness. There were protections against that. What in the world had she been thinking?

But she didn't say these things. Instead, she sat in stunned silence.

Wren leaned forward in the patio chair. "Please don't be mad. I can't handle you being mad at me."

Well, then, Jamie wanted to say, *you shouldn't have done something so impulsive.* Instead, she said, "I wish you had given it a little more time, a little more thought. I could have helped you. We could have figured it out."

And what about your health insurance? she wanted to ask. *How will you pay for that? How will you afford your rent? Where will you live? What will you eat? What about the hospital bills?*

But she did not ask these things. She didn't know where they stood in proximity to that invisible cliff edge. They were probably teetering right on the brink.

"I can't go back, Mom."

Jamie didn't disagree, which was precisely why she had done all the research that morning. She rubbed her forehead. "Okay. So, what exactly did you say to your supervisor?"

Wren said she told her she had done a lot of soul-searching on her vacation and had come to the conclusion she could no longer serve Bethel House well. It was too stressful an environment, and she had some health issues to attend to. Her supervisor was disappointed but didn't seem surprised. If Wren was sure she couldn't help them out for another couple of weeks while they searched for a replacement, then she could clean out her desk on Monday.

"Where is she now?" Dylan asked after Jamie called him with an update.

"Sitting outside, drawing in her sketchbook." She watched Wren through the kitchen window. "And please don't tell me I don't have control over any of this. I know I don't. But what will she do? How will she survive? She needs meds, counseling appointments, psychiatry appointments—how in the world will she survive?" This was how the mentally ill ended up on the streets, unemployed, sleeping under bridges, with no way to pay for the goods and services they needed.

"She won't be homeless," he said. "She can come here to regroup if she wants to. Or maybe Kit will put her up for a while. Have you mentioned it to her?"

"No, she's at New Hope today. She'll be back at dinner."

"Well, have a quiet conversation with her. Wren doesn't need to know you're working on contingency plans behind the scenes. See what the possibilities are. And let me know, will you? I've got more work to do on my sermon, and then I'll pick Phoebe up from school. She's still waiting to Skype with you."

"I know. I'm sorry. Maybe Wren can get on with her too."

"I'm sure she would love that. Call me later?"

"Okay."

"I'll keep praying, Jamie. Wish there was something else I could do for you."

"You're taking good care of the kids. That's plenty."

And what did it mean for her to take good care of an adult daughter? An "emerging adult" who didn't seem capable of making rational, well-considered decisions? Wren wasn't usually impulsive. Usually, she was cautious and conscientious, excessively so. This was uncharacteristically reckless and alarming. Was this a side effect of one of the meds?

She set her phone down on the counter and brewed herself another cup of coffee.

Never make an important decision in the midst of desolation. That was one of the most basic principles of discernment. And though Wren said she felt a huge sense of relief, how would she feel once the reality of what she'd set into motion began to sink in? Who would pick up the pieces then?

The patio door opened. "Mom?"

"Hmm?"

"Could you come be a hand model for me? I'm trying to draw something."

Yesterday if Wren had made such a request of her, Jamie would have felt a huge sense of relief. Now she heard only the familiar, insidious hum of fear. She wiped her palms on her jeans. "Sure, love. Be right there."

Her mother's hand was beautiful—delicately boned with fine wrinkles like complex quilling on milk-white skin. Casey's hands had been beautiful too, not large and rugged but the soft and graceful hands of an artist. The hands of Jesus were probably the rough and calloused hands of a carpenter, strong and sturdy.

And wounded.

Someday she would try to sketch a hand gouged like the cliff face she had seen when she prayed with Hannah. But for now, she would sketch her mother's hand as the hand of God, upholding and comforting.

On Hannah's desk was a small bronze sculpture of a curled infant sleeping peacefully in a hand. Wren would not draw an infant cradled in a hand. She would draw a woman kneeling, head in her hands, weeping. The tears would land in the wounds and become healing pools. But, as Vincent observed, the best drawings, the finest works, were the ones you dreamed about but never painted. Her vision would always exceed her talent and execution. She would never be able to render what she saw.

She held up her sketchbook and squinted at it. Not great. She might never master a hand. But it was adequate. "All done?" her mother asked.

Wren shaded a bit more. "Almost. I need one more thing."

"What's that?"

"I need to draw a woman kneeling. Like this." Wren rose from her chair and knelt on the grass, head in her hands. Then she stood and brushed off her jeans. "Would you do that?"

Without speaking, her mother lowered herself to the ground. "Even lower," Wren said. "With your elbows on the ground. Yes. Like that. Curved just like that, and then with your face in your hands."

Yes. That was perfect. She did a quick contour drawing to capture the shape, then began to fill in details. The hair would conceal most of the face like a mourning veil. The hands could be crudely drawn, a mere suggestion of fingers splayed. Yes. Like that. Just like that. Everything about her mother's form embodied the pathos she longed to convey.

If she herself were kneeling as her own model, Wren thought with a pang of sorrow and guilt, it could not have been more true.

17

Of course Wren could stay with her, Kit told Jamie as the two of them sat together at the kitchen table that evening. "For as long as she needs. But she might not want to."

"I know, but thank you. At least I can go home next week knowing she'll have a roof over her head." That was one burden checked off her list. As for health insurance, she would start making phone calls on Monday if Wren wasn't up to it. She would investigate student loans too. Maybe there was a provision for deferment. She didn't know how much progress Wren had made on debt over the past couple of years. She would talk with Dylan. They didn't have much to spare on his minister's salary, but maybe they could spare something. They wouldn't let her go under. They wouldn't let her starve.

How did people without advocates survive? What about people without family or friends or church support? Who cared for them?

She had peers who would caution her about coddling and enabling: "We kicked our kids out when they finished college and haven't let them come back. They need to figure life out on their own."

Yes, but maybe their kids didn't suffer from mental illness.

And then they might counter, "You can't support them forever. What happens after you're gone? Then what? They need to be independent."

Wren *had* been independent. But now—

Without support now, where might she end up?

Stop, she commanded herself. These verbal volleys would get her nowhere.

She stared at the kitchen ceiling. In the room above, Wren was reading a story to Phoebe on Skype.

She ought to rejoice that Wren was willing and able to do that. She ought to be amazed and grateful that she had stabilized a bit in the past twenty-four hours. But who knew how long it would last, or when the next crash would come, or what might trigger it?

"What about you, Jamie? What do you need?"

Jamie pressed her lips together and leaned her head back. She wasn't going to have Wren come downstairs and find her crying. "I don't know how to—"

Kit waited.

"—how to do any of it, how to help, how to trust, what to trust, how to pray. All these years, and I still don't have a clue how to do it. At least when she was younger, my role as mum was better defined. Now? It feels so much more complicated."

"If only there were a script," Kit said.

Right. If only. It might not make anything easier, but at least it would eliminate the uncertainty over the right steps to take. "How did you do it?" Jamie asked. "How did you survive"—she paused, searching for the right way to ask her question but lacking the courage to name specifics—"everything?"

Kit shrugged slightly. "I didn't think I would. I almost didn't. But I had good people alongside me, people who didn't give up on me, who kept believing for me when I couldn't believe for myself. And that made a difference. Their faith helped pull me through." She gently squeezed Jamie's arm. "So, whatever I can do for Wren or for you, know that I'll do it. But honestly, Jamie, the more trustworthy people holding you through this, the better. We can't make journeys like this alone."

No. She knew that. She would need to strengthen her support networks once she returned home. A few times she had gathered with some other local pastors' wives for prayer and conversation. Maybe she needed to take a leadership role in getting that small group established. Many of the other wives also felt lonely and isolated, scared to reveal the truth about their struggles because they had been burned by gossip and betrayal before. She probably wasn't the only one of them experiencing heartache over a child's suffering.

Maybe she should also try to find a spiritual director. She hadn't met with one since they lived in Kingsbury. She'd been so busy trying to navigate life with young kids, and then with a baby again, and being alongside Dylan to support his ministry and offer help in everything that needed to be done at the church—there was always something needing to be done. It wasn't an excuse, but a reason.

Or maybe she should return to her counselor for a few visits and gain fresh insights about establishing healthy boundaries, so she could fight a gravitational pull toward unhealthy caretaking. She needed wisdom about how to encourage Wren without trying to rescue her. No matter how many years passed, she always seemed to return to the same well-worn ruts.

"It looks like you're deep in thought," Kit said.

Jamie sighed. "Just running through a mental inventory of things that might help, all the things I neglect or forget when I get busy or overwhelmed." She paused. "What helped you, Kit? I mean, along with community support and prayer."

When she didn't respond right away, Jamie thought perhaps she had pushed too far. *It's not something our family talked a lot about,* Dylan's voice reminded her. *You didn't back then.*

Maybe you didn't now, either.

They had never talked about Kit's losses, even when they were living under her roof. They hadn't discussed any of her family's pain, even with all the time they had spent together at New Hope. All the retreats, all the seminars, all the conversations, all the many ways Kit had offered herself while they lived in Kingsbury—but not once had Jamie heard her share details about her own story. Maybe there had never been the right opportunity. Or desire. "I'm sorry," Jamie said. "I don't mean to pry."

"No, it's okay," Kit said. "It's good to talk about it." She thought a moment. "For me, it was all about discovering Jesus as the Man of Sorrows, the one acquainted with grief. I learned to keep company with him in his sufferings, to take time to meditate on the cross as the deepest evidence of his love. In fact, it was our friend Julian who helped me with that journey. She helped me see that if God could take the most evil moment in history and make all things well, then he could take all my suffering and anguish and make it well too. Even if 'making it well' didn't look like what I had pictured or hoped for."

Jamie nodded slowly. How many times had she heard somebody slap promises from Scripture onto someone else's pain and then walk away, expecting the sufferer to be immediately well? *All things work together for good for those who love God and are called according to his purpose.* That seemed to be a favorite verse to declare to someone gripped by anguish. But people like Kit, people who had been shaped by suffering and who could still speak a promise like that with integrity and conviction, their witness was gold.

"Do you still host that Holy Week event at New Hope?" Jamie asked. "I can't remember now what it was called, but the one with the art and prayer stations."

"Yes. Journey to the Cross. I have a wonderful local artist who has helped me the past few years. He always has a great vision for how to bring the Scripture texts to life."

Jamie remembered walking through the chapel not long after they moved to Kingsbury. It was powerful, seeing the art and reading the texts and imagining herself there in Jerusalem with Jesus. She had never done anything like that before. Wren had gone too, but she had been overwhelmed with sorrow at the first station and couldn't finish the journey.

"You're the one who first taught me to pray with my imagination," Jamie said, "to enter the story in a profound way. It was life-changing for me."

"I'm so glad to hear that." Kit folded her hands. "Know where I first encountered praying with imagination?"

Jamie shook her head.

"In the hospital. At the psychiatric hospital where I spent some time after Micah died. There was a chaplain there—oh, he was gifted, the best kind of pastoral presence, I tell you—and he was praying for me one day. I was about at the end of my rope, ready to give up, and he invited me to pray with the story of Jesus raising Lazarus from the dead. He told me to pretend I was Lazarus in the tomb, hearing Jesus speak my name."

As many times as Jamie had prayed with that text, she had never considered imagining herself as Lazarus, only as his grieving sisters.

Wren appeared in the doorway. "Mom?"

"Hmm?"

"Sorry to interrupt, but Phoebe wants you to say goodnight to her." She held out Jamie's phone.

"Oh. Okay." Jamie pushed back her chair. "Hold that thought, Kit, please. I'd love to hear more." Maybe Wren would join them at the table. It might be encouraging for her to hear that someone she respected had also spent time in a psychiatric hospital. If Kit would share with her.

Jamie waved at the screen as she walked toward the den. "Hey, Phoebe-girl! Did you hear a good story?"

Phoebe was sitting cross-legged on her bed, surrounded by stuffed animals. "Wren read me Winnie the Pooh."

"One of my favorites!" Jamie said. "Maybe she'll read it to me later."

Phoebe laughed. "You're a grownup!"

"Well, grownups like Winnie the Pooh too." She did her best impression of asking for a small smackeral of honey. Phoebe laughed again. "Are you heading to bed, sweetie?"

"Yep."

"Good girl. Is Daddy there? How about if we sing prayers?"

"Okay." Phoebe shut her eyes tight and began to sing, "Now I lay me down to sleep . . ." When it came time to say, "God bless . . ." she recited a litany of all her family members and friends and pets and stuffed toys. "And keep all the children kind and true. Amen."

"Amen," Jamie said. "Thank you for praying for us."

"Wren's feeling better."

"Yes, she is. And I've got your pretty fairy picture to give her. I'll do that tonight, okay?"

"Yep."

"Love you, sweetheart. I'll talk to you tomorrow, okay?"

They blew kisses until Dylan reached for the phone. "Wren sounds good," he said.

"Did you talk to her?"

"For a bit."

"I'm glad."

"Everything going okay?"

"Yes. I'll ring you later and fill you in. Are Joel and Olivia all right?"

"Yeah, fine. Want to talk to them? I think they're upstairs doing homework."

"I'll call them tomorrow," she said. "Just tell them hi for me, that I love them."

When she returned to the kitchen, she was glad to see that Wren was at the table. "Sorry about the interruption."

"That's fine," Kit said. "No problem."

Jamie picked up her mug and settled into her chair again, waiting to see if Kit would change the subject now that Wren was with them. They shared a moment's silence before Kit said, "I was telling your mom about my own experience at a psychiatric hospital."

Oh. Bless her.

A look of surprise crossed Wren's face. "You were at Glenwood?"

"No, not Glenwood. But one like it."

"When?"

"A long time ago, back when I was about forty. I was there a few weeks, trying to recover from a major depressive episode, a 'nervous breakdown,' they called it."

This was all new information for Wren. Jamie could tell.

"I was sharing with your mom that I was at the end of my rope, ready to call it quits on life when this chaplain suggested that I put myself into the story of Jesus raising Lazarus from the dead. He told me to imagine myself as Lazarus and hear Jesus speak my name. Well, I wasn't sure about that at first. For one thing, my mind was so muddled I didn't know if I could trust myself to imagine something like that. And for another thing, I'd led Bible studies for years, and this approach didn't seem very orthodox. But I trusted the chaplain, so I tried to do what he suggested. I used all my senses and pictured myself there in the tomb.

"At first all I could imagine was this awful stench, like death and decay mixed with spices—all very pungent and overpowering. And as I pictured myself as Lazarus, I was suddenly struck by the reality that the stench was coming from me. I was dead and decaying there in the grave. And it was awful. There was no hope for me."

Wren was leaning forward, her doe eyes fixed on Kit's face, her expression a blend of curiosity and compassion, the sort of sympathy Jamie imagined was often in Wren's eyes when she met with clients and heard their stories. She wondered if Wren would ever be well enough to return to that kind of work. Or if she would even want to. Or if it would be safe for her. But she had such gifts to offer, such beautiful and necessary gifts. *Lord, I believe . . .*

Kit shifted in her chair. "All of a sudden I heard a loud voice. Even though I was dead, I heard it. And something stirred deep within me when I heard the voice call my name. *My* name. Because in my imagination, I didn't hear, 'Lazarus!' I heard, 'Katherine!' And oh, when I heard my name . . . when I heard Jesus call my name . . ."

She removed from her sleeve a wadded-up tissue to wipe her eyes. "Well, something came to life in me. And when he commanded me to 'Come forth'"—she balled the tissue into her hand—"I mean, isn't that a remarkable command? How can you not obey a command like that? I was suddenly aware of the weight of everything, how the grave clothes were binding my whole body. And the smell! If I staggered out of that tomb, what would everyone think? They would all be gagging."

With gratitude Jamie watched a smile tug at the corner of Wren's lips, the first smile she had seen since arriving. More signs of life. *Thank God.*

"So, what did you do?" Wren asked.

"I pushed aside the shame, and I obeyed him. I tottered to the entrance and squinted at Jesus. He was standing there in blinding light, his whole face glowing. And he had his arms stretched out toward me, like a father welcoming home a beloved child. I knew one thing in that moment: if he had commanded me to come out of the tomb and live, then I needed to live. In the hospital room that day, I made a decision. No matter how hard life was—no matter how hard life would be—I would choose to live."

There was a Van Gogh painting, Wren said with as much animation as Jamie had yet seen in her, something Vincent had painted toward the end of his life while he was in the mental asylum in Saint-Rémy. She withdrew to her room and returned with one of the books Jamie had brought from her apartment. "It's the raising of Lazarus," she said as she flipped through pages. "While he was in the hospital, he was copying some famous works from Rembrandt, Millet, and Delacroix. Not copying, exactly. He called it 'translating' because he interpreted them with his own color and composition and said it gave him consolation while he was there. So he took Rembrandt's etching—here, look here"—she turned the book around so Jamie and Kit could both see—"and painted his version with his own face on Lazarus. See?"

Lying listless at the mouth of a cave was a pale man with red hair and a red beard, wrapped in white grave clothes. One of the sisters, painted with orange hair and a green dress, hands raised in surprise, had just removed his face cloth. Jamie leaned in for a closer look. It was Vincent, all right—a bit more crudely rendered than some of his self-portraits but a self-portrait nonetheless, his eyes vacant, his skin still displaying the pallor of death. But he was alive.

"Consolation," Kit murmured. "Is that what you said? That painting these things gave him consolation?"

"That's what he wrote to his brother."

"Extraordinary. I had no idea. I've never seen this before."

Wren said it wasn't very well known. She said some critics dismissed it because it wasn't original. Others dismissed it because it didn't fit the common narrative of Vincent's life, that he rejected faith.

"That's the story I've heard," Kit said. "But this is profound, Wren, how he placed himself in the narrative to make meaning of his experience—or to describe it."

Wren turned another page. "He did it with Jesus too—see? Here's his interpretation of Delacroix's painting of the Pietà." There in the arms of Mary lay the crucified Jesus, with flaming red hair and beard.

"Oh." Kit pressed her hand to her heart. "His identification with the suffering Jesus. He felt it deeply, didn't he? The anguish."

They stared at the painting in silence.

"Most people only know him as the famous artist who cut off his ear," Wren said after a few moments, "the artist who was crazy, a madman who killed himself. But he had deep faith. He wanted to be a minister when he was young, did you know that?"

Jamie did, because she had heard Wren speak passionately about Van Gogh ever since she was a teenager. That's when she began copying his paintings and sketches, reading all his letters, and devouring every biography she could find. Whenever Wren had the opportunity to introduce someone to her friend Vincent, she came to life. His passion and art had always managed to reach and rouse her, even in her darkest moments.

Thank God for Vincent.

Kit said, "I know that Henri Nouwen, one of my favorite authors, was profoundly influenced by his work and that he perceived something deeply spiritual in his life and paintings, but I don't know much else. I'd love to hear more, if you're up for sharing."

Thank God for Kit.

With complete and articulate sentences unlike most of what Jamie had heard from her the past two days, Wren proceeded to sketch an overview of his life, how he couldn't manage the rigor of theological training and saw no point learning ancient languages when what he wanted to do was comfort and serve the poor. So he abandoned his plans to be a minister and decided instead to serve as a missionary to miners in Belgium. But some said he was too zealous in his efforts to imitate Christ. Vincent wanted to identify with the miners' poverty, so he gave away his clothes, money, and food. He refused to live in even modest lodgings because they were better than what the miners had. So he chose to live in a little hovel where he slept on the corner of the hearth, alone. The missionary board praised his love for the sick and his compassionate self-sacrifice, but they decided he wasn't fit to continue beyond the probationary period and terminated his financial support. He wasn't a good enough preacher, they said. But the real reason seemed to be that Vincent was too radical. Some, including his father, thought he'd had a mental breakdown.

He was a failure, not even fit, it seemed, to preach to the poorest of the poor, to those who lived in darkness without light. So Vincent made a decision. In bitterness he rejected the institutional church and embraced a different kind of call. As an artist he would labor to show the beauty of the simple and the poor, the rejected and the despised. If he couldn't provide comfort as a minister or an evangelist, he might provide comfort through his art.

"Sorrowful, yet always rejoicing," Wren said, "that was his favorite phrase from the Bible, the verse he hoped would describe his life. There's a Dutch word he used in his letters—I can't think of it right now—but it has to do with melancholy and courage." She looked at Kit. "Like you were saying, that you had to make a decision to choose life."

Kit nodded. "And not just the one time, but many times since then."

Weemoed. That was the Dutch word Wren was searching for. After finding some pertinent passages in Vincent's letters, she brought the volume downstairs. Kit and her mother were speaking quietly in the front room, their prayer candle still lit. "Am I interrupting?"

"No," Kit said. "Come join us. We just finished."

Wren sat on the couch beside her mother. "I found the word I was talking about before. It's *weemoed*. It means 'melancholy.' Vincent wrote to his brother that the word could be a good word, as long as you understood it as two parts joined together—*wee* means 'woe,' and *moed* means courage. We all have plenty of woe, he said, but we need to join that word with courage so we don't despair." She pointed to a passage she had underlined. "Here, listen. I love what he wrote. 'So instead of giving in to despair I chose active melancholy, in so far as I was capable of activity, in other words I chose the kind of melancholy that hopes, that strives and that seeks, in preference to the melancholy that despairs numbly and in distress.'"

"Active melancholy," Kit said. "What a phrase! May I see that?"

Wren handed the book to her. Kit read in silence, then said, "To choose active melancholy, to choose a sorrow that hopes instead of a sorrow that despairs. I love that, Wren. Thank you. That's exactly what we must do."

It was the word "we" that caught Wren's attention. *We.* What a healing word that was, a fortifying, embracing, inclusive word to express solidarity and understanding and compassion. She stared at the glimmering flame and murmured, "Amen."

She didn't know many details, her mother said when Wren privately asked her what had caused Kit's nervous breakdown, but she knew her son, Micah, had died from a drug overdose when he was in high school. And her husband had an affair and filed for divorce. She wasn't sure about the sequence of events, whether he left before or after Kit was hospitalized. "I can't even imagine going through all that pain," her mother said.

No, Wren thought. Neither could she. She couldn't bear to.

Long after her mother said goodnight and went downstairs, Wren sat on her bed, knees tucked to her chest. Despite the magnitude of her own trauma, Kit affirmed her as a fellow sufferer, as belonging to the community of those who were called to choose hope in the midst of despair.

A companion in misfortune. In sorrow.

If Kit could persevere through that kind of darkness, she could manage skimming through texts and email. She turned on her phone.

Not nearly as bad as she anticipated: just a few friends hoping to get together after she returned from vacation. She would have plenty of time for lunch or coffee dates now. She just wouldn't have money to pay for them. Or the energy to explain herself. She would wait to reply to those.

She scrolled downward, hoping, hoping, hoping. But no, there was nothing from Casey. And why should there be? She wouldn't torture herself by clicking on his name. She wouldn't read again his final text from a month ago, the text reminding her Brooke was upset about how often they were communicating. She didn't need to read it. She had memorized it. He was sorry, so sorry, but he really needed to honor his wife's request and cut off contact completely. He hoped she understood. Maybe someday they could be in touch again. But not now. He was so very sorry. *Be well, Wrinkle,* he said.

But she had not been well. And Casey's heart would have broken to hear about it. He wasn't to blame. Brooke wasn't to blame. Her mental breakdown had nothing to do with his final text. It was the stress at work, her inability to sleep, her heartache over the women and children and how they had suffered and how powerless she felt in alleviating any of the pain or sorrow around the globe. Too many mama and baby whales. It was all too much to bear.

She should have replied to his final text after he sent it. She should have said, It's okay. I understand. I wish you well.

But she had not replied. And maybe he thought she was angry. She wasn't angry. She should have told him that.

She touched his name. She could write him a brief note now. She could say she was sorry she hadn't replied before, but she had just gotten home from Glenwood—he would want to know about that—and Theo had died—he would want to know about that—and she had quit her job—he would want to know about that. He would want to know about all of that, and he would say, "I'm so sorry. I wish there was something I could do."

But then he would remind her—again—that he had promised Brooke he would not be in touch, and please not to contact him again. And then how would she feel?

Or he wouldn't reply at all. And then how would she feel? That might be even worse, to receive no acknowledgment of what she had suffered or how she was grieving.

She turned off her phone. Better to leave things as they were. He had been a companion in struggle, in sorrow. He could be one no longer.

Downstairs Kit called goodnight to her mother. Her mother called back.

"We must choose," Kit had said. "That's what we must do. We must choose life."

Even when it wasn't the life she would choose.

Part Three

KEEPING

WATCH

They went to a place called Gethsemane, and Jesus said to his disciples, "Sit here while I pray." He took Peter, James and John along with him, and he began to be deeply distressed and troubled. "My soul is overwhelmed with sorrow to the point of death," he said to them. "Stay here and keep watch."

MARK 14:32-34

The moon still shines now, and the sun and the evening star, which is fortunate, and they often speak of God's Love and call to mind the words, lo, I am with you always, even unto the end of the world.

VINCENT VAN GOGH, LETTER TO THEO, JULY 1877

18

Wren stared out at a snow-covered courtyard at New Hope, where chickadees and cardinals flitted to and from feeders. She was weary of sketching winter landscapes and would have preferred practicing portraits. But apart from Kit, who had already kindly obliged her for a couple of sketches, she didn't have any models. So she labored over a cluster of pinecones dangling from a branch outside her window. On their lunch break Kit had told her about jack pine trees, how the thick cones protected the seeds and only released them in the heat of fire. Kit had a knack for speaking in metaphor.

She stepped back from her sketchbook to scrutinize her work. The attention to detail was true, but it wasn't artistic.

Now, if Vincent were painting them, they would come to life in all their different shades of russet and burgundy and brown. He would note the variety of form, the blended colors of the pine needles, the overlapping scales. Vincent could find a single blade of grass mesmerizing. He believed that looking at things for a long time could help you develop as an artist and give you deeper understanding and insight into the essence of things. So she would look longer at the pinecones and try to see them. Then she would set aside her sketchbook and try to paint them.

Paints were expensive, though. So were canvases and Claybord panels. She couldn't afford to be frivolous about anything. But without the freedom to experiment and to fail, she wouldn't grow as an artist, either.

An artist. She wasn't a real artist. She played at it, especially now that Kit had given her a designated space at New Hope, an unused classroom that almost felt like a studio, with wide windows and natural light and her paint-splattered tarps on the floor. Whenever she unlocked the door and entered, she was immediately transported to Gran's studio, which always smelled like creativity. And lavender and eucalyptus.

Voices in the hallway signaled the end of her art break. The afternoon contemplative prayer group had finished, and she would now have a short window of opportunity for vacuuming a couple of classrooms and the chapel. Kit didn't like noise in the building when groups were meeting for prayer. She frequently had to remind the maintenance crew about that.

There were three of them on the crew: the retired electrician who served as the handyman; the landscaper, whose primary job during winter was making sure the property was plowed and shoveled; and Wren, the part-time custodian. It wasn't the sort of job one boasted about. "I'm taking a break from social work," she told those who asked. "I was feeling burned out."

"So, what are you doing now?" they would ask.

"I'm working on my art."

And they would raise their eyebrows with surprise or admiration, and some would say that sounded cool, good for her, and others would lament how they wished they could take that kind of break from work but student loans, you know? And she would nod and say, I know. She didn't tell them she had negotiated a deferment. Or reveal the reasons why she couldn't work a full-time job.

"It's only temporary," her mother often reminded her. Wren knew this was the kind of hope her mother reassured herself with, that her daughter wouldn't spend the rest of her life sweeping floors and emptying trash, not when she had a graduate degree.

She closed her studio door and removed the vacuum from the maintenance closet. Kit had told her the story of Brother Lawrence, a seventeenth-century lay brother who served as a humble cook at a monastery in Paris and who learned to practice the presence of God as he went about the ordinary tasks of the day. He had as deep a sense of God's presence on his knees scrubbing floors as he did on his knees in the chapel. He viewed his work sacramentally, Kit said. He saw all of it as an opportunity to worship and adore God. Others marveled at his intimate communion with the Lord, how his work was his prayer and his prayer was his work, how he lived with fervor and gratitude and simplicity.

Wren didn't know how to aspire to such a continual awareness of God's presence. Most days she didn't have the energy for that kind of attentiveness. Hannah often reassured her that even a longing for God was prayer, and she could rest in being held and upheld in his hand. Still, she sometimes wondered what might emerge if she could bring to her relationship with God the same degree of intensity and attentiveness she tried to practice with her art. Brother Lawrence might tell her she could worship and love God by gazing with grateful wonder at a pinecone. Or at a gnarled tree laid bare beneath an ominous sky. Or at a face like Monica's. Or Sylvia's. Or at a stranger waiting for the bus, who avoided eye contact by checking her phone. Kit might say she could adore God by gratefully receiving his breath and life while she unwound a vacuum cord, being mindful of the weight and the texture in her hand, being astonished that her fingertips could send instantaneous messages to her brain that could be interpreted and categorized: coarse like sand, flexible like rope. Kit might say that.

She might say that Wren pausing to give thanks that her brain—her complicated, sometimes feeble and muddled brain—was able both to discern thousands of insignificant details she might never notice and to command tens of thousands of functions she might take for granted. That was a wonder. If she paid attention like that throughout the day, she might be in continual astonishment. Or in tears.

"Also prayer," Hannah would say. "Our tears can also be an offering, a prayer from the depths."

Wren finished sweeping the hallways and classrooms, then paused outside the chapel. It had become a ritual for her, first entering the space without the vacuum, acknowledging in some small way the significance of crossing a threshold into a room specially set apart for prayer and worship. She didn't want to blaze in carelessly without reverence.

Seating herself toward the back, she looked up at a painting of Jesus on the cross, his head bowed, his ribs protruding as if he was taking his final breath. Kit had told her a local artist had painted it, that every year he painted scenes from the last hours of Jesus' life for a special exhibition they hosted during Holy Week. A prayer journey, Kit said, with Scripture and art to help someone enter the narrative, similar to what she had described with her experience of imagining herself as Lazarus.

Wren had attended the event with her parents after they moved to Kingsbury. She remembered crying at seeing Jesus abandoned and tortured and bleeding. She couldn't bear to look at him suffering like that. But now she sat beneath the painting and was comforted by his anguish. He was the ultimate companion in misery, the Man of Sorrows, acquainted with grief, the One forever in solidarity with the despised, the rejected, the anguished, the abandoned. She was coming to better know and appreciate this Jesus. Art like the painting on the wall helped deepen her gratitude for what he had undergone in love.

She wished she could paint like that.

Vincent had destroyed a large canvas he had attempted to paint of Jesus and an angel in the garden of Gethsemane—"ruthlessly destroyed it," he wrote to a friend. She wished she could have seen it. He would have captured the essence of Christ's agony. And it would have been beautiful.

She was wiping down bathroom mirrors with a cloth when a heavyset woman wearing the bold colors and patterns of an artist entered. Their eyes met in the mirror, and the woman said hello. Wren stepped aside so she could check her reflection. "Ugh," she said, "even worse than I thought." She ran her fingers through her auburn hair, the white roots visible. Then she disappeared into a stall.

Wren turned on the faucet to give her some privacy. It still felt awkward to her, lingering in bathrooms while visitors used them. Most didn't speak to her or even seem to notice her, which wouldn't have surprised her if she had been working at an airport or a mall. But being disregarded at a retreat center where people were coming to explore deeper intimacy with God struck her as ironic.

The toilet flushed; the stall door opened. "Do you work here?" the woman asked.

"Yes." Wren expected her to say they were running low on toilet paper or the floor needed to be scrubbed.

Instead, she said, "I haven't seen you before. I'm Mara. Mara Payne." She stuck out her hand, and then said, "Whoops! Better wash it first. Hold on." She thrust both hands under a faucet and lathered up like a surgeon. "So, are you new?"

"Pretty new."

Mara tossed a paper towel into the bin, then rubbed her hands on her jeans. "Okay. Take two. I'm Mara."

Wren took her outstretched hand. Everything about the woman was soft: her eyes, her hands, her skin. Her mother would envy that kind of porcelain complexion. "I'm Wren."

"Wren? Oh, I love that name! Is it a family name or something?"

"Sort of." This was probably the sort of woman who would believe a story about a bird landing on a pregnant woman's lap to bring a message from God.

"Well, I love it," Mara said. "Are you a student around here or . . . ?"

"No, not a student. I'm taking a bit of a break from my job—I'm a social worker—and I wanted something a bit less stressful for a while—"

Mara nodded. "I totally get that."

"—so my aunt, Kit—Katherine—told me I could pick up some hours here."

"Wait! Katherine Rhodes is your aunt?" Mara looked as if Wren had just announced she was related to a celebrity.

"Well, not aunt-aunt, I mean, my dad—my stepdad's her nephew so . . ."

"Oh, wow! Katherine's amazing. I love her. She's my spiritual director."

"Oh. Cool."

"Yeah. Very cool." Mara pushed back lime green bangles to check her watch. "And I need to go. Appointment's starting."

Have fun, Wren almost said, then changed her mind. "Hope it's good."

"Oh, it will be. Always is. Nice to meet you, Wren. I'll probably see you again."

"Yes. Okay. Thanks." *Thanks for being kind,* she wanted to say, but didn't. Mara left the bathroom humming.

"I just met your niece!" Wren heard her exclaim out in the hallway, and then a door closed.

She wiped the remaining sinks and got her mop. Someday she would like to sketch Mara. Mara's eyes told a story. And she was beautiful.

Wren was getting ready to leave work to go to her counseling appointment when her mother called with news. "I sold *Weemoed!*" she exclaimed.

"You what?"

"Not my copy. I would never part with the one you drew for me. But I hosted a group of pastors' wives here this morning, and one of them was so captivated by your sketch and the meaning behind it, she said she had to have a copy. And then the others all chimed in too, how they also wanted one. So, I'm not sure how this works, whether I should just go and make special photocopies of it or—"

"Wait, Mom. Slow down." Wren rubbed her forehead. She had never sold any of her art before, not a single painting or sketch. She had never intended for the sketch of her mother kneeling in the hand of God to be copied. It wasn't good enough quality for that. But she could picture her mother showing it proudly to the group, telling them about "active melancholy" and her daughter, the artist.

She wasn't an artist. Not a real one. "They want to buy copies of it?"

"Yes. At least ten. And I told them I didn't know how much it would cost to reproduce them professionally on special paper, but I'd find out and let them know. I thought ten or fifteen dollars apiece. Is that okay? I mean, because they're copies, not originals."

Ten copies at ten or fifteen dollars each? She could buy paints. And a few more canvases.

"Is that too cheap? Did I do something wrong?"

"No, you did great! I just can't believe it." She sat down in a lounge chair beside the exit door.

"A couple of them thought people from their churches might also want to buy copies, or family members. It won't appeal to everyone, the depth of it, but it's speaking, Wren. It's already speaking."

The melancholy spoke. The lament and the hope and the longing to trust that God held all of it—the active melancholy spoke. *Jesus.*

Tell Vincent, she wanted to say. But that was silly. So instead, she murmured, *Thanks.*

"I'm glad to see you, Wren. How are you?" Dawn, her new counselor, settled into the chair across from her and folded her hands in her lap.

"Okay, I think."

Though it had taken a few weeks of trying, she had finally connected with someone on Hannah's recommended list of therapists who seemed like a good fit. At least for now. It was the Van Gogh print on Dawn's office wall—Vincent's *The Good Samaritan*—that had caught Wren's attention during their introductory visit and served as a possible confirmation of God's leading. She hoped it would work out. Her physician had agreed to oversee her medications, but only if she would commit to regular, ongoing therapy. And she didn't have the energy or patience for many more false starts, like the woman she'd seen in Dr. Emerson's old office, who ran half an hour late for their appointment and who, when she wasn't eyeing Wren over the rim of her spectacles or staring at the pad of paper in her lap, was glancing up at the clock on the wall. In their forty-five-minute session she said little more than, "So, what I hear you saying is . . ."

No. Not a fit.

In the silence she mentally sketched Dawn, whose tight ebony curls were restrained by her African print cloth headband, the navy spirals swirling on a lime background with hints of citron yellow, the movement reminding her of Vincent's stars. *Dawn.* That was a good name for a counselor. Sunrise. Light. Hope.

Dawn smiled at her, and her brown eyes were kind. "Tell me more, Wren. What does 'okay' mean?"

Wren did a quick mental inventory of the past week. "I've been sleeping okay, that's huge for me. And I think my new meds are working. I don't like being on them, but I know I need them. At least I'm not feeling completely numbed out. That always scares me when I feel numb. I'd rather feel sad than numb, if you know what I mean."

Dawn nodded.

"I mean, it hurts, and it's hard dealing with all the stuff we talked about last week, like losing Casey and Theo. I'm still grieving all that. Even though I know some people would say, It's only a cat."

"He was *your* cat," Dawn said, "and he was connected with your friend, with your friend leaving. And you loved both of them."

Wren bit her lip.

Like Dawn had told her last week, she needed to be patient with the grieving process and not let others' voices or the voices in her own head rush her through it. Or make her feel guilty for taking too long or being too sensitive. But those old scripts were hard to ignore and replace.

"I've been trying to paint, like you suggested, because that helps me process how I'm feeling and not be so scared of feeling the hard things. I guess it helps me get the feelings out so I can see them and work with them. Except I've mostly been sketching lately because painting can be expensive, especially if I don't really have something specific in mind. But my mom sold a sketch I made for her—I just found out a little while ago—so I'll be able to buy more art supplies."

On second thought, she would probably pay medical bills. That's what she should do with the money.

She would likely be paying off her medical bills for the next five years, given the payment plan she had negotiated with the hospital. But at least she was on a plan. She had given up her apartment—it didn't feel safe for now, living on her own—and Kit was letting her stay at her house indefinitely and wasn't charging her anything for rent or food or utilities, an extraordinary gift of generosity she felt guilty for accepting. But because of Kit's help she could pay her medical insurance bill and prescription costs and doctor office and counseling co-pays from her New Hope paycheck and her savings. She had enough money in savings to supplement her income for about four months. That was all. But it was more than most people had. And maybe soon she would be able to work full time again, if she could find a job that didn't completely stress her out. That was the nice thing about pushing a mop or a broom at New Hope. There was something soothing about it. But it wasn't a long-term solution.

Don't rush it, Hannah had said. It was important for her to take the necessary time to recover. And there was an emergency fund at the church, subject to a pastor's discretion, that she could access for help if she needed to.

But she didn't want to be a charity case. There were so many others who lived in more desperate need.

She already was a charity case. But Kit didn't make her feel like one.

She stared at Vincent's painting on the wall behind Dawn, the generous, uncomplaining Samaritan bent backward under the weight of lifting the limp, left-for-dead man onto his horse. In that moment of rescue the wounded man probably wasn't feeling guilty for accepting help. Only grateful. But it was still hard to receive.

"Tell me about your sketch," Dawn said.

"My what?"

"The sketch you said you made for your mom."

"Oh. Yeah." Wren shifted position in the armchair and crossed her ankles. "I drew it after I got out of the hospital. It's a picture of a woman kneeling in a hand, like the hand of God. My mom was the model."

"Why your mom?"

"Because she was the only one available. I didn't think I could draw it freehand"—she was like Vincent that way, better able to work from a model than from imagination or memory—"so I asked her to kneel with her head in her hands and pose for me."

"What was that like for you, sketching your mom in that pose?"

"I—" Wren stopped and tried to remember. She was in such a fog of grief when she first went to Kit's and when her mother arrived. She couldn't remember when she'd drawn it. She only knew they were outside in Kit's garden. "Sorry. I'm not sure."

"It's okay." Dawn paused. "How about the feelings behind the sketch?"

"You mean, while I was drawing it? Or what it means in general?"

"Either. Both."

"Well, I called it *Weemoed*, that's a Dutch word Van Gogh used in his letters. He said it means 'active melancholy.'"

Dawn raised her eyebrows. "That's an interesting phrase. What does that mean to you?"

"Vincent said it was a compound word with 'woe' and 'courage,' so it's like you have to combine both together. You can't have melancholy without courage. Because then it's just despair."

"And how about you? What do you say about the word?"

"Yeah, I think that's true, that we have to choose, as much as we're able to choose. Sometimes it's hard to choose hope when all you feel is sadness." *We must choose*, Kit had said. And keep choosing.

Dawn said, "Is that where you find yourself right now, that it's hard to choose hope?"

"Some days."

"What helps you on those days?"

Wren thought a moment and then said, "Art. Beauty. Being outside in nature, going for a walk. Prayer, when I can pray. But sometimes I can't come up with the words, and sometimes I don't have the mental energy to read my Bible or a devotional or anything. That's how I got the image for the hand, because my pastor came to the hospital to visit me, and we were talking about how I felt too tired to cling to God, like I was trying to climb this jagged cliff face, and I was losing my grip. But then it was like the cliff shifted into a hand, and I was held. And she told me that was a good image for me, that when I don't have the strength to cling, I can trust that God is holding me."

"So, you're the one in the hand."

"Yes."

"Even though you sketched your mom there."

"Yes."

"Is she in the hand too?"

Surprised by the force of emotion rising to the surface, Wren pressed her lips together and nodded. She had put her there.

"Your mom has her own journey to make," Kit commented as they sat in her living room that night in front of the fireplace.

"I know. That's what my counselor said too."

Yes, her mother had her own sorrow to process, Dawn had said, her own fears to navigate, but Wren wasn't responsible for her mother's feelings. She knew that, Wren said. But she still felt as if her mother was suffering because of her. All the emotions had returned while she sat in Dawn's office, the memory of her mother kneeling there in the grass, face in her hands, embodying sorrow. There was nothing false about her posture. That's what had helped give depth and passion to the sketch. All the emotion was true. Every bit of it.

"I think Mom's disappointed I'm not there for Thanksgiving."

Kit did not reply.

"Did she call and talk to you about it?" Wren asked.

"She worries about you. But I reminded her of the boundaries we set."

"Thanks." It was something the three of them had agreed to before her mother returned home in October: there would be no reporting back and forth without Wren's knowledge or approval, not unless there was an emergency. Kit wanted her home to be a safe place, a refuge for as long as she chose to remain. *That was really wise,* Dawn had said. *That's a good boundary for all of you.*

"But if you change your mind about your plans, Wren, you're welcome to come with me to Sarah's."

"I know. Thanks. But I think it'll be good for me to serve. I've been living so much in my own head lately, I think I need to be reminded of all the gifts I've got."

She wouldn't be responsible for anything other than showing up at the homeless shelter on Thursday with the other volunteers from her church. And afterward she would join Hannah and her family for their own dinner and celebration.

It was an honor, she'd told her mom, a privilege to be invited to her pastor's house for the holiday. And her mom had said, I'm happy you're going. We'll miss you, though. Maybe you can come for Christmas.

Yes, Wren had said. If she felt up to traveling, maybe Christmas. But no promises, okay? She couldn't think that far ahead. And her mother had said, Okay.

That night as she lay in bed, she took Kit's suggestion and visualized herself in God's hand. Then she pictured her mom in God's other hand, both of them upheld in anxiety, in sorrow, with love.

19

Thanksgiving Day dawned clear and bright without a trace of the forecasted snow in West Michigan, not even at the lakeshore. Before Kit drove to Grand Rapids to spend the day with her daughter's family, she dropped Wren off at Crossroads. Hannah met her at the entrance and ushered her into a large dining hall where tables were set with harvest linens and centerpieces. "We're expecting so many this year, we're going to run it as a buffet line rather than serving at tables," Hannah said. "Any preference for what you'd like to do?"

Wren scanned the auditorium, trying to ground and center herself in an unfamiliar, cavernous space. "I'm not sure."

Through the glass of the far double doors she saw guests lined up, three and four deep, clamoring to enter. Volunteers—none of whom she recognized—carried food from the kitchen to buffet tables, swerving to avoid one another. "Hot tray coming through! Careful! Hot tray!"

Wren jumped back to avoid a collision with two children who were ducking and dodging around tables in a game of tag, the girl managing to avoid the boy even while maneuvering with two canes. Wren had seen a lopsided gait like hers before. There was a little boy with cerebral palsy in one of her groups at Bethel House. Nicholas was one of the brightest six-year-olds she had ever met. She hoped he was okay.

"Hey, hey, son!" The father grabbed the boy by the arm as he tried to weave around another table. "Cool it, Collin. Stop the roughhousing. Leave your sister alone." The girl stuck her tongue out at her brother when her dad wasn't looking. Then she started the game again.

With all the noise and commotion, Wren hoped she didn't have a panic attack. Maybe she had overestimated her emotional and mental capacity.

"Wren!"

She spun around. "Mara!"

Mara wrapped her in the sort of hug one would offer a long-lost friend. "What are you doing here?"

"I'm serving with my church. This is my pastor, Hannah Allen."

Mara laughed. "I know Pastor Hannah. Hannah and I go way back."

"Mara's one of the directors here," Hannah said. "She oversees the food ministry side of things."

"I try to, anyway. It's loosely controlled chaos in here today."

"Hey, hey, Collin," the dad yelled. "I said enough! Do you need a time-out?"

"Well, put us to work," Hannah said. "What do you need?"

"Watch out!" someone called. "Hot tray!"

Mara said, "Another runner to make sure there's enough food in the trays. If you could do that, Wren. And Hannah, could you keep Charissa company at the drink station?"

"You bet."

One of the volunteers tripped trying to avoid the game of tag, and his tray of mashed potatoes crashed to the floor with a clatter. Wren clutched her chest.

"Clean up on aisle six!" Mara called, and returned to the kitchen.

Hannah touched Wren lightly on the elbow. "Are you okay?"

Wren wasn't sure.

"What can I do for you right now?"

She didn't know.

"I know a quiet place where we can sit a minute. Come with me."

They had plenty of volunteers, Hannah insisted. Wren didn't need to feel guilty about not serving. "If you'd like to stay here in Mara's office, that's fine. Whatever's best for you."

"I'm so sorry. I didn't think I'd—"

What? Nearly hyperventilate when she realized how many people would be there? Feel the need to crawl under a table to hide? Want to wrap herself in one of the harvest tablecloths and disappear?

She took a deep breath to steady herself. She needed a different focal point, something to distract her from the obsessive, racing thoughts. She scanned Mara's desk: a chipped mug filled with pencils, a World's Greatest Grandma mug half-filled with coffee, three blue binders, Post-it notes in bright tropical colors stuck onto a lampshade, a stack of cookbooks, photos in pink polka dot frames. She fixed her attention there: a tall, thin young man in combat fatigues, his red hair clipped into a crew cut, the name Garrison on his chest; a stocky twentysomething guy, also with red hair, holding a baby; and three dark-haired children eating ice cream cones in front of a small house with a Hacienda roof.

She closed her eyes and pictured herself eating an ice cream cone with Gran and Pop on their veranda. Tangara had his head in her lap, hoping she would let him have a lick. She would. But only after she had eaten all she wanted. He could have the cone. She always gave him the cone.

She missed Tangara. She missed Theo. She missed Gran and Pop and Casey. She should have gone to North Carolina. Soon they would be gathering at the table together. Dad would crack his knuckles and then carve the turkey. She could still remember him carving the turkey for her very first Thanksgiving after they moved to America.

She was not going to cry.

"Tell you what," Hannah said, "how about if we both head to my house right now? It'll be a lot quieter there. Just an old family friend who's in town for the weekend and our son and his fiancée."

Wren wasn't sure she had the energy to meet anyone. "I think I'd better go home. I'm not feeling well."

"Are you sure? I don't like the idea of you being alone."

"I'm okay. I'll be okay."

"I can drive you to Grand Rapids to be with Katherine. How about that?"

"No, that's okay." She didn't know Sarah and her family that well, and she didn't have the energy to interact with them, either. She didn't say that part aloud.

"Are you sure you don't want to come to our house and rest? You don't even have to join us for dinner. We've got a guest room where you can lie down or read . . ."

It was a very kind offer. But no. She shook her head.

Hannah looked as if she wasn't sure what to do. She leaned forward in her chair, hands clasped together. "I need to ask, Wren, do you feel like you're in any danger right now? Like you could cause yourself any harm?"

"No. It's nothing like that. It's mostly feeling anxious, like I'm on the verge of a panic attack. I just want to go home. I'm sorry." Talking about it would just make it worse.

Hannah nodded. "Okay. I'll take you."

The Potato Eaters. That's what came to mind as she followed Hannah down the hallway: one of Vincent's early paintings of peasants sharing a humble meal of coffee and potatoes in a dark, spartan, cheerless room, the potatoes like small round loaves of bread they offered to one another. The palette was somber gray, brown, and green—nothing like his later work with its vibrant swirling colors and bold brushstrokes. He told Theo he deliberately chose humble, unrefined models to show the truth and beauty and dignity of their life, how they ate with the same hands that had dug their food from the ground.

From the auditorium floated the sound of conversations, laughter, and music. Gathered around tables were the downtrodden and over-looked, the sort of people Vincent often tried to hire as his models in order to give them food and a warm place to stay while he drew and painted them, people whose faces were etched with stories, with suffering and beauty. *Companions in misfortune.*

Maybe instead of returning to an empty house and ruminating on what she did not have, she could remain for the meal and try to depict and offer what she saw. If she could have paper and a pencil.

"Let's see what Mara says," Hannah replied after Wren told her what she was thinking, and they went together to find her.

In a far corner of the room Wren sat with a stack of white printer paper, waiting. Mara needn't have worried she'd have a rush of people clamoring for sketches. A few children came but quickly grew impatient with sitting still. "We've got an artist here," Mara called out again. "Anyone who wants to take a sketch home, come this way!" But no one responded. "Wish my grandkids were here. My oldest grandchild loves art too. If Maddie were here, she'd be trying to draw with you."

"Are they the ones in the photo on your desk?"

"Yeah, they're in Texas. Madeleine's almost nine, Hillary's six, and Ben is five. My daughter-in-law's pregnant again—twins!" She reached out to grab the sleeve of the little boy who had been playing tag earlier. "Hey, Master Collin! How about posing for a picture?" He shook his head and raced off. Mara shrugged. "Wish I could find you some customers."

"It's okay. Everybody's having a good time doing other things."

"Yeah. Looks like it." Mara pulled up a chair. "Might as well take a load off. Did you get food?"

"No, I'm going to Hannah's house later." If she felt up to it. She wasn't sure yet. "How about you? Do you have a family dinner after this?"

"No, not anymore. All my sons are grown and live out of town. Jeremy—he's the one in Texas—I'm flying there in the morning to spend a few days with them. We'll have a big family dinner on Saturday. Brian, my youngest, is serving in Afghanistan. He'll be home in the spring, I hope. And Kevin, my middle son, lives in Colorado. He's got a little girl named Phoebe."

"Phoebe? That's my little sister's name." As they chatted about family and missing holiday traditions, Wren sketched Mara's face: dimpled cheeks and eyes that crinkled when she smiled. She probably looked like a cherub when she was a little girl. With the softness of her face, gray hair would look good on her. But the auburn color made a statement that she was playful. Or maybe that statement was made by her dangling pumpkin pie earrings. Wren drew those too.

"Oh, you're way too kind," Mara said when she finished sketching and handed her the paper. She held up the drawing next to her face and called to the little girl with the canes. "Bethany! What do you think? Does it look like me?"

Bethany shuffled closer to look. She pressed her hands on Mara's knees and squinted, first examining the picture, then Mara's face, then back to the picture. "Yep. It looks like Nana."

Mara scooped her up onto her lap, wrapped her arms around her tiny waist, and kissed her. Bethany leaned her head against Mara's ample breast. It was a sweet image, a small, thin-armed girl with braces on her legs, cradled in a soft nest. "Would it be all right if I drew you on your grandma's lap?" Wren asked.

Bethany laughed. "She's not my real grandma."

"I'm close enough, Bethie." Mara tickled her side, and she laughed again. "What do you think? Want Wren to draw a picture of you?"

"Okay."

"You have to hold still," Mara said, "just for a little while."

Unlike the other children who fidgeted, Bethany was still as a statue. Wren drew her angular face, her wide-set eyes and thick brows and lashes, her long dark hair pinned to the side with a pink and green felted owl. Her dress, too, was patterned with pink and green owls. She wasn't much bigger than Phoebe, but older. Wren could tell because of her missing front teeth.

Mara beckoned toward someone. "Charissa, come meet Wren."

Wren looked up to see a tall, slender woman with striking streaks of silver in her long, dark hair.

"Hi, Mom," Bethany said without shifting position.

"Hey, sweetie. What's this?"

"I'm sitting for a portrait."

"Oh. Okay. Well, it looks very good."

"Do you want one?" Bethany asked.

"No. Not today. We've got to get going. Your brother's having a meltdown." She and Mara exchanged a commiserating glance.

Mara said, "Charissa, meet Wren; Wren, meet Charissa."

"Hey," they both said.

Bethany said, "She's an artist."

"I can see that. Thanks, Wren. It's beautiful."

"And she's Katherine Rhodes' niece. Great-niece," Mara said.

"Are you?" Charissa said. "That's great." But her voice was flat, and Wren noted her vacant expression. Weariness, but possibly something more. "Are you still coming to our house tonight?" she asked Mara.

"Yep. I've got to let the dog out, and then I'll come over."

"Bring games," Bethany said. "And pie. Don't forget." She started to slide off Mara's lap. Charissa grabbed her arm to steady her.

"I won't forget," Mara said.

Wren handed Bethany her sketch. Charissa rested her hand on her daughter's head. "What do you say?"

"Thank you, Miss Wren."

"You're welcome. Thanks for modeling for me. You were great."

A companion in misfortune, Wren thought as she watched Charissa shepherd her daughter through the crowds and around the tables to the exit door. If you looked closely, you could recognize them everywhere.

20

Once, when she was a child, Wren was invited for tea at the minister's house. She sat in the paisley wallpapered room with the grownups, her ankles crossed primly, listening to Pop debate the doctrine of free will with the young new minister. Pop loved to debate. Though she didn't understand anything about what Pop or the minister said, she could see the minister was outmatched. He would tug at his collar and mop tiny beads of sweat from his brow with his sleeve and say, "Well, Joe, I'm not sure how to answer that," or "Another way to look at it would be . . ." Wren was fascinated by the way his Adam's apple wobbled when he spoke.

After they left the minister's house that day, Gran took off her gloves and swatted Pop with them. She said they would never be invited back. She was right. It was a shame, really, because the minister's wife made the loveliest lamingtons Wren had ever tasted. Even better than Gran's. She didn't tell Gran that.

"Tell me about your dinner," her mother said when she called.

Wren told her about how Hannah and her husband, Nathan, lived in a beautifully restored Victorian house with mahogany floors and high ceilings and leaded glass windows. They had guest rooms they made available to missionaries on furlough and to pastors who needed sabbaticals. "Anyone who needs rest," Hannah had said. The missionary family currently staying with them was out of town. But their son, Jake, and his fiancée, Erica, were there for dinner, along with a family friend a little older than Wren, a woman named Becca, who was like a daughter to them. It was low-key, Wren said, quiet and relaxed. Nathan made the best pecan pie she'd ever tasted. But she didn't tell her mother that.

"We missed you," her mother said, "but I'm so glad you had a good time."

As good a time as she seemed capable of having. She didn't tell her mother that, either. She didn't want her to worry. She didn't tell her about nearly having a panic attack at Crossroads or nearly changing her mind about going to Hannah's or nearly bursting into tears at the dinner table while listening to Becca tell stories about the refugee kids she taught at a public school in Detroit. Or how jealous she felt, listening to Jake and Erica talk about their plans to purchase a house in the inner city so they could be an incarnational ministry presence to people they felt called to serve. They were concerned about gentrification, they said. The poor were being displaced. If they could raise money to buy a few dilapidated houses that could be renovated, they could make sure a few needy families would have a low-rent option. Or maybe even be able to buy. They had already helped start a community garden. They were tutoring kids. And that was on top of their full-time jobs.

"And what do you do?" Erica had asked.

Wren told her she was in transition, praying to see what was next. Becca and Erica and Jake smiled and nodded while they chewed. Thankfully, Hannah changed the subject. They needed to decide what games to play after dinner. But as soon as dessert was done, Wren asked Hannah to drive her home.

It was a mental game she played, Wren thought as she crawled into bed shortly after seven, and she couldn't remember when she first started playing it, the game of calculating how old someone was when they started accomplishing great things. How old was that artist when he painted his first great work? How old was that composer when he wrote his first symphony, that author when she wrote her breakout novel? But it wasn't only for famous artists. It was for ordinary peers and colleagues too. How old was she when she bought her first house? How old were they when they got married? Had children? Traveled the world? Made a significant impact in the kingdom? If they were older, she felt consoled. She still had time. If they were younger, she felt deficient. She was lagging behind. Being around passionate people like Jake and Erica and Becca ought to be inspiring. Instead, being with them fueled her deep sense of failure and inadequacy.

Missionaries on furlough and pastors on sabbatical had no reason to be ashamed of staying rent-free in someone's house. But how long could she take advantage of Kit's hospitality? She needed to find a real job. She needed to find a real place to stay. She had claimed she was "praying about what's next." But she wasn't. Thinking about it made her head hurt.

The front door opened. Kit was home. Wren lay still. She didn't want Kit to know she was awake, didn't want to have another conversation about her day. She heard the jingling of keys, the rustling of a coat, light footsteps on the stairs, a soft knock, then the creak of her bedroom door as it slowly opened. She pictured Kit in the doorway, peering into the dark. Yes, she was home. She was in bed. She was safe. The door clicked shut.

Wren stared at the ceiling. She wondered where Casey and Brooke had spent their first Thanksgiving together. Not with his parents, she hoped. To think of him being only twenty minutes away made her heart hurt. Then again, what if he was only twenty minutes away? What if he had come into town for a few days? What if he longed to call or text but thought she was angry at him? What if there was a chance to meet for coffee to catch up in person? What if?

It had been almost three months since he'd last been in touch, plenty of time to demonstrate to Brooke that they weren't emotionally codependent, and they could be trusted to move forward with wise boundaries that honored both a new marriage and a platonic friendship forged in middle school.

What if his coming to mind right now was a holy nudge? She had marveled at those promptings over the years, how one of them could be in the middle of a crisis and the other would know. *Like twins,* they often joked.

Maybe Casey needed her help now. She sat up in bed and turned on the light.

Not long after she started working at Bethel House, she was awakened in the middle of the night, jolted out of a sound sleep by a sense of urgency. She needed to pray for him immediately. She needed to pray for his safety. She prayed, then called his number. He didn't pick up. She kept praying, then called again. Still no answer. So she threw on clothes and raced to his apartment. She found him with a few bottles of pills and a case of beer. He was having dark thoughts. So she got rid of the beer, took away the pills, and kept vigil on the floor beside his bed until the morning light broke and he could get to his counselor.

Maybe Brooke didn't know about his dark thoughts. Maybe he hadn't confided to her that he was bipolar and had been hospitalized a few times, that the scars on his arms weren't accidental cuts from a high school shop class. Maybe Brooke didn't know how to keep watch, how to look for the signs that he was sinking or that he had entered a manic phase. Maybe she didn't know.

Her heart began to race. He was in trouble. She could feel it. He needed help. She picked up her phone. She would send one text, a "You just came to mind" text, a "Hope you're okay" text. Not a "Miss you" text, not a "Need to hear your voice" text. Just, "Praying for you." Except she wouldn't say, "Praying for you." When he wasn't well, Casey resented God and prayer. He could get so angry sometimes. She didn't want to make him angry.

Her hands trembled as she typed the letters. She prayed. Then pressed Send.

Something was off, Jamie thought as she and Olivia put away the harvest china. There was something Wren wasn't telling her. It wasn't flatness in her voice. Jamie had grown accustomed to hearing that. Flatness was normal, part of her ongoing struggle with weariness and discouragement and grief. Flatness Jamie could deal with.

But today there had been something artificial and striving in her tone, as if she was trying to convince herself—or her mother—that all was well when it wasn't.

It wasn't. Jamie could tell. Her mother's intuition wasn't always correct, but it was accurate frequently enough. And that meant the alarm bells within her were pealing. "Thanks for your help today, Liv. I'll take care of the rest."

Olivia set one more plate in the cupboard and then checked her phone. "Jess is having a bunch of people over for a movie. Mind if I go?"

"Right now? Phoebe's been waiting to watch *A Christmas Story*." It was a tradition to watch that movie together on Thanksgiving, ever since Dylan introduced it to them on their very first Thanksgiving celebration as a new family of three in America. Phoebe was excited because she remembered getting to stay up late to watch it in her pajamas last year. She'd been talking about it all day. Even Joel, who was pretending it wasn't a big deal, had offered to make the popcorn.

That had always been Wren's job, making popcorn on the stove and flavoring it with cheese or cinnamon sugar. Then Wren, Olivia, and Joel would huddle together on the couch and quote lines to one another and laugh. Phoebe had sat on Wren's lap last year.

"Can't you go to Jess's another time?"

Olivia answered with a sigh.

"Or go. I don't care." The family had already been separated on Thanksgiving for the first time ever. What was one more family tradition broken?

Olivia hesitated.

"It's fine, Liv."

"Not if you're going to be mad."

"I'm not mad. Go, love. Have a good time." She gestured toward the counter. "Take one of your pies over to her. You guys can enjoy it." They had plenty left over, even if Joel and Dylan would disagree.

"Okay, fine. I'll stay."

"You don't need to stay."

"It's fine. I'll stay."

"Okay. Suit yourself. It's your choice."

"I'll tell Jess I'll come over later."

"Sounds good." Jamie put away the last of the utensils. "Tell Joel he can start making the popcorn, okay? I'll join you guys in a few minutes. I've got to make a phone call first."

"She's here, already in bed," Kit said. "I checked on her when I got home."

It was way too early for Wren to be in bed. That only confirmed something was wrong. Whenever Wren started sleeping too much, that was a warning sign. "Sorry to bother you, Kit, it's just, mother's intuition and all."

"I know. It's so hard not to worry. I don't think we ever stop worrying about our kids, no matter how old they are."

"So true." It seemed the older they got, the more complicated the worries became. Jamie tried to think of something to ask that wouldn't violate the boundaries they'd established, boundaries she knew were wise. And yet so difficult to honor. "But you'll let me know if . . ."

"I promise, Jamie. If I sense any kind of emergency, if I think she's in any danger, I'll let you know immediately."

Jamie sighed. "Okay. Thank you." At least Kit was there to keep watch. That ought to give her peace. "But the sleeping a lot—that's a danger sign. Or if she stops showering or getting dressed. She's been doing okay with that, right? With the basic life stuff?"

"She's keeping all her work commitments at New Hope and doing a fine job with everything I've asked her to do. I'm grateful for her help, for her attention to detail."

"That's good." That meant she was stable, and stability was a gift. The adjustments her doctor had made to her prescriptions must be working. That had become a problem shortly after she got out of the hospital, some troubling side effects with the medications she'd been put on. Wren had said they would probably be changing them, but Jamie hadn't asked her about it lately, not in a direct way. She didn't want to pry. "And painting—it sounds like she's doing some painting?"

"She's in her studio quite a bit. I haven't asked her what she's working on, but I think she's finding life in her art."

Also a very good sign. "And her counselor appointments—I mean, I'm not asking for any details. She told me she'd found someone she seems to like, who seems to be helping, so . . ."

Jamie knew she had been pushing toward the invisible line. Now she had crossed it. "So, we'll keep moving forward," she said, interrupting the awkward silence.

"Mommy?" Phoebe was bouncing up and down on her toes in the bedroom doorway. "We've got popcorn."

"Okay, love. Be right there."

Phoebe scampered away, calling, "She's coming!"

"Sounds like you need to go," Kit said.

"Yes. Thanksgiving movie night. Everyone's gathered downstairs." Except for Wren. But Wren was safe and working at being well. She had exerted her own desires and expressed her own needs, and that was healthy. Jamie wanted her to do that. She was relieved and grateful she was doing that.

"Enjoy it," Kit said. "And when you're feeling anxious, look at Wren's sketch and picture her in God's hand. Picture yourself in God's hand too."

After she hung up the phone, Jamie stared at the framed sketch she kept on her nightstand. She had no trouble placing her daughter in God's hand; she had trouble leaving her there. She had trouble trusting it was safe to leave her there.

Lord, I believe. Help my unbelief.

Her fingers hovered over the keypad. She wouldn't call. She wouldn't risk waking her. She could send a goodnight and "I love you" text, though, and if she was sleeping, she'd find it in the morning.

"You coming, hon?" Dylan called from the bottom of the stairs.

Or maybe she should let it go.

"Hon?"

She would let it go.

She would give Wren space to process whatever she needed to process and trust that if Wren needed her help, she would let her know.

She set her phone down on the nightstand. "On my way," she called, and headed down to join them.

Wren changed out of her pajamas into jeans and a sweatshirt. She would need to be dressed in case she got the news that yes, Casey was in town and there was an emergency. She would need to be ready to go. She put her sneakers beside the bed, then crawled under the covers again to wait.

She would want him to tell Brooke about her text, not to be secretive about it. And if he was too unwell to reply himself, Brooke might reply for him and say, "Tell me more about what he needs when he's like this. How do I help him?"

Wren would tell her to remind him that he had been in the dark before, and he had persevered. Remind him that he had made courageous choices before, and the despair wouldn't last forever. Wren would tell her how important it was not to avoid him or ignore him, how he needed to be listened to, even if what he was saying sounded angry or irrational. She wouldn't be able to argue him out of it. It was important to understand that. And it was important not to add to his burden of guilt or shame by pointing out that it terrified her to see him like this or that he needed to think about how his illness impacted the people who loved him. He couldn't think about that right now. It would just make things worse.

She checked the time again. Forty-five minutes since she sent the first text.

If he was at his parents' house, that could have pushed him over the edge. They'd had a very volatile relationship over the years. His parents had never understood his illness. They hadn't ever tried hard enough to work with it or be patient with him. She couldn't count the number of times they'd kicked him out of the house, demanding he get his act together. Wren had tried to get along with them, but it was hard when she felt so loyal to Casey and defensive about him. And there were times it seemed they resented how close she was to their son. "You've been more like a mom to me than she's ever been," Casey had sometimes said.

Maybe they'd had another terrible fight. His mother could get so angry. She could become so unreasonable. And Casey never stayed quiet. He always fought back.

She would send another text. "Sorry to bother you," she would say, "but I'm worried about you, and I need to know you're okay. Please let me know you're okay."

A thumbs up sign. That's all she needed. Just a thumbs up sign. She sent a second text and waited.

Though it seemed unlikely, maybe Brooke had never seen him unwell. When he left for his pilgrimage to Spain, he was well. Wren had been encouraged that he wanted to make such a trip, that he was open to self-reflection and seeking God again. And he was well—elated and hopeful—after he returned. Maybe Brooke had only ever seen him at his best. Their brief, mostly long-distance engagement probably wasn't long enough to observe any of the darkness.

Even if he had confided to Brooke about how he had battled over the years, she might not have believed it. Or she might have hoped it was all behind him. Because they were starting a new and wonderful life together, and she made him happy. Wren was so grateful he was happy. That was exactly what she had longed for, what she had prayed for him for many years, that he would be happy and hopeful. That's what he prayed for her too, when he was well.

She reached for his gray beanie on her nightstand and kept praying.

Shortly after midnight Wren's phone buzzed with a text. She fumbled for the lamp switch, then stared at her screen. A thumbs up sign.

He was alive. Her shaking hands were evidence that she had been holding her breath, fearing the worst.

He was okay. Or was he? Now that she thought about it, a thumbs up could mean many things: "Yes, I got your message," or "I'm doing great, nothing to worry about," or "I'm so glad I came to mind because I'm really struggling right now." So, which was it?

Impossible to know.

A thumbs up could mean, "I'm really glad you wrote, and it's okay for you to write again." Or "I wish you hadn't written, but since you did, here's the shortest reply I can give to let you know I'm okay."

It was impossible to interpret. She stared at her phone. Now that she knew he was alive, she wanted him to either confirm or refute her discernment. She needed to know whether she'd heard correctly. Because maybe she was muddled about all of that too. And if she couldn't trust her discernment in a small thing like feeling led to pray, then how could she trust her discernment in larger things like knowing how to move forward in life?

No. This was important. She needed to know if he was really, truly okay. She sent one more clarifying text and waited.

He had his phone with him. He would see that she had replied. If he didn't send a text right away, did that mean he was angry? That Brooke was angry? Maybe they were talking about it right now. Maybe he was telling her he would send one last message and make it clear—again—that she shouldn't contact him. Maybe Brooke was saying, You need to change your number. I want you to change your number.

And then what? What would she do if the conduit for reaching him permanently closed? Casey didn't have any social media accounts; he thought it was all ridiculously narcissistic. And Wren didn't want to return to social media, even if it meant she could possibly track Brooke online. At Dr. Emerson's urging, she had shut down all her accounts months ago. It wasn't good for her, being continually bombarded with others' success stories or subjected to the constant acrimony or an endless scrolling feed of bad news. For the sake of her mental health, those avenues needed to remain closed. Permanently.

She stared at her screen.

She wasn't a stalker. And she wouldn't keep sending him text messages. She probably should have made that clear in her last message, that she knew the boundaries and had violated them only because she had been worried. She had violated them only because she had been led to reach out and pray.

Had she been led to contact him?

Now she wasn't sure. Maybe it was all her imagination. That's what she needed to know.

Her phone buzzed again. *Everything's fine. No need to worry. Happy Thanksgiving. Take care.*

He was okay! Thumbs up meant he was well and truly okay. That was good. It was good he was okay.

Everything's fine. It wasn't just him that was fine. *Everything* was fine. Everything with him, everything with Brooke, everything with life. It was all fine.

No need to worry. Her instinct had been wrong. The two of them were no longer connected by deep intuition. Her sense of urgency, her gut feeling that he was in danger, all of it was wrong. There was no need for her to worry. Because everything was fine.

Happy Thanksgiving. That was the polite greeting to offer on a holiday. Even strangers said Happy Thanksgiving on Thanksgiving. Friends might say, Hope you had a happy Thanksgiving. Friends who wanted to engage in further conversation might say, How was your Thanksgiving?

He was fine. He didn't need her support. He had moved on with life.

Take care. He hoped she would move on with hers.

21

W e're entering a time of amplification," Hannah reminded the congregation. Christmas was the time of year when everything was amplified, the joys and the sorrows, the celebration and the grief, the gift of community and the pain of isolation. That's why it was so important to be mindful of Advent, she said. Advent was a season for keeping watch in darkness, for naming the anguish of waiting, and for pressing forward with hope, even when everything seemed bleak and desolate. So, along with their songs of praise—which were right to sing, she said—they would also sing songs of lament. And they would remember in prayer those who found the season particularly painful, those who were grieving losses, those who were unemployed, those who battled chronic illness, whether physical or mental, those who—

Wren clicked the pause button on the audio file and removed her headphones. She would listen to the rest of the sermon later.

She tidied the bottles on the housekeeping cart and pushed it down an empty hallway at New Hope. Though she had spent more than half her Christmases in the northern hemisphere, and though she appreciated the symbolism and poetic synergy of winter and Advent, she longed for the Decembers of her childhood when Christmas signaled the start of summer, and Pop and Gran and Mum and a host of friends would gather for a picnic and bonfire at the beach near Thirroul.

She hadn't appreciated it then. As a child she pined for the kind of Christmas described in the books she read and films she watched: Christmas in winter, with snow blanketing the earth and twinkling lights brightening the darkness. As she buried her toes in hot sand on Christmas Day, she imagined children across the world, bundling up to build snowmen or barrel downhill on sleds or saucers. That was what Christmas was supposed to look like.

"You'll have that now," her mother had said when they moved to Michigan. Wren was excited. Instead, she discovered that the short, gray days of winter exacerbated her homesickness and sense of disequilibrium. Her new dad bought her a special lamp that simulated sunlight. It was supposed to help, but most days it didn't. She didn't tell him that. She didn't want to hurt his feelings; he was trying so hard.

She paused at the threshold of the chapel, then entered with her cart. Kit was rearranging evergreens and berries around an Advent wreath. "Ahhh, here's the artist," she said. "I'm making a mess of this." She stepped back and motioned for Wren to give it a try.

"Is it all right if I start over?"

Kit laughed. "Of course! Have at it."

Wren removed a plastic garbage bag from her cart and spread it out on the floor so she had a place to lay all the branches. Then she began to weave them back together.

"I want to ask you something," Kit said, "and feel free to say no."

Wren said, "Okay." But given Kit's generosity, it was hard to imagine saying no to any of her requests.

"I got a call the other day from the artist who has painted some of the Journey to the Cross stations for me. He's had some health trouble and isn't going to be able to do it this year. Now, we have plenty of art from our past events, and I'm happy to use some of it again. But I wondered, given your gifts, whether you'd be willing to paint for me?"

Wren was so surprised, she pricked her finger on the sharp edge of a branch and began to bleed.

Kit took a tissue box from the cart and handed it to her. "I wish I could offer you a living wage to paint," she said. "I'm a big believer in patrons for the arts. And we do have a stipend set aside. It's not much. But I'd also buy all your materials—paints, brushes, canvases, anything you might need—and then you would be free to sell your work after the exhibition."

Wren pressed a tissue more firmly against her finger. She wasn't a real artist, not like the man who had painted Jesus on the cross. She could see it from where she stood. She couldn't paint like that. There was no possible way her art could equal what had been displayed before. And to accept a stipend when she wasn't even sure she would be able to deliver the final product? No. She couldn't do that. It was an incredibly kind and generous offer, but she couldn't accept it.

Kit smiled at her as if reading her thoughts. "Think about it. And if you'd like someone to help you process any resistance you might feel about saying yes, I'm sure your dear pastor would be happy to be alongside."

That afternoon in her studio Wren stared at a painting that was going nowhere. She had hoped to paint a corner of the New Hope courtyard, where a memorial bench had become a favorite gathering place for birds. She wanted to capture the scarlet of the cardinals against the white linen of fresh-fallen snow dusting the weathered gray beams. She liked the sturdy horizontal lines of the bench beneath an arbor laden with bare twining vines. The scene had good structure, good balance. But if she couldn't even paint a snow-covered bench and some birds, what chance did she have of painting Christ's suffering?

She dipped a wide brush in white paint and smeared it all over her work.

It was one thing to draw sketches for people at a psychiatric hospital or homeless shelter; it was another to paint meditative art designed to usher people into the presence of God.

She couldn't do it. She wasn't skilled enough.

But Kit thought she was. Or maybe she only felt sorry for her.

They had enough art from past years, Kit had said. They could use that. So really, it wasn't a huge risk asking her to paint, was it? If she failed, the exhibition would still move forward. The event didn't rest on her shoulders.

That was good. Because she couldn't manage that burden of responsibility. She couldn't bear the thought of people counting on her and then disappointing them, either by not being able to paint anything or by painting mediocre, useless work. And then how would she feel?

"But it's a commissioned work," Casey would say. "How could you say no? Artists dream about that kind of opportunity. You need to get over yourself and go for it, Wrinkle."

She wished she could hear a real pep talk from him. When he was well, there was no better encourager.

She stared out the window again. Maybe that's why the memorial bench had caught her attention. It was a marker, a way to honor someone who was beloved. But what type of memorial could you create for someone who was gone but not dead?

It felt like death, losing him again, losing again the hope of reconnecting with him.

Like a divorce. She hadn't made that connection before, but she imagined that kind of heartache was similar, losing someone you loved, not because of death, but because he had moved on with his life, leaving you behind.

But it wasn't Casey's fault. He hadn't willingly abandoned their friendship. There had been no loss of love between them. At least, she didn't think there had been. And that was why they couldn't be in contact. Because it wasn't fair to Brooke or to their marriage. Logically, she knew this. But oh, how her heart hurt with the weight of fresh grief layered on top of an unhealed wound.

She never should have texted him. It had only made things worse. If not for him, for her.

She needed to move on. And maybe the timing of Kit's request was providential, something to help her focus so she wouldn't be overwhelmed by loss. But was that a good enough reason to say yes to painting the prayer stations?

She reached into her bag and removed Casey's beanie. It was only a small piece of him. But at least it was something tangible she could carry with her as she tried again to move forward without him. With a heavy sigh, she placed it on her head and picked up her phone.

It was no bother, Hannah said. She was glad Wren called. In fact, she was just getting ready to call her. "I noticed you weren't in worship yesterday. Are you okay?"

It was nice to be missed. "I don't do too well this time of year, so sometimes it's easier to stay home." That was the short answer. She would save conversations about Casey for her meetings with Dawn.

"I understand," Hannah said. "I know the season can be hard."

Wren waited to see if there would be a caveat, an admonition to remember it was important not to isolate yourself when you suffered from depression, that spiritual disciplines ought to be practiced whether you felt like it or not, that gathering together in corporate worship ought to be a high priority every week. But there was only silence.

"I was wondering," Wren said, "if you'd have any time to get together this week? Kit thought it might be helpful for me to talk with you about something."

As it so happened, Hannah said, her next appointment had just canceled, so she had the rest of the afternoon free. She could come to New Hope for conversation, no problem at all.

An hour later they were sitting together in the chapel beneath the crucifixion painting. "I could never paint something as profound as that," Wren said. "The best I could do would be to copy it. But then that wouldn't feel like it was coming from an authentic place. It would have to be worship, painting the prayer stations."

"Is that where you think most of your resistance is coming from? From measuring your own offering or talent against someone else's?"

"Maybe." She knew better than to compare herself with others. But that didn't keep her from doing it. "I think it's more than that, though. I'm not sure I have the capacity to take on a project like this. When I can barely hold myself together most days, how do I manage immersing myself in Jesus' suffering? I'm afraid it might take me under." The betrayal, the abandonment, the torture, the forsakenness —how could she enter the depth of that kind of suffering for an extended period of time?

"You're wise to consider that," Hannah said. "Meditating on the cross takes courage. Most people—churches, even—want to skip right to Easter. We tend to prefer a sanitized cross. An empty one we can wear as jewelry."

Exactly, Wren thought.

She remembered Mrs. Hoffman calling her aside after art history class one day to ask if she was all right. "I noticed you weren't looking at any of the slides," she said. Wren offered an excuse about the crucifixion paintings being too gory and disturbing and that she felt squeamish. But the real reason she didn't look was because she didn't want to burst into tears in front of the class. She didn't want to hear people mock her for being too sensitive, for taking things too much to heart. An empty cross was much easier to look at. And disregard.

She glanced up again at the painting on the wall. That painting didn't disturb or depress her. That painting comforted and enlarged her. That painting beckoned her and urged her to respond.

Maybe spending a few months meditating on Jesus' sacrifice was exactly what she needed as she worked to recover. Maybe Kit knew that. Maybe that's why she had invited her to paint the Scriptures.

"What are you thinking?" Hannah asked.

Wren closed her eyes. Even if the paintings never were displayed, maybe she still needed to paint them as an act of worship. Maybe she needed to push through her resistance and trust God with the results. "I think I need to pray for courage and say yes."

It would be important, Kit said as they drove home together from New Hope, crucial to pay attention to her limits and not push herself beyond them. Since she was the one who had asked Wren to consider doing the work, she said, she was also taking on a measure of responsibility for her wellness while she did it. "I won't be intrusive, but I'll watch to make sure it's not too much for you. And I want you to be honest with me along the way. Because remember, I have other options. I don't want this to become a burden or source of anxiety for you. But I do hope it will be an opportunity, not just for you to share your gifts with others but for you to discover something new and beautiful about Jesus and his love for you."

Wren turned toward her. "Is that why you started doing it every year, the Journey to the Cross? Because you discovered that?"

Kit nodded. "There were prayer stations at the psychiatric hospital where I stayed. All around the chapel walls were stone carvings of Jesus in his last hours, along with the Scripture texts. And every day I would go in there, even the days when I could hardly put one foot in front of the other, and I would make my way around those stations. And cry. I couldn't read the texts. That was too much for my brain to take in. But I could look at the art. And it reached me. At a very deep and empty place it reached me, and I began to heal. Slowly. Like I said to you and your mom, I came to see the cross as the deepest evidence of the love of God. I saw with fresh eyes that the Lord had withheld himself from none of our pain, none of our suffering. And I was able to move forward with hope. Very gradually."

Wren stared out the front windshield. "Do you tell your story at the retreats you lead?"

Kit paused a moment, then said, "No. I've never wanted to make those about me. I've never wanted my story to distract anyone from listening prayerfully to their own life, to their own story with God."

"But would you tell it? I mean, if someone asked you?"

"If I thought it would be helpful, yes. Under the right circumstances I would. A few friends have encouraged me to write my story. But there are already so many good books about enduring through suffering and encountering Jesus in the midst of it, I'm not sure what I could add."

"I'd read it."

"Thank you. I appreciate that."

Wren gave a slight smile. "And if you'd like to talk with someone about your resistance to writing it, I know this pastor . . ."

Kit laughed and nudged her with her elbow. "Well, now. I may just need to think and pray about that."

22

Jamie blew kisses to Phoebe at the bus stop, then returned to her car. If Kit thought Wren could manage a project like this, then she ought to trust her judgment. And, as Wren said, it gave her direction, something concrete to focus on during her most difficult time of year.

But wouldn't it be better to focus on something happier? Wouldn't it be better to invest whatever emerging or limited energy she possessed into something that might help her be less isolated? Like reconnecting with friends? Wren needed to socialize with peers her own age. It wasn't good for her to be so withdrawn.

Then again, Wren had never sought a wide social circle. A few close relationships, and she was fulfilled. Or actually, one close friendship with Casey had evidently been enough.

Jamie watched the bus round the distant corner. If she had taken time in February to consider the implications of Casey moving away—and not been so caught up in her own assessment of what might benefit her daughter—she might have predicted Wren's decline. And if she could have predicted it, she might have been able to—

Stop.

She couldn't have stopped it.

She needed to let that go.

She also needed to let go of her hopes that Wren would spend Christmas with them. Every time she'd asked about her plans, Wren had been noncommittal. Jamie didn't want to pressure her, but the clock was ticking on booking a flight.

Maybe Casey was coming to Kingsbury for Christmas. He and his wife probably hadn't visited his parents for Thanksgiving. Wren would have mentioned him being in town. But, come to think of it, Wren hadn't mentioned him in weeks. No, months.

As Jamie drove back home, she tried to remember the last extended conversation they'd had about him. The spring, probably, when Wren couldn't attend his wedding because she couldn't afford a trip to the Caribbean. She was okay with it, Wren said. It was going to be a small wedding, and she didn't know Brooke, so it made sense she wasn't included in the wedding party. After that disappointment Jamie had been careful not to ask probing questions about him for fear of upsetting her. Once, though, when Wren mentioned their frequent texts and video chats, Jamie gently offered unsolicited advice, reminding her about the need to give the newlyweds space to figure out life together. She wasn't stupid, Wren snapped. And anyway, they were just friends, and friends could continue to support and encourage each other, no matter what.

But maybe they'd had a falling out Wren didn't want to discuss. Or perhaps they had simply drifted apart. Not a bad thing. People grew and changed and moved on. Now that Wren seemed more stable, growing and changing and moving on seemed a possibility again, not just in forging new friendships but in pursuing other significant relationships.

Here was a thought Jamie hadn't yet allowed herself to entertain: since Wren was no longer working a stressful job, she might have more time and energy to try dating. That had always been her excuse in the past, that she didn't have margin for a boyfriend. But now . . . if she kept moving toward health . . .

"Don't even try to go there with her," Dylan said when Jamie got home and shared her thoughts. "That's all she needs right now, her mom prying into her love life. Or lack of it."

Jamie crossed her arms and leaned back against the kitchen counter. "That's not what I'm talking about. I'm not stupid."

"Didn't say you were."

"You kinda did."

"I'm just saying, give her some space to figure her life out."

What did he think she'd been doing the past few months? *"I'm* just saying, I'm not sure painting the prayer stations is the best use of her energy right now, not when she seems to be settling into a new normal. Or trying to. I'm afraid that meditating on Jesus' suffering might take her under again."

Wren never did anything half-heartedly. She would explore Jesus' anguish in the deepest possible way. She would feel his torment and agonize with him. Jamie had seen it. She had been the one to hold her years ago in a dark corner at New Hope while she sobbed and hyperventilated over the cruelty of what the soldiers did to Jesus. There was no quieting her, not even by reminding her the story had a happy ending. She couldn't bear the pain.

Jamie reminded Dylan of this.

He poured himself another cup of coffee. "She was twelve."

"I know that."

"And painting is good for her."

"I know. I just wish she'd start with something easier."

"Like what?"

Jamie sighed. "I don't know. How about Christmas?"

He scoffed. "Have you read those stories? Unwed mother? Slaughter of the innocents? Refugees on the run?"

"You know what I mean. A manger scene. Angels lighting up a night sky. Joy. Celebration. I wish she'd take time to enter into that."

"So, suggest that to her." He kissed her on the forehead. "Gotta go. Is your group coming over?"

"At ten."

"Hope it goes well."

"Thanks. I'm sure it will."

Though they had met together only twice, already the masks were off. The other four pastors' wives who planned to gather in her kitchen every week brought gut-wrenching prayer requests: children with special needs, teenagers battling addictions, adult children who had rejected faith, husbands whose private lives contradicted their public personas, marriages on the verge of disintegrating. They came hungry for connection and desperate for a safe place where they wouldn't be condemned for voicing their fears, doubts, and resentments.

She glanced at the pile of dirty clothes in the laundry area, the toys and books scattered in the living room, and the mail stacked on the kitchen counters. She could either give the illusion of a clean house by quickly shoving clutter out of sight as she had done before or—as she thought about it, this seemed the better option—she could embrace and mirror their common desire to find freedom from the burden of living under scrutiny and judgment and make peace with what was true.

Maybe she should place a sign on the door: Welcome to the mess. Feel free to bring your own.

John, chapter one. That's where they would begin. Jamie retrieved her Bible from a basket of books beside the couch and sat down to read while she waited for the group members to arrive.

Now that they had spent time sharing a bit about their stories and longings, she hoped to ground them in the practice of meditating on Scripture together, similar to what she had experienced in various classes and groups at New Hope. Without that kind of structure to frame their discussions, they might become only a talk-therapy group. Which wasn't bad, she reminded herself. Sharing their needs and concerns had already been healing and liberating. It just wasn't the fullest expression of what she sensed they needed. And what she knew she needed.

In him was life, and that life was the light of all mankind.

Together they would fix their eyes on the Word made flesh and marvel at how he had come to bring light and life to a dark and weary world. They would pray for their loved ones, asking God to help them glimpse light shining in the darkness. And they would pray for themselves, asking God to help them trust the power of that light and the promise that darkness would never overcome it.

But the Word, the living, breathing, sharper-than-any-two-edged-sword Word, could not be controlled or tamed. The Word had a life of its own. And though Jamie expected to concentrate on the image of light and dark when the group gathered around her table half an hour later, what penetrated her as she listened to one of the women read the passage was the phrase, "the Word became flesh."

The Word became flesh.

She turned the phrase over in her mind.

The Word that spoke everything into being took on the frailty, poverty, and suffering of human flesh.

The Word became flesh and dwelt among us.

The Word that created all things seen and unseen became flesh and revealed God's glory. The Word became flesh and came to his own people for a welcome but was rejected. The Word became flesh and that flesh would be beaten, bruised, and torn. There was no escaping the sorrow of the cross even in the beauty of the incarnation. The two were woven together into one seamless garment and could not be separated. Not one dark thread could be removed.

Not a single one.

While the other women wrote in their prayer journals, Jamie covered her face with her hands and kept listening.

That night, with Phoebe asleep and Joel doing homework, with Olivia out with friends and Dylan at a board meeting, Jamie lay in bed reading Julian's *Showings*. "Just as the blessed Trinity created everything from nothing," Julian wrote, "just so the same blessed Trinity will make well all things which are not well."

The cross convinced her. Everything Julian saw in her vision of Christ's suffering and death on the cross convinced her of his love. Everything she saw revealed his delight in making atonement for sin and his thirst for humanity to comprehend the extent to which he was willing to suffer in order to prove once and for all the perfection and passion of the love of God.

That's what Julian saw, that all the power of the enemy was safely shut in the hand of her friend, that even when Satan was doing his best to tempt and torment, he was only serving God's larger purpose in redemption. "All will be well. Trust in him for everything." Julian's words rang with joyful confidence.

Lord, I believe. Help my unbelief.

It wouldn't depress her, Wren had insisted. Meditating on Christ's sufferings gave her comfort. She had already begun to discover that. And perhaps it was her path toward deeper healing. Kit had found that to be true, Wren said. She had no reason to believe it couldn't be the same for her.

Jamie flipped pages back to the beginning, where Julian described the extraordinary requests she had made of God when she was young. First, she wanted to know Christ's sufferings. She wanted to look upon the cross and experience the same kind of anguish those who loved him suffered when they watched him die. Julian had seen paintings of the crucifixion. She had read the Scriptures. She had "great feeling" for the Passion of Christ. But she wanted more. She wanted deeper gratitude for what he had suffered for her, deeper devotion. And so she asked for that grace.

She asked, too, for a bodily sickness that would bring her to the verge of death. She wanted to face every kind of physical and mental and emotional and spiritual pain, to confront all her fears of dying so she might live with more faith until she went home to meet the Lord.

Then she asked God for three wounds: the wound of contrition, the wound of compassion, and the wound of longing for more of God.

Jamie shut the book.

Wren wasn't asking for bodily illness. She wasn't asking for a mystical vision. But she did want to know the sorrow and suffering of Christ in a deeper way. And Kit would be alongside her for the journey. She wouldn't be alone.

Given what the other women had shared that morning, any one of them might trade their worries over their children for her worries about a daughter who, in her weakness, was reaching for Jesus and longing for more of him.

Jamie set her book on the nightstand. Then, opening her hands, she let go of her fears. Again.

23

Maybe Vincent had the right idea, that it was possible to depict the presence of Christ without painting Jesus. At her studio worktable Wren pressed open the page in her book showing his interpretation of the raising of Lazarus beside Rembrandt's original.

Rembrandt included Jesus in the scene; Vincent did not. Instead, he painted a glowing citron yellow sun, a rising sun, he told Theo. Some said his decision to reinterpret the original without Jesus revealed his rejection of faith. But Vincent painted his faith with color, and his Lazarus was bathed in yellow light, a symbol for Vincent of "something from on high." To Wren the painting revealed not only Vincent's identification with the dead man but also his hope for deliverance and his longing for resurrection.

It was a good thing she had nearly four months to paint the stations. Before she even began to pray with the Scripture texts, she would need to practice her technique. And if Vincent was convinced he could grow as an artist by copying the masters, perhaps she needed to start there too.

She placed a sheet of tracing paper on top of his painting and outlined the sister with her arms outstretched in astonishment as she leaned forward to see her brother, her right hand gripping the handkerchief that had covered his face. He was alive!

Given her position in the center of the painting, one might say this orange-haired sister had prominence. But her gaze was directed toward the supine Lazarus, the lines of his body paralleling the mouth of the cave. And it was the sun—the brightly glowing, heavily outlined orb in a swirling yellow sky—that drew a viewer's attention and anchored the work, a sun made all the more prominent by its contrast with the blue and lavender hills on the distant horizon.

He had depicted the presence of Christ without painting Christ. That's what she might need to do.

Through color, through symbol, through lines and composition, perhaps she could portray his presence without showing him. The paintings might be more abstract than she was accustomed to painting, but if she gave up trying to be literal and accurate, she might capture something transcendent.

She wondered if Kit would be okay with that concept. Kit had offered to show her the other painter's work, but she didn't want to be influenced by it. Or feel discouraged by the skill and depth of it. She needed to approach each blank canvas without pressure or expectation and see what emerged. And in order to paint without pressure, she told Kit she didn't want to take the stipend. Not until she knew the paintings were viable. If Kit could pay for her materials, that would be enough for now. She had already given so much.

"How about a lunch break?" Kit called from the hallway. "Are you at a stopping point?"

"Sure." She removed the tracing paper and held it up to look. Next step, draw it freehand. Then interpret it. And reinterpret it. She would do the same with his Pietà.

"I'm a bit tired of peanut butter sandwiches," Kit said, "so I thought we'd head out to eat for a change. How about the Corner Nook?"

Her mother had sent her a check for the *Weemoed* prints, and Corner Nook wasn't too expensive so—

"My treat," Kit said. "If you won't accept a stipend now, at least accept the occasional meal out. Patrons need to take care of their artists."

Wren felt her face flush. "Thank you," she said, and followed Kit to her car.

As they ate their soup and sandwiches, Kit explained there would be fourteen Scripture texts to choose from, beginning with Jesus wrestling in the garden of Gethsemane and journeying forward until he was laid to rest in the tomb. Usually, they included only eight each year, though she was willing to have more. "I'll go through my notes and compile a list of the texts we've used over the past twenty—no, more than that!—it's been almost thirty years." She rubbed her forehead. "Some days I forget how old I am. I suppose that's a good thing."

Wren nodded and took another small bite of her veggie panini. She had forgotten how delicious a grilled sandwich could be. While she was working at Bethel House, she often ate dinners out with friends and had taken most of those meals for granted. The friendships too. Amazing how quickly people fell away from your life when you didn't have money to go out.

Amazing, too, that no one other than her family and pastor bothered to find out how she was doing. Not that she would have told the truth to anyone else. But it would have been nice to have been asked.

The reality stung and might always sting: Casey had been her one true friend and confidant. The others didn't know about the struggle or the darkness. The others didn't know how desperately she needed someone she could call in the middle of the night after waking up with a panic attack, thinking she was going to die. They didn't know. It wasn't their fault. She hadn't told them. Most people didn't have margin to be alongside someone with her kind of needs. And many people with her kind of needs didn't have anyone alongside. She had her family, her pastor, a counselor. It should be enough. It needed to be enough.

At least she wasn't alone in her apartment anymore. If she awoke in the middle of the night, she could call for help, and someone would come. At least she had that. She could be grateful for that. And like Casey, Kit wouldn't judge. She had been there herself. She understood.

That was a priceless gift, having even one person who had lived the struggle from the inside and who had been shaped with compassion. *A companion in sorrow.*

The words tumbled out of her mouth. "Have you thought any more about writing your story?"

Kit smiled. "A bit. I've been praying about my hesitation—my resistance—thanks to your astute observation. And I'm seeing where some of it is coming from."

Wren nodded.

"My friends always said I should write my story as a memoir. But I don't feel called to that. I think the most I could manage would be small bits of narrative woven around Scripture that has been meaningful to me."

"Like a devotional?"

"Maybe."

"With the Journey to the Cross verses?"

Kit stared at her, her brow furrowing in concentration. "Now, there's an interesting thought," she said slowly. "I never even considered using those texts as a way to help frame my story. But you're right. Some of those passages have been at the heart of my journey. That's something for me to ponder."

Wren shrugged. "If I'm going to be painting them, maybe you could write about them. Like a joint project." As soon as she said the words, she realized how ridiculous it sounded, that her art could be paired with Kit's wisdom. "I'm sorry. Ignore that. The pairing together part, not the writing your story part."

But Kit reached across the table and squeezed her hand. "I can't think of anyone I'd rather share that journey with, my dear girl. So, I say yes. Let's both try. And see where it goes."

They would need to figure out how best to work the process. Kit wanted both of them to be open to the Spirit's leading, even with regard to selecting the passages they felt most drawn to explore. And with all her other commitments during Advent, Kit said, she knew she wouldn't have time to prayerfully begin until after the New Year.

That was okay, Wren said, because she needed time to work on her technique and possibly explore a more abstract way of approaching art.

"I'm fascinated with abstract art," Kit said as the server filled their water glasses. "I had a friend who painted that way, and she said she was always surprised by what emerged. She'd come to an empty canvas barefoot—she always painted barefoot as a declaration that she was standing on holy ground—and then she'd pray and ask the Spirit to guide her with color and form and shape. Texture too. She used a lot of texture in her paintings, sometimes even incorporating objects from nature right onto the canvas."

Wren had never considered intentionally incorporating natural forms into her paintings. She might experiment with that too. And approaching a canvas barefoot as a declaration of worship? That would frame everything in the right kind of prayerful, open posture. She liked that idea. "In some of Vincent's paintings there are grains of sand because he sometimes painted at the beach. There's even a grasshopper embedded in one of them. Not intentionally. Just from painting outside."

Kit laughed. "What a place for a grasshopper to land! Vincent must not have noticed."

"No, probably not. It's in one of my favorite paintings too, one of his paintings of an olive grove. Have you seen any of those?"

"I don't think so."

While Kit listened intently, Wren described the first time she saw it. She was at a conference in Kansas City, and she skipped one of the afternoon sessions to go to the Nelson-Atkins Museum of Art. Standing in front of Vincent's olive grove, she quietly wept, not caring if others in the hallway saw her. "I felt like I should take off my shoes—just like you were saying—like I was standing on holy ground, and I didn't understand why that particular painting grabbed me. Until later, when I remembered how Vincent had been thinking about the garden of Gethsemane while he was at the asylum. And it was like all of his deep emotion went straight into the canvas and reached out to touch me too." It wasn't the first or the last time she had wept over one of his paintings.

"I'd love to see it," Kit said. "And it sounds like that might be an important one for you to spend time with, especially if you end up painting the Gethsemane text."

As soon as they returned to New Hope, Wren retrieved one of her art books from her studio and showed Kit a few of his olive groves, all painted while he was at the asylum, some with yellow and lilac skies, others with blue and purple or pink and green skies. The soil, too, was diverse: ochre and bronze and green and yellow. After obsessing for months about painting the trees and telling Theo they were too beautiful and full of character to capture on canvas, he had finally found ways to render them, each work uniquely shimmering.

Kit shook her head slowly. "Incredible, what he saw. You can almost feel the heat and hear the cicadas buzzing."

"That's exactly what he wanted," Wren said, "to give the sensation of being in nature, not just seeing it but experiencing it with all the senses." She pointed to the painting she had encountered in Kansas City. "This is the one I was telling you about, the one that made me cry."

Kit picked up the book for closer observation. "So much movement and emotion. I can't decide if it's turbulent or jubilant." She paused. "Maybe both."

Yes, Wren thought. That was the beauty of it, the intense pathos and breathtaking radiance intertwined. It was chaotic and churning and swirling and glorious.

"And what about this?" Kit asked, pointing to the left side. "The red—or are they orange splotches?"

Wren leaned closer. "Wildflowers, I think. Poppies, maybe?"

"They look like drops of blood," Kit murmured. "Do you think that was intentional?"

"I don't know. I've never thought about that."

"It came to mind because you mentioned he was thinking about Gethsemane."

Wren nodded. "He was frustrated by some paintings his friends Gauguin and Bernard had done of Christ in the garden. He said they had failed to observe the scene—whatever he meant by that. Maybe they didn't capture the passion of it? He told Bernard that an artist could express anguish without literally painting Gethsemane."

"*Anguish* is a good word," Kit said. "I can feel it in this. Something agitated and yearning. Writhing, even. It's as if he revealed the presence of Jesus wrestling there in the garden without showing him."

Wren felt her throat burn. Kit understood. She saw it. She felt it. She knew it. "Yes," Wren whispered. "That's it exactly."

That night after Kit went to bed, Wren sat in her room, reading Mark's account of Jesus in Gethsemane. Was there any other time when Jesus requested something for himself? It was such a simple thing to ask for. He was overwhelmed with sorrow—her Greek lexicon on her phone indicated the word meant he was "engulfed"— and he asked his closest friends to keep him company. *I am engulfed in grief. Keep watch with me.*

But they couldn't even do that. They couldn't stay awake. No one shared his anguish. No one provided the comfort of presence. He was alone in his wrestling, abandoned even before they ran away.

She set aside her phone. She couldn't bear to read any more.

24

Much as Wren wished she could have stayed in bed Friday morning, there was a retreat group gathering that evening, and the bathrooms needed to be cleaned. "We can manage if you're not up to it," Kit had said. But Wren suspected "we" meant "I," and she wasn't going to let Kit spend her day of preparation scrubbing toilets and sinks.

She extended her duster to reach cobwebs in the corner, then ran it over the tops of picture frames in the hallway.

At least no one depended on her to be high functioning, mentally or emotionally. That was a gift. She might not be able to assess risk factors for a child, but she could dust and scrub without jeopardizing anyone. Vincent had frequently expressed to Theo his conviction that if the asylum patients had been given work to do, it might have benefited them. Having simple, menial tasks to perform might have given them a sense of purpose.

"All of this is part of your recovery work right now," Dawn had reminded her at her weekly appointment, "and having even a part-time job to go to will help you keep a regular schedule." She felt so foolish whenever Dawn commended her for doing simple things like taking a shower, getting dressed, eating regular meals, or going to bed on time. But if she focused on how remedial her current skill level was, that would only cause her to spiral into guilt and shame, which wouldn't do her any good.

"Oh, you're thorough," Kit said as she emerged from her office. "Thanks for dusting those." She motioned toward the wall with her chin. "What do you think? Time for a change? These prints have been here as long as I have. Longer. And I've never paid much attention to them."

Wren glanced at an unexceptional seascape—Vincent would have said there was nothing observed in it—and shrugged.

Kit said, "They're not very inspirational, are they? Nothing inviting or soul-enlarging about them. Just decor. We can do better, don't you think? How about if I put you in charge of picking new work? Maybe from your friend Vincent?"

"Sure, I'd love to." She could look again at his notes about which paintings belonged together for complementary and contrasting colors and then group them together according to his directions to Theo. She would definitely choose several of his olive groves. And the reapers and sowers and wheat fields were visual parables.

Kit scanned the hallway. "Come to think of it, what we need is a larger vision for how to incorporate art into this whole space. Not just the hallway here but throughout the building. We could give an ongoing opportunity for prayer and contemplation in the larger space, something more than once a year during Holy Week. What do you think?"

"I think that would be amazing."

"Good. Let's talk about it later and dream about what the space could become." She squeezed Wren's shoulder. "See what you've stirred in me? I'm so glad you're here. Thank you."

No, Wren wanted to say, no, you don't understand. I'm the one who—

But Kit's compassionate smile stopped her mid-thought. She *did* understand. She understood it all.

"Thank you," Wren murmured, and returned to her dusting.

"It's called *visio divina*," Kit said as they ate peanut butter sandwiches in the lounge, "Latin for 'sacred seeing.' Like *lectio divina*— slow, prayerful reading and meditation on Scripture—but with art."

Wren brushed crumbs into a napkin. "Like when you saw the wildflowers in the olive grove and thought about Jesus sweating blood in the garden."

"Exactly. It's about how art opens us to prayerful contemplation as we notice details that stir us, something that comforts or agitates us. It might be the gaze of a figure in the painting or the expression of light or color or texture or form—anything that catches our attention and leads us to pondering, any detail that invites us to encounter God."

Wren had been doing that for years with art. She just didn't know there was a Latin term for it. Even the discipline of choosing images for the life collage at Glenwood was a type of *visio divina*. Or could be, if someone was prayerful about the process.

"Have you ever done a life collage with photos?" Wren asked.

"Like a prayer collage?"

"Maybe." She hadn't heard it called that before. "It's where you have a lot of different clipped photos or words from magazines, and you see which ones speak to you, and then you glue the images onto cardboard or paper."

Kit said, "I sometimes offer that as an exercise at prayer retreats. In fact, I've got file folders filled with hundreds of images, all categorized by theme. I set out lots of pictures on tables, scramble them up, and ask people to pray and see which images attract and repel them. In fact—thank you very much again—maybe I'll bring out those folders for the retreat this weekend. And buy fresh glue sticks." She reached for her phone. "Better send myself a note or I'll forget."

Wren watched her type. "We did that exercise at Glenwood. The social worker had us choose images from a table, then assemble them together and see if a theme emerged." She hadn't had the energy to think about it in much depth then. "Maybe I should try it again."

"We could do it together if you like. A quiet evening at home."

"Sure. That sounds good. Thank you."

Kit set her phone aside. "It always strikes me, the process of trimming away the excess so the collage fits together. Somehow the things we trim away are just as revealing and important as the things we keep."

Wren stared at her. Another metaphor to chew on. All that had been removed, everything that seemed to be missing from her current life collage . . . that was something to ponder. The difference was, she hadn't made most of the decisions about what had been trimmed and discarded. Someone else held the scissors. That was her ongoing grief. And as for what remained, most of it seemed a chaotic jumble, not organized around any particular theme. Except loss. That was ironic, how the images that remained revealed what had been lost. Dawn would probably encourage her to reflect on that.

Her phone rang in her pocket—unusual these days for her phone to ring at all, apart from her mother or Hannah—and she pulled it out to find a number she didn't recognize.

"Feel free to take that," Kit said.

"No, it's okay." Wren put it back in her pocket and took another bite of her sandwich. "You were saying . . . about keeping images or trimming them away."

Kit nodded. "It's a process, isn't it? Knowing which is which. But if we're prayerful about it, we might be surprised what we see." She paused. "I often think about how Jesus painted with word pictures, or how the prophets saw visions of dry bones or almond branches or rivers of life. I think God uses images to reach us in ways we don't expect. You and I, we've both experienced that, how art has a way of sneaking past our defenses, getting right around all we think we already know or understand, and penetrating the soul in ways we might not grasp. Not at first, anyway. Like you being moved to tears in front of an olive grove."

Or in front of a painting of Jesus hanging on a cross.

Come to think of it, even before she fell in love with paintings by Vincent or Monet or Renoir or any of the other masters inhabiting Gran's studio, the stained-glass windows in her childhood church spoke to her, not only the images of Jesus tending sheep or calling the disciples or calming the storm or blessing children on his lap, but also the way the sunlight streamed through the glass and cast prisms of color on the polished wood floors, the slivers of light dancing and shifting during worship. The beauty moved her, sometimes to tears. Her mother would wrap her arm around her and draw her close and never demand to know why she was crying or tell her to stop. She knew. She understood.

In her memory Wren surveyed the sanctuary, the life story of Jesus from his birth to his resurrection unfolding before her. But—she had never thought of this before—there were no depictions of him on the cross, no stained-glass panels showing his suffering or his death. Only the resurrected Jesus aglow in white, his hands extended to bless the circle of disciples gathered together as he rose and returned to heaven. She had cried at that panel too, at the sadness of saying goodbye to a beloved friend and not knowing when they would see him again. If she entered that story with her imagination, she wasn't sure she could let Jesus go like that, not without many tears.

"You look like you're deep in thought," Kit said.

She wasn't going to cry now, thinking about goodbyes and departed friends. "I was just thinking about how our church in Australia had these beautiful stained-glass windows showing the life of Jesus, but nothing about the cross. Well, an empty one draped in lilies at the front of the sanctuary, but nothing with Jesus on it. Like it's not necessary to focus on that, as if it's not a significant part of the story because there's a happy ending."

"That's been my experience too," Kit said. "It wasn't until I saw the stations of the cross at the hospital years ago—not a Catholic hospital, either, where I might have expected them—that I first realized how much I was missing in my life with God by not meditating on Christ's sufferings. A whole new way of intimacy and communion opened for me. And would I have discovered it if I hadn't been so ill? Maybe God in his providence would have led me to it in a different way. But I'm so grateful I encountered the cross when I did."

Wren's phone buzzed with a text. "Sorry, I should have turned it off." She pulled it from her pocket again. But just before hitting the power button, she glanced at the screen, a surge of adrenaline rushing through her as she read three words.

Wrinkle it's me

Their connection—it was still there! She had just thought of him, of all that had been trimmed away in her life, of all the losses she hadn't chosen and couldn't control, and at that very moment her phone had rung. At that exact moment! Maybe the Spirit had prompted him to call. A way of saying, *You're not forgotten. See?*

She quickly excused herself from the table and hurried down the hallway to her studio. He had obviously changed his number to a Nevada number and wanted her to know. That meant the door to communication wasn't closed. He hadn't disconnected his phone without telling her. He hadn't cut off contact forever. Maybe Brooke was feeling less threatened by his old friendships.

She leaned against the wall and stared at the screen again.

Oh! She had so much to tell him. But she wouldn't bombard him with all her sorrow and struggles first. She would want to hear about his life, how he was enjoying marriage and whether he had managed to find more freelance editing work as he'd hoped. Maybe he had even found a job working for the same nonprofit Brooke worked for, a small company that helped to facilitate micro-loans in impoverished communities around the world. Totally millennial, he had joked, with its employee play days and free yoga classes and massages.

Her hand trembled as she typed her reply. *Hey! How are you?*

Immediately, the words appeared on her screen. *Call me*

It was almost like getting him back from the dead.

She pressed the new number. "I'm in town," Casey said before he even said hi. "When can I see you?"

Wren lowered herself onto her painting stool. "You're here?"

"Yeah. Where are you? At work?"

"Yes."

"I'll come by. Have you had lunch?"

Only a few bites of her sandwich. "No, not yet."

"Okay, I'll meet you in about fifteen."

"Okay, sure." But it was only after he ended the call that she realized he would be heading to their old meeting place near Bethel House. It was too long a story to narrate over the phone. She wanted to tell him in person—in person! Casey was in town and wanted to see her! She could hardly believe it. She typed, *New job. Meet me outside New Hope Retreat Center,* and pressed Send.

Inside the lobby Wren fiddled with her coat zipper while scanning the parking lot entrances for the first sight of him. It had been nine months since he'd packed up his apartment, loaded his pick-up truck with boxes, and hugged her goodbye. She had stood on the front steps, her blurry gaze fixed on his waving hand as he turned the corner and disappeared with a final honk of his horn.

She should have asked if Brooke was in Kingsbury with him, but it had all happened so fast.

A silver sedan pulled into the lot. The closer it came, the faster her heart raced. Yes, it was Casey. She glimpsed him through the windshield, alone in the front seat. She stepped back out of view so she could assess him more fully before he saw her. The car stopped. He got out. Long dark trench coat, skinny jeans, boots. Red hair pulled back in a man bun, beard unkempt.

Her stomach churned. It was Dark Casey. Maybe her intuition at Thanksgiving hadn't been off after all.

She rubbed her hands together to warm them, then exited the building. "Hey, you!"

"Hey." He stooped to embrace her in a rocking hug as he always had, her head only coming up to his chest. A gentle giant and a little bird, that's who they had always been. He pulled away first. "Get in," he said, opening the car door. "It's freezing."

Wren stared at his left hand, where there was no ring. He saw her staring and smiled wryly. "Yeah," he said. "Lots to tell you."

The more he said on the drive to the restaurant, the more her heart sank. He couldn't handle Brooke's nagging and insecurity. He couldn't handle her expectations and desire for control. "Yeah, okay, so I slipped back into some online stuff, but the way she lost it when she found out, it was scary. You think I'm scary when I'm angry? You should've seen her throwing things and shrieking. I thought for sure the neighbors would call the police. Maybe I should have. You would've been proud of me, though. Never raised my voice at her, just made sure I kept ducking. Then, when she finally wore herself out, I threw some clothes in a box and drove fifteen-hour days to get here. Got to my parents' place a little while ago. But you know how they are. I can't stay there, not with them lecturing me about what I need to do. So, can I crash at your place a few days until I figure things out?"

"I don't have a place anymore," she murmured.

"What do you mean?"

So she told him everything about Glenwood and Theo and Kit and Bethel House. And when she finished telling him everything, he cursed and said, "Guess we're both a total mess."

She bit her lip and did not reply.

He would figure it out, he said between mouthfuls of greasy cheese-covered fries. A group of guys from the documentary film project had a house downtown. He figured the universe owed him; he'd let people crash with him plenty of times.

She stirred her soup. An hour together already, and he hadn't once said, "I'm so sorry to hear what you've been through," hadn't once asked, "How are you doing now?" That's how it was when he wasn't well: it was all about him. Depression could do that to people. It did it to her too; she would never throw stones. Over the years they had occasionally been depressed at the same time, and it wasn't pretty. Amazing that their friendship had survived. But when Casey was well, there wasn't a more compassionate person on the planet. She wondered if Brooke had ever seen that side of him. Or maybe she had fallen in love with the carefree, adventurous Casey, the one with a quick wit who could brighten a room with his smile. Dark Casey, though, was a challenge. And when he spiraled into depression or entered a manic phase, his anger and addictions could be brutal. Wren still bore the scars of words thoughtlessly spoken. He wouldn't remember most of them. She wished she didn't, either.

She checked her watch. "I should get back."

"I thought you said you're just working as a maid."

She pushed her bowl of soup away. "I am. But I still have work I need to do."

"Well, I'm not done yet. Not gonna waste perfectly good food."

They could argue about what constituted good food, or she could stay quiet and let him finish. She stayed quiet. All these weeks, building him up in her mind as a shoulder to cry on, a support in darkness, a companion in suffering, and now that he was across the table from her, she wanted to bolt. Maybe she hadn't been sincere after all when she texted at Thanksgiving to see if he was okay. Maybe that had also been about her, about wanting him to know she wasn't all right. Maybe she had only wanted to garner sympathy, even pity.

Depression could make a person very self-absorbed and self-deceived.

Sorry, she said silently. She wasn't well enough herself to buoy him up, that much she knew. There was that verse in Ecclesiastes about two being better than one. Because if one fell, the other could help him up. But woe to the one who was alone and fell. Because then who would help him up? And what about when both had fallen? Then what good were they to each other?

Casey would need others to help him up. A counselor, to start with. She would remind him of that as soon as it was appropriate. His medications too. He needed to stay on them faithfully.

But if he was angry at Brooke for being a nag, she wasn't going to risk him getting angry at her too. Let his parents say the hard things for now. When it came to Casey and his illness, they had said and done plenty of hard things over the years. One thing they could never be accused of was being codependent in their relationship with him.

That's what Brooke had accused her of, being codependent with Casey. Maybe she was right.

But this new crisis could provide an opportunity to do things differently in their friendship, to love one another without taking on responsibility for the other. That seemed healthy. Dawn would affirm her in that. Casey would benefit from the same resources she was pursuing in recovery—counseling, work that didn't overwhelm him but kept him engaged, a hobby that could motivate and give life. Like his photography or filming. Not prayer or church, though. Dark Casey always scoffed at faith, and, given her own struggles to persevere in hope, she didn't have the strength to listen to or defend herself against his beleaguering doubts about the trustworthiness or goodness of God.

She stared at her empty soup bowl.

She would do everything she could to support him through this current episode, without becoming codependent. She would try to be as faithful and nonjudgmental a friend as she could possibly be, which might not be much right now, but it was something.

"Okay, fine," he said. "If you're just gonna sit there, we'll go." He pushed his chair back and swore again. "Where's the server?"

"I'll get him." She could at least spare the young man a verbal tirade. She got up from the table, went to the counter, and put the total with a large tip on her credit card. Casey brushed past her and strode to the car. She returned to the table to retrieve her coat. "Thank you," she called to the server, then hurried out into the cold.

25

Casey didn't ask for her new address when he dropped her off at New Hope, and she didn't offer it. Who knew when he might show up on a doorstep, pounding to be let in? When she lived in her apartment, he had sometimes shown up in the middle of the night, desperate and despairing, afraid to be alone. It hadn't happened often, only a few times over the past five or six years. But Kit didn't need to be frightened out of a sound sleep.

She watched him drive out of the parking lot, his car swerving on a patch of snow as he took a turn too quickly. That's how he had totaled his pickup a few months ago, he'd said, by driving too fast on a narrow, winding road.

"How was your visit?" Kit asked when Wren entered the lobby.

"Good." She didn't have energy to recount the long version of the story. It had been enough to say an old friend had returned unexpectedly to town and had surprised her with a phone call. "Sorry it took longer than I expected."

"No worries. The bathrooms look good. That's the main thing people tend to notice when they come. As far as cleaning goes, anyway. Thanks for doing those."

"Sure."

Kit resumed her conversation with the part-time receptionist, who had come in specially to help her prepare for the retreat. Wren could have made the registration spreadsheet and name tags for the guests. It wouldn't have been too taxing. But maybe Gayle needed the money. She suspected Kit hired people others might not, people who, for whatever reason, couldn't manage the rigors of a stressful job environment. Like a great-niece who, Casey had reminded her, was a "total mess."

A charity case, Wren thought as she headed to her studio. How humbling to be in a position of needing charity.

In fact, that was likely what broke Vincent in the end: his despair over never being able to support himself as an artist, his worries over Theo's financial stress, and his unwillingness to continue to be a burden, especially when Theo had a wife and baby to care for, a little son who had been unwell. All those years relying on Theo to send money and paints and canvases and other supplies took a toll.

It is better to give than receive, the Bible said.

Easier too, Wren thought as she closed her studio door behind her.

Paint your feelings, Gran's voice said. What color is shame? What color is worry? What color is disappointment with a friend? What about with yourself?

Wren opened her box of paints and mixed her palette with brown and gray.

What was Casey going to do? her mother asked on the phone that night. He wasn't just going to abandon his marriage, was he?

Wren said she didn't know. But it didn't sound as if he had any plans to return to Reno. Brooke was unstable, he said. And it didn't work to have two unstable people living together. It wasn't safe. Not for anyone.

There was a long pause, and then her mother said, "Be careful, Wren. Please."

Wren opened Kit's fridge to pour herself a glass of milk. "I know. I will."

"I mean, about everything. Not just about trying to take care of him while you're still working to recover, but about not getting in the middle of him trying to figure things out with his wife. That's not a safe place to be."

Her face flushed. She didn't like the subtext. "There's nothing inappropriate between us. There never has been, never will be."

"I know, love. I'm just saying, be careful, especially when he's in such a vulnerable place. When you both are."

Wren shoved the milk carton back into the fridge. She didn't need a lecture. She also didn't need to be accused of things she had never done. Or warned about things she would never do. "I need to go."

"Wren—"

"I've got to go. I'll call you later." But she had only just set down her phone when it rang again. She sighed and picked it up to look. It wasn't her mother. "Hey," she said.

"Hey," Casey said. "My mom is driving me nuts."

Join the club, she almost said.

"Can I come over?" he asked.

She checked the clock on the wall. Kit would be at New Hope for another couple of hours, leading the retreat. "How about if I meet you somewhere?"

"You don't want me to see where you live?"

"What? Of course not."

"Of course you don't?"

"No—I mean, of course that's not it."

"So, what's the address?"

It tumbled out of her mouth before she could reconsider.

"Be there in twenty minutes," he said.

And she said, "Okay."

She ended the call and flung her phone onto the sofa. What was wrong with her? Hadn't she already decided it wasn't wise for him to know where Kit lived? But now if she called him back with a change of plans, he would sulk or get angry. Or do something stupid. She couldn't risk that.

She changed out of her pajamas into jeans and a hoodie. She could lie, and it wouldn't hurt anything. She could meet him on the porch, already wearing her coat, and say Kit had just gotten home and was tired and it would be better if they went out for coffee. But he might say, I'd like to meet her, and then what would she do? Lie again and say she was already in bed.

Or she could meet him at the door, already wearing her coat, and say, I'm tired of being at the house. Let's go for coffee. And he might say, Okay, whatever. But it still wouldn't solve the problem of him knowing the address and being able to show up any time of day or night.

Like Vincent with Theo. Vincent had grown tired of living in Belgium. He was sick and hungry, and he showed up unexpectedly at Theo's apartment in Paris four months earlier than they'd planned. After a year of living together, Theo complained to one of their sisters. No one came to visit anymore because Vincent was so filthy and argumentative. It was like living with two different people, Theo said: the compassionate, sensitive, gentle, talented brother he loved and the churlish, selfish, slovenly, unfeeling man who seemed more like a stranger. Even before his seizures began, Vincent was difficult. Bipolar, maybe. That kind of diagnosis might have made sense of his erratic behavior. Theo hoped he would leave but couldn't bear to throw him out.

She wondered how long it would be before Casey's parents threw him out. If he wasn't returning to Reno, he would quickly need to find a place to live. He probably wouldn't be averse to showing up at a place like Crossroads. He had gone there before when his parents threw him out. And then, once he got stabilized on his meds again, he worked multiple freelance jobs and signed short-term leases on apartments and paid his bills on time. And sometimes he took spur-of-the-moment trips, like flying across the world to walk an ancient pilgrim path and sleeping out under the stars when he didn't feel like staying in hostels. Brooke might have thought it was romantic, sleeping under the stars with him. She probably hadn't had any inkling of the darkness that lurked beneath the smile, waiting to be awakened. If Casey had mentioned it at all, he probably hadn't given her details. When he was well, he assumed he would always be well. When he was well, he decided he didn't need the medications that helped him remain well. And then he spiraled. It was a vicious cycle.

Wren put on her boots and coat and watched for headlights from behind the blinds. As soon as she saw the sedan slow in front of the neighbor's condo, she locked the door behind her and met him in the driveway. "I'm tired of being at the house," she said before he could ask for an explanation. "How about The Beanery?"

"Okay, whatever."

She knew him so well. "So, what's your mom doing?" She latched her seatbelt and folded her hands in her lap.

"Being a nag, telling me it's my responsibility to go back and try to work things out. Same old, same old." He modulated his voice to mimic her. "'You're the one who decided to get married so soon, you made promises you need to keep, you made your bed so now sleep in it,' and on and on. I swear, if she keeps it up, I'll go full-bore Brooke on her and start throwing things."

"Don't, Casey."

"Don't what?"

"Don't joke about that."

"It's not a joke. I'm saying I'll snap if I have to stay there."

"What about the guys from the film project? Did you call them?"

"They don't even have a spare couch right now. And they weren't cool about me sleeping on the floor, not even for a night." He tapped his dashboard. "So if I need to, I'll sleep in the car."

"Not in this weather, you won't. You'll freeze."

"You're such a mom."

"Well, don't be ridiculous. You're not sleeping outside." Too bad Hannah's rooms were occupied by the visiting missionary family. She would have asked if he could stay there. Then again, Hannah probably didn't need Casey's brand of chaos in her personal space, especially a place designed to be a refuge for the weary and burned-out.

She eyed his hair—when had he last washed it?—and scraggly beard.

A large, shaggy dog. That's how Vincent described the way his parents viewed him when he showed up on their doorstep, needing a place to stay. A shaggy dog with wet paws who barked loudly and might bite.

But he was a dog with feelings, he told Theo, a dog with a human history and human soul who knew what people thought of him and felt it all so deeply. That letter, along with many of his others, had always made her cry.

Poor shaggy dog.

She mentally sketched Casey's profile, the lines of sorrow beneath the resentment, the fear beneath the bravado. Yes, he might bite. But she had always had a heart for strays.

When Wren entered shortly after midnight, Kit was seated at the kitchen table, her Bible open, her Christ candle flickering. "I was worried when I got home and you weren't here," she said. "And then I realized all my phone calls and texts were ringing inside the house."

"I'm so sorry!" She had completely forgotten about the phone she'd flung onto the couch.

"I know you're not a teenager, but next time, as a simple courtesy, please leave me a note." Kit rose and blew out the candle. "Your mother called several times, also worried. I had to tell her I didn't know where you were."

The disappointed expression on Kit's face and the pinch in her voice were things Wren had never experienced from her. She felt as if she was going to throw up.

Kit closed her Bible and tucked it under her arm. "I have an early start for the retreat tomorrow. I'll leave it with you to call your mother and let her know you're okay."

Wren nodded and murmured "goodnight" to her back. If she replied, Wren didn't hear her.

She stared at the candle, the wisp of smoke still rising and curling above the wick. She could follow her down the hall to her bedroom, apologize for being inconsiderate, ask for her forgiveness, and work to mend what was broken. So why were her feet anchored in place?

And her mother. She couldn't bear the thought of enduring her reproach either, whether verbally or through silence. She would send a text. That would have to be enough for now. She typed, *I'm at Kit's and I'm fine,* and pressed Send.

Several long minutes passed before the words appeared: *Thank you.* There was nothing more.

No apology, no acknowledgment of any stress she had caused, nothing. Jamie lay back in bed and stared at the ceiling. "Let it go for now," Dylan said as he turned off the light. "You can work it out with her in the morning."

How could she let it go?

It was one thing to expect nothing from Wren the day she disappeared on the walk, when she was catatonic with grief and unable to respond to anyone around her. Kit was right to counsel not confronting or chastising her then. It would have done no good.

But what about now, when she'd seemed relatively stable for a few weeks, able to get out of bed and go to work and carry on coherent conversations and find life in her art again? Was it still prudent not to confront?

Even Kit, who was usually so calm and levelheaded and gracious, even she hadn't disguised her anxiety or frustration on the phone. She was already poured out after leading an evening retreat group, and she had a full retreat day planned for tomorrow. She was tired. And when she was tired, she said, her mind went in a million unhelpful directions. Jamie had apologized profusely. Even though Kit had told her it wasn't her responsibility to apologize, it was her daughter causing the stress, and she was sorry for that.

How was it possible for Wren to be so intuitive and sensitive while also being so selfish and inconsiderate? Where was the line between accommodating her illness and naming sin? And how did they overlap or intertwine?

And how well was she? Could she manage a declaration of truth about how she had impacted others? Was she well enough to bear that responsibility without being crushed by guilt and shame? Where was the edge of the cliff, and how close was she?

Over and over again Jamie asked herself the same questions without ever finding answers. So, what was the point asking?

Wren might never understand the terror Jamie felt after not being able to reach her, knowing she had upset her by offering a warning about Casey. She had lost three hours of her life, frantically worrying and chiding herself for saying too much, for going too far. She had lost three hours of her life. And someone might say, "It was your choice to ruminate and worry. It was your choice not to spend the time more fruitfully." True. She could have made different choices about where to turn. That was easy to see in hindsight and hard to practice in the midst of fear.

Dylan adjusted his side of the blanket. "Jamie, you've got to let it go." She closed her eyes. Easy for him to say. He wasn't her mother.

The longer Wren thought about it, the more irritated she became. She'd told Kit she was sorry. What more did she need? Assurance it wouldn't happen again? Kit was right: she wasn't a teenager. She certainly didn't need a curfew. And if Kit thought she needed one, then this living arrangement would be even more short-term than she'd initially planned.

She brushed her teeth vigorously and spit with force into the sink.

She'd been forgetful, not malicious. Maybe she should have known Kit and her mother would be worried. But she hadn't planned to be out that long with Casey, and when their conversation stretched on—a conversation she was grateful to have with a wounded friend, no matter what her mother might presume—she wasn't thinking of anything other than being fully present and giving him every ounce of energy and attention, exhausting as it was. If there wasn't grace for being forgetful, if there wasn't mutual understanding about offering incarnational presence to a companion in misery, then maybe she needed to take to heart Casey's suggestion after all, that the two of them find a couple of housemates and move into one of the artist communities on the west side of town.

Especially if Kit and her mother were going to make a habit of disregarding boundaries by discussing her whereabouts or monitoring her wellness.

She changed her clothes in the dark, then crawled into bed and texted him: *Let's go look at houses.*

The screen immediately buzzed: *You're the best Wrinkle. Thanks.*

26

Kit was already gone when Wren shuffled downstairs Saturday morning. Good. She would be away all day at New Hope, and by the time she got home for dinner, Wren would be there. Or maybe not. Maybe she would leave a note to say she had plans for the evening and wouldn't be back until late. Casey had already texted links to several houses he thought looked promising and was waiting to hear back from landlords. He would pick her up by nine, and they could have breakfast together and brainstorm about people who might make good housemates. Already, he sounded less like Dark Casey and more like Adventurous Casey. She was grateful for that.

She made herself a cup of coffee. She had often witnessed it at Bethel House, how women, after they first escaped abusers, blamed themselves and felt guilty for leaving. If they had scars or bruises, it was sometimes easier to convince them they were right to escape. But when the abuse was psychological or emotional, it was harder to name. Once they became more aware of the common patterns and were able to identify the twisted methods of control and manipulation and name them as evil, many of them began to flourish and grow in self-confidence and courage.

All the victims she had worked with had been women. But everything Casey had described at the coffee shop the night before—the constant monitoring, the cutting off of his old friendships, the verbal berating, the angry outbursts, the physical assaults of striking him or throwing objects—all of it fit the profile of an abuser. Even his "Everything's fine" text at Thanksgiving was consistent with abuse.

When Wren asked him about it, he'd shrugged and said, "I didn't want you to worry, and I was afraid she would find out I was in touch with you." On top of that he felt ashamed, he said, ashamed for making such an awful decision to marry her and ashamed for being weak and not standing up to her. So yes, the stress of it all had driven him back to his longtime addictions to alcohol and pornography, but now that he was free of her, he had every expectation of being well again. *Thanks to you, Wrinkle. Thanks for never giving up on me.*

"So, what do you think?" he asked when she got into his car an hour later. He rubbed his trimmed beard. His hair, still pulled into a man bun, didn't have the oily sheen of twenty-four hours ago. "I'm going for 'artist,' not 'homeless and unemployed.'"

She smiled. "I think you nailed it."

"Well, you'll pull up our respectability factor." He tucked a loose strand of her hair behind her ear. "You look nice."

"Thanks." She smoothed her pleated skirt. "I'm going for the I'm-on-sabbatical-from-a-real-job-while-I-work-at-my-art look."

"Crushing it," he said.

It was just like old times, the two of them talking in the car, Casey tapping on the steering wheel to the beat of his playlist songs while she listened attentively and gave input when he asked for it. There wasn't much she could offer in terms of ideas for potential house-mates. Most of her friends—former friends? acquaintances?—were married or getting married. The others already had roommates or were living in studio apartments or with their parents. She couldn't picture anyone in her contact list jumping at the opportunity to live in a fixer-upper on Kingsbury's west side.

But the more she thought about it, the more perfect it seemed. Why not pool limited resources and share life in common? Why not surround herself with other artists who could inspire and encourage creativity? That's what Vincent had hoped for when he envisioned creating an artists' community in the south of France. He asked Gauguin to be the leader, the abbot. Theo finally persuaded—bribed, more accurately—Gauguin to move into the Yellow House with Vincent. But it didn't go well.

She wasn't going to dwell on that part of the story. She and Casey had enough history together to know one another's idiosyncrasies and weaknesses. Though they had never roomed together—neither one of them had ever had more than a one-bedroom apartment— they could learn how to be respectful of each other's need for privacy. She would need her own room. That was non-negotiable. He would need to keep the common areas tidy and not expect her to clean up after him. With the other residents they could mutually negotiate house rules and responsibilities and have regular meetings to talk frankly about how it was going. Even if it was only for a year or so while they regrouped and transitioned toward next things, it could be a rich and fruitful time.

If he would make the commitment to take his medications and address his addictions. She would need to have a firm conversation with him about that.

Her phone rang—her mother again. She should have texted her before she left Kit's house. But she hadn't wanted to talk about what happened last night. She didn't want to hear the anxiety or sorrow or disappointment in her mother's voice. And she didn't want to be grilled again about Casey or his plans.

Our plans, she thought. If her mother had freaked out about her quitting her job suddenly, she would be beside herself over this. Wren could hear her now: "But he's a married man! What are you thinking?" And they could argue about whether that was anything other than a technicality at this point.

Casey had escaped an abusive marriage. That was the bottom line. And he would be moving forward with a divorce. In the meantime, he needed a place to live, and it wasn't unreasonable that he should first go to his oldest and closest friend to see if she was interested in sharing rent.

The logic of his request wouldn't matter. Her mother would still regard a man and woman living together, even in separate rooms, as inappropriate. She was old-fashioned that way, probably because of her own past.

Wren turned off her phone and shoved it into her purse.

"Your mom?" Casey asked.

"Yeah."

"Did you tell her we're looking at houses?"

"No." She was a grown woman, and she could make her own decisions without feeling guilty. If they found a house and room-mates to share it, then she could make her announcement. But until then it served no good purpose. "No promises about any of this, okay, Casey? If it doesn't seem like the right situation, for whatever reason, then don't be mad at me for saying no. We both need to figure out what's best. Without pressure."

"I know, but wait until you see the one on Holly Street. I think you're gonna love it."

She *did* love it: the hardwood floors, the arched doorways, the cozy reading nooks, the tiled fireplace, the tall windows. She loved everything about it, except for the rent. "But split four ways," Casey said after they told the landlord they would think about it and call him. "Or even five or six ways. I could share a room. A couple of those bedrooms are big enough to share."

Yes, but who would they find to share the rooms? And did she really want to share a house with five other people, especially people she didn't know? Maybe the whole thing was a really ill-conceived plan.

"Leave it to me," he said. "I'll find the people. But I think we should snatch it up while we can. I've got a bit of savings I can throw at a deposit. What about you?"

"I've got nothing. It's all going to health insurance right now."

"That's ridiculous. Total waste of money."

Typical Casey, she thought, blithely playing roulette. But if she needed to be hospitalized again, then what? Or what if there was another medical emergency? No. She needed insurance. Her mom had already helped her find the cheapest available option that covered her needs, and even then, as a single woman without a full-time job, she could barely make ends meet. She was stuck. Indefinitely. She knew people who raved about healthcare sharing ministries, but those didn't usually help with prescriptions and counseling appointments. And that's what she needed: help with mental health expenses because she was "mentally ill."

Her eyes welled with tears.

"Oh, Wrinkle," he said, enfolding her in a bear hug. "It'll be okay. You'll see."

As she and Casey wound through other neighborhoods on the west side, Vincent's sketch *Sorrow* came to mind, a portrait of a naked, pregnant woman seated on a rock, head bent to her knees, breasts sagging, profile hidden by her clasped arms. His model was Sien, the pregnant prostitute he had found wandering the streets with her little daughter one day. Moved by compassion, he decided to care for her so she wouldn't be destitute. Because, he told Theo, what man worth anything would abandon such a woman to the streets? Didn't God's law of love command something more?

His family didn't approve.

Wren looked up at a house with torn sheets in the grimy windows and a sagging balcony that looked as if it would collapse if anyone stepped onto it. None of the more affordable properties they'd viewed after the Holly Street house bore any resemblance to photos posted online, and they weren't in the sort of neighborhood she would feel safe walking around at night.

But this was exactly the sort of community where people like Jake and Erica planted themselves as an incarnational presence. This was the sort of neighborhood they ran toward, not away from. "We filmed somewhere around here for the documentary," Casey said as he stared through the windshield. "I remember they had this story about this girl, thirteen. Her mom had been pimping her out for months—"

Wren held up her hand. "Sorry. I can't."

"No, it's got a good ending, Wrinkle. Promise."

She grasped her knees.

"So, this girl, she's home alone one day when the doorbell rings. She answers it, and it's a Jehovah's Witness, and they start talking. I think maybe the girl had met the woman a few times before or something. Anyway, the girl ends up saying something to the woman that makes her suspicious. She makes a call, gets the police involved, and the girl's rescued, mom's sent to jail." He smiled at her. "See? Told you. Happy ending."

It was never that simple. The wounds from abuse and trauma didn't get healed overnight, if ever. The poor girl would face years of recovery, if they even managed to get her to a safe place where she could heal. That was never a given. Some of the vulnerable ones remained vulnerable to predators. But she wasn't going to say that to him. If the story had been a bright spot in his research on trafficking and gave him hope, then that was a good thing.

"Living in a neighborhood like this," he said, "we could do a lot of good, right? Isn't that what you always used to say, take the light into the dark?"

Yes. And shine. That's what she used to say. Before she got overwhelmed by all the helpless, stranded whales. Before she ended up stranded herself.

But if Casey was saying it . . .

If Casey was experiencing a nudge from the Spirit, and if living together in a place like this could help inspire him and fan the embers of his faith, would she not be willing to do everything possible to help him rediscover his passion and sense of purpose? She would give her life for that. She would. She wasn't being melodramatic thinking that. She would lay down her life for her friend, even if it meant upsetting her family. She was a grown woman. She needed to make her own way. And maybe this was part of God's rescue plan. For both of them.

The way Casey saw it, there were two possibilities. "Obviously, the Holly Street one is my favorite," he said as they drove back to Kit's house later that afternoon. "But if we can't get enough people to share it, we probably can't afford it. That last one on Green Street, that's doable with three or four people, don't you think?"

"With four people, yes." It was musty. It was cramped. She would never walk barefoot on the carpets. But yes, four people sharing the two bedrooms could afford it. With the right female roommate, she would be willing to let go of her desire for a private room. But they still didn't have any ideas about who to invite into the arrangement. And honestly, how many women would be willing to live in a place like that, in a neighborhood like that? When she thought of her own comfortable room at Kit's, it made no sense, giving that up for relative squalor.

Someone might call her crazy. She might call herself that. But Jesus sometimes called his followers to do crazy, sacrificial things for the sake of love.

And besides. The thought of living in community appealed to her. The thought of keeping a close eye on Casey appealed to her. It wasn't safe for him to be on his own. And strangers wouldn't know the warning signs to watch for. If they lived together, they could support each other. If one fell, the other could help him up. That's what companions in sorrow could do.

"I'll keep texting people to see if anyone's interested," he said. "And if anyone comes to mind from your circles, let me know."

She didn't have circles anymore. Maybe she never had.

He pulled into the driveway and turned off the ignition. "Okay if I come in and lie down for a while? I'm beat. And I don't want to go back to my parents' house. They'll just pick up where they left off, beating me up over my choices and grilling me about my plans." Before she could reply, he opened his car door. Wren stayed glued to the front seat. "What? You don't want me to come in?"

"No, it's not that." She mentally calculated how long it would be before Kit returned.

"What, then?"

"Nothing." She fiddled with her boot buckle.

"What is it with you and your aunt? Are you ashamed of me or something?"

"No, of course not. It's just—she's not home, and I don't know how she'd feel about someone she doesn't know sleeping in her house."

Casey scoffed. "You're kidding, right? It's a nap, I'm not moving in."

"No, I know." She opened her car door. "You're right." If Kit objected to her best friend taking a rest on the futon, then that might be one more indicator it was time to move.

She fumbled in her purse for her key. She had seen a copy of the retreat schedule. It would finish at five. And then Kit would need to put away supplies and lock everything up, and it would be at least six o'clock before she arrived home. Casey would be long gone by then. Kit would never even need to know.

On the front porch Wren stomped the snow from her boots and motioned for him to do the same. "And then take them off"—she opened the door—"and put them on the mat there."

"Yes, ma'am." He stooped to unlace them. "What is she? An older version of Brooke or something?"

"No. I just don't want to mess up her floors."

"Whatever." He exaggerated the motion of placing the boots on the mat, making sure each one was perfectly straight and parallel to the other. "Anything else I need to do to enter?"

"I'll hang up your coat," she said as he was about to fling it onto the back of a chair.

With a sigh and shake of his head, he handed it to her. "Where's your room?"

"Upst—"

He raised his eyebrows.

"But it's a mess," she said quickly. "There's a futon in the den. I'll show you."

"Man! What is it with you?" He followed her around the corner. "You're acting totally weird."

"No, I'm not."

"You are. You're acting completely bizarre. Chill out. It's not like I bite."

"No one said you—"

"Okay, stop. You can be such a mom, you know that?" He brushed past her through the doorway and plopped down onto the futon.

"I'll get you a blanket."

He yanked an afghan from the back of the futon and covered himself up. "Make sure you lock me in. Not safe to have me wandering around, right? Might mess something up? Freak someone out?"

"Stop."

"Just saying, you can never be too careful about welcoming a strange man into the house."

"Casey, please." Maybe it wasn't a good idea to leave him alone in the room. Whenever he became irritable like this, he could be unpredictable. She motioned for him to scoot over. There was room for two. If two lay down together, Ecclesiastes said, they could keep each other warm. She crawled in beside him, a shaggy dog and a little bird defending themselves against the cold.

27

Wren was sitting on the living room sofa, reading from a volume of Vincent's letters, when Kit entered just after six. "How was the retreat?"

She unwound her scarf and removed her gloves. "It went well, I think. The Spirit did beautiful work."

"That's good." Wren flipped a page and pretended to keep reading. It was ridiculous, the way her heart was racing as if she had narrowly averted a catastrophe. Like a teenager cleaning up the mess of a party before her parents came home.

But she wasn't a teenager. And there had been no mess to clean up. And nothing improper to conceal. So why did it all feel so furtive and deceitful?

After a long nap Casey, thankfully, had left without her needing to hurry him out the door. A well-timed text from a potential housemate had been an act of grace, keeping her from having to concoct an excuse for him to leave. "You go and meet with him," she'd said. "Then let me know what you think."

She yawned casually and set her book on the coffee table. "I wasn't sure what to fix for dinner."

Kit said, "There's not much here, I'm afraid. I'll need to get to a store tomorrow. I'm too tired tonight." She hung her coat in the closet. "In fact, if you'd be happy with eggs or cereal, I might just eat light and head to bed early. I'm feeling a bit poured out."

"Oh, okay, sure." Wren rose and went to the pantry to get some granola.

Kit followed her into the kitchen. "I'm sorry I went to bed last night without having a conversation with you, Wren. But I was tired and frustrated and didn't trust what might come out of my mouth."

Wren set the cereal box on the counter.

"When I didn't know where you were, I reacted out of my own fear and trauma, and I'm sorry. Please forgive me."

"I'm sorry too. I should have left a note. It won't happen again." Especially since she probably wouldn't be living under Kit's roof much longer.

"I'm glad you're doing well," Kit said, "that you have friends who are important to you and that you're going out to socialize. All of that is a good sign, a sign of healing." She kissed Wren's cheek. "I love you, and I'm glad you're here."

A lump rose in her throat. "Thank you," Wren said. She didn't trust herself to say anything more.

In the middle of the night she was awakened with her heart pounding out of her chest. A nightmare, she thought. But no, it wasn't a nightmare. It was real. A rush of adrenaline flooded her. Within minutes her T-shirt was drenched in sweat, her breathing shallow and ragged. She was having a heart attack. She knew it. This time was different.

She tried to cry out but couldn't find her voice. She was going to die alone. *Help!* But it was only a shaking whisper. *Help me!* She rolled over in bed and tucked her knees to her chest, trying to slow her pulse. But every attempt for breath was a shallow gasp. Her chest was tight. She couldn't swallow. She was going to die. She curled her fingers into a fist but couldn't feel her hand. *Jesus!* She couldn't breathe. She was hovering outside her body. *Bye, bye, little bird.* She clawed at the wall, trying to sit up, and knocked a lamp onto the floor.

God, help me.

No air. Nothing solid. Only darkness and the sound of blood rushing in her ears.

And then, bright light and a voice saying, "I'm here." Suddenly, she was swept up into an embrace. Someone pushed her hair away from her forehead. She was held. She would not die alone.

"I've got you. I'm here."

But just when she felt her mind and body reconnecting, another wave of panic crested, her heart revving up again until she was sure it would explode.

"I've got you, ride it out, you're doing great. Ride it out."

She clung to Kit's nightgown.

"Here, look at this, Wren. See this button here? What color is it, can you tell?"

She tried to focus on what Kit was pointing to. But she was spinning, floating.

"You can touch the button, see?" Kit gently moved her quivering hand. "Can you feel it there? It's smooth, isn't it? Smooth like a pebble. That's it. Fix your eyes right there. Can you tell what shape it is?"

A heart. It looked like a heart. She tried to murmur the word but couldn't find the breath for "h."

"You're so brave. You're doing great."

Wren fixed her eyes on the button and tried to hold on.

She'd had them too, Kit said after the last wave finally subsided. "They're awful." She stroked Wren's forehead with a slow and steady motion, almost as if she was making the sign of the cross over and over again. "How about if I bring you a glass of water? Or would you like herbal tea?"

Wren shook her head slightly, her hand still clutching Kit's nightgown. She didn't want to be left alone even long enough for Kit to go to the kitchen.

"How about if I read Scripture to you, then? Maybe some Psalms?"

She nodded. The sound of Kit's voice soothed her. She closed her eyes and listened as the words washed gently over her.

A prayer of one afflicted, when faint and pleading before the Lord: Hear my prayer, O LORD; let my cry come to you. Do not hide your face from me in the day of my distress. Incline your ear to me; answer me speedily in the day when I call. For my days pass away like smoke, and my bones burn like a furnace. My heart is stricken and withered like grass; I am too wasted to eat my bread. Because of my loud groaning my bones cling to my skin. I am like an owl of the wilderness, like a little owl of the waste places. I lie awake; I am like a lonely bird on the housetop.

Wren opened her eyes. She had never heard those verses before. But there was her heart, described by a poet worshiper long ago. She was like a little owl hooting forlornly in the wilderness, like a lonely bird scanning for companions. Her heart was stricken and weary, she was exhausted by her groaning, she felt withered like grass. The psalmist knew. So did Kit. Companions in sorrow, in suffering and distress. Throughout the centuries, the millennia, so many companions. Wren grasped Kit's hand while she continued reading her heart. Then, exhausted and quieted, she drifted off to sleep.

In the beaming morning sunlight, particles of dust floated above her head, strangely mesmerizing. Wren watched them swirl and dance on the current of her breath.

She could breathe. She could fill her lungs with rich, deep breaths. Glorious gift. She inhaled slowly, then exhaled.

From the kitchen rose the genial clatter of pots and pans. Kit was awake and cooking breakfast.

Poor Kit, jolted from sleep in the middle of the night. It was a wonder she had been able to be so calm and so present, especially when she already felt exhausted after leading the retreat.

Wren felt a pang of guilt and shame. One more thing to apologize for.

"Don't be silly," Kit said when Wren joined her downstairs. "I know what it feels like, waking up with a panic attack."

"But I'm really sorry. That's two nights in a row when you've been up late because of me."

Kit cracked an egg into a bowl and smiled. "I don't mind. It's nice having someone in the house again."

Another pang of guilt, this one even sharper.

She hadn't considered the possibility of Kit being anything other than a generous benefactor in their living arrangement. But if she was enjoying the companionship of sharing her house, that complicated departure plans.

"Don't tell me you're backing out," Casey said when she called him after breakfast.

"No, not backing out. Just still trying to discern what's best, what I can manage. Maybe the panic attack was a sign, like I'm not ready to make a change right now. Not that I won't ever be ready, but maybe this is all too quick."

"Well, I need to move ahead. And fast. If you're not with me, I'm not sure who else I can find. So, it kinda screws me over."

Wren sat down on the edge of her bed, a sick feeling rising from the pit of her stomach.

"But hey, don't you worry about it. I'll figure it out." It was the voice of Dark Casey, Cynical Casey.

Before she could reply, he was gone.

Wren had intended to skip church. But the longer she thought about it, the more she realized what she needed: someone objective who could listen prayerfully to her quandary without their own desires or worries contaminating their counsel. And the only person she could think of who fit that description, apart from her counselor, was her pastor. She wouldn't see Dawn until Friday, and given Casey's state of agitation, the sooner she talked with someone, the better.

It was a selfish reason for attending worship, she thought as she mouthed the opening songs from the far back corner of the sanctuary, but it was the best she had to offer. *Sorry.*

When the senior pastor, Neil, invited them to take their seats for a time of prayer, Wren expected him to lead them in a time of thanksgiving and celebration. Instead, she was surprised to hear him read words of lament.

"Out of the depths I cry to you, O LORD. Lord, hear my voice!"

For the second time in less than twenty-four hours, she found herself mirrored in the emotions and longings of an ancient worshiper. *My soul waits for the Lord more than those who watch for the morning, more than those who watch for the morning.*

Name your longings to God, the pastor said. Offer the cry of your heart, the ways you are waiting for light to dawn in the darkness. Ask God for the courage to wait with hope.

She opened her hands on her lap.

It was the cry of Advent, Neil said in his sermon following the time of prayer, the cry for Jesus to come and save and rescue and redeem, the cry for Jesus to come as Light and Life, to come and enter the dark chaos of the world and shine like the dawn upon all who walked in the shadow of fear and despair and death. It was the cry of Advent, the cry for him to come. And come again.

She needed Jesus to come. She needed Jesus to come and bring light, to penetrate the dark fog of confusion and anxiety and show her the way forward, to be the Way, the Truth, the Life.

She whispered the cry of Advent. *Lord, come.*

As she waited after worship to speak with Hannah, words from the psalm continued to resonate in her soul: *Out of the depths I cry to you, Lord. Hear my prayer.*

Out of the depths.

De profundis.

Vincent had written to Theo about *De profundis,* about those dwelling in the abyss. That's why he had journeyed as an evangelist to Belgium. He wanted to bring the light of the gospel to the miners who labored without light in the bowels of the earth. He joined them there in the stifling, oppressive darkness, staring up the mineshaft at a tiny square of light no bigger than a star shimmering in the night sky. He tore up his clothes to make bandages for the injured. He shared his bread with them. He kept vigil at their bedsides. In every way he inhabited the abyss with them and tried to shine light. And when the missionary board rejected him, he remained in the village and practiced sketching, wanting to capture and reveal their dignity and worth.

She had hoped to offer something similar as a social worker, to bring light and comfort to those who dwelt in the abyss of fear, to those who needed a safe harbor. For a few short years she was part of the rescue mission. She had carried bucket after bucket of mercy. But no longer. There was no returning to the stress and strain of that kind of work. She knew that. But what if she was part of God's rescue mission for Casey? Wouldn't she be willing to descend into the darkness for that, even if it was dangerous?

Hannah finished speaking with a young couple and came over to give her a hug. "Hey, Wren, thanks for waiting."

"Sure."

"How are you?"

She shook her head slightly. "I hate to bother you, but . . ."

"No bother," Hannah said. "I've got time."

In the privacy of Hannah's office, Wren told her about Casey's unexpected return, the breakdown of his marriage, their long history of friendship and companionship in depression, and his request that they share a house. Hannah listened without interrupting, her body language and facial expressions betraying nothing about her personal opinions, only a commitment to compassionate attentiveness.

"He needs to move quickly," Wren said. "It's not a good situation for him with his parents. It never has been. And that means I would need to move quickly too, definitely before Christmas, but probably in the next week."

"There's nowhere else he can stay while he regroups?" Hannah asked.

"No. I don't think so. I mean, Casey isn't exactly easy to live with when he's not well. And he's not well right now." Her voice cracked.

Hannah passed her a box of tissues. "And what about you, Wren? How are you?"

She shrugged. "Some days I think I'm doing pretty well, and I have some hope for moving forward and getting stronger. But other days I feel like I can barely get out of bed, and I wonder if I'll ever be able to work full time again or live on my own. And then I have a panic attack like I had last night, and I realize I can't be alone right now. Because I don't know when the next attack could hit and take me under—not just the anxiety but the depression. It all feels fragile."

Hannah nodded. "And knowing that about yourself right now, what are the benefits of staying with Kit? Does it seem like a good situation?"

"She says it is, that she enjoys having me there. But then that makes me feel guilty for thinking about leaving. And then I feel guilty about staying there and not helping Casey. Because he really needs the help."

"But what about you, Wren? What seems best for you? Don't think long-term, just for right now."

She shrugged again. "It's peaceful at Kit's house."

"Does that help with your recovery? Being in a peaceful place?"

"I think so."

"And what about living with Casey? Would that be peaceful for you?"

"No. Definitely not."

"Why not?"

"Because, like I said, even when he's well, he can be difficult. Draining. And on top of that there would be all the added stress about money for rent and food and utilities. But I worry about him if I say no. I worry about what he might do to himself. He's not in a good place." She blew her nose.

"No. It doesn't sound like he is." Hannah leaned forward slightly. "It's agonizing, watching people we love suffer, wanting to help, to do what's loving and kind. But to love people well without taking responsibility for their well-being or for their choices, that's hard to do. And it sounds like that's part of what you're trying to figure out, how to be alongside as a friend without trying to rescue him. Because you can't rescue him. That's not your job."

Dawn would tell her the same thing. "I know that. In my head. But there have also been a couple of times when my being there at just the right time made the difference between life and death for him. I know it did. And what if he needs me, and I'm not there? Then what?" She would never recover from that kind of devastation and regret.

Hannah looked at her with a deep kind of knowing. "What a heavy burden, trying to be constantly vigilant for him. I wonder if there's a different way forward?"

Like what? Just trusting Jesus that Casey would be okay? Trusting Jesus didn't mean he would keep him safe. And if she couldn't trust Jesus to keep him safe, then she needed to do it.

She buried her face in her hands. What a heavy burden, indeed.

Part 4

EVEN THE

DARKNESS

If I say, "Surely the darkness will hide me,
and the light become night around me,"
even the darkness will not be dark to you;
the night is bright as the day,
for darkness is as light to you.

PSALM 139:11-12

It is precisely in learning to suffer without complaining, learning
to consider pain without repugnance, that one risks vertigo a
little; and yet it might be possible, yet one glimpses even a vague
probability that on the other side of life we'll glimpse justifica-
tions for pain, which seen from here sometimes takes up the whole
horizon so much that it takes on the despairing proportions of
a deluge. Of that we know very little, of proportions, and it's
better to look at a wheatfield, even in the state of a painting.

VINCENT VAN GOGH, LETTER TO THEO, JULY 2, 1889

28

As soon as the worship service finished, Jamie maneuvered through the sanctuary and down the back stairs to check her phone for messages from Wren. Nothing. Not a thing since Friday's "I'm at Kit's and I'm fine" message. No explanation, no apology.

"Jamie! I was hoping to find you."

No. Not today. She didn't have the margin for a conversation. Or complaining. Or gossip under the guise of prayer requests. She shoved her phone into her pocket, commanded her mouth to smile, and turned to greet one of the church matriarchs, who had followed her. "Good morning, Florence. Nice to see you."

"I was hoping to speak to Pastor, but he's in his office with someone, so can you give him a message for me?" Before Jamie could reply, she plowed ahead. "I was talking to some people after service this morning—"

I'm sure you were, Jamie thought. *You always are.*

"—and some people are saying—"

Yeah, it's always "some people."

"—they aren't happy about—"

Take a number. Get in line.

"—not singing many Christmas carols."

Uh-huh. She watched Florence's lips form words like "guitar" and "tradition" while waiting for her to take a breath. "It sounds like something you'll need to talk with Dylan and the worship committee about," Jamie said when Florence finally stopped talking.

"Well, just let him know I mentioned it to you."

Not my job. "Sure. I'll pass it along."

"And as long as I've got you—"

Jamie lightly touched Florence's arm. "I'm sorry, I've got a daughter home sick today and need to get back to check on her."

"Oh, that's too bad. I've been meaning to ask you, how's Wren doing with all her job stress?"

"Great. She's doing great, thanks."

"My granddaughter, the one in Charleston, you've heard me talk about her—"

Oh, God. Please. If she didn't cut her off at the pass, it would either be a half-hour litany of every trophy the girl had won since preschool or every hangnail she had suffered. "Hey, Phoebe!" Jamie called down the hallway. "Sorry, Florence. There's my other one, and I've got to catch her while I can."

Without waiting for a reply, Jamie hurried down the hallway and up a different stairwell, successfully dodging conversations. She found Phoebe sitting in a corner of the sanctuary, coloring. "C'mon, Feebs, we've got to go."

"Wait until I finish—"

"No. Now. We need to get home." Before anyone else accosted her and she lost her cool. That would go over great—the pastor's wife snapping at a church member. She took Phoebe by the hand. "C'mon, put your coat on. You can bring your picture with you."

"I'm almost done."

"I said now." She pulled her to her feet, helped her into her coat ("I can do it!" Phoebe protested), and trotted her out the side door. Once they had safely made it across the street and up the hill to the house, Jamie let go of her hand and checked her phone again. Still nothing from Wren. If there wasn't trouble brewing, then it was extremely thoughtless of her not to return a phone call. Or send a text.

Phoebe held up an acorn from their yard. "Look, Mommy! This is a funny one!"

"Is it?"

"Yeah. See?" She thrust out her arm. "Look!"

If there's an emergency, I'll call you. That was Kit's promise; that was their rule.

"Look, Mommy, it's funny!"

Jamie stared at an ordinary acorn. "What makes it funny?"

"The face."

"The face you're going to draw on it?"

"Yep." She had plans for each of the acorns she picked up from the grass for her collection: the sad one with no hat, the old one with white streaks on his chin, the little baby one. Phoebe kissed that one because it was soooo cute. "Olivia! Look!" Phoebe waved to her sister and skipped across the lawn to meet her, her skirt a cradle for her treasures. Olivia, evidently, had miraculously recovered from the migraine that had kept her home from worship and, car keys in hand, was heading toward the driveway.

"Hey!" Jamie called. "Where are you going?"

"Jess called and invited me to—"

"No. Absolutely not. If you're not well enough to go to church, you're not well enough to go out with friends."

"Mom!"

"No. I mean it."

"But that's not even fair!"

"My car, my rules."

Olivia gave an exasperated sigh, stormed into the house, and slammed the rickety door behind her. Phoebe stared at her mother, eyes wide. "Go change your clothes and get ready for lunch."

"But I want to play with—"

"Now!"

Phoebe raced inside, her acorns scattering behind her.

"What's this about Olivia not getting to go out with friends?" Dylan said when he entered the house half an hour later.

Jamie stirred the Crock-Pot stew. "Don't even start with me about it. What did she do? Text you?"

"Yeah."

"Well, I don't like being lied to. If she's"—Jamie mimed air quotes—"'too sick' to go to church, she's too sick to go out with friends."

"Cut her some slack, hon."

"No. She could have just said she was tired. But she turned it into an elaborate pretense about suffering with a migraine, so, no. She's not going out with friends."

"Okay." He hung up his church keys on the rack and took off his coat. "I'll talk to her."

She covered the stew again and turned the dial to warm. Dylan draped his coat on the banister and trudged up the stairs. She heard him rap quietly on the door and call, "Liv?" The door creaked open, then shut again.

Whatever he said to her, it had better result in Olivia apologizing. Jamie could tolerate many things. Deceit was not one of them.

Joel appeared in the doorway. "Phoebe's crying outside."

"I know," Jamie said. "Tell her it's time for lunch." She peered out the kitchen window to the yard, where Phoebe was wandering in circles, head back, mouth open in loud sobs, periodically glancing over her shoulder to see if anyone was watching.

As soon as Joel opened the side door and went outside, the wailing became louder.

She checked the rice on the stove. Two more minutes. The broccoli too—almost ready. She poured baby carrots into a bowl for Phoebe and spooned out some peanut butter. There would be no forcing her to eat green vegetables today.

At the sound of footsteps on the stairs, she turned to find Dylan. No Olivia. "Well?"

"She says she didn't lie; she had a headache."

"She said migraine. A migraine is different than a headache."

"Okay, migraine. So maybe she exaggerated. But she still wasn't feeling well."

"A miraculous recovery, then. Praise God."

"Don't do this, Jamie."

"Do what?"

"Whatever anger or frustration you're feeling with Wren right now, don't displace it toward Olivia."

"I'm not."

"I think you are."

The side door banged shut again. "She lost her acorn family," Joel said.

"Oh, for cryin' out loud!" Jamie exclaimed. "Have you seen her room?"

Dylan held up his hand, motioning for her to calm down. "Help her find them, will you, Joel? Or just pick up some other ones and call it good."

"I tried that. She says there's a baby one that's lost, and she has to find it."

"Okay," Dylan said. He grabbed his coat again and went outside. Joel followed him.

Jamie stared at the stove. *Fine.* Everyone could figure out their own lunch. She clicked off both burners, tromped up the stairs, and kicked the bedroom door shut with the side of her foot. Olivia's headache? Amazing. It seemed to be contagious. Or maybe just *displaced*.

No, Wren insisted to Casey on the phone Sunday afternoon, she wasn't going to "keep stringing him along."

"Well, the guy I talked to yesterday annoyed the crap out of me," he said, "so I'm running out of options. If you back out . . ."

"Nobody's backing out. I just need a few days to think about it, pray about it."

He scoffed. "Pray. Yeah. A whole lot of good that does." He paused. "You know what I've decided?"

She braced herself. She shouldn't have mentioned prayer. "What?"

"That it's not a question for me about whether there's a God. I settled that one a long time ago. No, the big question for me is, What kind of God is he?" He paused again. "And you know what? That question's way worse."

"Casey—"

"I'll talk to you later."

His hanging up on her was becoming routine.

She set her phone on her nightstand and went downstairs to make herself a cup of coffee. One thing he had learned over the years was how to wound her, how to manipulate her into worry.

But she wasn't going to make this about her, she told herself as she poured fresh water into the reservoir. If he had abandoned every shred of hope in God's goodness, then he was in even more danger than she'd feared.

She wished he could be persuaded to listen to Neil's sermon. What kind of God? A descending God. A self-emptying God. A compassionate and humble God. The manger, the incarnation demonstrated what kind of God.

So did the cross.

Maybe if she moved in with Casey and he watched her paint the suffering of Jesus, he would come to see again what kind of God. Maybe she could help him see.

"Everything okay?" Kit asked as she entered the kitchen with a book tucked under her arm.

"Mm-hmm."

Kit poured a glass of water from the fridge.

Wren chose a hazelnut blend from the box of assorted cups on the counter. "Actually, no. Everything's not okay."

Kit eyed her with concern. "Would you like to talk about it?"

Sure, she thought. Why not? Maybe Kit would make the decision easy for her and tell her she wanted her to stay. Needed her to stay. Then at least she wouldn't feel selfish for choosing the easier, more peaceful place.

"Please don't tell my mom, okay? I know that sounds really juvenile but . . ."

"No, it's fine. We made an agreement, remember? That I wouldn't carry information back and forth without your permission."

"Okay, thanks." Wren waited for her coffee to brew, then sat down at the table. Everything she had told Hannah that morning she repeated, adding the latest information about Casey playing the "What kind of God?" card.

Kit nodded slowly. "I'm very sorry to hear about your friend. It sounds like he's in a lot of pain."

"He is."

Kit sat in silence a moment and then said, "When we're in that kind of pain, we don't have the ability to think about how we're impacting others. We're just trying to survive."

How beautiful that Kit had immediately enfolded Casey into their collective "we," their "companions in misfortune" community. Wren loved her even more for offering that gift.

"It's like drowning," Kit said. "If we're going under, we panic and instinctively grasp for anything we can cling to, anything we can push down in order to keep ourselves afloat. It's how rescuers can drown trying to save someone, because the one who's going under pushes down on them in order to survive. It's not deliberate—it's a desperate survival instinct. So that's why rescuers need to throw out a lifeline. Something buoyant to keep the victim afloat so he doesn't hang on to the rescuer and push him under."

Wren nodded. She understood the metaphor. It was the same caution Hannah had given her. "What I can't figure out is what kind of lifeline to throw him," she said. "If I'm not the one stepping in to help, then I don't know what to offer him."

Kit reached across the table and grasped her hand. "Well, that's something we can pray about together, if you'd like."

Wren wished Casey could have heard Kit's prayer for him, how tenderly she named to God his need for help and hope, how passionately she pleaded for his deliverance from everything that bound him and held him captive. "Set him free to see what kind of God you are, full of mercy and compassion. Show him your grace and power. Let him see that you're full of steadfast love and affection for him even when it seems dark and overwhelming. Come, Lord Jesus. Come quickly and rescue him."

Please, Wren silently prayed.

And then Kit thanked God. She thanked God for the beauty of Wren's soul, for her gift of compassion and her deep desire to love and serve her friend. "You call us, Lord, to love one another and lay down our lives for each other. We need wisdom about how best to love Casey in this and to know what kind of lifeline to offer in your name. Let our thoughts be your thoughts. Deliver us from fear. And may we know your way and walk humbly in it, trusting in your love."

Wren sniffed back tears.

Beauty of soul. Really? Is that what Kit saw in her? Not fearful codependency and fragility but beauty of soul?

That's not what she saw in herself.

She longed for it to be true. She longed to possess even a portion of the kindness and goodness and generosity and patience and compassion and wisdom she had received from others. She was surrounded by people with extraordinary beauty of soul, the blessed beneficiary of their Christlikeness.

And who was she to receive such a bounty of care when so many suffered with no one to help them? It wasn't fair, all the generosity she had received when others despaired alone, discarded.

Every Vincent needed his Theo. Not every Vincent had one. And even those who did, even those with a Theo alongside to help shoulder the burden and offer love and care—even with a Theo, the strain of melancholy and fear might become too much to endure.

29

Thanks to Dylan, Olivia got her way and went out with friends. Phoebe got her way too. Not only did he spend half an hour traipsing around the yard with her, hunting for the exact acorns she'd lost, but when they didn't find them, he decided to placate her by taking her to a movie. "To give you some space," he'd said to Jamie before leaving.

Translation: to give you time to figure out how to get a handle on your anger so you don't cause our children harm.

Well, he needed time and space to figure out how not to be manipulated by them.

From the bedroom window she watched the car head down the hill. Even Joel had decided to go—not, to be sure, because he had any interest in sharing a theater with a five-year-old, but because he probably didn't want to share a house with an irritated mother. Smart boy.

She rinsed her face and went downstairs to see what could be salvaged from lunch. The stew was still warming in the Crock-Pot, and the rice and vegetables were stowed in the fridge. Had any of them bothered to eat what she'd prepared? She removed the lid to inspect. No. Still full. That meant Dylan was probably taking Joel and Phoebe to a drive-thru right now.

Fine. They could eat leftovers for dinner. And if they complained about it, she wasn't fixing anything else.

She heated up some rice and spooned stew over it.

What was it Dylan had accused her of? Projection? Transference?

Displacement. That was it.

She sat down at the kitchen table and stirred her food. Maybe she could concede the possibility that her nerves were frayed because of Wren, and her emotions were leaking sideways. But that didn't alter the reality of Olivia's deception or her need to apologize.

How difficult would it have been for her to say, "I'm tired, and I don't feel like going to church this morning"? She would have told Olivia she could stay home and rest. And her choice to stay home wouldn't have impacted her going out later with friends. She wasn't an unreasonable mother. She just wanted honest, open communication. Was that too much to ask?

She spit out a piece of stringy beef. The whole thing was ruined. With a heavy sigh, she dumped the contents of her bowl into the trash and went back to bed.

"Does Casey have his heart set on renting a house?" Kit asked as she and Wren ate dinner.

"Instead of getting an apartment, you mean?"

"Or just having a room somewhere. Is he hoping to live in community?"

"I'm not sure. But the thought of him living somewhere alone doesn't thrill me. I don't know if it would be safe for him right now." Wren scooped more salad onto her plate. "Why?"

Kit shrugged. "Something just came to mind—I'm surprised it didn't occur to me earlier—and perhaps it's a lifeline, at least temporarily. But it wouldn't be in community like you're hoping." She slowly buttered a piece of bread. "There are a couple of bedrooms at New Hope. We used to offer quite a lot of overnight retreats, but we haven't for years. You probably haven't even noticed them. I keep the doors locked."

Wren had assumed they were storage closets.

"They're very spartan, just a twin bed, desk, chair, and an attached bath. But I would be willing for him to stay there—not indefinitely, but for a few weeks. I wouldn't charge him rent, but I'd ask him to help with some maintenance projects. Painting, carpet cleaning, that sort of thing. Do you think he might be interested?"

It was impossible to predict. But what a kind offer. And with a concrete option like that, she wouldn't feel guilty for saying no to sharing a house. It might be the perfect lifeline for both of them.

"So, you're backing out?" Casey said when she called to extend Kit's invitation.

She shifted position on her bed. "I can't make it work financially, and I'm not strong enough right now to handle that kind of stress."

"The stress of living with me."

"No, the stress of trying to afford rent, utilities, food—all the things I don't have to worry about right now."

"Yeah, lucky you."

She tried to ignore the barb. He didn't know he was tapping on her guilt and shame. Or maybe he did. "Well, you wouldn't need to worry about it, either. The rent and utilities, anyway. It buys you time, Casey. In a really peaceful place."

"And then what? After a few weeks, then what? I'm back to trying to find a house and no one to share it with."

"You were able to afford your apartment before. Once you start freelancing again—"

"Yeah. Right. Kinda burned those bridges when I moved away."

"I thought that's what you were doing in Reno, freelance projects from here."

He laughed. "Not with a wife who didn't trust me being online late at night. She took away my computer, so I couldn't meet the deadlines. Screwed some people over. Not pretty."

Classic abuser move, Wren thought. Thank God he had escaped. "I'm really sorry," she said. "You went through hell."

"*Went?* Not exactly past tense."

"No. I know. But maybe this is an answer to prayer—even if you don't believe it right now. Maybe this is God's way of providing for you."

He did not reply.

"I'm there at New Hope almost every day. We'd probably even get to work on some of Kit's projects together. And you could move in right away. Even faster than if you'd rented a house."

"Stop trying to sell it."

"Okay." She sat up and leaned back against the wall. "Text or whatever and let me know what you decide. But I hope you'll say yes."

"Yeah, so you don't have to feel guilty."

Wren felt a surge of anger. "I'm the one trying to help you, remember? Don't act like I'm being the selfish one here."

"Oh, right. 'Cause you're not looking out for yourself at all."

This time she was the one to punch "End Call."

When her phone rang again a few minutes later, she picked up without checking the number. "What?" she snapped.

"Wren?"

It wasn't Casey. She cursed silently. She didn't have capacity for a conversation with her mother right now. "Hey, Mom, sorry. Thought you were Casey."

"Oh."

"Can I call you back?"

"I don't know. Can you?"

The uncharacteristically curt words landed an unexpected, well-placed blow to her gut. "I'm sorry," Wren said, once she caught her breath again. "I've had a lot going on."

"Evidently."

She swung her legs over the side of the bed. "I meant to call earlier but I've been trying to help Casey sort out some things, and it's taken all my attention the past few days. Sorry."

There was silence. And then, "We had a rule years ago, a rule I taught you when you were little: never go to bed angry. Well, I've broken my own rule. My fault. But I'm not going to bed angry again tonight."

Over what? Wren thought. *Not calling you? I'm not twelve!* But she didn't say that. Instead, she waited, the pit in her stomach widening.

"Maybe someday if you're a mother—"

Oh, God. Not this lecture.

"—you'll understand how it feels to worry over the safety of your children, even grown children. Especially when they haven't been well. Maybe you'll understand how it feels when your worry is over, but in the relief you feel, you also feel anger. Especially if they don't seem able to acknowledge the worry they've caused and the stress they've put you through. And you end up feeling confused because you know they aren't usually inconsiderate and selfish."

Wren leaned forward, head on her knees. Casey had just accused her of the same thing.

"But here you are, and here I am, waiting for an apology that may never come because you don't seem to understand how worried I am about you. And so, I just get angrier and more resentful and take it out on everyone around me rather than being direct with you to say I feel disappointed. And hurt."

Tears dampened her flannel pajamas. Maybe it was true. Maybe she was inherently selfish and inconsiderate. Maybe she couldn't blame depression for causing her to be preoccupied. Maybe this was who she was. Not forgetful. Selfish.

"I'm sorry to have to say these hard things to you, Wren. Believe me, I've battled all kinds of fear just to be able to be honest with you. Because a big part of me worries you won't hear the love in what I'm saying, that you'll only go to shame, and then I worry something I've said will cause harm and—"

She was an awful daughter.

"—send you over the edge."

Wren grasped the bedspread. She wanted to say, "There's no edge. I'm okay." But she wasn't sure if those words were true. So she said nothing. And tried not to burst into alarming sobs.

As soon as Jamie hung up the phone, she called Kit. She was sorry to bother her, she said, and she wasn't trying to draw her into the middle of a situation. But she was worried about Wren's state of mind. "I said some difficult things to her just now, and I don't know how she took it. I'm wondering if you could please keep an eye on her?"

"Of course," Kit said.

A car door slammed. Then another. She peered out the bedroom window. Dylan was home. He waited for Phoebe to unbuckle herself from the car seat, then held her hand as she hopped out. Joel went over to the garage, picked up a basketball, and starting shooting hoops on the driveway.

Jamie said, "I debated all weekend whether to tell her how upset I was Friday night. I feel like I'm constantly weighing the cost of being truthful against my fear of saying or doing something that triggers her."

"I understand that," Kit said. "So hard to know."

Dylan held up his arms for Joel to pass to him, then took a long shot. When he sank it, Phoebe jumped up and down, clapping.

"I don't want you to betray anything, Kit. I know what we agreed. But can you tell me how you think she's doing, just in general?"

"Pretty well, I think, considering everything."

Jamie wondered what "everything" referred to. "A lot going on" and "everything" were words that meant little without flesh on them.

"I know about Casey," Jamie said.

"Oh, good. I'm glad she told you."

Wait, Jamie thought. That sounded like something more specific than "Casey's back in town, and he's under a lot of stress right now."

Phoebe was running back and forth, arms raised, begging for a pass. Joel fired one too hard at her, and when Dylan scolded him, he sent a softer one her way. She missed and chased after the ball.

"It sounds like she's been under a lot of stress this weekend," Jamie said. "I'm glad you're there for her."

"I'm happy to try to help. And I'm hoping he'll say yes to the room at New Hope. Between you and me, I was a bit worried when she told me their plans. Not that it's my business, who she lives with, but . . ."

Wait. What? Jamie leaned against the windowsill. "Sorry. I think maybe you've got some information she didn't share with me."

There was silence on the other end of the phone.

"Do you mean she's planning to move in with him?"

Another moment of silence. "Jamie, I'm sorry. When you said you knew about Casey, I thought—"

"I knew he left his wife and came back to town and that Wren's been spending a lot of time with him. But I didn't know anything about moving in with him. You mean, like, living together?" She felt sick to her stomach.

"Just as roommates," Kit said, "to share rent. But if she didn't tell you about all of this . . . I was very wrong to assume. I'm sorry."

Jamie stepped away from the window. "So, do you think that's still a possibility, the two of them living together?"

Kit hesitated, then said, "I wouldn't want to speculate on that. But I know Wren is praying about the way forward, so we'll keep praying too."

Jamie could tell from her tone of voice that she was unwilling to discuss any further details. She rubbed the back of her neck. "Well, like I said, if you can keep an eye on her, especially right now . . ."

"I will."

Jamie thanked her again and hung up the phone. There were many things she could tolerate. But deceit from a daughter was not one of them.

At the sound of a knock, Wren wiped her eyes and sat up on the bed. "Yes?" she called.

Kit opened the door slowly. "Thought I might make a cup of tea. Would you like anything?"

"No, thanks."

Kit hesitated, then said, "Mind if I come in a minute?"

Wren shook her head.

Kit pulled the desk chair closer to the bed and sat down. "In the spirit of full disclosure, your mom just called me, worried about you. I told her I would keep an eye on you and make sure you're okay." She paused. "Are you?"

Wren shrugged.

"Your mom didn't go into specifics with me, and I don't need to hear them. But could we make an agreement that if you find yourself struggling in any way, you'll let me know?"

"Okay."

"I won't nag you. I know the frequent monitoring can feel intrusive. But please know I'm here for you. Anything you need."

"Thanks."

Kit placed her hand on the edge of the bed. "On top of everything else you're processing right now, I've managed to step right into something I'm afraid has only made things more complicated for you."

Wren stared at her.

"I don't even remember how it came up now, and it doesn't matter. But in the course of the conversation with your mom, she said something that caused me to assume—incorrectly—that you had mentioned to her the possibility of getting a house with Casey."

Wren closed her eyes.

"I'm so sorry. I didn't mean to betray your confidence, but I did. And I'm sorry."

Wren brought her knees to her chest.

"I didn't give your mom any other details. Whatever else you want to tell her is up to you. But she knows I offered him a room at New Hope and that I'm hoping he'll say yes."

Wren pulled her hood over her head.

"I wish I could do or say something to make it better for you, Wren. I'm so sorry I've made it worse."

Wren did not reply.

After a few moments of silence, the chair creaked. Footsteps padded across the floor. The door brushed the carpet but did not click closed. Wren waited until the footsteps receded downstairs. Then she rose and closed the door the rest of the way.

30

The building needed to be cleaned after the weekend retreat. That was the only reason Wren dragged herself out of bed Monday morning after a restless night.

Perhaps the simple rhythm of scrubbing and wiping and spraying and dusting and mopping would help break her cycle of rumination. That's what Dawn would probably recommend: redirect your focus.

She stared out the window of Kit's car as they made their way to New Hope in silence, not a punishing silence—Wren knew what that felt like—but a pregnant one. Kit had been honest about divulging confidential information, and it was clear she wasn't going to rehash her indiscretion or keep apologizing. The next move toward reconciliation, Wren knew, was hers to make.

She cleared her throat. "Thank you for being honest with me, about my mom and everything."

Kit turned toward her briefly, then fixed her gaze on the road again. "That's a gracious way to put it. I think if I were you, I'd be saying, I'm mad at you, I can't believe you did that, or, You crazy old woman, what were you thinking?"

Wren smiled. "Okay. Maybe that too."

"Which one?"

"The 'What were you thinking?' one."

"I wasn't thinking. That was the problem, making assumptions. Will you forgive me?"

"Yes."

"And you'll find a way to work it out with your mom?"

"Somehow."

"If I can help with that, let me know. Especially since I'm the one who muddied things."

"Not really. I could have told her about Casey, but I knew she'd get upset."

"Well, we moms, we worry about our kids, no matter how old you get."

Wren shifted in her seat. "Yes. But not telling Mom about Casey wasn't about trying to spare her worry. I was trying to spare myself a lecture. I wasn't protecting her, I was protecting myself. And that was selfish."

Kit eyed her again. "That's a beautiful insight."

"It's a terrible insight."

"Well, it feels terrible, true. But seeing our sin—awful as it feels—is always a work of the Spirit. The enemy doesn't want us to see the truth. He'd rather have us stay in deception and darkness. So when we see the ugliness, we can be confident the light's shining and exposing us so we can be healed. So, yes. I say that's a beautiful insight. A gift."

"Okay . . . if you say so."

Kit laughed. "Trust me. I see the ugliness in myself all the time. As long as we don't head into shame and condemnation over it but into gratitude for God's grace and forgiveness, then we're heading in the right direction." She leaned forward in her seat to peer over the steering wheel. "Somebody's here early." She motioned toward the entrance. "I'm not expecting anyone for another hour."

Wren followed her gaze to a tall figure leaning against the building, a backpack beside him. "It's Casey!"

The shaggy dog had decided to come in from the cold.

Kit welcomed him as if he were a long-lost grandson. "I'm sorry it's so small and plain," she said after unlocking the guestroom. "But I hope you'll be comfortable here, Casey."

"Thanks," he said, and tossed his backpack onto the floor.

"There's a microwave and small fridge in the kitchenette down the hall. Are you a coffee drinker?"

"Yeah."

"I'll bring you a small pot to use." She smoothed the green chenille bedspread. "And a few extra blankets. There's a wall unit there to control the heat in the room. I haven't turned it on in ages, so hopefully everything will still work okay for you."

Wren said, "It's all great. Thank you." If she could have nudged a polite response out of Casey without Kit seeing, she would have.

"You're probably exhausted," Kit said, "so let's not plan on talking shop until tomorrow. Sound good?"

"Yeah."

"Okay. Great."

He flopped onto the bed with his shoes on, arms folded across his chest.

"We'll let you get settled in, then," Kit said. "Rest well."

"Yeah," Wren said. "I'll just be here cleaning, so . . ."

He closed his eyes.

"I guess I'll see you later." Wren backed out of the room and closed the door softly behind her. Kit was silent as they walked down the hall, her brow furrowed. "Thanks again for doing this," Wren said.

Though Kit's brow relaxed, her smile was uneasy. "Of course."

Wren couldn't help wondering if she was already regretting her invitation.

An hour later she was pushing the cleaning cart out of the bathroom when she nearly collided with Mara rounding a corner. "I was hoping to run into you," Mara said. "I mean, not literally, but . . ."

Wren smiled. "Sorry. Did I bump you?"

"No, I'm fine."

She straightened the spray bottles. "How was Texas?"

"Aren't you sweet to remember! I had a wonderful time. Always hard to leave, though. They keep threatening in a nice way to move me down there, but I'm not ready to give up my job, much as I'd love to be near the grandkids." She reached into her large embroidered bag. "Here, since you asked, I'll show you pictures." Holding out her phone so Wren could see, she scrolled through images of kids playing catch and riding bikes and holding guinea pigs.

"They're beautiful," Wren said.

Mara smiled at the screen. "They're my happy place, that's for sure." She put her phone back into her bag. "And how about you? How's everything going?"

"Okay."

"Just okay?"

Wren shrugged. "Some days are better than others."

"Boy, isn't that the truth! Which is why I come here for a monthly tune-up. Your aunt helps me see how God is with me, even in all the crappiness of life. Especially in all the crappiness."

"Yes, she's great at that," Wren said. "I guess that's one of the things she's been helping me with too, seeing how Jesus keeps me company in everything that's hard. A companion in sorrow."

"Ooh, that's good. I like that. I should write that one down." Mara rummaged in her bag for a pen, then scribbled the phrase on her hand. "A companion in sorrow." She held her hand out to stare at the words. "Yep. That's who he is. It makes me think of that painting in the chapel—you know the one I mean? The one with Jesus on the cross?"

"Yes. I love that one."

"Me too. But it used to creep me out. Can I say that, or is that sacrilegious?"

"No. I know what you mean."

"There's something to it," Mara said, "something comforting, you know? That probably sounds weird, saying that a painting of the crucifixion could be comforting. Disturbing too, I guess. But mostly comforting. At least, to me it is."

"Yes. Me too." Whatever the details of Mara's journey, it sounded as if she was also a companion in affliction and sorrow. "My aunt asked if I would paint the prayer stations this year for the Journey to the Cross. Have you been to that before?"

"Every year for the last ten, probably. Wouldn't miss it. How cool that you're painting them! I'll look forward to it even more, knowing that."

"Well, I don't know if I can manage it, but I'm going to give it a try. As a spiritual exercise, I guess."

"I think you'll do great. Just seeing the sketch you did of my friend's daughter at Crossroads—that was amazing. It's like you caught Bethany's spirit, like you saw into her soul and drew what was most important."

Wren swallowed hard.

Mara grabbed her arm. "Oh, sorry! Did I say something wrong?"

"No. It's just . . . That's one of the best things anyone's ever said about one of my sketches."

Mara feigned wiping her brow. "Phew! Because if someone's gonna put her foot in it, that'll be me."

Wren brushed her eyes with the back of her sleeve.

"Ahhh . . . c'mere," Mara said, opening her arms wide. "Honey, c'mere."

Vincent would have painted her. He would have painted Mara Payne over and over again, just as he had done with Augustine Roulin, the wife of his dear friend Joseph, the postmaster who brought him letters and money and art supplies from Theo. Vincent loved that family. They were kind to him when many others were cruel.

In her studio that afternoon, Wren studied his multiple portraits of Augustine seated in a chair, her hands clutching a rope to rock an unseen cradle. *La Berceuse,* he called the paintings. A lullaby. By leaving the cradle out of sight, Vincent had placed the viewer within it, to be lulled and comforted to sleep by a watchful, peaceful, loving mother. He envisioned the work as the centerpiece between paintings of sunflowers, a sort of triptych portraying an ordinary saint flanked by golden, fiery candelabras.

Augustine, with her ample breast, sturdy hips, red hair, and soft gaze, reminded her a bit of Mara. Some women might be offended by that comparison. But Vincent thought Augustine was beautiful, and he captured her spirit in his depictions of her. That's what he longed to do in all his portraits: show the dignity and beauty cloaked in the humility and humanity of his subjects. That's what he managed to do so profoundly, to convey a radiance, a holiness. For all his faults, Vincent knew how to see with compassion.

She longed for the same gift. And Mara said she'd seen it in her. *It's like you caught her spirit, like you saw into her soul and drew what was most important about her.*

Mara could have spoken no greater praise. Hers was a word of encouragement for Wren to treasure and replay whenever she felt discouraged by her limitations, both as an artist and as a human being.

"I've never really understood your obsession with him."

Wren jumped at the sound of Casey's voice, her hand lurching to her heart.

He laughed. "I mean, look at that woman, all distorted and hideous. I can see her now, staring at the portrait after he finished and thinking, What the——"

"Okay. Stop. You know what?" Wren closed the book. "He didn't paint portraits to be accurate. He painted them to speak a deeper truth."

"Well, that one says, 'butt ugly.'"

"You don't have to be mean."

"And you don't have to be touchy."

She should have kept her door shut. This was her sacred space, and if he was going to be snarky and unkind, then he didn't need to have access to it.

He stretched and yawned. "What's to eat around here?"

"We usually pack lunches."

"Did you pack me one?"

"Did I know you were coming?"

"You don't have to be rude, it was just a question."

A dumb one, she thought. "I keep granola bars on the counter over there. And you can have my banana."

"I think I'll go out to eat. Wanna come?"

"I've got to keep working."

"On what?"

"I promised Kit I would choose new art for the walls."

He scoffed. "That can wait." He picked up her coat from the table and handed it to her. "C'mon. I need some food."

Wren sighed. "Okay, fine. But only for a little while."

"You're no fun."

No, Wren thought. *And neither are you.*

"What's with you, anyway?" he said from across the booth. "You're the one who was all keen on me staying in that room—'We'll get to see each other, work together,' blah, blah, blah—and now you act like you don't even want me around."

"I'm not acting like that."

"You are."

"Well, you barged into my studio—"

"Oh, *sorry.* Didn't know it was *your studio.*"

"See? You can't even hear yourself, can you?" She almost said—oh! she was so close to spitting, *No wonder Brooke* . . . But she caught herself in time. "You're not the only one trying to heal and regroup, okay? I am too. And art is helping me do that. Vincent is helping me do that." *Jesus is helping me,* she wanted to say, but she couldn't bear it if he scoffed at that too. And given his anger with God right now, he might.

She bit her lip.

He stared at her, his face softening. "Okay. I'm sorry, Wrinkle." He reached across the table. "Can we call a truce?"

"Okay." She set down her fork and shook his hand.

"I'm sorry I made fun of his painting. And I'll knock next time."

"Thanks. And don't accuse me of not wanting you around or not caring about you. It hurts me when you do that."

"Okay. Deal. Anything else?"

"Don't be a jerk."

He laughed. "You've known me too long to expect me to change now. That's like me saying to you, Don't be sensitive."

She stared at him, on the verge of being offended. But his expression was so tender, so sincere, that she laughed too. And it felt like grace, two old friends sitting across the table from one another, laughing at their own frail and absurd humanity.

31

O kay," Casey said after they returned to New Hope, "gimme another chance on the ugly woman painting." He picked up her Van Gogh book and started flipping pages.

She snatched it from him. "I'll find it." She turned to the section of his paintings from Arles, then held the page open, showing five different versions.

He squinted at it. "What is it? Like a spot the difference game?" He leaned closer and started pointing. "Black top, green top, yellow face—doesn't she look jaundiced? Look! Her hands aren't even the same color as her face in that one. Grouchy eyes, bored eyes, 'How long do I have to sit here?' eyes. And in this one she looks constipated or something."

"Okay. Enough." Wren started to close the book.

He shoved his hand onto the page. "No, wait, I'm not done. I haven't even started on the psychedelic floral wallpaper. Look"—he pointed to one in the bottom row—"her head is the same color as that flower. Trippy."

She ran her finger across the arm of Augustine's chair, where Vincent had signed his name. "I'll have you know, that's the one Augustine picked to keep for herself, and Vincent told her she had good taste, that it was the best one."

"Not much of a competition, is it?"

She elbowed him. "Stop being such a hater. You said you wanted another chance."

"Okay. So explain it to me. Because I don't get it."

No, she thought, most of Vincent's contemporaries—even the

Impressionists who were pushing boundaries in the art world—hadn't understood or appreciated his art, either. What he wanted to do was convey emotion, whether he was painting portraits or landscapes, and he attempted to do that with the imaginative use of color. "Look at her face and hair," Wren said, "the way he wove threads of green and blue. He wasn't going for a realistic portrayal of her, he was trying to show her spirit, a glow from within. He was trying to express deep feeling."

She wondered what Vincent had felt when he was painting her. Was he longing for home? For his mom? For a sense of intimacy and connection? For nurture? For love? Maybe just for a safe place to belong. To rest. "He had his first major breakdown not long after he painted her," she said quietly.

She could tell by Casey's expression that he was about to say something snide but reconsidered.

"What he wanted to do was paint works that comforted people," she went on, "and he hoped this would do that. He was thinking about sailors being rocked by the waves, and he wanted to paint something they could hang inside the cabin of their fishing boat, something that might soothe them when they were in danger, like a mother rocking them and singing lullabies to comfort them."

The sailors were like children and martyrs, he wrote to Theo. Wren had often wondered if Vincent viewed himself the same way, unmoored in a stormy sea, vulnerable and self-sacrificing.

"I still don't get it," Casey said. "If that thing were hanging in my bedroom, I'd have nightmares." He motioned for her to hand him the book, then held it out at arm's length, shifting his head from right to left and back again as he looked at the pages, then holding the book higher above his head with the same maneuvering back and forth. "You can't catch her gaze," he said. "Ever notice that? No matter where you stand, you can't make her look at you." He handed it back to her. "Maybe that's what he was trying to say, that no matter how hard you try, you're never gonna please them. They're always going to be disappointed and disapproving."

She shook her head. "He had huge respect for mothers. He thought motherhood was a high and holy calling. He always longed to have a family, to be a husband and a father. But his dreams of that kept getting dashed."

Casey scoffed. "Overrated, if you ask me." Thrusting his hands into his pockets, he strode out of the room.

Wren let him go. If the art had provoked an emotional response, then it had achieved Vincent's aim. Even if it wasn't the emotional response he intended when he painted her.

That was the power of art, she thought as she continued gazing at Augustine, the power to mirror someone's soul and reveal what was true, the power to agitate or comfort, perplex or inspire. Like what Kit said about *visio divina*. Except Casey probably hadn't been provoked to prayer, just resentment.

She mimicked his trick of trying to catch Augustine's eyes, back and forth, up and down. Wren had always interpreted her gaze as pensive and reflective. That's why Augustine seemed removed and detached; she was absorbed in her own thoughts. But Casey was right. No matter which angle you tried, there was no catching her attention.

It would have been more disturbing, though, if her gaze had followed you no matter where you went.

The longer Wren looked, the more she had to concede his point about the painting not oozing maternal affection. But was it disappointment and disapproval etched on her face? Or was it sorrow? Perhaps Augustine was a companion in misfortune, a mother acquainted with grief. That could have drawn Vincent to her, a sense of affinity with someone wearied by the burdens and trials of life. It wasn't easy, being a mother.

She closed the book.

Okay. I hear you, she murmured, and picked up her phone.

After telling her mother everything that had happened with Casey—the plan she had contemplated and the solution he had agreed to—she apologized for being thoughtless and inconsiderate. She said she was sorry for being so self-absorbed that she hadn't considered the worry she'd caused. She was sorry for not trusting her mother to listen to her wrestling without becoming angry or judgmental. "Please forgive me," Wren said. "I'm sorry I hurt you."

She was sorry too, her mother said. She was sorry for not trusting Wren to make reasonable decisions. She was sorry for allowing her fear to turn into resentment and anger. She was sorry for lecturing her and being quick to silently reproach her. "I hate being that kind of mom," she said. "I love you. And I'll try to find a new way forward so my anxiety doesn't cause you more stress. Or make you feel like you can't be honest with me."

"Thanks, Mom." If only all conflicts could be resolved as gracefully.

"So, tell me more about Casey," her mother said. "You don't think he'll head back to Reno?"

"No."

"No hope for reconciliation?"

"Not with the kind of abuse he's described, no. I wouldn't say so."

Her mother sighed. "It's all so sad. So broken."

"Yes. And I don't know how to help him."

Her mother paused, then said, "He's got to make his own choices about how to be well. You can't make those for him."

"I know." Wren exhaled slowly. "The truth is, I didn't really want to move in with him, but I was terrified of what he might do if I didn't. So I guess I convinced myself of all the good reasons why I should do it, why it was the loving thing to do. But really, I was just afraid. Afraid of moving in with him, afraid of not moving in with him. It feels like I'm constantly monitoring and watching him, afraid of making him upset, or causing harm, or saying or doing the wrong thing."

"I understand," her mother said.

Yes, she did understand, Wren thought after she hung up the phone a few minutes later. Her mother knew that kind of anxiety from the inside. And she was sorry for that too.

"So, it's all worked out?" Dylan asked as he poured himself another cup of coffee for sermon-writing inspiration.

"With Wren, yes."

But she had some repair work to do with Olivia, which she would undertake as soon as she got home from school. She would apologize for losing her temper and overreacting. She would apologize for accusing her of lying and for not taking time to listen or communicate why she was feeling upset. And she would thank her for helping around the house, especially while she was away taking care of Wren. She hadn't expressed any appreciation for that. In fact, she'd been so preoccupied with Wren's needs, she hadn't taken much notice at all of Olivia. Or Joel. She would apologize to Joel too.

And Phoebe. Poor Phoebe and her lost acorn family.

She found Phoebe upstairs in her room, coloring at her desk.

"Hey, Phoebe-girl, mind if I come in?"

She shook her head without looking up.

Jamie sat down on the pink bedspread. "I'm really sorry you lost your acorn family. I know it was important to you, and I'm sorry I didn't take time to listen to why you were upset. Will you forgive me?"

Phoebe took another crayon from her box. "There was a baby one."

"I know, sweetheart. And I'm sorry. I'm sorry you and Daddy couldn't find it."

She didn't reply.

Jamie reached into her pocket. "I know it's not the same as finding your baby one, but I collected a special acorn, too, when I was visiting Wren. Did I tell you that?"

Phoebe looked up from her drawing and shook her head again. Jamie patted the bedspread. "C'mere. Let me show you."

Silently, she obliged. It seemed her curiosity was strong enough to overcome any remaining hurt feelings or any renewed sadness at being reminded of what she had lost. Jamie wrapped one arm around her. "This is a very special acorn because I found it when I was feeling a bit sad and afraid. It was like a message from God, reminding me that he loves us and takes care of us. And he's always with us, even when we're feeling sad and afraid." Jamie handed it to her daughter. "Would you like to keep it in your collection to remind you?"

Phoebe nodded solemnly and kissed it. "I'll take good care of it," she said, and nestled close.

Wren wandered down the back hallway to Casey's room, where the door was open. "Knock, knock," she called. No answer. She peeked into the room. No sign of him. She glanced out the window toward the parking lot. His car was still there.

She found Kit in her office, working at her desk. "Have you seen Casey?"

"A little while ago. He was in the chapel."

She never would have thought to look for him there. "Oh! Thanks." She strode down the hall. Maybe the Holy Spirit was stirring him. Maybe he was already being drawn by the sense of peace in the place, a sense of Presence. She hoped so.

Pausing at the threshold of the chapel, she peered in. There he was, sitting near the painting of Jesus on the cross, looking up at it. He turned when he heard her footsteps.

"Hey," she said.

"Hey."

She sat down next to him.

He gestured toward the painting. "This is the sort of thing you're going to do? Paint him?"

She shook her head. "No, I'm not good enough to do something like that. But maybe something more simple or abstract. I'm not sure yet."

"Your aunt was telling me about what she asked you to do. How come you didn't?"

"Didn't what? Tell you?"

"Yeah."

Wren shrugged slowly. "I knew you were struggling with your faith, so it just didn't seem like the right moment."

He sat in silence a long time. Then he said, "I haven't stopped believing, Wrinkle. It's just what kind of belief. Like some of the answers I used to trust don't fit anymore." He shifted back and forth in his seat. "I've been sitting here, doing the same trick I did with that Van Gogh woman, trying to see if I can catch his gaze. What do you think? Does he look disappointed to you?"

She stared up at the painting. "Disappointed? No, of course not."

"Really? 'Cause that's what I see."

"I see sorrow," she said. "Compassion. Love. Mercy. But not disappointment, no."

"You're lucky." He shifted back and forth again, still looking up. "No matter which way I look, that's all I see. Like he can't bear to look at me."

"Casey . . ."

"I'm just saying, that's what I see. I'm not saying that's what I know. I know what I'm supposed to see, I just don't see it."

She nodded. "I think that's why Kit invited me to paint his journey to the cross, because she wanted me to see the love that led him there. I think she wanted me to see how he's with me, no matter what, how he keeps me company in everything that's hard and sad. That's why I said yes to painting the stations, because I want to see his love more clearly."

He turned to face her. "You think Vincent saw it?"

She thought a moment and then said, "He saw the suffering. But love? Maybe only glimpses." His favorite Bible verse came to mind. "Sorrowful, yet always rejoicing," she murmured, "that was his motto, his life verse. I know he tried to live it, but . . ."

"Yeah, but in the end . . ." He mimed firing a shotgun.

She flinched.

"A lot of sorrowful, not much rejoicing," he said.

Vincent had to have had glimpses. He couldn't have painted with

such radiance and exuberance without perceiving the hope of redemption, of resurrection. He painted hope in the cycle of the
seasons, in the blossoming of trees in spring, in the delicate wings of
a butterfly, in the seeds planted by a sower, in the golden fields of
wheat ripe for harvest.

In her mind's eye she re-created his haloed stars, swirling like
celestial flowers pollinating the dark with golden grains of light.

Despite the work later being deemed a masterpiece, Vincent
viewed his starry night as a failure, convinced he had been led astray
into painting dangerous abstractions that hindered his recovery at
the asylum. He told Bernard and Theo he could not permit himself
to venture there again. He'd had enough of reaching for stars that
were too big. Something about the vision seemed to frighten him, the
emotions, perhaps, too intense. He was terrified of bringing on another attack of hallucinations. For the sake of his health, he had to
try to remain calm. But the seizures were happening more regularly
and were more debilitating. And since he could only paint when he
was well—

"Did he do it?" Casey asked, his voice low.

"Do what?"

"Kill himself."

She hesitated, then shrugged slightly. All the research and con-
spiracy theories and speculation . . . there would never be a definitive
answer. "He told the innkeeper and his doctor and the authorities
that he shot himself in the fields. And that the police shouldn't blame
anyone else." Which was an odd thing to say. But even if he had
been covering up the truth to protect some bullying boys, as some
claimed, he still seemed to embrace the end as an opportune conclusion for his tormented, lonely life. "Theo was with him when he
died," she said, "and he believed it was intentional, that life was too
heavy for Vincent to bear."

Casey nodded. "The grand finale in the story of the tortured
artist. Poetic, don't you think?"

No, she thought, *not poetic. Tragic.*

The sadness will last forever, he told Theo as he was dying.

But she liked to imagine Vincent surprised and awed by the splendor of everlasting light.

32

Though Kit invited him to join them at the house for dinner, Casey said he was tired and would probably go to bed early. "Well, let me give you a full set of keys." She opened a cabinet in the office and pulled out a ring of them. "This one is for the front door. I'll lock up when we leave, but if you decide to head out, please remember to lock up again. And this one is for your room. Do you think you need one for the office?" She glanced around the room. "I guess if you need access to a printer or paper or anything, that's this one. And that should be it. All the outside doors are on this main key. Am I forgetting anything?"

When he didn't reply, Wren said, "I don't think so. Can you think of anything else you need, Casey?"

He was staring off into space.

"Casey?"

"No, I don't think so. Thank you, Mrs. Rhodes."

"Please call me Kit." She patted his shoulder. "I hope you have a very restful sleep."

"Thanks."

"I'll call you later," Wren said.

"I'll probably just turn off my phone so I can sleep."

"You want Augustine to keep you company? I'll leave my book here for you."

He laughed. "I'll pass."

"Are you sure you don't want to eat with us?"

"I'm sure."

"And you're sure you're okay, that I don't need to worry about you?"

"You're such a mom, you'll worry no matter what I tell you."

Wren fiddled with the collar of her coat. "I guess you're right about that."

He kissed the top of her head. "Well, don't. Everything's fine."

She studied his face a moment, looking for congruity. Relaxed brow, a bit of light in his eyes, no shadow of darkness. He looked at peace. Tired, but at peace.

"Okay." She stood on her tiptoes to embrace him. "I'll see you in the morning."

He rocked her in a bear hug. "Yeah," he said. "Be well, Wrinkle."

And she said, "You too."

With a quiet evening at home, Wren turned again to the texts Kit had supplied for the prayer stations. If she had any hope of painting them, she needed to start thinking and praying about images that might capture and define each scene. A cup, perhaps, for Gethsemane. Or trees like Vincent's, not only his olive grove trees, but his trees in the asylum garden, which were crooked and dark. She turned in her art book to his painting of the tree struck by lightning, then set it on her bed beside her open Bible.

It was no surprise such a tree had caught Vincent's attention while he was recuperating, its harsh amputation highlighted in black. But resilient and defiant it stood, a living parable, with vegetation growing around its base and one side branch soaring upward. To the left of the amputated tree stood an empty stone bench, which, painted at an angle, resembled a coffin. She wondered if that was intentional.

She read the accompanying letter from Vincent to friend and fellow artist Bernard. "You'll understand that this combination of red ochre, of green saddened with grey, of black lines that define the outlines, this gives rise a little to the feeling of anxiety from which some of my companions in misfortune often suffer, and which is called 'seeing red.'" He was also working on another canvas, he said, a painting of a sun rising over a field of new wheat, a painting meant to express great calm and peace. "I'm speaking to you of these two canvases, and especially the first, to remind you that in order to give an impression of anxiety, you can try to do it without heading straight for the historical garden of Gethsemane; in order to offer a consoling and gentle subject it isn't necessary to depict the figures from the Sermon on the Mount."

An impression of anxiety.

✗ She read that portion of Vincent's letter several times, then looked again at Mark's description of Jesus. *Distressed* and *agitated.* Those were the words that caught her attention. "He began to be distressed and agitated."

Those words had nothing to do with most of the paintings she had seen of Christ in the garden of Gethsemane. Most of them depicted Jesus perfectly at rest, his face tranquil, his eyes lifted heavenward, his hands clasped in composed surrender, the light of God's presence and favor engulfing him in a warm glow. Perhaps the artists wanted to assert that this phlegmatic Jesus was meant to be the model for prayer and that those called by his name were to yield with equanimity to the will of God, no matter what the cost.

That's what those paintings had always communicated to Wren. She had never been comforted by them, had never felt any sense of Jesus identifying with her in her own fearful moments of wrestling to yield her will to God's.

But *distressed* and *agitated.* She looked the words up on her phone. The Greek conveyed the idea of being terror-struck, troubled, and fearful. This was no stoic Savior yielding without wrestling. He was overwhelmed—engulfed in grief and agonizing. He was anguished and agonizing. But terror-struck?

Was it possible Jesus had felt afraid?

She stared at her open Bible.

She had heard years ago at a youth retreat that it was impossible to please God without faith, that any fear was sin. And so, by corollary, it was impossible that Jesus had ever been afraid. He was always perfect in obedience and trust.

But was it possible trust and terror weren't mutually exclusive? That someone could be full of trust while being terrified?

She read the story again. Here in the darkness of the garden . . . Was it here that he entered even more fully into the experience of human frailty by feeling afraid?

Through his sacrifice he shared the fellowship of human sorrow and suffering. She was grateful for that. But had he also shared the fellowship of human anxiety?

Was it possible he hadn't withheld himself even from terror?

Was that also a demonstration of his compassion and love?

She closed her eyes and pictured him in his anguish, pleading with the Father, terror-struck, his sweat falling like blood in the dark.

And she loved him even more.

There was one painting of the olive groves meant to be a daytime companion piece to *Starry Night*, a scene with swirling clouds and sculpted mountains, the rock formations like shadowy figures keeping watch over gnarled trees, the clouds like white angelic robes billowing above an earth that churned and flowed with movement mirroring the whirl of the sky. With no visible external light source portrayed, the whole painting seemed illumined from within.

She turned the pages in her book until she found it, then set it on her bed.

This was what she wished she could convey through her own work, that the beauty and terror of Gethsemane could not be separated from one another, that concealed within the sorrow and suffering was a mysterious, shimmering seed that when planted, opened the way to an encounter with the divine.

But how could it possibly be done? And who would see what she saw?

She wished Casey could see it.

Maybe now that he knew about Kit's commission, he would be interested in her painting process and reflections. Despite their long-standing disagreement over Van Gogh, she had always admired Casey's artistic sensibilities, his knack for capturing on film the same fusion of pathos and beauty Vincent had captured in his portraits and landscapes. Casey, when he was well, knew how to see. He just needed to be reminded.

Maybe she could persuade him to return to his art and find healing through it. Maybe he could find in the Man of Sorrows a companion for the journey and be drawn into the love of God. Maybe there was a joint project they could do, she with her painting, he with his film, something that could illustrate hope in spite of suffering, something that could illustrate the astonishing beauty of courage and faith in the midst of it.

Sorrowful, yet always rejoicing.

What a paradox.

Rustling in the doorway caught her attention, and she looked up to see Kit in her bathrobe and slippers. "Am I interrupting?"

"No. Just studying Gethsemane again."

"Feel like you're ready to try painting it?"

Wren smiled. "I'm not sure I'll ever be ready. I don't think I'll ever be able to translate the emotion onto the canvas. It's way beyond me."

Kit sat down in the chair at the desk. "It's beyond all of us, I think, the horror and grace, the awe of Gethsemane."

Awe. That was a good word.

In fact, that was one of the possible renderings of the Greek word. Terror. Awe. Fear. She told Kit what she had seen about Jesus experiencing terror. "Just knowing he felt afraid—that he knows what fear feels like—makes me even more grateful for what he did."

Kit was silent.

"Or maybe that's not right? Maybe that's not what the verse means?"

"No, I read it that way too. And it's been a deep comfort to me over the years, remembering that Jesus knows how it feels to wrestle with resistance and fear." Kit paused. "I don't think you can be truly human if you never wrestle with those things. It's where we move with it that matters. And that's what we see in him, his fearful anguish and his trusting surrender. Both awe-inspiring. Both beautiful."

Yes, Wren thought. *All of it. An awful beauty.*

"I'm about ready to light my Christ candle and pray," Kit said after a while. "Care to join me?"

It had been years since Wren had prayed the examen. But the language of noticing both consolation and desolation resonated with her, especially after having seen with fresh eyes the desolation of Gethsemane becoming her consolation. Mystery, all of it.

In the companionable silence with Kit, she named to God her gratitude. She confessed to God her fear. She asked for the grace to trust him more completely, in both light and darkness. And she prayed his blessing on all those she loved, that each one of them would encounter his faithfulness in life-giving ways. *Especially Casey,* she prayed.

When she opened her eyes, Kit was staring at the flickering candle. "Amen?" Kit asked.

Wren nodded. "Amen."

That night, consoled, she slept more soundly than she had in years.

33

I was up late last night," Kit said as she shuffled into the kitchen in her robe and slippers, her white hair endearingly mussed.

Wren set down her coffee mug. "I'm so sorry! Was I snoring or something?"

Kit laughed. "No, dear one, nothing to do with you. Or, actually, yes. Something to do with you." She wagged her finger. "It's your friend Vincent. I stayed up way past my bedtime, reading some of his letters online. Fascinating man. And the way he painted with words! I think I'm hooked."

"Oh, good. I'm so glad. What were you reading?"

"His early letters, including his first sermon. Oh, how the Word poured out of him, didn't it? Such conviction and passion."

Wren nodded. So much Word, so much conviction and passion that even his pastor father was worried. Vincent never did anything by halves.

Kit filled the kettle with water from the fridge. "It's the theme of consolation that runs through everything in his life, like you were saying when your mom was here. It seems he wanted nothing more than to comfort the poor and poor in spirit, whether he was trying to do that as a minister or evangelist or painter."

That was the bitter irony, Wren thought, that though he longed to comfort and console others with his art, and though he longed to receive comfort and consolation, neither desire was fulfilled during his lifetime.

"And then after reading those letters, I started thinking about the paintings you said he destroyed, so I searched for anything I could find from him about Gethsemane." She sat down across from Wren as she waited for the water to boil. "It's the angel comforting Jesus that seemed to capture his attention, isn't it? That's the scene he wanted to paint?"

"Mm-hmm. Did you read his description of what he planned? The colors he wanted to use?"

"Yes. Blues and yellows, with a starry night background, right?"

"Right." Vincent had envisioned the brightest blues for Jesus and lemon yellow for the angel and a landscape of all different shades of purple.

"When I read that," Kit said, "it reminded me of what you said about him painting his faith with color. So, I started clicking through links and found something intriguing. Have you heard the theory that *Starry Night* is his painting of Gethsemane?"

"What? No." She'd heard the theory about his *Café Terrace at Night* being a representation of the Last Supper, with the robed figure in white glowing beneath the lantern and eleven people sitting around tables while one exited. But Vincent hadn't ever identified it as such. At least, not in his correspondence with Theo.

Kit shrugged. "I don't know if it's multiple scholars or not, but what I read was interesting, how he'd been obsessed with the idea of painting a starry night and how the image brought consolation to him, just like the angel in the garden brought consolation. So then, the theory goes, when he wasn't able to paint Jesus and the angel in Gethsemane, he used those same colors for the sky, moon, and stars."

It was possible, Wren thought, especially since he intended it to be paired with the olive grove. If that theory was true, then *Starry Night* was a painting of both intense agony and intense consolation. Like Gethsemane.

She visualized the masterpiece, with the monumental, sepulchral cypress dominating the left side, its vertical line echoing the church steeple in the center, like two celestial antennae probing the darkness, and to the right, a grove of olive trees nestled beneath the churning sky. Many insisted that the dark church, one of the few unlit buildings in the village, revealed Vincent's rejection of institutional religion, even faith. But what if instead it was an image of the church abandoning him? He'd once told Theo he was no fan of contemporary Christianity, though he thought its founder was sublime. What if the painting represented his identification with the One who knew abandonment and rejection at the hands of the so-called religious? Maybe the images from the garden were embedded after all, the wrestling and sorrow and agony, as well as the light shining in the darkness, bringing hope and strength and consolation to the ones in anguish and affliction. Like an angel appearing in Gethsemane.

"I know it's all conjecture," Kit said. "But I guess that's the beauty of these things, right? How art is open to interpretation and how we can each find something within it that mirrors our own longings or desires."

Exactly, Wren thought. And everyone, it seemed, wanted to claim Vincent as their own, whether atheists, skeptics, or believers. Which was also ironic, given how few people wanted to associate with him when he was alive. Whatever images or themes he had deliberately or subconsciously woven into the work would remain a mystery. But it was a testimony to his genius, how his art could be received at such a deep spiritual and emotional level by so many people. Vincent had achieved, in far greater measure than he ever could have imagined, what he longed to achieve. He provided comfort and consolation.

"There's not a lot of cleaning to be done today," Kit said, "so take your time in the studio. Do you have everything you need? Paints? Canvases? Brushes?"

"Not yet. But maybe Casey and I can go shopping."

"That's a great idea. And remember, I'm reimbursing you."

"Thank you so much."

"Thank *you*, Wren. You've stirred something new in me with your passion. I'm grateful for that." She rose to pour herself a cup of tea. "And how about if we stop at a bakery on the way? It might be nice for Casey to have some treats to enjoy." She smiled. "Before I put him to work."

When they arrived at New Hope with a box of pastries, the parking lot was empty. "Maybe he went out for breakfast," Wren said. She checked her phone in case she had missed a text from him. But there was nothing. And when Kit turned her key in the front door, she discovered it had been left unlocked. She didn't need to voice her annoyance; her pursed lips spoke.

"I'll talk to him," Wren said, "and remind him." She hoped he wouldn't commit too many other offenses. She wasn't sure how tolerant Kit would be. And if his forgetfulness or negligence began to reflect poorly on her as his friend . . .

Kit pushed open the door. A sheet of paper anchored by a ring of keys fluttered on the carpet. Wren stooped to pick it up. *Heading home,* the scrawl read. *Thank you for everything.*

She stared at the note, her body responding before her mind could process anything, her hands trembling, her mouth dry, a wave of nausea causing her to be unsteady on her feet. Gripping the note, she careened down the hallway to the guestroom, which was empty, the bed showing no signs of having been slept in, the towels still folded neatly on the desk.

Kit met her in the doorway. "He's gone?"

"He said he's heading home."

"Which home? With his parents?"

"I doubt it." Wren pulled out her phone and texted him. If he was going back to his parents' house, he would have texted her something like, *Hey! Decided not to stay here. Heading to my folks. I'll call you later.*

She read the note again. *Heading home.* To Reno? To Brooke? Was he returning to abuse? She'd seen it so many times, how even some of the women who seemed to benefit most from the programs at Bethel House had returned home, unable to break free. And if he was heading back to Reno, he wouldn't have wanted her to know about it until he had a few hours of driving under his belt. Maybe he had bolted right after they hugged goodbye.

She checked the time on her phone. If he had left then, he could be almost halfway to Reno by now.

Forget texts. She dialed his number. It went straight to voicemail.

"What about contacting his parents?" Kit asked.

But when she called the house, his mother said she hadn't heard from him. "He's not coming back from Reno until Christmas," she said.

"You mean"—Wren lowered herself onto a bench in the foyer—"you mean he wasn't with you over the weekend?"

"With us? No. He lives in Reno." Her tone of voice indicated she thought perhaps Wren had suffered a mental breakdown. "You know he's married, right?"

"Yes. Yes, I know. I—never mind. I guess I misunderstood his text. I'm sorry to bother you." If he hadn't told his parents about leaving Brooke, then she wasn't going to tell them he was returning to her. He obviously hadn't wanted them to know.

"I don't understand," Kit said after Wren relayed the information. "I thought he said he was staying with his parents."

"He did."

So, where had he been staying? And what else had he lied about?

There was nothing she could do except wait to hear from him. *If* she heard from him. If he had decided to return to control and abuse, then maybe he had also decided he would submit again to Brooke's demand that he cut off contact.

In the quiet of her studio she replayed their final interaction. Had there been a tell she had missed? Something in his tone of voice? In his facial expression? Anything false or final?

He had seemed a bit preoccupied, but she had believed him when he said he was tired. She'd offered to let him sleep with *La Berceuse*. But he said he didn't want to have nightmares. Or maybe that was from earlier in the day. Had he laughed when she offered to leave Augustine with him? She couldn't remember. But she could hear his laugh in her mind, so it was possible he laughed. She had told him she would call him, but he said he would be turning off his phone.

Had he manipulated her right then? Did he already have in mind what he was going to do? Or did he decide later?

She dialed his number and left another "Please call me" message. Soon his mailbox would be full.

He'd told her not to worry about him, that he was fine. He'd teased her about being a mom. He had often teased her about that. She had studied his face, looking for darkness, for anything to indicate she should be worried, but she had seen peace in him. Maybe he was at peace because he had wrestled and made his decision to leave.

And then he'd rocked her and said, "Be well."

Her throat burned.

That was his goodbye. She hadn't realized it at the time. But it was the same benediction he'd given when he told her he would have to cut off contact. *Be well, Wrinkle.*

How could she have missed it?

Casey had said his farewell. There would be no reaching him.

"Maybe he'll call you when he gets there," Kit said as they ate their sandwiches in her office.

"I doubt it. He won't want to be lectured."

She stared at the extra sandwich she had packed for him and tried not to cry. *Such a mom,* she heard him say, a smile in his voice. Or was it sorrow? If she hadn't been so prone to anxiety, would he have confided in her? Had he confided in anyone?

"There's no one else you can think to call? No one else he might be in touch with?"

"I don't know." She had texted the only friends she had contact information for. No one had seen him, though one confirmed he had called to ask whether he could stay with them, but they didn't have room. At least he hadn't lied about that. "I guess he could have been at a hotel, though I can't imagine him wanting to spend the money.

Or maybe he slept in his car." The temperatures had been cold, but if he kept his insulated sleeping bag in the trunk . . .

She stared at Kit's desk, another possibility dawning. He had stayed at Crossroads before. What if he had stayed there again?

"Sure, he was here a few days," Mara said when Wren reached her by phone later that afternoon. She recognized the physical description. "He said his name was Kevin, though. I remember 'cause that's my son's name. His wallet had been stolen, so he didn't have any ID. And no credit cards to pay for a hotel. Nice guy, very polite. He told me he was just passing through, and he didn't plan to stay longer than a couple of days. He was from somewhere out west, I think. Vegas, maybe?"

"Reno," Wren murmured.

"Yeah, Reno. And his wife had died, and he was distraught about that. Hadn't been married long, I don't think, poor guy."

Oh, Casey. "Do you happen to know when he arrived?"

"Well, let's see. He was here when I got back from Texas last Wednesday." Wren hadn't seen him until Friday. That's when he said he arrived in town. "But I wasn't here over the weekend, so I don't know when he left. Why? Is he in trouble?"

She pressed her free hand against her forehead. "I think he might be."

No, she told Kit, he didn't have schizophrenia. Bipolar, yes, sometimes with delusions. But as long as he was taking his medications, he remained fairly stable. When she'd questioned him, he had insisted he was taking them, so she had interpreted his depressed and dark state of mind as being consistent with someone who had endured and escaped abuse—not as an indicator of an acute episode.

She should have seen it. She should have known.

"Don't berate yourself over that," Kit said, reaching for her hand. "Even doctors can have trouble diagnosing these things."

"I'd almost rather believe he's been deliberately lying and manipulating everyone," she said. "That would make me less frightened for him."

"I understand."

She picked up her phone. She needed to call his parents again. And this time she would tell them everything.

34

Her parents were praying. Mara was praying. Hannah was praying. Kit was praying.

Good thing, too, because Wren could not pray. Or read. Or concentrate. So she smeared paint onto her only blank canvas, bright blue and burgundy and violet. She swirled the colors into a churning vortex, watching the form become a black hole of darkness that threatened to pull her in. Sometimes she whispered, *Help* or *Please.* That would have to be good enough.

Hour after hour she waited for even a morsel of information from his parents. But they did not call. When she called them again that night, his father said they were doing everything they could to locate him. And in the background she heard his mother cry, "It's her fault. Tell her it's all her fault!"

"Why in the world would they blame you?" Kit asked as she put away the soup Wren could not eat.

Wren blew her nose. "I don't know." She dialed Casey's number for the hundredth time. No answer.

She wished she could call Brooke. But there was no way she was asking his parents for her number.

"Well, don't let an accusation like that stick," Kit said. "We say lots of things when we're distraught. And I understand how distressed his parents must feel. But maybe he's doing exactly what he said— he's heading home and just hasn't gotten there yet. Like you said, he may not want to talk to you because he knows you won't approve. And if his parents didn't know he'd left in the first place . . ."

It was a logical scenario. But she didn't trust that Casey was operating from logic. No. He was in danger. She felt it in her gut.

But then again, how reliable was her intuition? She had slept soundly last night without once sensing anything amiss. She hadn't once been prompted to call or text to make sure he was okay. She had taken him at his word. And his word had been false.

"Did he say anything to you in the chapel yesterday?" Wren asked. "He mentioned you told him I was painting the stations. Did he say anything else?"

Kit thought a moment. "He came in while I was there praying. He didn't see me over in the corner and sat down in front of the crucifixion painting. I was going to leave through the back door so I wouldn't disturb him, but he saw me. So I mentioned something about where the painting had come from and how I'd asked you to paint some work based on Scripture for our prayer journey in the spring. But I don't remember him responding. Or if he did, it was something simple like, That's good. Or maybe, She's good." Kit paused. "Obviously, I don't know him well, but he didn't seem in a mood to talk, so I let him be."

Wren ran her hands through her hair. If only she had recognized the signs when she was with him in the chapel: his questions about Vincent, his comment about Jesus looking disappointed. But she was so happy he was noticing the painting and so hopeful about the Spirit stirring him, she'd been blind to the undercurrents of despair. His mother was right. It *was* her fault. The impulsivity, the mood swings, the flashes of anger—she should have recognized the warning signs. She should have alerted someone. But she'd believed his story. She'd trusted him.

And if he'd lied about staying with his parents, what else had he lied about? What if he'd lied about Brooke? What if she wasn't an abuser? What if she'd been a victim of his unpredictable mood swings and aggression? What if his addictions, mixed with the manic and depressive episodes, had proven too much for her? What if she'd asked him to leave?

And if he was now returning, what if Brooke was the one in danger?

Oh, God.

Wren felt sick to her stomach.

She had to reach her. She had to warn her.

She was about to dial his parents' number again when another idea came to mind. If Brooke had been monitoring his texts, then maybe she still had Casey's old phone. It was worth a try.

Wren texted the old number: *Brooke, if you get this, please call me.*

She set her phone on the table and checked the clock. She would give the plan half an hour. And then she would call—bother—his parents again.

This whole business with Casey, this was the very sort of thing Jamie worried could be a tipping point for Wren. Why this? Why now?

She tucked Phoebe into bed and kissed her goodnight. "I need my Bumble," Phoebe said.

"I'll get your Bumble. You stay in bed." Jamie retrieved the stuffed bee from the floor.

"And Biggie."

"Okay, Biggie too." She rummaged through the mesh bag of stuffed animals until she found the pink elephant. "Here you go. Bumble"—she made buzzing and kissing noises as she nuzzled Phoebe's face with the bee—"and Biggie." She did her best impression of an elephant trumpeting.

Phoebe laughed. "Daddy does it better."

"I know. I'll get Daddy for you. But no more stories tonight, okay? You need to go to sleep."

"Did I hear a pig squealing in here?" Dylan called from the doorway.

Phoebe giggled and thrust Biggie into the air.

He leaned his head back, raised his arm like a trunk, and blew out air through closed lips. Phoebe mimicked him. "Good one, Feebs!"

He sat down on her bed. "But keep your lips even tighter. Like this."
He blew again. Phoebe joined him, louder this time.

"She's already had her stories," Jamie said.

"Okay."

Phoebe said, "Shadow puppets!"

Jamie shook her head. "Not tonight."

"Pleeeeease?"

"Mommy says no," Dylan said.

Jamie shot him a look he immediately interpreted correctly.

"Daddy says no," he said.

Phoebe pouted.

"You need to get to sleep, pumpkin." He kissed her on the forehead.
"We'll do shadow puppets another time."

"But I want a Bible story!"

Oh, she was good.

Dylan looked at Jamie. "One," she said. "But let's sing prayers
first."

Phoebe shut her eyes tight and clasped her hands together. Jamie
sang along, her heart disconnected from the words. The only one on
her mind for prayer right now was Wren. She had promised to pray
for Casey, for his safety and state of mind, but all those words had
rung hollow. What she felt toward him was resentment. Resentment
that he had swept into town, caused chaos, and left again, leaving
more chaos in his wake.

"Maybe he left the way he did for a good reason," Dylan said
when he joined her in the kitchen after finally settling Phoebe.
"Maybe he made a choice to return to his marriage and work on it."
He paused. "I hope they can get good counseling and see what can
be salvaged and restored."

"But the abuse piece," Jamie said. "Wren only ever heard his side
of the story, but she believed him. And now to hear that he was lying
about these other things, it's devastating to her."

Dylan's phone buzzed in his pocket. He looked at the message,
then shook his head. "And speaking of marriages in crisis, there's

one imploding as we speak. Sorry, hon. I hate to leave right now
but—"

"I know," she said. "Go."

Half an hour passed with no reply from Brooke. Not that Wren
had expected one. It had been a long shot, first thinking the message
might reach her, then thinking she might reply.

Wren stared at her phone.

Wait.

What if—?

He said his wife had died, Mara had told her, *and he was distressed.*

What if he hadn't been lying?

And why hadn't she thought of this sooner?

Oh, God.

What if Brooke had caused him to snap? There were news head-
lines all the time about that sort of thing. What if he'd done something terrible and then fled? What if he came to Kingsbury to hide
out?

Oh, God.

Her heart pounding in her chest, she picked up her phone and
dialed his parents' number again. His mother answered. "Why can't
you just leave us alone?"

"I'm sorry, I was just hoping to reach Brooke to make sure she's
okay."

"*Okay?* Of course she's not okay! How could she be? She's worried
sick."

Present tense, worried. Brooke wasn't dead. *Thank God.* Wren sank
into a chair. "No, I understand, I mean—"

"You *understand*? How dare you say you understand!" In the background his father was saying, *Leave it alone, Sue.* "No! I won't leave it
alone! You—do you have any idea the chaos you caused for them,
the strain you put on their marriage? You just couldn't let him go,
could you? Always running to him for support."

"No, I—"

"And what did you do? Lure him here? Promise him what?"

"Nothing! I—"

"That he could move in with you? Leave his wife and baby behind?"

Wren gripped the phone, leaned into the table, and pushed out the word. "Baby?"

"Oh!" his mother exclaimed. "Not such a confidante after all, huh? Never told you?"

"No." Wren's eyes stung.

His mother laughed a horrible, cynical, spiteful laugh. "Classic," she said. "Absolutely classic." And the call went dead.

"But none of this makes any sense, Wren." Jamie stared out their bedroom window, hoping Dylan would be home soon. "Why wouldn't Brooke have called his parents when he left? Wouldn't she have been worried then?"

Wren said she didn't understand it, either. Maybe the abuse story was true, she said, and Brooke didn't want his parents to know. Or maybe Casey had told her he was going away on a business trip. Or visiting a sick friend. Or that a long-lost uncle had died and left him an inheritance. Who knew what tale he had spun? Or what delusions he might have suffered? She said she had imagined all kinds of possible scenarios, and none of them made sense.

"And a baby!" Jamie said. "Do you mean a baby-baby or just that she's pregnant?"

"Mom!"

"I'm sorry. I'm just trying to wrap my head around this. How could he not tell you about that? You were his closest friend!"

Wren started to cry again.

"Oh, love. I'm sorry. What can I do?"

"I don't know."

"Is Kit there?"

It sounded like she said yes.

"Put her on, sweetheart, will you?" She paced back and forth. "Jamie."

At the sound of her name spoken with steadiness and strength, her eyes filled with tears. "Thank God you're there, Kit. Again."

"I'm not going anywhere, just work tomorrow. But we'll both be there."

"And tonight? Do you think she's safe?"

"I think so. I'll talk to her about it."

"Thank you. I know I promised not to go around her, but please. If you sense any danger . . ."

"Of course. I'll let you know right away."

She picked up Wren's *Weemoed* sketch from her nightstand and clutched it to her chest. "None of it makes any sense, Kit. And I know I've asked the question before, and there's probably no answer this time with Casey, either. But with all the deception and dysfunction and chaos he's caused, what's mental illness and what's sin?"

There was silence. And then Kit said, "We can't parse it, can we? We don't know anything about his state of mind. It's enough to say it's all broken. All hard."

"Yes." Jamie stared at the empty driveway. "All of it."

Wren slipped off her jeans and pulled on her flannel pajamas, a new possibility dawning. What if it was the image of the mother rocking the unseen cradle that provoked Casey into making his decision to return home?

She had thought he was only responding to what he deemed an ugly portrait. But as she replayed that scene again, she glimpsed the goad. He'd stormed out of her studio after she mentioned Vincent's admiration for mothers and his unfulfilled longing to be a father. *Overrated.* That's what Casey had muttered.

Never had she imagined when he spit the word that he was a dad.

It made sense now, his reaction to Augustine's expression, his interpretation that she couldn't be pleased, that she didn't approve, that he couldn't catch her eye and see any tenderness. It wasn't about his mother. Or rather, it wasn't *only* about his mother. Maybe it was about Brooke too.

Or maybe it was about himself. He had reacted to the painting of Jesus on the cross in the same way he had reacted to Augustine. "He looks disappointed, doesn't he?" he'd murmured in the chapel. "Like he can't bear to look at me."

Maybe Casey couldn't bear to look at himself.

"Heading to bed?" Kit called from the doorway.

Wren balanced herself against the bureau and removed her socks. "I don't know. I can't tell if I'm tired or not."

"Well, I'm just getting ready to pray, if you'd like to join me."

"I don't know. I don't feel like I can concentrate on anything right now."

"That's understandable." She entered and sat down on the bed. "I promised your mom I'd make sure you're safe, though. How are you feeling?"

Wren tossed her discarded clothes into a laundry basket. "I feel sad. Anxious. Confused." She paused. "Angry too. It's all kind of a messed-up jumble."

Kit nodded. "All those things are normal. And it's a good sign that you can articulate all those feelings."

Wren sat down beside her. "I keep replaying our conversations from yesterday, looking for things I missed. But I can't see it. I can't see any hints he dropped along the way. Nothing. Going back months, I mean."

She ran it through her head again. If Brooke had already had the baby, then she could do the math. It explained their short engagement and the wedding out of the country. It explained a lot, actually. What it didn't explain was why Casey hadn't told her.

"I know I shouldn't make this about me," she said. "I know I should be happy he decided to go back to his wife and baby. And I hope that's a good thing for all of them. But after everything we've been through together, it hurts that he didn't feel like he could confide in me. And it makes me wonder what else he hid over the years."

Everything she thought she'd known and understood about their friendship had died. And she didn't know what to do with that. There was nothing she could do about it if they could never have a conversation to work it out. She wiped her eyes with her wrist. "You think you know someone and . . ."

Kit pulled a tissue from the box on the desk and handed it to her. "I know. I understand."

From the expression on her face, Wren knew they shared this particular grief in common too. Companions in sorrow. In bewilderment. And in betrayal.

Maybe she could pray after all, if she approached prayer in a different way. "Do you have any magazine pictures here for a collage?"

A dirt path winding through golden woods, a shelf of books with bindings in many different colors, a flock of birds in flight, a gauzy pink sunrise over mountains. At the kitchen table, with the Christ candle lit, Wren sifted through images from Kit's collection, scanning for photos that comforted or agitated, attracted or repelled.

There. She found one: the wreckage of a plane in a field, still smoldering.

She picked up the photo for a closer look. What news story had accompanied it? Were there any survivors?

She set it back on the table and covered it up with other pictures. Why would Kit have cut out an image like that? Who would choose it?

She scanned for a mental reset. A pair of red high heels. A little boy holding a yellow balloon. A man and woman walking along a beach, sharing deep conversation. She covered that one up too.

Across the table from her, Kit was arranging images in a preliminary way on her cardstock, shifting and rotating and layering them.

Wren stood and reached for photos she hadn't yet explored: a bowl of apples, an open pink polka dot umbrella, and a breakfast tray with a small vase of flowers, muffins, and fruit.

But no matter how hard she tried, she couldn't shake the image of the plane crash. Just like she hadn't been able to shake the image of the whales. *Work with it,* urged the voice inside her head. She stared at the pictures she had stacked on top, then removed it again.

She didn't want that one in her collage. It was too sad, too violent.

Too honest.

Too true.

Be open to what the image might want to reveal, Dr. Emerson had counseled her about the stranded whales. Don't try so hard to ignore it. You'll just give it more power.

Okay, fine.

She set the image of the charred fuselage on her cardstock square, right in the center. Then she took the one with the man and the woman walking along the beach and cut it in half, dividing them.

A dark and stormy sky streaked with jagged edges of lightning, that was hers. So was the tiny fishing boat being tossed upon churning seas. And the ridiculous polka dot umbrella, because really, what kind of protection did that offer against a storm?

All these she laid onto her cardstock square, arranging and re-arranging, trimming and layering, then fixing them into place with glue.

Wrecked. That's what she would title her prayer collage.

She was just about to declare it finished when one small photo, one Kit had collected and then discarded, caught her attention and beckoned her, the photo of a tiny premature baby hooked up to wires, crying. Wren picked it up. The baby was so small, she fit entirely into the palm of a hand. Whose hand? A doctor's? A parent's? Wren stared at the fingers cradling the child and marveled. How could one so fragile and vulnerable survive? And yet, there she was, alive and strong enough to cry.

She picked up her scissors again and carefully trimmed around each finger. Then she set the hand with the crying baby on top of the wreckage, right in the center. There were survivors. There was a rescue. She would not be abandoned or forsaken. She was safely held, even here.

As she stared at her collage, words from Psalm 139 came to mind. She opened the Bible that Kit had set on the table. She didn't need to find her own words for prayer. They had been given to her by a companion in sorrow and hope long ago:

> Where can I go from your Spirit? Where can I flee from your presence? If I go up to the heavens, you are there; if I make my bed in the depths, you are there. If I rise on the wings of the dawn, if I settle on the far side of the sea, even there your hand will guide me, your right hand will hold me fast. If I say, "Surely the darkness will hide me and the light become night around me," even the darkness will not be dark to you; the night will shine like the day, for darkness is as light to you.

Amen, she whispered. *For me. And for Casey. Please.*

The next morning Wren was emerging from the women's bathroom with her cleaning cart when Kit met her in the hallway, a plain white office envelope in her hand. "This was in the chapel, on a chair beside the crucifixion painting."

For Wren, Casey's scrawl read.

Wren clutched it to her chest.

"I guess I wasn't in there yesterday," Kit said. "I only just found it."

Wren hadn't been in the chapel, either. She had spent all day in the studio. But she went to the chapel now and sat where Casey had left it for her to find. Hands trembling, she removed a single unlined sheet of printer paper.

If you paint a rooster crowing, think of me.
If you paint him saying, "Father, forgive them," think of me.
And if you paint the thief on the cross who said he was sorry, paint my face and think of me.

Be well, Wrinkle.

Love, Casey

She looked up at the painting of Jesus, his arms extended, his head bowed. As she sank to her knees, the letter pressed to her heart, she thought she heard him cry out with a loud voice. But the cry was from her own lips, out of the depths.

35

When her phone buzzed with a text late that afternoon, Wren knew it wouldn't be Casey. It was his father. The authorities had found his car in Utah, overturned in a ravine. The family asked that she respect their desire for privacy during this difficult time. There would be a private memorial service in Reno.

She handed Kit the phone so she wouldn't have to open her mouth.

"My God, my God . . ." Kit murmured as she stared at the screen. "Why?"

If Wren could have formed her own words, she wouldn't have spoken any better.

Manila, Utah. Victim in single-car crash identified. That was the headline Jamie found after hours of searching online. Casey Matthew Wilson, 28, of Reno, Nevada. Witnesses said he was driving erratically on Highway 44 when his car went off the road into a ravine. The medical examiner's office said Wilson, the sole occupant of the vehicle, died from injuries related to the crash. Additional testing was underway.

She sent the link to Kit, in case she thought Wren should see it.

"There won't be any closure for her," Jamie said to Dylan as she shut her laptop and set it on the coffee table. "Especially if his family won't let her come for the funeral."

And even if she went to the funeral, what kind of closure could there be when none of the questions about his intentions could ever be definitively answered? All the questions Jamie was asking were no doubt the ones that would torment Wren. Had he left Kingsbury intending to return to his wife and child? Had he changed his mind along the way? Was it an accident? Was the letter he left for her a temporary goodbye and "I'm sorry" letter, or a suicide note?

Dylan wrapped his arm around her and pulled her closer on the couch. "I don't get it," he said. "Why are his parents treating Wren like she's the culprit here?"

"I don't know. Maybe Brooke is telling them Wren broke up their marriage. Evidently, she was insecure about their friendship and had asked Casey to cut off contact." A detail Wren had only just disclosed.

"Like an emotional affair?" he asked.

"She thought they were codependent. Too attached."

"Well . . ."

"I know." Maybe Brooke wasn't wrong.

Dylan said, "I guess it makes sense they would believe what his wife says. They'd want to support her, especially with a grandchild. If I were them, I'd do everything I could to make sure I'd remain part of the baby's life."

"I know. Me too."

And, oh! What would that be like for Wren, knowing he had left behind part of himself and never having the opportunity to meet his child?

If the stress of losing his friendship before had been enough to plunge her into danger and despair, what now?

She slept. Day and night Wren slept. In the mornings Kit would wake her and sometimes persuade her to eat some toast, and then she would drive her to New Hope, where she would sleep again, not in Casey's guestroom, but in the one adjacent to his. Kit did not want her to be left alone at the house. Wren understood this. She did not want to be left alone, either.

Her mother offered to come. No, Wren said. Not right now. Her mother asked her to come for Christmas. No, Wren said. She didn't have the strength to travel. Or celebrate anything.

Kit drove her to appointments with Dawn—how many, she didn't know. Dawn said she might want to consider going back to Glenwood for more help. No, Wren said. No more hospitals. She wasn't in danger of harming herself. She just wanted to sleep. And not wake up. Or wake up and discover it had all been a horrible nightmare.

Her mother sent a link to his obituary. She could not read it. Her mother told her his baby's name was Estelle Rose, but she didn't know how old she was. The obituary didn't say. Someday maybe she would read it herself. Or not.

Kit read psalms to her while she lay in bed. My tears have been my food day and night. Out of the depths I cry. My God, my God, why have you forsaken me?

Her parents sent her money so she could buy more art supplies. She didn't want to paint again. Even though Dawn said she needed to. But she couldn't.

Hannah came to see her, sometimes at New Hope, sometimes at the house. Wren didn't know how many times. When she offered to serve her communion, Wren opened her mouth so Hannah could place a bit of bread on her tongue. She chewed it slowly and tried to believe the words Hannah spoke. Then Hannah gently held a cup to her mouth so she could sip. And she tried to receive.

Kit gave her two framed prints: *Starry Night* and *Olive Trees.* Wren set them side by side on the long bureau in her room. Sometimes she looked at them and thought of Jesus or Vincent. But mostly, she slept. And hoped she would not be tormented by dreams of cars crashing and abandoned babies crying and voices screaming it was all her fault.

She prayed. Day and night, because she couldn't sleep, Jamie prayed. Or tried to. Mostly it felt as if she was talking to herself. There were no moments of encouragement and no signs of deliverance or rescue. So, she took Kit's suggestion and started praying through lament psalms. Has God forgotten to be gracious? I am overwhelmed with troubles. How long, Lord? Why do you hide your face and forget our misery and oppression?

Jamie told herself Wren had all the support she needed and that her being physically present in Kingsbury wouldn't make a difference, even though she wished she could be there with her. Dylan said he knew it was hard, but the kids needed her to be mentally and emotionally present with them, especially with Christmas coming. It was such a busy time of year, he needed her to be present too. She knew, she said. She was sorry. She would try.

She bought gifts. She hosted parties. She helped make costumes for the nativity play. But her heart was far from all of it.

The Word became flesh, she reminded herself. The Word descended into all the suffering and sorrow of the world. But she wanted Jesus to do more than that. She wanted him to fix it. He did not fix it. She wished she could fix it. She could not fix it. And she was sad and disappointed that he would not. When he had the power to do it, he did not.

My God, my God, why?

36

Estelle, her mother had told her. His baby's name was Estelle. Like a star. Estelle Rose. Celestial flower. That was his baby. He had left his baby. He had returned to his baby. He had not made it safely there. He was gone.

He had a baby named Estelle. Like a star. Like flowery stars in a starry night. They had named their baby after the stars. Poor baby. Poor little baby.

Estelle. Like a star twinkling in the dark.

Wren rolled over in her bed and stared at the ceiling.

Casey had named her after the stars he loved to sleep beneath. What a beautiful name, Estelle. She could pray for her. Pray for Estelle, his tiny star.

Baby Estelle would never hear him laugh. She would never be enfolded in his arms in a bear hug or hear his voice say, Don't be afraid. The only stories she would ever hear about him would be stories her mother or his parents told. She wouldn't know how he rescued Theo and the other kittens from the dumpster. She wouldn't know how he once dreamed of making films that would change lives. She wouldn't know. There was no one to tell her.

Poor baby. Poor sad little star.

She would write to the baby. She would tell Baby Estelle about her daddy.

Did her daddy love her?

She didn't know.

She would not write to the baby.

She wanted to see his obituary.

Kit printed out a copy so Wren could hold it in her hands. Then Kit sat on the couch with her while she read.

Casey Matthew Wilson, 28, passed away on December 13. He is survived by his loving wife, Brooke, and newborn daughter, Estelle Rose . . .

Wren shook her head. She couldn't read any more.

"How long?" she asked.

Kit took hold of her hand. "How long until what, dear one?"

Wren stared at the paper. "How long since Casey . . ."

"A few weeks," Kit said.

"I missed the funeral."

"It was far away."

Wren nodded.

"Hannah offered to lead a memorial service for him," Kit said.

"Did she?"

"Do you think you might like that? To have a service to remember him?"

"No one will come."

"I'll come," Kit said. "We can sit in the chapel near the painting and remember him."

Wren remembered him sitting near the painting in the chapel and wept.

"I'll come," Jamie told Kit on the phone. "If she decides to do that,

I'll be there." Now that Christmas was behind them, the schedule with
the kids and the church had opened up. Dylan wouldn't begrudge her
going, even with the cost of it. If Wren was thinking about a memorial
service, it was a sign of life. An odd sign of life, but a sign of life nonetheless. At this point, Jamie would take anything she could get.

"Tell me about you, Jamie. How are you holding up?"

No one had asked her that question lately. Dylan had been preoccupied with various tasks and crises at church, the small group of
pastors' wives had stopped meeting during the Christmas season and
was awaiting her leadership to launch it again, and she hadn't yet
made any move toward finding a spiritual director or renewing a
relationship with a counselor. Her own fault, she knew. But it all
required energy she didn't have. "I'm tired," she said.

"Of course you are. Suffering alongside a loved one is exhausting.
A hard cup to drink."

She sat down on her bed. That was a good way to describe it,
especially when there didn't seem to be a bottom to the cup. Or
maybe it kept refilling. "I just feel so helpless in everything," she said.
"It's hard sometimes to see how any prayers are being answered. And
then that feeds my cycle of wanting to take control again, to step in
and try to manage things. Fix things. But I can't. And then that feeds
the discouragement."

"I know," Kit said, "but you've done so well in persevering."

It didn't feel that way to her. "All I've done is worried. I haven't
been attentive to the kids or Dylan, not really. I've tried, but . . ."

Kit was silent a moment, then said, "You've tried and you're still
trying. You're still hoping and watching for how God is revealing
himself in all of this. And that's enough."

37

S he wanted to see Estelle Rose. She needed to see her. She needed to know when she was born and whether she looked like her daddy.

Wren reached for her phone on the nightstand, then sat up in bed. She had promised herself she would never stalk Brooke online. Even after Casey sent the text saying Brooke had asked him to cut off contact, Wren had kept that contract with herself. As a matter of integrity.

She stared at her screen. She was the one who had made the rule for herself; she could break it. Just this once.

Brooke, as it turned out, didn't have private settings on her social media accounts. There was Brooke in the hospital. There was Casey in the hospital. He was holding Estelle Rose. He looked happy. And afraid. She saw anxiety in his eyes. Terror, even.

Estelle was born on Thanksgiving Day.

She had known something was wrong. On the day that should have been joyful for him, he had been afraid. Everything's fine, he texted. Everything was not fine. Maybe he wanted it to be fine. But it was not fine.

It could not have been fine. He would not have left if it had been fine.

Baby Estelle went to the funeral. She wore a black headband with a bow wrapped around her tiny head. Brooke wore a short black dress. She posted selfies. *Missing my beloved Casey.* She posted pictures of Estelle. *Missing my daddy.* She posted pictures of the two of them together. *We love and miss you forever. Hugs and kisses from your favorite girls.* The photos had hundreds of likes and hearts and sad faces and comments:

Sending love.

Be strong!

So sad.

Praying for you.

You're so beautiful.

Love you!

Casey is watching over you and your little angel from heaven.

He'll always be with you.

She shouldn't envy and resent Brooke for getting so much support. But she did. She shouldn't judge a grieving woman for wanting attention or seeking it. But she did. She scrolled through the posts again. Whatever story Brooke needed to tell herself, whatever she needed to believe about Casey's life, death, and their life together in order to grieve and heal, that was her business.

She shouldn't care. But she did. She cared about the truth. There was no knowing the truth. Not about anything. Not now.

She stared at the photo of Casey holding Estelle in the hospital. What kind of man abandoned his baby? And then lied about it? What kind of man?

She shouldn't be a stalker. But she couldn't help it. Having an open conduit to his life with Brooke was irresistible. She spent hours examining every post over the past year, every photo of him, every photo of them together, every update about what they ate or where they went and with whom. Pictures of them walking the Camino, pictures of their engagement, pictures of their wedding, their honeymoon. Some of them she had seen. Casey had sent them to her. But after Brooke announced she was pregnant, her updates became entirely about herself. The few pictures Casey did appear in, he seemed vacant.

She touched his face on the screen.

If she had been sketching the progression of his life with Brooke, she would have seen it, how his eyes stopped lighting up when he smiled, how a cloud of melancholy began to descend. And then remained.

He should have told her. Why hadn't he told her?

What reason had she ever given him not to trust that she would love him and support him through anything?

It was selfish of him to conceal and deceive. But he knew that. He knew he was wrong, and he was sorry. He had left a note. She had his note. She would always have his note.

If only he'd had the courage to speak his regrets aloud. She could have helped him. She could have saved him. If only she'd checked Brooke's profile months ago, she would have discovered the truth about her being pregnant, and she could have confronted Casey about his secrecy. If only, if only, if only.

She scrolled back to the posts from the day he died. *Terrible news. Accident. On his way back from a trip. Lost our beloved Casey. Miss you, babe. Love you forever. Can't stop crying.*

Was Brooke hiding the truth? Telling the truth? Deceived about the truth?

Casey had hidden the truth. Had he spoken any truth? Been deceived about the truth?

What was the truth?

He left Reno to escape abuse; he left Reno to escape responsibility.

He arrived in Kingsbury planning to stay; he arrived in Kingsbury planning not to stay.

He left Kingsbury intending to return to his family; he left Kingsbury knowing he would never get there.

Wren clutched his beanie to her chest. It was her fault; it wasn't her fault.

It's not your fault, Hannah said.

It's your fault, Brooke said.

It's not your fault, Kit said.

It's your fault, his parents said.

It's not your fault, her parents said.

It's your fault, the voice inside her said.

It's not your fault, Dawn said.

It is, Wren said. *It is my fault.* But whenever anyone asked her why it was her fault, she didn't know the answer.

There would never be any answers. Because the only one who knew the truth—if he knew the truth—was Casey.

She set her phone aside. She would not be a stalker. But she could watch for posts about Estelle and see if she grew to resemble her daddy. She could read posts and see pictures and videos about her rolling over or sitting up or eating solid food or learning to crawl or saying her first words or taking her first steps or going off to school or getting married. Brooke would publicly chronicle their life together, and Wren could watch and pray.

Casey was gone. But he had left behind his little star. She could see her whenever she wanted. And Brooke would never know. It would be her secret. Her secret with Casey.

Wren rose from bed and washed her face. Maybe she would even take a shower. That would be enough for the day.

Kit looked up from her reading as Wren, wearing something other than sweats or pajamas for the first time in weeks, came downstairs Sunday afternoon. "Did you tell me about a funeral?" Wren asked, sitting down across from her. "Or did I imagine it?"

Kit hesitated. "That was about six weeks ago. They had it out in Reno."

"No. I know. I remember. I couldn't go."

"That's right."

"But another funeral Hannah offered to do. Did you tell me that?"

"Yes. She offered to lead one in the chapel."

Brooke had put together her own version of whatever she thought had honored him. But Brooke didn't know him like she did. Brooke would never know him like she did.

Wren made her decision. She needed to be the one to organize Casey's memorial service, the real one. "I'd like to do that," she said.

Kit nodded. "I'm glad. Shall I call Hannah and arrange it?"

"No. I'll do it."

Six weeks. Had she really sleepwalked through six weeks?

No more. Even if it hurt, she needed to be awake. Estelle needed a godmother who would watch over her, even from a distance. Casey would want it that way.

For the service, she wanted flowers. Sunflowers, like Vincent had at his. If the florist could get sunflowers in January. Casey wouldn't have cared about flowers, but Hannah said memorial services were as much about the people who were grieving as about the ones who had died. And she wanted sunflowers. She would use the money her parents sent her for Christmas to buy them.

"What else would you like to include?" Hannah asked when they met in the New Hope chapel on Monday afternoon. "Did he have any favorite songs?"

"Just secular stuff. Nothing that would work well for a service, I don't think."

"How about Scripture? Any favorite passages?"

Wren thought a moment and then said, "I'm not sure. When we were younger, he liked the Beatitudes. And he liked the verse from Philippians about forgetting what lies behind and pressing forward. But he didn't talk much about his faith the past couple of years. I don't know if he just became jaded, seeing all the suffering, or cynical because of things going on in his own life or . . ."

Hannah waited.

Wren's eyes filled with tears. "I think he did it on purpose."

If Hannah was surprised, she didn't show it.

"I know that no one will ever know for sure, but he wasn't well. And I couldn't help him."

Had she already had this conversation with her pastor? She couldn't remember. Maybe she had rehearsed it every time Hannah came with the bread and the cup, always searching for closure that would never come because she would never know the truth. "I couldn't save him."

Hannah leaned forward. "No," she said, her face filled with compassion. "That wasn't your job. You were his friend. And you loved him well."

"It wasn't enough."

"You did the best you could, Wren. You aren't responsible for any decisions he made or wasn't able to make. You can't carry the weight of that burden. It will crush you."

Dawn had probably told her the exact same thing during their last appointment. The words sounded familiar.

She reached into her sweatshirt pocket and removed the letter Casey had left her. "Did I already show you this?"

Hannah hesitated, then nodded.

"Lots of times?"

"A few."

She would never be able to re-create the past six weeks in her mind. Perhaps it was best that way, like a gentle anesthesia administered to the traumatized and bereaved.

"I'd love to see it again, though."

Wren gave it to her. Hannah read in silence.

"Do you think it's a suicide note?" Wren asked after a while.

Hannah did not reply.

"It's a goodbye letter, isn't it?" Wren said. "He was saying goodbye. I just don't know if it was a permanent one or not. I mean, he could have decided to return home and obey whatever rules Brooke had set up for him, about us not being in contact, I mean. So, it could have been that kind of goodbye. Or the other kind. It could be the other kind."

Hannah placed her hand on top of Wren's. "Here's what I know," she said. "It's a letter that says he loves you, and he's sorry he hurt you. It's a letter that says he was thinking about Jesus and turning toward him, seeking forgiveness. And that's a beautiful gift he left you."

Wren nodded and blinked back tears. If that was all she ever knew, maybe it would one day be enough.

38

O f course I'll come," Jamie told Wren on the phone Tuesday
morning. She tried not to sound enthusiastic about a memorial
service, but finally, there was movement forward, an answer to prayer.
She sliced the crusts off Phoebe's sandwich and put it in her lunchbox.
"I'll talk to Dad and figure out the schedule here, but plan on me
flying in on Friday and then back on Monday, probably. And if the
florist can get sunflowers, we'll pay for them. Use your Christmas
money for something else."

"Thanks, Mom."

Wren sounded good. Strong. Like there was a hint of life in her
again. "I'm glad you're doing this, love. It's important to have an
opportunity to say goodbye and celebrate his life. Not that this will
be the only time for that, but . . ."

"No, I know." Wren paused. "I found something last night in one
of Vincent's letters to Theo, something he had written to the minister he worked for in England. He was apologizing for his sudden
decision to leave and asked the minister and his wife to remember
him and to wrap his"—her voice broke—"wrap their memory of
him in the cloak of charity."

Jamie placed her hand on her heart. Wren was reading again.
And she was carrying on a coherent conversation about what she
read and what she remembered. Thank God for Vincent. Again.
"That's beautiful, honey."

Wren blew her nose. "That's what I want to do for Casey. I
don't want to become bitter about anything he did. Even though

sometimes I think if I could stay angry at him, it might hurt less." She started to cry.

"I know, love. I know." On Friday she would wrap her daughter in her arms and hold her while she wept. She wished she could do it now.

Phoebe shuffled into the kitchen in her elephant slippers and pajamas and stood on tiptoe to peer into her lunchbox. "I don't want carrots."

Jamie held the phone away from her mouth and whispered, "You've got to eat some carrots. Carrots are good for you." She ruffled Phoebe's hair. Phoebe smoothed it down. It was going to be that kind of morning. Still eyeing Phoebe, she said, "Are you headed in with Kit today?"

Wren sniffled. "Yes. And then I've got a counseling appointment. I'd rather just stay in bed, though."

"A routine is good." Jamie hoped the words sounded like an affirmation rather than a lecture. "And it's good you're meeting regularly with your counselor."

"I know. I don't remember a whole lot from our appointments the past few weeks. I guess that's okay."

She hoped Wren had mentioned—or would mention—to Dawn that she was tracking Brooke online and viewed herself as Estelle's godmother. Sometime, if the opportunity arose, Jamie might gently suggest that it wasn't healthy for her to do that.

Then again, maybe she shouldn't try to interfere.

Be patient with the growth process, Kit might say. Not just for Wren. For herself too.

Phoebe snatched the bag of carrots out of the lunchbox and carried it over to the trash can. "Phoebe Noelle, don't you dare."

Phoebe stared at her, the bag dangling above the pit.

"Put them back. Now." She watched Phoebe's mental wheels turn: How angry would her mother be? How much trouble would she get into? Then, with a dramatic sigh, she slammed the bag onto the table and ran upstairs.

"I'm sorry, Wren, I've got a situation here with Phoebe. Okay if I call you later?"

"Sure."

"I mean, are you sure you're okay if I—"

"I'm okay."

"Okay, love. I'll call you with my flight info later."

She was heading up the stairs as Dylan was coming down, briefcase in hand. "What's wrong with Phoebe?" he asked.

"I'll handle it. Battle of the wills today." She took a few more steps, then said, "I just got off the phone with Wren. She's going to have a service for Casey on Saturday. I told her I would check the schedule with you but that I didn't think there was anything going on."

He stared at her. "This Saturday?"

"Her pastor's going to lead it. I told her I would probably fly in on Friday, back on Monday."

"Jamie."

From the look on his face, she was forgetting something. But the wall calendar in the kitchen was clear. She had checked. And if she was able to find a last-minute travel deal . . .

Oh, no. Wait.

She exhaled slowly. "Saturday is the 27th, isn't it?"

He nodded.

"Joel," she murmured. She hadn't marked his thirteenth birthday on the wall calendar because what mother forgot one of her children's birthdays?

She pivoted and followed Dylan downstairs, hoping Joel hadn't heard any of their conversation from his room.

"He might not care," Dylan said when they reached the kitchen.

"I care. I can't believe I forgot."

He didn't want a party, Joel had said. His friends weren't having birthday parties any more. But she and Dylan had offered to take him out to dinner and a movie without his little sister tagging along. And he'd said, "Okay. That sounds good," which, for Joel, was about as enthusiastic as he got.

Honestly, what kind of mother was she? No matter how hard she tried . . .

"Don't stay here out of mom guilt," Dylan said as he grabbed his coffee mug and headed for the door. "Do what you need to do, and we can figure the rest out."

But from the tone of his voice, she knew which decision he thought she should make.

Just as she picked up her phone to call Wren, Olivia entered the kitchen with her backpack. "Phoebe's in her room, crying. I tried to find out what's going on, but . . ."

Jamie set her phone down. "Thanks, Liv, I've got her." And she headed upstairs.

Wren said she understood. "I mean, I'll miss you, but I understand."

Jamie waved to Phoebe on the bus and blew her another kiss before returning to her car. "I wondered if you could push it back a few days? Then I could come. I'd love to be there."

"I can't, Mom. I've already worked out the details with Kit and Hannah, and I need to move ahead while I have the courage and desire to do it. Sorry."

Jamie felt her heart sink. She had hoped she wouldn't have to choose between her children. She had hoped to avoid the inevitable feeling of guilt for missing something important, no matter which she chose. "No, I'm sorry. Sorry I can't be there to support you."

"I've got lots of support."

"Are you just saying that to try to make me feel better?"

"No. I've got everything I need."

"You'd tell me if . . ."

"If I need you, I'll let you know. But right now, I've got really good people around me."

"I know you do, love. I'm so grateful for that." She ought to feel relieved and reassured. Instead, her heart hurt.

"I've got to go, Mom. I've got to get to work."

She ought to feel relieved and reassured about that too. Instead, her heart hurt.

It wasn't the life she would have chosen for her daughter, not this affliction, not these limits, not these ongoing needs. "I'll keep praying," Jamie said.

And Wren said, "Thanks."

"I think my fear has been replaced by sorrow," Jamie said when she called Kit later that morning from the church office. "At least for now."

"That's an important noticing," Kit said.

Jamie stared at a copy of *Weemoed*, which she had framed and placed on her desk. "Now that the crisis has eased up, I think it's hitting me again that she's back in the mode of trying to manage something chronic. And I feel sad about that. Sad I can't do anything to help and sad that this is the battle she faces, maybe for the rest of her life."

"It's a bitter cup," Kit said. "For both of you."

Jamie's eyes stung with tears. "And I don't think it's going to be removed, no matter how hard I pray."

Kit was silent a moment. "It may not be, dear one. And that's such a hard thing. But if the Lord does not remove the cup of suffering, I've come to trust that he gives us the grace to drink it. And drinks it with us."

Jamie traced the outline of Wren's sketch with her finger. The hand almost looked like a cup. Maybe the woman was kneeling to drink, safely held. "I wish it weren't so hard for me to trust. I wish I were quicker to recognize where I get stuck and why it's hard for me to let go."

"It's hard for all of us," Kit said. "Especially when the stakes are high."

Dylan's office door opened, and he exited with the estranged husband and wife, who appeared to be standing a few inches closer to one another than when they entered. Jamie turned aside to finish her conversation with Kit, then waited for the couple to disappear down the hallway.

"Is Wren okay?" Dylan asked.

For the moment, Jamie thought, *yes.* "She says she doesn't need me to be there, that she's got lots of support."

He moved closer to her desk. "What about you? Are you okay?"

She glanced again at Wren's sketch. "I will be," she said. And for the moment, that was enough.

Late that afternoon Wren sat with Kit in her office. "I'm wondering if I could paint a rooster," she said. "I was talking with Dawn today about Casey's letter, and she thought it would be good for me to paint a rooster. Even if we don't use it for the prayer stations, it might be a way for me to process my grief."

"I think that would be wonderful," Kit said. "And whenever you feel up to it, I'm happy to take you to get whatever supplies you need."

"I don't know. It might not work for the stations, so I don't want you to buy—"

"My gift," Kit said, "without any pressure or strings attached, all right? Just see where it goes. Whether you end up painting the stations or helping me curate someone else's art for them, I want it to be a healing journey for you, not a stressful one. We've got plenty of time to figure it all out. So just paint what you feel drawn toward and see where it goes."

If you paint a rooster crowing, Casey had written, *think of me.*

What was it he wanted her to know?

Hannah had said his letter revealed he was thinking about Jesus, seeking forgiveness. But what if all of it was about despair rather than hope? What if he only saw his failures and what he perceived as Jesus' disappointment? Then he was more like Judas, not Peter. And what hope was there for Judas? Peter persevered, but Judas gave up before restoration. What about the ones who gave up? Was there grace for them?

In her imagination she saw a rooster, its blood-red comb becoming a mane of hair, the wattle a beard, the face Casey's.

Or Vincent's.

She'd never made the connection before—the physical similarities between them, their hair and beards like flame. In that moment she saw again Vincent's face on the face of Lazarus. But now it was Casey's.

"Was it real?" Wren asked. "When you heard Jesus speak your name and call you out of the tomb like Lazarus, was that real or just your imagination?"

Kit tilted her head slightly and closed her eyes, as if watching the scene unfold again. "The impact on my life was real," she said. "Very real. So even though it happened in my imagination as I placed myself in the story, I trust that the Lord was guiding what I saw as I prayed." She breathed deeply, slowly. "That was such a significant turning point in my recovery. A resurrection of life and hope. So, yes. It was real in that it was fruitful. The Spirit accomplished something very real in me, something beyond my own imagining or inventing."

"But what happened to you doesn't happen for everyone."

"No. You're right."

"So, even if someone prayed with a text like that and imagined themselves as Lazarus, they might not hear or see anything like what you saw."

"True. But I would hope they'd still encounter Jesus in a significant way, that the Word would come alive and reveal who Jesus is as the Resurrection and the Life. Whether we see it and embrace it or not, that's who he is."

Wren nodded. Maybe she would try to copy Vincent's painting of Lazarus and paint Casey's face there as a declaration of her longing and hope.

"It's a painful mystery, isn't it," Kit said, "how some are healed or delivered, and others aren't?" She had a sad, faraway look in her eyes. "No matter how much you pray."

The words seemed an invitation. "Like your son?" Wren asked softly.

"Like my son."

They shared the gentle cloak of silent solidarity.

"Did he believe?" Wren asked after a while.

Kit stared at her folded hands as if collecting herself. "I don't know what Micah's thoughts about faith were at the end," she said. "As a little boy he went to church, said his prayers, and learned about Jesus. Whatever darkness of addiction overtook him, I have to trust that God's grace is enough, that the Lord is compassionate toward those who are sick and captive." Her voice cracked. "There was no miraculous healing or deliverance for him, though I begged and pleaded with God for it. Jesus knows that too."

The pines in the courtyard sighed and creaked. A branch tapped on the window.

Kit sat up straighter in her chair. "I was thinking about my own story the other day. Odd, how memories come back to you, and I don't know why I didn't think about it when you and I were talking about the angel in Gethsemane. But after Micah died, I went into such a terrible depression, not knowing where I was most days, not able to function. And then one day in the hospital I read that passage and felt so angry and resentful that Jesus got an angel when it felt like I was getting nothing. Like it wasn't fair—a cheat, almost, that he received a visitation in the midst of his agony when I felt so forsaken and alone. Doesn't that sound awful?"

Wren hesitated, then said, "No." She had never thought about it that way before, but she understood.

"I see it differently now," Kit said. "Now I'm glad Jesus received that gift in his time of need. If the Son of God needed reassurance and strengthening, how much more do we?" She paused. "And it comes. Not in the way we hope or ask for or imagine sometimes, but it comes. Even if it doesn't come until we see him face to face. The ultimate consolation."

Wren followed Kit's gaze to the unlit candle on the coffee table. "You know," Kit said after a while, "the older I get and the more grief I accumulate, the more I long for that day. And I like to think that Micah has received it, that he's had every tear wiped away and every wound restored. Every sin forgiven. The cross is big enough for that. And my love for him—great as it was, great as it is—it's nothing compared to Jesus' love for him. There's comfort in that. Consolation."

Yes, Wren thought. Maybe there would be consolation in that for her too. Someday.

"There's something here for you," Kit said as she sorted through her mail at the house that evening.

Wren looked up from viewing new pictures of Estelle on her phone, surprised to see her own handwriting on the envelope. Then she noticed the return address: Glenwood. She had forgotten. She had requested that the letter to her "future self" be sent to her in three months, and it had been forwarded from her apartment.

She stared at the address of her former life. What could she possibly have written to herself that would speak any word of hope or help? The losses she had experienced before Glenwood were nothing compared to the losses afterward. She thanked Kit and went upstairs to her room to read.

Dear Wren,

As you write this, a man is telling the story of three failed suicide attempts. He says, See? I can't even do that right. A woman is telling him it's the mercy of God that has saved him. But he says, It would be mercy to let me die. Sylvia has gotten up from her chair and gone over to sit in the empty seat next to him. She is patting him on the shoulder, and there are tears in her eyes. She tells him he is beautiful. Then she looks at you and smiles.

I don't know what else to say. Remember, I guess. When you get discouraged and feel like there's no hope, remember that there is a communion of sufferers. And Jesus sits at the center of it.

Hannah would say, Go gently. Be kind to yourself. Know that you are God's beloved daughter, and He is with you in all of this. No matter what happens, you are seen, you are known, you are loved, you are held.

I hope you—I—can believe that.

Always,

Wren

She folded the letter and tucked it into the envelope, remembering Sylvia's face as she held the communion cup, the cross etched into her broken flesh. *Jesus is beautiful, isn't he?* she'd asked. *Don't you think he's beautiful?*

And Wren answered again, Yes. He is.

39

She needed to paint her rooster. She needed to paint him not just for herself but for Casey. If she could manage it, she might even be able to set it out for his memorial service.

"I love that idea," Kit said as they ate lunch together in the New Hope lounge. "What a beautiful way to honor him."

"I'm not sure what else to do," Wren said. "I don't even know what he meant when he asked me to paint one and remember him. Maybe he was thinking that if I painted one for the prayer stations—if I thought about Peter failing and denying Jesus, then that would make me think of him because of all the ways he failed. I don't know. Maybe it would be weird for me to put it out for others to see, like it was a testimony about his failures or shame. I'm not sure."

"Is that what the rooster brings to mind for you? Failure and shame?"

She hadn't read the story in a while, but yes. That was the gist of it. Jesus had predicted Peter would lose his courage and deny him three times before the rooster crowed, and it happened just as he said. "Is there another angle I'm missing?"

Kit set her sandwich down. "Obviously, we can't know what connection Casey was making with it, but one way to read the text is that the moment Peter heard the crowing is the moment he came to himself. It was the moment he realized his own capacity for weakness and failure, when all his bravado was broken and there was nothing left of his pride. Those awakenings—as devastating as they feel—can be gifts that open us up to repentance and receiving grace."

Wren wished she could believe that hope and restoration were on Casey's mind at the end, not despair and condemnation. She would love to believe that his connection to the rooster and the thief on the cross meant he was searching for grace, like Hannah had said.

"Amazing birds, roosters," Kit continued. "We had them on the farm where I grew up. It was always such a happy sound for me, hearing them sing in the dark. They just knew—even when there was no light visible—they knew that morning was coming. So they sang." She glanced toward the window. "I remember this one time, we had a terrible storm come through with hurricane-force winds and torrential rain, like people were up on the roof, emptying buckets. My parents weren't sure the old farmhouse would still be standing when it was all said and done, though they didn't tell me or my sisters that until it was all over. But after the storm finally passed, I was lying in my bed in the dark, and suddenly I heard our rooster crow for the first time in days. And I knew somehow that everything would be okay, that morning would come." She paused. "I think the rooster is a beautiful image to paint as you remember your friend."

As they sat in silence, an image took shape in Wren's mind: a thickly layered blue and purple background for the dark of night, brightly colored impasto strokes giving dimension to the feathers, and the head thrown back in profile, with the open beak gold and shimmering against the pre-dawn sky.

She would paint her rooster singing in the dark, heralding the arrival of morning before any glow appeared on the horizon. She would paint her rooster as a messenger of grace and hope. She would paint him and remember Casey. But not only Casey. She would paint him and remember her companions in suffering and sorrow—all who kept watch from the depths, longing for shades of light.

"Knock knock," a voice called from her studio doorway.

Wren turned on her stool to find Mara, clad in turquoise and orange. Vincent would have loved the bright colors she always wore.

"Hey, Mara!"

"Hey! Your aunt said I'd find you here." She motioned toward the easel. "Sorry to interrupt."

Wren rose from the table where she had been looking again at *The Raising of Lazarus*. "No, it's fine. You're not interrupting."

Mara entered and enfolded her in a warm embrace. "I haven't seen you since your friend . . . I'm so sorry, Wren. How awful for you."

"Thank you."

Mara stepped back and eyed her with compassion. "Sometimes all you can say is, this world sucks. And it's a good thing it's not all we get."

That was a good way to put it. "We're having a memorial service here on Saturday. Hannah's leading it. If you can make it, I mean, I know you don't—didn't know him, but . . ."

"Oh, honey, I wish I could. But I'm heading down to Texas for the twins' birth, if they cooperate."

"That's wonderful. I'm happy for you."

"Thanks. But Hannah, she'll do a great job. Does that sound weird, 'doing a great job' at a funeral? Sorry."

"No, I know what you mean."

Mara motioned toward the easel again. "Did you do that?"

Wren glanced over her shoulder at the last canvas she had painted, the dark whirlpool of blue and violet an honest expression of her anxiety and sorrow while she waited for news about Casey. "Yeah."

"I like it."

It was only a swirl of colors, nothing special, nothing luminous about it, only the churn of her heartache. "Really?"

"Oh, yeah." She moved closer. "Okay if I touch it?"

"Sure."

Mara lifted it off the easel. She tilted it, then turned it upside down. "Yeah, I thought so," she said. She set it back on the stand. "You had it turned the wrong way, see?" She pushed back her sleeve to reveal a tattoo of an eye. "Got this a long time ago to remind me how God is watching over me. Just like in your painting."

Wren stared at it. Mara was right. It wasn't a vortex or black hole. It was a benevolent, watchful eye. "I had no idea," she murmured. "Thank you for seeing that."

Mara laughed and tapped her forehead. "Well, sometimes I get it." She picked up the painting again. "So, what are you gonna call it?"

"I have no idea."

"It's gotta have a name. You'll think of something." She handed it to Wren, then checked her watch. "I gotta get back to work. But after I get home from Texas, let's get together for lunch or coffee or something, okay? I mean, no pressure or anything."

"No, I'd love that. Thank you so much."

She laid her hand on Wren's shoulder. "And you keep painting, okay? When I get back, I expect to see something new. Maybe something with Jesus."

"Oh, I don't think I'm good enough to paint him."

Mara smiled at her. "I think you might be surprised."

"Maybe I'm thinking about it the wrong way," Wren said to Kit as they stood together in the painting supply aisle at the store that evening.

"What do you mean?"

"I mean, I've been trying to think of the prayer stations in terms of colors and symbols because I don't think I can paint scenes with Jesus. But maybe I'm overthinking it. Maybe I just need to take the same approach I do when I sketch someone quickly: try to find the essential lines so I capture the spirit, you know? Maybe I don't even try to use color—at least, not at first—but make it look like a sketch. In black or gray."

"I like the idea," Kit said. "If that's how you're feeling led."

"I don't know. I guess I could try and see where it goes, right? No pressure."

Kit smiled and set several large canvases into the shopping cart. "Right. No pressure."

Wren chose a gray paint tube from the rack, then stepped aside so a woman with two children could reach for sketch pads on a nearby shelf. As the woman thanked her, their eyes met, and Wren felt her face flush. Monica stared awkwardly at her, then turned away. No need for any introductions or revealing conversation. They were two strangers briefly crossing paths in an art supply aisle, not women who had shared an experience at a psychiatric hospital. "My girls like to draw," she said, still avoiding eye contact. "Don't you, girls?"

They both nodded, and one of them said, "Mommy's teaching us."

"What a great mom," Wren said.

And Monica said, "Thanks."

Wren watched them walk away, both girls clinging to their mother's coat. As Monica turned the corner, she looked back and gave a shy smile. Wren nodded her encouragement.

"You ready?" Kit asked.

Wren looked down to survey all the supplies in their cart, then squeezed Kit's hand. "Ready."

40

On Saturday the florist brought sunflowers to the New Hope chapel. Wren set the vases on either side of her favorite photo of Casey, a picture of him with his camera, his inspiration cap on his head, his smile broad and true. Then she placed on an easel her painting of the rooster, its comb the color of Casey's hair.

Casey, she knew, would have been pleased.

A few of his college friends came to pay their respects, a couple of them smelling like marijuana. Together they gathered in a small semi-circle of chairs around the painting of Jesus on the cross, and Hannah read Scripture. *Blessed are the poor in spirit, for theirs is the kingdom of heaven. Blessed are those who mourn, for they will be comforted* . . .

Hannah spoke of Casey's hope, how one of his favorite passages was Paul's testimony about moving on from the past and being found in Christ, not having a righteousness of his own that he achieved by keeping the rules, but a righteousness from God given as a gift to all who put their faith in Jesus. "Casey wasn't perfect," Hannah said. "None of us are. But as a young man he wanted to know Christ. And as best he could, he pressed forward, trusting that Jesus had made him his own. And we trust that as he belonged to Jesus—as he had received the gift of Christ's life through faith—he also received the resurrection Jesus promises to all who believe in him. Death is not the end. Death—no matter what kind of death—never has the final word. In Christ, death has been defeated. Death has been swallowed up by life."

Wren leaned her head against Kit's shoulder. Kit wrapped her arm around her.

"Casey knew his own brokenness," Hannah said. And with Wren's permission, she read the note he'd left her. "Jesus promised the thief on the cross, 'Today you will be with me in paradise.' Perhaps," Hannah said, "we can all imagine our faces there like Casey did and receive the same good news."

"Yeah," one of his friends said, "that's cool."

For a moment Hannah looked taken aback. But when one of the potheads echoed the same enthusiasm, she led them in a prayer to say yes to Jesus. When they finished, Wren could hear Casey laugh, a ringing, hearty, unhindered-by-any-darkness kind of laugh. *Crushed it*, she heard him say. And she laughed too.

"She made it," Jamie said to Dylan Saturday afternoon. "Thank God."

"Made what?" Phoebe asked from the table where she was coloring.

"Phoebe Noelle," Dylan said, "when Mommy and Daddy are talking . . ."

"Made this," Jamie said, pulling up a photo on her phone. "Look at the rooster Wren painted. Isn't it pretty?"

Phoebe stopped coloring and leaned forward to inspect. "It looks like a guy."

"It is a guy," Dylan said. "Roosters are guys."

"No. It looks like a *man*. Like a man singing."

Jamie enlarged the photo on her screen. Phoebe was right. It did have a human quality to it, like a bearded man in profile. "Good call, Feebs." She would ask Wren about that sometime, whether it was intentional.

"And everything else went okay?" Dylan asked.

"She said her pastor did a beautiful job. It was everything she hoped for." She paused. "I'm not sure how much closure she'll ever get, though, not with everything that can't be answered about what happened and why." She hoped the ambiguity wouldn't haunt or crush Wren.

Lord, I believe. Help my unbelief.

"It's a step," Dylan said. "A big step forward."

"Right. And now she wants to try to move ahead with painting the prayer stations."

"If she does that," he said, "it's important for you to go and see them. Even if she only manages to do one of them."

"Thank you." It wouldn't be the same, looking at photos. She wanted to stand in front of them and pray.

"Can I go?" Phoebe asked.

"Maybe, love. We'll see." It wasn't a bad idea for a family road trip, if Olivia and Joel were willing. Dylan wouldn't be able to get away from the church during Holy Week, but maybe they could all go out during spring break. They could even combine the trip with some college visits. Olivia might say yes to that. They would need to find something special for Joel too.

"There's the birthday boy!" Jamie exclaimed as he entered the kitchen and headed toward the fridge. "Don't spoil your dinner, okay? We're going early." Before Phoebe could protest again that she wasn't going with them, Jamie said, "And you're helping Olivia with the surprise, remember?"

Phoebe nodded solemnly. Olivia had promised to let her ice the cake.

Jamie took one last look at Wren's rooster before setting her phone aside. *All shall be well,* she reminded herself. And all shall be well. And all manner of things shall—somehow—be well.

Back in her studio later that afternoon, surrounded by sunflowers, Wren turned in her art book to one of Vincent's last paintings, *Wheatfield with Crows,* the thick indigo sky churning and troubled above a golden, ripe field with three diverging red and green paths, the center path disappearing into the horizon. Black crows punctuated the scene, at first glance ominous and brooding. Were they approaching or retreating? Some interpreted the painting as a suicide note, more articulate and transparent than the perplexing partial letter to Theo that Vincent was carrying in his pocket when he presumably shot himself. Years later Johanna, Theo's widow, would reveal that Vincent's suicide had taken her husband completely by surprise. Vincent had seemed relatively calm, moving forward with work, even including sketches and descriptions of current projects in what would be his final letter.

So, was the painting a declaration of his despair and his intent?

She read again an earlier letter in which Vincent mentioned the painting, a letter written a little more than two weeks before he died. In it he expressed his profound gratitude for his sister-in-law's kind letter of reassurance. Her words were "like a gospel," he said, serving to mitigate the distress he felt after a difficult and trying visit with them. Jo and Theo were under financial strain, Theo's employment was uncertain, and baby Vincent had been unwell. Vincent was worried about being a burden to them, afraid they would view his need for ongoing support as "intolerable." The storm that threatened them, Vincent wrote, weighed heavily on him as well. And what was to be done? "I usually try to be quite good-humored," he wrote, "but my life, too, is attacked at the very root, my step also is faltering."

And then he described his current paintings: "They're immense stretches of wheatfields under turbulent skies, and I made a point of trying to express sadness, extreme loneliness."

Yes, Wren thought as she gazed again at the one with the crows, he had certainly accomplished that. But the very next sentence read, "You'll see this soon, I hope—for I hope to bring them to you in Paris as soon as possible, since I'd almost believe that these canvases will tell you what I can't say in words, what I consider healthy and fortifying about the countryside."

So, which was it? A painting of sadness and loneliness, or a painting about the invigorating, restorative nature of the landscape? Was it a painting of despair or hope?

The crows, some said, were evidence of Vincent's despair. But he had frequently painted crows in his landscapes, in summer and

winter, and above sowers and reapers. They weren't ominous har-
bingers in those paintings.

Vincent, who often painted images of sowing and reaping as
symbols of life, death, and rebirth, had written other letters about
death not being something to be feared as a final destination, but as
a passageway to the eternal, into the presence of God. Yes, he was
weary. He was losing hope. He felt the strain of his illness and the
weight of melancholy and anxiety. But what if he also remembered
that he knew something else, something deeper? And what if the
painting communicated that? What if it was a work, not predicting
a tragic end, but expressing a resilient hope that the journey would
end not in death, but in life?

"Death is not the end," Hannah had declared. Death, no matter
what kind of death, never had the final word. The resurrection of
Jesus was the final word. The tomb was empty. Christ is risen! Death,
with all its terror and fear, had been defeated, once and for all. Death
had been engulfed—overcome—by life.

She traced her finger along the red and green path from the left
toward the center. That combination of complementary colors
would have been deliberate and significant. Vincent knew that by
painting those colors together, they would draw the eye toward a
focal point. The viewer could step right into the painting and follow
the path through the golden, waving wheat into the bright, luminous
blue of infinity. Sorrowful? Yes. But also rejoicing. *Always* rejoicing.

Perhaps even here Vincent had painted his longing, his testimony,
his vision.

His desolation, yes. But also his consolation and hope.

She stared at her painting of the swirling blue and violet, at the
kind and watchful eye that, unbidden, had emerged in the midst of
her sorrow and fear. "You've got to name it," Mara had said.

Wren picked up the canvas and held it near the window, the un-
filtered winter sunlight illuminating the curved lines, dark accents,
thick strokes, and shades of blue. Mara was right. There was something oddly luminous and comforting about it.

As she stared at the painting, words from one of David's prayers came to mind. *Even the darkness is not dark to You.*

That's what she would call it: *Even the Darkness.*

That was her song, her prayer. Even here. In the place she had not chosen, in the life she must continue to choose, she was known, loved, seen, held. In all the wreckage, in every stranding, there was One who would not forsake or abandon her. No matter what. That was her hope, her testimony, her vision, her consolation.

With Casey's inspiration cap on her head, she placed an empty canvas on the easel and picked up her brush to pray.

ACKNOWLEDGMENTS

Unlike the Sensible Shoes series, which emerged out of my work as a pastor and spiritual director, *Shades of Light* required extensive research into fields in which I have no professional expertise, namely, issues of mental health, art, and the life and work of Vincent van Gogh. I'm grateful to all who contributed their gifts as I wrote this book.

First, I'm humbled and honored by the courage of those who were willing to share with me their personal stories of how mental illness has impacted their lives or the lives of those they love. Many have suffered in silence. Though you are not named here, know that I have heard you and seen you. I hope this book gives voice to your pain and helps ease the burden of isolation and shame. Thank you for being vulnerable and brave. You have so much to teach us about perseverance and hope, and I thank God for you.

Many people generously gave their time in interviews and offered input on early drafts, including counselors, psychiatric nurses, physicians, chaplains, social workers, artists, and art historians. I am deeply grateful. Special thanks to James Johnson, Jane Gray, Cathline DeWitt, Nancy Betker, Elizabeth Bates, Barbara Hoffman, Elizabeth Ivy Hawkins, and Peter Berg.

Thanks to Debra Sportel, who first invited me to watch painters in action and served as inspiration for Gran's style and philosophy of painting.

Thanks to Heather Monkmeyer, Jennifer Andersson, and Rachel Sangster, who introduced me to the beauty and creative possibilities for prayer collage.

Thanks to Jenni Jessen for the gift of her inspiring painting, *Dancing in the Dark*, a beautiful image of God's hand being a safe and sturdy resting place.

Thanks to Curtis Dykstra and Marjo Jordan, who shared their passion for birding with me. I now listen and watch in an entirely new way to our feathered friends.

Thanks to Jo Barrie for stepping out in faith and inviting me to Australia to lead retreats in 2017. Seeds of Wren's story were planted while I was there, and I'm grateful for the connections with new friends Down Under.

Thanks to Donna Kehoe, who took me to the Nelson-Atkins Museum after a speaking engagement in Kansas City. Vincent caught my attention that day and became firmly implanted in my heart.

Thanks to Hugh Cook for editing an early draft of the manuscript with skill, perception, and the gifts of a teacher.

Thanks to my faithful team of early readers who challenged and encouraged me by asking great questions and offering insightful suggestions. Special thanks to Lisa, Rebecca, Debra, Amy, Michelle, Therese, and Kathleen. You gave me pages of feedback and ideas, and this is a better book because of you.

Thanks to Krisha and Sharon for midwifing this book with me from its first breath. You held me in prayer the whole time, and I'm so grateful.

Thanks to Mary Peterson for holding my story with love and compassion, and challenging me to prayerfully explore God's invitations to do something new with art.

Thanks to my niece, Meaghan, for helping with art research and showing me how to paint. You are fearlessly creative, and I'm so proud of you.

Thanks to the gifted team at InterVarsity Press. It is such an honor and privilege to partner in ministry with you! Special thanks to my discerning and encouraging editor, Cindy Bunch; my creative and passionate marketer, Lori Neff; and the talented cover designer, David Fassett, who caught the vision for the heart of the book and expressed it so beautifully through art. Thanks, too, to Stephanie Jewell, who helps me connect with readers; Kathryn Chapek, who often works wonders in supplying books for events; Allison Rieck, who generously accommodates my style in her copyediting; and Jeff Crosby, who embodies grace and humility in his leadership.

Thanks to my readers, who encourage me on this journey. So many of you are already working on behalf of those who need support, compassion, and advocacy. I know you will continue to say yes to God's invitations to travel deeper into his heart and extend his love and grace to others. I hope Wren's story inspires you, comforts you, and enlarges you as you seek to be faithful to God's call. And I hope you continue to pursue life in community. May you find trustworthy companions, in joy and in sorrow.

Thanks to my family. I love you and couldn't do any of this without you. To my sister, Beth, who always picks up the phone. You tell the truth, make me laugh, and endure adversity with your own inimitable brand of moxie. To Mom and Dad, who have always been my biggest cheerleaders. I'm so grateful for your love and generosity. To my son, David, who partnered with me in the development of this story, from start to finish. Your creative gifts and profound insights astound me, and I'm always learning from you. To my husband, Jack, who faithfully pours out his life in loving sacrifice to enable all my yeses. In the words of a favorite song, "God blessed me with you."

Thanks to Vincent, whose story has deeply touched my soul. I hope this book tenderly honors both his frailty and his faith.

And to Jesus, our Man of Sorrows, acquainted with grief. Thank you for calling me to the journey with you. Thank you for the privilege of serving you. Thank you for what you endured for the sake of love. All of this is for you.

*The Word became flesh and made his dwelling among
us. We have seen his glory, the glory of the one and only
Son, who came from the Father, full of grace and truth.*

JOHN 1:14

RECOMMENDED RESOURCES

FOR MENTAL HEALTH

- National Suicide Prevention Lifeline: 800-273-8255. This is a 24/7 line. If you or someone you love is in crisis, please call this confidential number for immediate care. You can also text HOME to the Crisis Text Line at 741741 or go to www.suicide preventionlifeline.org.

- National Alliance on Mental Illness (www.nami.org) works to raise awareness and provide support for those afflicted with and impacted by mental illness through advocacy, local support groups, and education.

- Grace Alliance (www.mentalhealthgracealliance.org) provides Christian mental health resources and programs for individuals and families, as well as leadership tools for developing active community support.

- Fresh Hope for Mental Health (www.freshhope.us) provides Christian mental health resources through support groups, an award-winning blog, podcasts, and webinars.

- InterVarsity Press publishes many excellent nonfiction books about mental and emotional health. Here are a few that may be helpful:

  - *Grace for the Afflicted: A Clinical and Biblical Perspective on Mental Illness*, Matthew S. Stanford

  - *Troubled Minds: Mental Illness and the Church's Mission*, Amy Simpson and Marshall Shelley

- *Grieving a Suicide: A Loved One's Search for Comfort, Answers, and Hope*, Albert Y. Hsu

FOR GRIEF AND SPIRITUAL FORMATION

- *A Grace Disguised: How the Soul Grows Through Loss*, Jerry Sittser
- *A Sacred Sorrow: Reaching Out to God in the Lost Language of Lament*, Michael Card
- *When Heaven is Silent: Trusting God When Life Hurts*, Ron Dunn
- *Broken Hallelujahs: Learning to Grieve the Big and Small Losses of Life*, Beth Allen Slevcove

FOR ART AND SPIRITUAL FORMATION

- *Contemplative Vision: A Guide to Christian Art and Prayer*, Juliet Benner
- *Spiritual Formation: Following the Movements of the Spirit*, Henri Nouwen with Michael J. Christensen and Rebecca J. Laird

FOR VINCENT VAN GOGH

- All his letters are available to read online: vangoghletters.org
- *Learning from Henri Nouwen and Vincent van Gogh: A Portrait of the Compassionate Life*, Carol A. Berry
- *Vincent van Gogh: His Spiritual Vision in Life and Art*, Carol A. Berry
- *At Eternity's Gate: The Spiritual Vision of Vincent van Gogh*, Kathleen Powers Erickson
- *The Shoes of Van Gogh: A Spiritual and Artistic Journey to the Ordinary*, Cliff Edwards

LIST OF VINCENT
VAN GOGH WORKS

ALSO BY
SHARON GARLOUGH BROWN

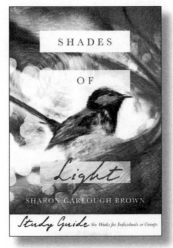

Shades of Light Study Guide
978-0-8308-4664-1

Remember Me
978-0-8308-4670-2
<small>AVAILABLE DEC. 10, 2019</small>

Shades of Light Study Guide
978-0-8308-4667-0

Visit sharongarloughbrown.com *for book club resources*

The Sensible Shoes Series

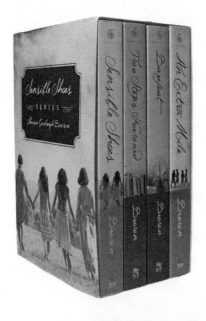

Sensible Shoes
Two Steps Forward
Barefoot
An Extra Mile

STUDY GUIDES

For more information about the Sensible Shoes series,
visit ivpress.com/sensibleshoesseries.
learn more from Sharon Garlough Brown or to sign up for her newsletter,
go to ivpress.com/sharon-news.

formatio

**TRADITION. EXPERIENCE.
TRANSFORMATION.**

Formatio books from InterVarsity Press follow the rich tradition of the church in the journey of spiritual formation. These books are not merely about being informed, but about being transformed by Christ and conformed to his image. Formatio stands in InterVarsity Press's evangelical publishing tradition by integrating God's Word with spiritual practice and by prompting readers to move from inward change to outward witness. InterVarsity Press uses the chambered nautilus for Formatio, a symbol of spiritual formation because of its continual spiral journey outward as it moves from its center. We believe that each of us is made with a deep desire to be in God's presence. Formatio books help us to fulfill our deepest desires and to become our true selves in light of God's grace.